A M

MCR

ZOYA

Also by Danielle Steel

DANIELLE STEEL

ZOYA

THE DELACORTE PRESS LARGE-PRINT COLLECTION

LP
F
Steel

Published by
Delacorte Press
The Bantam Doubleday Dell Publishing Group, Inc.
1 Dag Hammarskjold Plaza
New York, New York 10017

Library of Congress Cataloging in Publication Data

Steel, Danielle.
Zoya.

I. Title.
PS3569.T33828Z4   1988   813'.54   87-30372
ISBN 0-385-29649-5
Large-print edition 0-385-29674-6
Limited edition 0-385-29679-7

Manufactured in the United States of America

June 1988

10 9 8 7 6 5 4 3 2 1

BG

**The Production Review Committee of the
NATIONAL ASSOCIATION
FOR VISUALLY HANDICAPPED
has found this book to meet its criteria
for large type publications.**

Darling Maxx

Be never too young, never too old,
always strong enough
to live and love and inquire,
ever loving,
always kind.
May life share its many blessings
with you,
and may its burdens be ever light.
The wind at your back,
the sun in your soul,
and our love in your heart,
now and forever.

For you, and your Daddy,
my heart ever yours,
my love and my life
yours forever.

DS.

Zoya

Wandering the world
   in magic places,
    treasured
     faces
whispering
   from the past,
   clouds
    of memories
    soaring past
and life
   her very name,
  nothing ever
    quite
    the same
as it was
  so long before,
the palaces,
  the memories,
   the dreams,
the scheme
   of all that was,
of all that would
   and could

have been,
and what she once
had seen,
a magic life
of palaces
and balls,
all of it to fall
like snow,
all of it to go,
swiftly gone
like rain,
the laughter,
music,
beauty, pain,
the friends,
the smiles
they left
behind,
the memories
as soft as dew,
like satin
on her cheek . . .
a lifetime left
to seek
anew
what was all
so swiftly gone,
gentle, treasured
winter song,
wrapped in love's
cocoon,

life of fire
quickly
burned,
and gone so much
too soon.

St. Petersburg

Chapter 1

Zoya closed her eyes again as the troika flew across the icy ground, the soft mist of snow leaving tiny damp kisses on her cheeks, and turning her eyelashes to lace as she listened to the horses' bells dancing in her ears like music. They were the sounds she had loved since childhood. At seventeen, she felt grown up, was in fact almost a woman, yet she still felt like a little girl as Feodor forced the shining black horses on with his whip . . . faster . . . faster . . . through the snow. And as she opened her eyes again, she could see the village just outside Tsarskoe Selo. She smiled to herself as she squinted to see the twin palaces just beyond it, and pulled back one heavy fur-lined glove to see how much time it had taken. She had promised her mother she would be home in time for dinner . . . and she would be . . . if they didn't spend too much time talking

. . . but how could they not? Marie was her very dearest friend, almost like a sister.

Ancient Feodor glanced around and smiled at her, as she laughed with excitement. It had been a perfect day. She always enjoyed her ballet class, and even now, her ballet slippers were tucked into the seat beside her. Dancing was a special treat, it had been her passion since early childhood, and sometimes she had secretly whispered to Marie that what she wanted most was to run away to the Maryinsky, to live there, and train day and night with the other dancers. The very thought of it made her smile now. It was a dream she couldn't even say out loud, people in her world did not become professional dancers. But she had the gift, she had known it since she was five, and at least her lessons with Madame Nastova gave her the pleasure of studying what she loved best. She worked hard during the hours she spent there, always imagining that one day Fokine, the great dance master, would find her. But her thoughts turned swiftly from ballet to her childhood friend, as the troika sped through the village toward her cousin Marie. Zoya's father, Konstantin, and the Tsar were distant cousins, and like Marie's, her own mother was also German. They had everything in common, their passions, their secrets, their dreams, their world. They had shared the same terrors and delights when they were children, and she had to see her now, even though she had promised her mother that she wouldn't. It was stupid really, why shouldn't she see her? She wouldn't visit the others in their sickroom, and Marie was perfectly fine. She had sent Zoya a note only the day before, telling her how desperately bored she was with the others sick around her. And it wasn't anything serious after all, only measles.

The peasants hurried from the road as the troika sped past, and Feodor shouted at the three black horses that drew them. He had worked for her grandfather as a boy, and his father had worked for their family before him. Only for her would he have risked her father's ire and her mother's silent, elegant displeasure, but Zoya had promised him no one would know, and he had taken her there a thousand times before. She visited her cousins almost daily, what harm could there be in it now, even if the tiny, frail Tsarevich and his older sisters had the measles. Alexis was only a boy, and not a healthy lad, as they all knew. Mademoiselle Zoya was young and healthy and strong, and so very, very lovely. She had been the prettiest child Feodor had ever seen, and Ludmilla, his wife, had taken care of her when she was a baby. His wife had died the year before of typhoid, a terrible loss for him, particularly as they had no children. His only family was the one that he worked for.

The Cossack Guard stopped them at the gate and Feodor sharply reined in the steaming horses. The snow was heavier now and two mounted guards approached in tall fur hats and green uniforms, looking menacing until they saw who it was. Zoya was a familiar figure at Tsarskoe Selo. They saluted smartly as Feodor urged the horses on again, and they rode quickly past the Fedorovsky chapel and on to the Alexander Palace. Of their many imperial homes it was the one the Empress preferred. They seldom used the Winter Palace in St. Petersburg at all, except for balls or state occasions. In May each year they moved to their villa on the Peterhof estate, and after summers spent on their yacht, the *Polar Star,* and at Spala in Poland, they always went to the Livadia Palace in September. Zoya was often with them there until she returned to school at the Smolny Institute. But the Alexander Palace was her favorite as well. She was in love with the Empress's famous mauve boudoir and had asked that her own room at home be done in the same muted opal shades as Aunt Alix's. It amused her mother that Zoya wanted it that way, and the year before she had decided to indulge her. Marie teased her about it whenever she was there, saying that the room reminded her far too much of her mother.

Feodor climbed from his seat while two young boys held the prancing horses, and the snow whirled past his head as he carefully held out a hand to Zoya. Her heavy fur coat was encrusted with snow and her cheeks were red from the cold and the two-hour drive from St. Petersburg. She would have just enough time for tea with her friend, she thought to herself, then disappeared into the awesome entranceway of the Alexander Palace, and Feodor hurried back to his horses. He had friends in the stables there and always enjoyed bringing them news from town, whenever he spent time with them, waiting for his mistress.

Two maids took her coat while Zoya slowly pulled the large sable hat from her head, releasing a mane of fiery hair that often made people stop and stare when she wore it loose, which she did often at Livadia in the summer. The Tsarevich Alexis loved to tease her about her shining red hair, and he would stroke it gently in his delicate hands, whenever she hugged him. To Alexis, Zoya was almost like one of his sisters. Born two weeks before Marie, she was of the same age, and they had similar dispositions, and both of them babied him constantly, as did the rest of his sisters. To them, and his mother, and the close family, he was almost always referred to as "Baby." Even now that he was twelve, they still thought of him that way, and Zoya inquired about him with a serious face as the elder of the two maids shook her head.

"Poor little thing, he is covered with spots and has a terrible cough. Mr. Gilliard has been sitting with him all day today. Her Highness has been busy with the girls." Olga, Tatiana, and Anastasia had caught the measles from him and it was a virtual epidemic, which was why Zoya's mother had wanted her to stay away. But Marie had showed no sign whatsoever of the illness, and her note to Zoya the day before had begged her to come. . . . *Come to see me, my darling Zoya, if your mother will only let you. . . .*

Zoya's green eyes danced as she shook out her hair, and straightened her heavy wool dress. She had changed out of her school uniform after her ballet lesson, and she walked swiftly down the endless hall to the familiar door that would lead her upstairs to Marie and Anastasia's spartan bedroom. On her way, she walked silently past the room where the Tsar's aide-de-camp, Prince Meshchersky, always sat working. But he didn't notice her as, even in her heavy boots, she walked soundlessly up the stairs, and a moment later, she knocked on the bedroom door, and heard the familiar voice.

"Yes?"

With one slender, graceful hand, she turned the knob, and a sheaf of red hair seemed to precede her as she poked her head in, and saw her cousin and friend standing quietly by the window. Marie's huge blue eyes lit up instantly and she rushed across the room to greet her, as Zoya darted in and threw her arms wide to embrace her.

"I've come to save you, Mashka, my love!"

"Thank God! I thought I would die of boredom. *Everyone* here is sick. Even poor Anna came down with the measles yesterday. She's staying in the rooms adjoining my mother's apartment, and Mama insists on taking care of everyone herself. She's done nothing but carry soup and tea to them all day, and when they're asleep she goes next door to take care of the men. It seems like two hospitals here now instead of one. . . ." She pretended to pull her soft brown hair as Zoya laughed. The Catherine Palace next door had been turned into a hospital at the beginning of the war, and the Empress worked there tirelessly in her Red Cross uniform and she expected her daughters to do the same, but of all of them, Marie was the least fond of those duties. "I can hardly bear it! I was afraid you wouldn't come. And Mama would be so angry if she knew I had asked you." The two young women strolled across the room arm in arm and sat down next to the fireplace. The room she normally shared with Anastasia was simple and austere. Like their other sisters, Marie and Anastasia had plain iron beds, crisp white sheets, a small desk, and on the fireplace was a neat row of delicately made Easter eggs. Marie kept them from year to year, made for her by friends, and given to her by her sisters. They were malachite, and wood, and some of them were beautifully carved or encrusted with stones. She cherished them as she did her few small treasures. The children's rooms, as they were still called, showed none of the opulence or luxury of her parents' rooms, or the rest of the palace. And cast over one of the room's two chairs was an exquisite embroidered shawl that her mother's dear friend, Anna Vyrubova, had made her. She was the same woman Marie had referred to when Zoya came in. And now her friendship had been rewarded with a case of measles. The thought of it made both girls smile, feeling superior to have escaped the illness.

"But you're all right?" Zoya eyed her lovingly, her tiny frame seeming even smaller in the heavy gray wool dress she had worn to keep her warm on the drive from St. Petersburg. She was smaller than Marie, and even more delicate, although Marie was considered the family beauty. She had her father's startling blue eyes, and his charm. And she loved jewels and pretty clothes far more than her sisters. It was a passion she shared with Zoya. They would spend hours talking of the beautiful dresses they'd seen, and trying on Zoya's mother's hats and jewels whenever Marie came to visit.

"I'm fine . . . except that Mama says I can't go to town with Aunt Olga this Sunday." It was a ritual she above all adored. Each Sunday their aunt the Grand Duchess Olga Alexandrovna took them all to town, for lunch with their grandmother at the Anitchkov Palace, and visits to one or two of their friends, but with her sisters sick, everything was being curtailed. Zoya's face fell at the news.

"I was afraid of that. And I so wanted to show you my new gown. Grandmama brought it to me from Paris." Zoya's grandmother, Evgenia Peterovna Ossupov, was an extraordinary woman. She was tiny and elegant and her eyes still danced with emerald fire at eighty-one. And everyone insisted that Zoya looked exactly like her. Zoya's mother was tall and elegant and languid, a beauty with pale blond hair and wistful blue eyes. She was the kind of woman one wanted to protect from the world, and Zoya's father had always done just that. He treated her like a delicate child, unlike his exuberant daughter. "Grandmama brought me the most exquisite pink satin gown all sewn with tiny pearls. I so wanted you to see it!" Like children, they talked of their gowns as they would of their teddy bears, and Marie clapped her hands in delight.

"I can't wait to see it! By next week everyone should be well. We'll come then. I promise! And in the meantime, I shall make you a painting for that silly mauve room of yours."

"Don't you dare say rude things about my room! It's almost as elegant as your mother's!" The two girls laughed, and Joy, the children's cocker spaniel bounded into the room and yipped happily around Zoya's feet as she warmed her hands by the fire, and told Marie all about the other girls at the Smolny. Marie loved to hear her tales, secluded as she was, living amongst her brother and sisters, with Pierre Gilliard to tutor them, and Mr. Gibbes to teach them English.

"At least we don't have classes right now. Mr. Gilliard has been too busy, sitting with Baby. And I haven't seen Mr. Gibbes in a week. Papa says he is terrified he'll catch the measles." The two girls laughed again and Marie began affectionately to braid Zoya's mane of bright red hair. It was a pastime they had shared since they were small children, braiding each other's hair as they chatted and gossiped about St. Petersburg and the people they knew, although things had been quieter since the war. Even Zoya's parents didn't give as many parties as they once had, much to Zoya's chagrin. She loved talking to the men in brightly hued uniforms and looking at the women in elegant gowns and lovely jewelry. It gave her fresh tales to bring to Marie and her sisters, of the flirtations she had observed, who was beautiful, who was not, and who was wearing the most spectacular diamond necklace. It was a world that existed nowhere else, the world of Imperial Russia. And Zoya had always lived happily right at its center, a countess herself like her mother and grandmother before her, distantly related to the Tsar on her father's side, she and her family enjoyed a position of privilege and luxury, related to many of the nobles. Her own home was but a smaller version of the Anitchkov Palace, and her playmates were the people who made history, but to her it all seemed commonplace and normal.

"Joy seems so happy now." She watched

the dog playing at her feet. "How are the puppies?"

Marie smiled a secret smile, and shrugged an elegant shoulder. "Very sweet. Oh, wait. . . ." She dropped the long braid she had made of Zoya's hair, and ran to her desk to get something she had almost forgotten. Zoya assumed instantly that it was a letter from one of their friends, or a photograph of Alexis or her sisters. She always seemed to have treasures to share when they met, but this time she brought out a small flacon and handed it proudly to her friend.

"What's that?"

"Something wonderful . . . all for you!" She gently kissed Zoya's cheek as Zoya bent her head over the small bottle.

"Oh, Mashka! Is it? . . . It *is*!" She confirmed it with one sniff. It was "Lilas," Marie's favorite perfume, which Zoya had coveted for months. "Where did you get it?"

"Lili brought it back from Paris for me. I thought you'd like to have it. I still have enough left of the one Mama got me." Zoya closed her eyes and took a deep breath, looking happy and innocent. Their pleasures were so harmless and so simple . . . the puppy, the perfume . . .

and in the summer, long walks in the
scented fields of Livadia . . . or games on
the royal yacht as they drifted through the
fjords. It was such a perfect life, untouched even by the realities of the war,
although they talked about it sometimes.
It always upset Marie after she had spent a
day with the wounded men being tended
in the palace next door. It seemed so cruel
to her that they should be wounded and
maimed . . . that they should die . . .
but no crueler than the constantly threatening illness of her brother. His hemo-
philia was often the topic of their more
serious and secret conversations. Almost
no one except the intimate family knew
the exact nature of his illness.

"He is all right, isn't he? I mean . . .
the measles won't . . ." Zoya's eyes were
filled with concern as she set down the
prized bottle of perfume and they spoke
of Alexis again. But Marie's face was reassuring.

"I don't think the measles will do him
any harm. Mama says that Olga is a great
deal sicker than he is." She was four years
older than either of them, and a great deal
more serious. She was also painfully shy,
unlike Zoya or Marie, or her two other
sisters.

"I had a lovely time at ballet class to-day." Zoya sighed as Marie rang for a cup of tea. "I wish that I could do something wonderful with it."

Marie laughed. She had heard it before, the dreams of her beloved friend. "Like what? Be discovered by Diaghilev?"

The two girls laughed, but there was an intense light in Zoya's eyes as she spoke. Everything about Zoya was intense, her eyes, her hair, the way she moved her hands or darted across the room, or threw her arms around her friend. She was tiny but filled with power and life and excitement. Her very name meant life, and it seemed the perfect choice for the girl she had been and the woman she was slowly becoming. "I mean it . . . and Madame Nastova says I'm *very* good." Marie laughed again, and the girls' eyes met, both of them thinking the same thing . . . about Mathilde Kschessinska, the ballerina who had been the Tsar's mistress before he married Alexandra . . . an entirely forbidden subject, to be spoken of only in whispers on dark summer nights and never within earshot of adults. Zoya had said something about it to her mother one day, and the Countess had been outraged and forbidden Zoya to mention it

again. it was most emphatically not a suit-
able subject for young ladies. But her
grandmother had been less austere when
she'd brought it up again, and said only in
amused tones that the woman was a very
talented dancer.

"Do you still dream about running away
to the Maryinsky?" She hadn't mentioned
it in years, but Marie knew her well, well
enough to know when she was teasing and
when she was not, and how serious she
was about her private dreams. She also
knew that for Zoya it was an impossible
dream. One day she would marry and
have children, and be as elegant as her
mother, and she would not be living in the
famous ballet school. But it was fun to talk
about things like that, and dream on a
February afternoon as they sipped the hot
tea and watched the dog gambol about
the room. Life seemed very comfortable
just then, in spite of the current imperial
epidemic of measles. With Zoya, Marie
could forget her problems for a little
while, and her responsibilities. She wished
that one day, she would be as free as Zoya
was. She knew full well that one day her
parents would choose for her the man that
she was to marry. But they had her two
older sisters to think about first . . . as

she stared into the fire, she wondered if she would really love him.

"What were you thinking just then?" Zoya's voice was soft as the fire crackled and the snow fell outside. It was already dark and Zoya had forgotten all about rushing home for dinner. "Mashka? . . . you looked so serious." She often did when she wasn't laughing. Her eyes were so intense and so blue and so warm and kind, unlike her mother's.

"I don't know . . . silly things, I suppose. . . ." She smiled gently at her friend. They were both almost eighteen, and marriage was beginning to come to mind . . . perhaps after the war . . . "I was wondering who we'll marry one day." She was always honest with Zoya.

"I think about that sometimes too. Grandmama says it's almost time to think about it. She thinks Prince Orlov would be a nice man for me. . . ." And then suddenly she laughed and tossed her head, her hair flying free of the loose braid Mashka had made for her. "Do you ever see someone and think it ought to be him?"

"Not very often. Olga and Tatiana should marry first. And Tatiana is so serious, I can't even imagine her wanting to get married." Of all of them, she was the closest to their mother and Marie could easily imagine her wanting to stay within the bosom of her family forever. "It would be nice to have children though."

"How many?" Zoya teased.

"Five at least." It was the size of her own family, and to her it had always seemed perfect.

"I want six," Zoya said with absolute certainty. "Three boys and three girls."

"All of them with bright red hair!" Marie laughed as she teased her friend, and leaned across the table to gently touch her cheek. "You are truly my dearest friend." Their eyes met and Zoya took her hand and kissed it with childlike warmth.

"I always wish you were my very own sister." She had an older brother instead and he teased her mercilessly, particularly about her bright red hair. His was dark, like their father's, although his eyes were also green. And he had the quiet strength and dignity of their father. He was twenty-three, five and a half years older than his sister.

"How is Nicolai these days?"

"Awful as usual. But Mama is terribly glad he's with the Preobrajensky Guard here and not off at the front somewhere. Grandmama says he stayed here so he wouldn't miss any parties." They both laughed and the serious moment passed, as the door opened quietly and a tall woman silently entered the room, watching them for a moment before they became aware of her presence. A large gray cat had followed her into the room and also stood watching beside her. It was the Empress Alexandra, fresh from the sickroom where she had been ministering to her three other daughters.

"Good afternoon, girls." She smiled as Zoya turned, and both girls immediately stood up, and Zoya ran to kiss her. The Tsarina herself had had the measles years before, and she knew there was no danger of infection.

"Auntie! How is everyone?"

She gave Zoya a fond hug and sighed with a tired smile. "Well, they're certainly not well. Poor Anna seems to be the worst of all." She was speaking of her own dearest friend, Anna Vyrubova. She and Lili Dehn were her closest companions. "And you, little one? Are you well?"

"I am, thank you very much." She blushed as she often did. It was what she hated most of all about having a redhead's complexion, that and the fact that she was always getting sunburned on the royal yacht, or when they went to Livadia.

"I'm surprised your mother let you visit us today." She knew how desperately afraid the Countess was of infection. But Zoya's even deeper blush told her what Zoya had done, even without a confession, and the Tsarina laughed and wagged a finger at her. "So! Is that what you've done? And what will you tell her? Where have you been today?"

Zoya laughed guiltily, and then admitted to Marie's mother what she planned to tell her own. "I have been hours and hours at ballet class, working very hard with Madame Nastova."

"I see. It's shocking for girls your age to tell such lies, but I should have known we couldn't keep you two apart." And then she turned her attention to her daughter. "Have you given Zoya her gift yet, my love?" The Empress smiled at them both. She was usually restrained, but her fatigue seemed to make her both more vulnerable and warmer.

"Yes!" Zoya spoke up instantly with delight, waving toward the bottle of "Lilas" on the table. "It's my very favorite!" The Tsarina's eyes sought Marie's with a question, and her daughter giggled and left the room swiftly, while Zoya chatted with her mother. "Is Uncle Nicholas well?"

"He is, although I have barely seen him. The poor man came home from the front for a rest, and instead he finds himself here in the midst of a siege of measles." They both laughed as Marie returned again, carrying something wrapped in a wisp of blanket. There was a strange little peep, almost as though it were a bird, and a moment later, a brown and white face appeared, with long silky ears, and shining onyx eyes. It was one of their own dog's puppies.

"Oh, he's so sweet! I haven't seen any of them in weeks!" Zoya held out a hand and he let out a series of squeaks and licked her fingers.

"It's a she, and her name is Sava," Marie said proudly, looking at Zoya with excited eyes. "Mama and I want you to have her." She held the puppy out to her as Zoya stared at her.

"For me? Oh my . . . what will . . ." She had been about to say, "What will I tell my mother?" but she didn't want them to take back the gift so she stopped instantly, but the Empress had understood all too clearly.

"Oh, dear . . . your mother's not fond of dogs, is she, Zoya? I had forgotten. Will she be very cross at me?"

"No! . . . no . . . not at all." She fibbed happily, taking the puppy in her own hands and holding her close, as Sava licked her nose and her cheeks and her eyes, and Zoya tried to duck her head before the little spaniel could gobble at her hair. "Oh, she's so lovely! Is she really mine?"

"You would be doing me a great service, my dear, if you took her." The Empress smiled and sank down in one of the two chairs with a sigh. She looked extremely tired, and Zoya noticed then that she was wearing her Red Cross uniform. She wondered if she'd worn it to take care of the sick children and her friend, or if she'd worked at the hospital that day as well. She felt strongly about her hospital work, and always insisted that her daughters do it too.

"Mama, would you like some tea?"

"Very much, thank you, Mashka." Marie rang for the maid, who came quickly, knowing that the Tsarina was there with them, and a cup and fresh pot of tea arrived almost at once. Marie poured, and the two women joined her. "Thank you, darling." And then she turned to her husband's distant cousin. "So, is your grandmother well these days, Zoya? I haven't seen her in months. I've been so busy here. I never seem to get into St. Petersburg anymore."

"She's very well, thank you, Aunt Alix."

"And your parents?"

"Fine. Mother's always worried that Nicolai will be sent to the front. Papa says it makes her terribly nervous." Everything made Natalya Ossupov nervous, she was terribly frail, and her husband catered to her every whim and turn. The Tsarina had often said to Marie in private that she thought it was unhealthy for him to indulge her so constantly, but at least Zoya had never put on languid airs. She was full of life and fire, and there was nothing of the shrinking violet about her. Alexandra always had an image of Zoya's mother, reclining on a chair, dressed all in white silk, with her pale skin and blond hair, with her incredible pearls, and a look of terror in her eyes, as though life was simply too much for her. At the beginning of the war, she had asked her to help with her Red Cross work, and Natalya had simply said that she couldn't bear it. She was not one of life's sturdier specimens, but the Tsarina refrained from comment now and only nodded.

"You must give her my love when you go home." And as she said it, Zoya glanced outside and saw how dark it had gotten. She leapt to her feet and looked at her watch in horror.

"Oh! I must go home! Mama will be furious!"

"As well she should!" The Tsarina laughed and wagged a finger at her as she rose to her feet, towering over the young girl. "You mustn't lie to your mother about where you are! And I know she'd be most upset about your being exposed to our measles. Have you had them?"

Zoya laughed. "No, I have not, but I won't catch them now, and if I do . . ." She shrugged with another burst of laughter as Mashka grinned. It was one of the things Marie loved about her, her courage and sense of devil-may-care. They had gotten into considerable mischief together over the years, but nothing dangerous or truly harmful.

"I shall send you home now. And I must go back to the children, and poor Anna. . . ." She kissed them both and left the room, as Marie swept up the puppy from where she was hiding and wrapped her in the blanket again, and handed her to Zoya.

"Don't forget Sava!"

Their eyes met again and Zoya's were filled with love for her. "Can I really have her?"

"She's yours. She was always meant to be, but I wanted to surprise you. Keep her in your coat on the way home. You'll keep her warm that way." She was only seven weeks old, born on Russian Christmas. Zoya had been wildly excited when she saw her on Christmas Day for the first time, when their family came to visit the Tsar and his family for dinner. "Your mother will be furious, won't she?" Marie laughed, and Zoya laughed with her.

"Yes, but I'll tell her your mother will be frightfully put out if we send her back. Mama will be too afraid to offend her."

The girls both laughed as Marie followed her downstairs and helped her on with her coat, as she held the puppy in the blanket in place. She pulled the sable hat back over her red hair, and the two girls embraced.

"Take care of yourself, and don't get sick!"

"I have no intention of it!" She handed her the bottle of perfume as well, and

Zoya took it in a gloved hand, as the maid told her that Feodor was ready.

"I'll come back in a day or two . . . I promise . . . and thank you!" Zoya gave her a quick hug and hurried back outside to the troika where Feodor was waiting. His cheeks and nose were bright red and she knew he had been drinking with his friends in the stables, but it didn't matter. He would need it to keep warm as they sped home to St. Petersburg. He helped her into her seat and she was relieved to see that it had stopped snowing.

"We must hurry, Feodor . . . Mama is going to be very cross at me if I'm late." But she already knew that there was no way she would arrive in time for dinner. They would already be sitting down when she arrived . . . and the dog! . . . she laughed out loud to herself, as the whip cracked in the chill night air, and the troika leapt to life behind the three prancing black horses. It was only an instant later when they sped through the gates, and the Cossacks on their horses were a blur behind them, as they sped through the village of Tsarskoe Selo.

Chapter 2

As Feodor raced the troika down the Nevsky Prospekt, Zoya sat clutching the tiny puppy to her, trying to compose herself and desperately inventing excuses to tender her mother. She knew that with Feodor driving her, they would not be afraid for her safety, but her mother would surely be outraged at her coming home so late, and bringing the tiny puppy with her. But the puppy would have to be introduced later. At Fontanka, they turned sharply left, and the horses plunged ahead, knowing full well that they were almost home, and anxious to return to their own stable. But knowing the terrain well, Feodor gave them their head, and within moments, he was handing her down, and in sudden inspiration, she pulled the blanket-wrapped puppy from her coat and thrust her into his hands with an imploring look.

"Please, Feodor . . . the Empress gave her to me . . . her name is Sava. Take her to the kitchen and give her to Gallina. I will come downstairs for her later." Her eyes were those of a terrified child as he laughed out loud at her and shook his head.

"The Countess will have my head for this, mademoiselle! And perhaps yours as well."

"I know . . . perhaps Papa . . ." Papa, who always interceded for her, who was always so kind, and so gentle to her mother. He was a wonderful man and his only daughter adored him. "Quickly, Feodor . . . I must hurry." It was after seven o'clock, and she still had to change her dress before she could appear in the dining room. He took the puppy from her, and she hurried up the marble steps of their small but very beautiful palace. It seemed to be both Russian and French, and had been built by her grandfather for his bride. Her grandmother lived in a pavilion across the garden now, with a little park of its own, but Zoya had no time to think of her now. She was in a great hurry. She slipped quickly inside, pulled off her hat, and handed her coat to a maid standing nearby, and flew up the main staircase toward her bedroom, but as she did so, she heard a familiar voice boom out behind her.

"Halt! Who goes there?"

"Be quiet!" She turned toward her brother standing at the foot of the stairs with a furious whisper. "What are *you* doing here?" He was tall and handsome in his uniform and she knew that most of her friends at the Smolny swooned at the sight of him. He wore the insignia of the famed Preobrajensky Guard, but she was not impressed by it now.

"Where's Mama?" But she already knew without asking.

"In the dining room, where would you expect? Where have you been?"

"Out. I have to hurry. . . ." She still had to change, and he was delaying her even more. "I'm late."

He laughed and the green eyes so like her own flashed in amusement. "You'd best go in like that. Mama will be furious if you're any later."

Zoya hesitated for an instant as she looked down at him. "Did she say anything? . . . Have you seen her?"

"Not yet. I just arrived. I wanted to see Papa after dinner. Go and change. I'll distract them." He was fonder of her than

she knew, she was the little sister he
bragged about to all his friends, all of
whom had had an eye on her for years.
But he would have killed them if they'd
touched her. She was a little beauty, but
she didn't know it yet, and she was far too
young to dally with his cronies. She would
marry a prince one day, or at least someone as important as their father. He was a
count and a colonel, and a man who inspired the respect and admiration of all
who knew him. "Go on, you little beast,"
he called after her. "Hurry!"

She flew on toward her room, and ten
minutes later she was downstairs in a navy
blue silk dress with a lace collar. It was a
dress she detested, but she knew her
mother always liked her in it. It was very
proper and very young, and she didn't
want to upset her even further. It was impossible to appear in the doorway of the
dining room without attracting attention,
and as she walked sedately into the room
looking subdued and chaste, her brother
grinned at her mischievously from where
he sat between their grandmother and
their mother. The Countess was looking
unusually pale in a gray satin dress with a
beautiful necklace of black pearls and diamonds. Her eyes seemed almost the same

color as the dress as she lifted her face slowly and looked unhappily at her only daughter.

"Zoya!" Her voice was never raised, but her displeasure was easy to read as she looked at her. Zoya's eyes met hers honestly, and she hurried to kiss her cool cheek, and then glanced nervously at her father and grandmother.

"I'm terribly sorry, Mama . . . I was delayed . . . at ballet class today . . . had to stop and see a friend . . . I'm terribly sorry . . . I'm . . ."

Her mother's voice was chill as the rest of the family watched. "Just exactly where were you?"

"I . . . I had to go . . . I'm . . ."

Natalya looked her straight in the eye, as Zoya tried to smooth her hair into place. It still looked as though she had combed it in great haste, which of course she had. "I want to know the truth. Did you go to Tsarskoe Selo?"

"I . . ." It was no use. Her mother was too cool, too beautiful, too frightening, and too much in control. "Yes, Mama," she said, feeling seven years old again instead of a decade older. "I'm sorry."

"You're a fool." Natalya's icy eyes flashed and she glanced unhappily at her

husband. "Konstantin, I specifically told
her not to. All the children there have the
measles, and now she's been exposed to
them. That was a wanton act of disobedi-
ence." Zoya glanced nervously at her father, but his eyes were filled with the
same dancing emerald fire as her own,
and he could barely repress a smile. Just as
he loved his wife, he also adored his
daughter. And this time Nicolai interceded for her, which was unusual, but she
looked so uncomfortable, he felt sorry for
her.

"Perhaps they asked her to come,
Mama, and Zoya felt awkward refusing."

But with her other qualities, she was
honest, and Zoya faced her mother
squarely now as she sat quietly in her seat,
waiting for the maids to bring her dinner.
"I wanted to go, Mama. It was my fault,
not theirs. Marie has been so very lonely."

"It was very foolish of you, Zoya. We will
discuss it again after dinner."

"Yes, Mama." She lowered her eyes toward her plate, and the others carried on
their conversation without her. it was only
a moment later that she looked up and
realized her grandmother was there, and
a smile lit up her face as she saw her.

"Hello, Grandmama. Aunt Alix said to send you her love."

"Is she well?" It was her father who asked. Her mother sat looking silently beautiful, still obviously displeased with her daughter.

"She is always well when she tends the sick," her grandmother answered for her. "It's an odd thing about Alix. She seems to suffer every possible malaise, until she is needed by someone sicker, and then she rises to the occasion remarkably." The elderly Countess looked pointedly at her daughter-in-law, and then smiled proudly at Zoya. "Little Marie must have been happy to see you, Zoya."

Zoya smiled gratefully. "She was, Grandmama." And then to reassure her mother, "I never saw the others. They were all closeted somewhere. Even Madame Vyrubova is sick now," she added, and then regretted it bitterly as her mother glanced up in obvious terror.

"How stupid of you, Zoya . . . I can't understand why you would go there. Do you wish to catch the measles?"

"No, Mama. I'm truly very sorry." But there was nothing in her face to make one believe that she was. Only her words were filled with the expected contrition. "I didn't mean to be late. I was going to leave when Aunt Alix came in to have tea with us, and I didn't want to be rude to her. . . ."

"As well you should not. She is, after all, our Empress as well as our cousin," her grandmother said pointedly. Her own eyes were the same green as Zoya's, and her father's and brother's. Only Natalya's were a pale bluish gray, like a cold winter sky with no hope of summer. Her life had always been too demanding of her, her husband was energetic and robust, he had always loved her enthusiastically and well, and he had wanted more children than she was able to bear. Two had been stillborn, and she had had several miscarriages, and both Zoya and Nicolai had been difficult to bear. She had spent a year in bed for each of them, and now slept in her own apartments. Konstantin loved his friends, and he had also wanted to give innumerable balls and parties, but she found all of it far too exhausting, and used ill health as an excuse for her lack of joie de vivre and her almost overwhelming shyness. It gave her an air of icy disdain, behind which she hid the fact that people terrified her, and she was far happier reclining on a chair near the fire. But his

daughter was far more like him, and after
Zoya made her debut in the spring, Konstantin was looking forward to the prospect of having her accompany him to parties. They had talked for a long time about
abandoning the idea of a ball, and Natalya
had insisted that they shouldn't consider it
with a war on, but finally Zoya's grandmother had decided the matter for them,
and Konstantin was much relieved. There
was to be a ball as soon as she graduated
from the Smolny Institute in June, perhaps not as grand a ball as they might have
given if there were no war going on, but it
was still going to be a very lovely party.

"What news of Nicholas?" Konstantin
inquired. "Did Marie say anything?"

"Not much. Aunt Alix says he's home
from the front, but I think he's going back
soon."

"I know. I saw him last week. He's well,
though, isn't he?" Konstantin looked concerned, as his handsome son watched him.
He knew then that his father must have
heard the same rumors he had heard in
the barracks, that Nicholas was exhausted
beyond what anyone knew, and that the
strain of the war was wearing on him.
Some even spoke in hushed whispers
about the possibility of a breakdown. With

the gentle kindness of the Tsar and his constant concern for everyone, that was almost impossible to imagine. It was difficult to think of him breaking down, or giving up. He was deeply loved by his peers, and most especially by Zoya's father. Like Zoya and Marie, they had been childhood friends, and he was godfather to Nicolai, who had been named after him, and Nicholas's own father had been extremely close to Konstantin's father. Their love for each other went beyond family, they had always been extremely close, and had teased each other about their both marrying German women, although Alix seemed to be a little hardier than Natalya. At least she was capable of rising to the occasion when necessary, as she did with her Red Cross work, and now when her children were sick. Natalya would have been constitutionally unable to do anything like it. The old Countess had been fiercely disappointed when her son had not married a Russian. The fact that a German had been good enough for the Tsar was only small consolation.

"What brings you here tonight, by the way?" Konstantin turned to Nicolai with a warm smile. He was proud of him, and pleased that he was with the Preobrajensky and not at the front, and he made no secret of it. He had no desire to lose his only son. Russian losses had already been great, from the Battle of Tannenberg in the summer of 1914 to the terrible reverses in Galicia's frozen fields, and he wanted Nicolai safely in St. Petersburg. That at least was a great relief to him, and to Natalya.

"I wanted to chat with you after dinner tonight, Papa." His voice sounded quiet and strong, as Natalya glanced nervously at him. She hoped he didn't have something unnerving to share, she had heard from a friend recently that her son was involved with a dancer, and she was going to have a great deal to say if he told his father he was getting married. "Nothing important." His grandmother watched him with wise old eyes, and knew that whatever it was he had to tell his father, he was lying about its importance. He was worried about something, worried enough to drop by and spend an evening with all of them, which was most unlike him. "Actually," he smiled at the assembled troupe, "I came to make sure that the little monster here was behaving." He glanced over at Zoya, and she shot him a look of extreme annoyance.

"I've grown up, Nicolai. I don't 'misbehave' anymore." She sniffed primly and finished her dessert, as he laughed openly at her.

"Is that right? Imagine that . . . it seems like only moments ago when you were flying up the stairs, late for dinner as usual, wearing wet boots on the stairs, with your hair looking as though you'd combed it with a pitchfork. . . ." He was fully prepared to go on and she threw her napkin at him, as her mother looked faint and glanced imploringly at their father.

"Konstantin, please make them stop it! They make me so terribly nervous."

"It is only a love song, my dear," the Countess Evgenia said wisely. "That is the only way they know to converse with each other at this point in their lives. My children were always pulling each other's hair, and throwing their shoes at each other. Didn't you, Konstantin?" He gave a crack of laughter as he looked sheepishly at his mother.

"I'm afraid I wasn't very well behaved when I was young either, my dear." He looked lovingly at his wife, and then happily around the table as he stood up, bowed slightly to all of them, and preceded his son into a small adjoining sitting room, where they could converse in private. Like his wife, he hoped that Nicolai had not appeared to tell them he was getting married.

And as they sat down quietly near the fire, the elegant gold cigarette case Nicolai took from the pocket of his uniform did not go unnoticed. It was one of Carl Fabergé's more typical designs, in pink and yellow gold with a very pretty sapphire thumbpiece. Konstantin was almost certain that the workmaster was either Hollming or Wigstrom.

"A new bauble, Nicolai?" Like his wife, he had also heard the story of Nicolai's allegedly very pretty little dancer.

"A gift from a friend, Papa."

Konstantin smiled indulgently. "That's more or less what I was afraid of." Both men laughed and Nicolai furrowed his brow. He was still young but he was wise for his years, and he had a sharp mind in addition to his good looks. He was most emphatically a son to be proud of.

"You have nothing to worry about, Father. In spite of what you hear, I'm only having a little fun, nothing serious, I promise you."

"Good. Then what brought you here tonight?"

Nicolai looked worried as he stared into the fire, and then into his father's eyes. "Something a great deal more important. I'm hearing unpleasant things about the Tsar, that he's tired, that he's sick, that he shouldn't be in charge of the troops. Father, you must be hearing it too."

"I am." He nodded slowly and watched his son. "But I still believe that he will not fail us."

"I was at a party with Ambassador Paléologue last night. He paints a very gloomy picture. He thinks the shortages of food and fuel are far more serious than we admit to ourselves, the strain of the war is taking its toll. We are supplying six million men at the front, and we're barely able to take care of our own at home. He's afraid that we might crack . . . that Russia might crack . . . that Nicholas might crack . . . and then what, Father? Do you think he's right?"

Konstantin thought about it for a long time, and finally shook his head. "No, I don't. Yes, I think we're feeling the strain of all that, and so is Nicholas. But this is Russia, Nicolai, this is not a tiny, weak country in the middle of nowhere. We are a people of stamina and strength, and no matter how difficult the conditions without or within, we will *not* crack. Ever." It was what he believed, and Nicolai found it reassuring.

"The Duma reconvenes tomorrow. It will be interesting to see what happens then."

"Nothing will happen, my son. Russia is for always and forever. Surely you must know that." He looked warmly at his son, and the youth felt better again.

"I do. Maybe I just needed to hear it."

"We all do sometimes. You must be strong for Nicholas, for all of us, for your country. We must all be strong now, and the good times will come again. The war can't go on forever."

"It's an awful thing." They were both aware of how severe had been their losses. But none of that had to mean an end to what they held dear. Now that he thought of it, Nicolai felt foolish for having been so worried. It was just that the French ambassador had been so convincing with his predictions of doom. He was glad now that he had come to talk to his father. "Is Mother all right?" Nicolai had found her even more nervous than usual, or perhaps it struck him more now because he saw her less often, but Konstantin only smiled.

"She worries about the war too . . .

and about you . . . and about me . . . and about Zoya. . . . She's quite a handful."

"Lovely, though, isn't she?" He spoke of Zoya with a warmth and admiration he would have denied vehemently had anyone told her. "Half my regiment seems to be in love with her. I spend most of my time threatening to murder them."

His father laughed, and then shook his head sadly. "It's a shame she has to come out during wartime. Perhaps it'll all be over by June." It was a hope they both shared, but which Nicolai feared wasn't likely.

"Have you anyone in mind for her?" Nicolai was curious. There were several of his friends he thought might make excellent suitors.

"I can't bear to think of losing her. It's foolish, I suppose. She's too lively to stay with us for very much longer. Your grandmother thinks a great deal of Prince Orlov."

"He's too old for her." He was every bit of thirty-five, and Nicolai frowned protectively at the thought. In fact, he wasn't sure if anyone was good enough for his fiery little sister.

Konstantin stood up and smiled at his

son as he patted him on the shoulder. "We'd best go back to them now. If we don't, your mother will get worried." They walked out of the room, with Konstantin's arm around Nicolai's shoulders. And when they joined the ladies in one of the smaller drawing rooms, Zoya was pleading with her mother about something.

"Now what have you done, you little monster?" Nicolai laughed at the look on her face, and he could see that his grandmother had turned her back to hide a smile. Natalya's face was as white as paste, and Zoya's was bright red as she looked angrily at her brother.

"Don't you get involved in this!"

"What is it now, little one?" Konstantin looked amused until he saw the look of reproach on his wife's face. She thought he was entirely too easy on his daughter.

"Apparently," the younger Countess spoke in outraged tones, "Alix gave her a totally ridiculous gift today, and I absolutely will *not* let her keep it."

"Good God, what is it? Her famous pearls? By all means, darling, accept them, you can always wear them later." Konstantin was in good spirits after his visit with Nicolai, and the two men exchanged a warm glance over the heads of the women.

"This is not amusing, Konstantin, and I expect you to tell her just exactly what I did. She must get rid of it at once."

"What is it, pest? A trained snake?" Nicolai teased.

"No, it's one of Joy's puppies." Tears shone brightly in Zoya's eyes and she looked imploringly at her father. "Papa, please . . . if I promise to take care of it myself, to never let it out of my sight, or my room, and keep it away from Mother . . . please? . . ." Tears trembled in her eyes and her father's heart went out to her, as Natalya stormed across the room, her eyes like her diamonds flashing in the lamplight.

"No! Dogs breed diseases! And you all know perfectly well how delicate my health is!" She looked far from delicate just then, as she stood in the center of the room, a vision of exquisite fury. It reminded Konstantin of how taken he had been with her the very first time he laid eyes on her, but he also knew now that Natalya was not an easy woman.

"Perhaps if it lives in the kitchen . . . perhaps then . . ." He looked hopefully at his wife, as she strode to the door and pulled it open.

"You always give in to her, Konstantin, don't you?"

"Darling . . . it can't be a very big dog. Theirs is quite small."

"And they have two others and a cat, and their child is constantly hovering on the brink of death." She was referring of course to Alexis's chronic ill-health.

"That has nothing to do with their dogs. Perhaps Grandmama would keep it at her house. . . ." He looked hopefully at his mother and she smiled, secretly enjoying the storm. It was just like Alix to give Zoya a dog, knowing full well how furious it would make her mother. There had always been a secret rivalry between the two women, but Alexandra was, after all, the Tsarina.

"I'd be quite willing to have him," the elder Countess offered.

"Very well." Konstantin felt he had found the perfect solution, but the door slammed with a resolute bang, and he knew he would not see his wife again until the next morning.

"And on that happy note," Nicolai said, smiling around him, and bowing to his grandmother formally, "I shall return to my extremely peaceful barracks."

"See that you do," his grandmother said pointedly with an ill-concealed smile, and then chuckled as he kissed her good night. "I hear that you're becoming quite a rake, my dear."

"Don't believe everything you hear. Good night, Grandmama." He kissed her on both cheeks, and gently touched his father's shoulder as he bid him good night. "And as for you, you little beast . . ." He gave the bright red hair a gentle tug as he kissed her, and she looked up at him with the love she felt for him scarcely hidden. "Behave yourself, goose. And try not to come home with any more pets. You're going to drive your mother crazy."

"Nobody asked you!" she said pointedly, and then kissed him again. "Good-bye, you utterly awful boy."

"I'm not a boy, I'm a man, not that you would ever know the difference."

"I would if I saw one."

He waved at them all from the door with a look of amusement, and then he was gone, more than likely to visit his little dancer.

"What a charming boy he is, Konstantin. He reminds me a great deal of you

when you were young," the elderly
Countess said with pride, as her son
smiled, and Zoya threw herself into a
chair with a look of disgust.

"I think he's perfectly awful."

"He speaks of you far more kindly, Zoya
Konstantinovna," her father said gently.
He was proud of them and loved them
both deeply. He bent to kiss her cheek,
and then smiled quietly at his mother.
"Are you really going to take the dog,
Mama?" he asked the Countess Evgenia.
"I'm afraid Natalya will put us all out of
the house if I press her any further." He
stifled a sigh. There were times when he
would have liked his wife to be a trifle
easier to deal with, particularly when his
mother was looking on in barely silent
judgment. But Evgenia Ossupov had
formed her opinions of her daughter-in-
law long since, and nothing Natalya did
now was likely to change them in any
case.

"Of course. I would like to have a little
friend." She turned to Zoya with a look of
amusement. "Which of their dogs sired
this one? The Tsarevich's Charles, or Tatiana's little French bulldog?"

"Neither, Grandmama. It's from Marie's cocker spaniel, Joy. She's so sweet,

Grandmama. And her name is Sava."
Zoya looked radiant and childlike as she
went to sit at her grandmother's knees,
and the older woman put a gnarled but
loving hand on her shoulders.

"Ask her only not to christen my favorite Aubusson and we shall be fast friends, I
promise." She stroked the fiery red hair
that fell across Zoya's shoulders. She had
loved the touch of her grandmother's
hands since she was a child, and she
reached up and kissed her tenderly.

"Thank you, Grandmama. I so want to
keep him."

"And so you shall, little one . . . so you
shall. . . ." She stood up then and walked
slowly toward the fire, feeling tired but at
ease, as Zoya disappeared to retrieve the
little puppy from the servants. The Countess turned slowly to Konstantin, and it
seemed only moments before when he
had been Nicolai's age, and much, much
younger. The years seemed to fly by so
quickly, but they had been kind to her.
Her husband had led a full life. He had
died three years before at eighty-nine,
and she had always felt blessed to have
loved him. Konstantin looked like him
now, and it reminded her of him in happy
ways, particularly when she saw him with

Zoya. "She's a lovely child, Konstantin Nicolaevich . . . a beautiful young girl."

"She's a great deal like you, Mama."

Evgenia shook her head, but he could see in her eyes that she agreed with him. There were times when she saw a great deal of herself in the girl, and she was always glad that Zoya was very little like her mother. Even when she disobeyed her mother, the old Countess somehow thought it admirable, and had long since felt it was a sign of her own blood running in Zoya's veins, which annoyed Natalya even more. "She is someone new . . . she is her own. We must not burden her with our quirks and failings."

"When have you ever failed? You have always been good to me, Mama . . . to all of us . . ." She was a woman who was respected and well liked. A woman of purpose and sound values. He knew her wisdom and depended on her countless but generally sensible opinions.

"Here she is, Grandmama!" Zoya had reappeared with the little dog. She was scarcely bigger than Zoya's hands, and the countess took the puppy carefully from her. "Isn't she sweet?"

"She is wonderful . . . and so she shall be until she eats my best hat, or my favorite shoes . . . but not, please God, my favorite Aubusson carpet. And if you do," she said, stroking the puppy's head as she had Zoya's only moments before, "I shall make soup of you. Remember that!" Little Sava barked, as though in answer. "That was very nice of Alix to give her to you, little one. I hope you thanked her properly."

Zoya giggled and covered her mouth with a graceful hand. "She was rather afraid Mama would be upset."

Her grandmother chuckled as Konstantin tried not to smile, in deference to his wife. "She knows your mother very well, I see, doesn't she, Konstantin?" She looked him straight in the eye and he understood everything that she was saying.

"Poor Natalya's health has not made things easy for her lately. Perhaps eventually . . ." She tried to defend her.

"Never mind, Konstantin." The dowager countess waved an impatient hand, as she held the puppy close and kissed her granddaughter good night. "Come and see us tomorrow, Zoya. Or are you going back to Tsarskoe Selo? I should go with you one of these days and pay a call on Alix and the children."

"Not while they're ill, Mama, please

. . . and the drive will be too much for you, in this weather."

His mother laughed out loud. "Don't be foolish, Konstantin. I had measles almost a hundred years ago, and I have never been worried about weather. I'm quite well, thank you very much, and I plan to stay that way for at least another dozen years, or perhaps more. And I'm mean enough to do just that."

"That's excellent news." He smiled. "I'll walk you back to the pavilion."

"Don't be foolish." She waved him away as Zoya went to find her cloak and returned to put it over her shoulders. "I'm quite capable of walking across the garden, you know. I do it several times a day."

"Then don't deny me the pleasure of doing it with you, madame."

She smiled up at him, seeing him as a child again, in her heart anyway, where forever he would remain a small boy for as long as she lived. "Very well then, Konstantin. Good night, Zoya."

"Good night, Grandmama. And thank you for keeping Sava for me." The old woman gave her a fond kiss, and Zoya went upstairs to her mauve room as they went out into the cold night air. Zoya yawned to herself, and smiled as she thought of the little dog Marie and her mother had given her. It had been a lovely day. She softly closed her bedroom door, and promised herself she would return to Tsarskoe Selo in a day or two. But in the meantime, she would have to think of something wonderful to take to Mashka.

Chapter 3

Two days later, Zoya was planning to return to Tsarskoe Selo to see Marie, and instead a letter came that morning before breakfast. It was delivered by Dr. Fedorov himself, Alexis's doctor, who had come to town to bring back some more medicines, and he brought the unwelcome news that Marie had also succumbed to the measles. Zoya read her note with dismay. It meant not only that she could not visit her, but that they might not see each other for weeks, as Dr. Fedorov said that she would not be able to have visitors for quite some time, depending on how ill she became. Already, Anastasia was having trouble with her ears as a result of the disease, and he greatly feared that the Tsarevich was developing pneumonia.

"Oh, my God . . ." Natalya wailed. "And you've been exposed as well. Zoya, I had forbidden you to go and now you've exposed yourself . . . how could you do this to me? How dare you!" She was nearly hysterical at the thought of the illness Zoya might unwittingly have brought into the house, and Konstantin arrived on the scene in time to see his wife swoon, and he sent her maid rapidly upstairs for her vinaigrette. He had commissioned a special case for it by Fabergé, in the shape of a large red enamel, diamond encrusted strawberry, which she kept ever near her, by her bedside.

Dr. Fedorov was kind enough to stay long enough to see Natalya upstairs while Zoya dashed off a quick note to her friend. She wished her a speedy recovery so they could be together again, and signed it from herself and Sava, who had generously watered the famous Aubusson rug only the night before, but her grandmother had kept the puppy there anyway, while still threatening to turn her into soup if her manners did not improve very quickly.

". . . I love you dearly, sweetest friend. Now hurry up and get well, so I can come and see you." She sent her two books, one of them *Helen's Babies*, which she herself had read and loved only weeks before and had planned to give her anyway. And she

added a quick postscript, warning Mashka
not to use this as an excuse to cheat at
tennis again, as they had both done the
summer before, while playing at Livadia
with two of Marie's sisters. It was their
favorite game, and Marie was better than
the rest of them, although Zoya always
threatened to beat her. ". . . I will come
out to see you as soon as your Mama and
the doctor will let me. With all my heart,
your loving Zoya. . . ."

That afternoon, Zoya saw her brother
again, which at least distracted her, and
while waiting for their father to return
home, he took her out for a spin in their
mother's troika. She had not emerged
from her room all day, so upset was she by
the news that Marie had contracted measles and Zoya had been inadvertently exposed. Zoya knew she might not come out
for days, and she was grateful for the distraction provided by her brother.

"Why have you come to see Papa again?
Is something wrong, Nicolai?"

"Don't be silly. Why would you think
something's wrong? What a twit you are."
But a smart one. He marveled at how she
instinctively knew that he had returned to
see Konstantin because he was worried.
The previous day when the Duma con-

vened, Alexander Kerensky had made a
dreadful speech which included an incite-
ment to assassinate the Tsar, and Nicolai
was beginning to fear that some of what
Ambassador Paléologue had said was true.
Perhaps things were worse than they all
knew and the people were more unnerved by the shortages than they all suspected. Sir George Buchanan, the British
ambassador, had said as much too before
leaving for Finland for a ten-day holiday.
Nicolai was hearing a great deal these days
and it worried him, and once again he was
anxious to hear his father's opinion.

"You never come to visit unless something's wrong, Nicolai," Zoya pressed him
as they sped along the beautiful Nevsky
Prospekt. There was fresh snow on the
ground and it had never looked prettier
than it did then, but Nicolai still staunchly
insisted that nothing was amiss, and although she felt an odd twinge of fear, she
decided to believe him.

"That's a charming thing to say, Zoya.
And besides, it's not true. More to the
point, is it true that you've driven Mama
to distraction again? I hear she's taken to
her bed thanks to you, and has had to be
visited twice by her doctor."

Zoya shrugged, with an impish grin.

"That's just because Dr. Fedorov told her that Mashka has the measles."

"And you're next?" Nicolai smiled at her and she laughed at him.

"Don't be stupid. I never get sick."

"Don't be so sure. You're not going back there again, are you?" For an instant he looked worried, but she shook her head with a look of childlike disappointment.

"They won't let me. No one can visit now. And poor Anastasia has a terrible earache."

"They'll all be fine soon and you can go back again."

Zoya nodded and then grinned. "By the way, Nicolai, how's your dancer?"

He gave a sudden start and then pulled a lock of her hair peeking from beneath her fur hat. "What makes you think I have a 'dancer'?"

"Everyone knows that, stupid . . . just like they did about Uncle Nicholas before he married Aunt Alix." She could speak openly with him, after all he was only her brother, but he looked shocked anyway. Outspoken though she was, he expected at least a little decorum.

"Zoya! How dare you speak of such things!"

"I can say anything I want to you. What's yours like? Is she pretty?"

"She is not anything! She doesn't exist. Is this what they teach you at the Smolny?"

"They don't teach me anything," she said blithely, discounting a very solid education she had gotten there in spite of herself, just as he had years before at the Imperial Corps des Pages, the military school for the sons of noblemen and high-ranking officers. "Besides, I'm almost finished."

"I imagine they'll be awfully grateful to see the last of you, my dear." She shrugged and they both laughed, and he thought for an instant that he had fobbed her off, but she was more persistent than that as she turned to him with a wicked smile.

"You still haven't told me about your friend, Nicolai."

"You're a terrible girl, Zoya Konstantinovna."

She giggled and he drove her slowly home, returning to their palace on Fontanka, and by then their father was home, and the two men closeted themselves in Konstantin's library, which overlooked the garden. It was filled with beautiful leather-bound books, and objects her father had collected over the years, particularly the malachite pieces he was so fond of. There was also a collection of elaborate Fabergé Easter eggs that Natalya had given him each year, similar to the ones the Tsar and Tsarina exchanged on memorable occasions. As Konstantin stood at the window, listening to his son, he saw Zoya bounding across the snow, on her way to visit her grandmother and Sava.

"Well, Father, what do you think?" When Konstantin turned to face him again, he saw that Nicolai was genuinely worried.

"I really don't think any of it means anything. And even if there's a bit of trouble in the streets, General Khabalov can handle anything, Nicolai. There's nothing to worry about." He smiled comfortingly, pleased that his son was so concerned about the well-being of both the city and the country. "All is well. But it never hurts to be alert. It is the mark of a good soldier." And he was, just as he had been when he was younger, and his father before him. If he could, Konstantin would have been at the front himself, but he was far too old, no matter how much he loved his cousin the Tsar and his country.

"Father, doesn't Kerensky's speech to

the Duma worry you? My God, what he's suggesting is treason!"

"And so it is, but no one can possibly take this seriously, Nicolai. No one is going to assassinate the Tsar. They wouldn't dare. Besides, Nicky is wise enough to keep himself well protected. I think he's in far more danger at home just now, with a houseful of measles-ridden children and servants"—he smiled gently at his son— "than he is at the hands of his people. But in any case, I will call on Ambassador Buchanan when he returns and speak to him myself if he's so concerned. I would be interested to hear his point of view on the matter, and Paléologue's as well. When Buchanan returns from his holiday, I'll arrange a luncheon with them, and of course you're more than welcome to join us." Most of all he wanted to assist his son's career. Nicolai was a bright boy, with a brilliant future ahead of him.

"I feel better talking to you, Father." But still this time the fears were not so easily stilled, and when he left the house, he still had a gnawing sense of impending danger. He was tempted to go to Tsarskoe Selo himself and have a private meeting with his cousin, but he knew from what he'd heard about how exhausted the Tsar was, and how worried about his son, that the time was not appropriate. It was an unfortunate time to intrude on him, and it seemed wiser not to.

It was fully a week later, on March 8, that Nicholas left St. Petersburg to return to the front, five hundred miles away in Mogilev. And it was on that very day that there was the first sign of disorder in the streets when the breadlines erupted into angry, shouting people and they forced their way into the bakeries, shouting, "Give us bread!" And at sunset, a squadron of Cossacks arrived to control them. And still, no one seemed overly concerned. Ambassador Paléologue even gave a very large party. Prince and Princess Gorchakov were there, Count Tolstoy, Alexander Benois, and the Spanish ambassador, the Marquis de Villasinda. Natalya still wasn't feeling well and had insisted that she couldn't possibly go out, and Konstantin didn't want to leave her. He was just as glad they hadn't gone, when he heard the next day that a tram had been overturned by rioters on the fringes of the city. But on the whole, no one seemed unduly alarmed. And as though to reassure everyone, the day after had dawned bright and sunny. The Nevsky Prospekt was filled with people, but they seemed happy enough and all of the shops were open for business. There were Cossacks on hand to observe what was going on, but they seemed on good terms with the crowd. But on Saturday, March 10, there was unexpected looting, and the following day, several people were killed during assorted disorders.

And that night, the Radziwills nonetheless were to give a very elaborate party. It was as though everyone wanted to pretend nothing was happening. But it was difficult to ignore reports of turmoil and disturbance.

Gibbes, Marie's English tutor, brought Zoya a letter from Mashka that day, and she pounced on him with open arms, but she was dismayed to read that Marie was feeling "terrible," and Tatiana had developed ear problems too. But at least Baby was feeling a little better.

"Poor Aunt Alix must be so tired," Zoya told her grandmother that afternoon as she sat in her drawing room holding little Sava. "I'm so anxious to see Marie again, Grandmama." She had had nothing to do for days, her mother had absolutely insisted that she not go to ballet because of the problems in the streets, and this time her father had endorsed the order.

"A little patience, my dear," her grandmother urged. "You don't want to be on the streets just now anyway, with all those hungry, unhappy people."

"Is it as bad as that for them, Grandmama?" It was difficult to imagine in the midst of all the luxuries they enjoyed. It hurt her heart to think of people so desperately hungry. "I wish we could give them some of what we have." Their life was so comfortable and easy, it seemed cruel that all around them people were cold and hungry.

"We all wish that sometimes, little one." The fiery old eyes looked deep into her own. "Life is not always fair. There are many, many people who will never have what we take for granted every day . . . warm clothes, comfortable beds, an abundance of food . . . not to mention the frivolities like holidays and parties and pretty dresses."

"Is all of that wrong?" The very idea seemed to startle Zoya.

"Certainly not. But it is a privilege, and we must never forget that."

"Mama says they're common people

and wouldn't enjoy what we have anyway. Do you suppose that's true?"

Evgenia looked at her with irritated irony, amazed that her daughter-in-law was still so blind and so foolish. "Don't be ridiculous, Zoya. Do you suppose anyone would object to a warm bed and a full stomach, or a pretty dress, or a wonderful troika? They would have to be awfully stupid." Zoya didn't add that her mother said they were that too, because Zoya understood that they weren't.

"You know, it's sad, Grandmama, that they don't know Uncle Nicky and Aunt Alix and Baby and the girls. They're such good people, no one could be angry at them if they knew them." It was a sensible thing to say, and yet so incredibly simplistic.

"It isn't them, my love . . . it is only the things they stand for. It's incredibly hard for people outside palace windows to remember that the people inside them have heartbreaks and problems. No one will ever know how much Nicholas cares about all of them, how much he grieves for their ills, and how his heart has been broken by Alexis's illness. They will never know, and never see . . . it makes me sad too. The poor man carries so many terrible burdens. And now he's back at the front again. It must be difficult for Alix. I do wish the children would get well so I could go to see them."

"I want to go too. But Papa won't even let me step outside the house. It's going to take me months to catch up with Madame Nastova."

"Of course it won't." Evgenia was watching her, it seemed as though she grew more beautiful each day as she approached her eighteenth birthday. She was graceful and delicate with her flaming red hair and her huge green eyes, her long, lovely legs and the tiny waist one could have circled with both hands. She took one's breath away as one watched her.

"Grandmama, this is so boring." She twirled on one foot as Evgenia laughed at her.

"You certainly don't flatter me, my dear. A great many people have found me boring for a very long time, but no one has ever said so quite so bluntly."

"I'm sorry." She laughed. "I didn't mean you. I meant being cooped up here. And even stupid Nicolai didn't come to visit today." But later that afternoon, they knew why. General Khabalov had had huge posters put up all around the city, warning everyone that assemblies and public meetings were forbidden now, and all strikers were to return to their jobs the following day. Failure to comply would mean being drafted immediately and being sent to the front, but no one paid any attention whatsoever to the posters. Huge crowds of protesters swarmed from the Vyborg quarter across the Neva bridges and into the city, and by four-thirty that afternoon, the soldiers had appeared and there was shooting on the Nevsky Prospekt opposite the Anitchkov Palace. Fifty people were killed, and within hours, two hundred more died, and suddenly there was dissent among the soldiers. A company of the Pavlovsky Life Guards refused to fire, and instead turned and shot the officer in charge, and suddenly pandemonium reigned, and the Preobrajensky Guard had to be called in to disarm them.

Konstantin got word of it that night, and disappeared for hours, attempting to find out what was happening elsewhere and secretly wanting to reassure himself that Nicolai was all right. Suddenly, he felt panic sweep him knowing that his son was in danger. But all he could find out was that the Pavlovsky Guards had been dis-

armed with very little loss of life. "Very
little" seemed suddenly too much, and he
returned home to wait for news. On his
way back, he saw the lights at the
Radziwills and wondered at the madness
of a city that went on dancing while people were being murdered. Suddenly, he
wondered if Nicolai had been right all
along to be so worried about what might
be coming. Konstantin was anxious to talk
to Paléologue himself now, and decided to
call on him the next morning. But it was
only when he turned into Fontanka and
saw the horses outside his own home that
his heart froze and he wanted to stop and
run away. He suddenly felt terror seize his
heart and pressed his own horses forward.
There were at least a dozen of the Preobrajensky Guard outside, there was running and shouting and they were carrying
something as he heard a shout fly from his
own mouth and he abandoned Feodor and
his troika almost before it stopped, shouting to himself, "Oh my God . . . oh my
God . . ." and then he saw him. He was
being carried by two men and there was
blood everywhere on the snow. It was Nicolai. "Oh my God . . ." There were tears
streaming down Konstantin's cheeks as he

stared at them and rushed forward. "Is he alive?"

One of the men looked at him and nodded, speaking softly to Konstantin. "Barely." He had been shot seven times by one of the Pavlovsky Life Guards, one of their own . . . one of the Tsar's men . . . but he had been fearless and he had felled the other man. "Bring him inside . . . quickly . . ." He shouted for Feodor, who appeared at his side. "Get my wife's doctor *now!*" he roared as the young Guards looked at him helplessly. They knew that nothing could be done, it was why they had brought him home, and Nicolai looked up at his father with glassy eyes, but he recognized him and he smiled, looking like a child again as Konstantin took him in his own powerful arms, and carried him inside. He set him down on the tapestry-covered couch in the main hall, and all of the servants came running. "Bring bandages . . . sheets . . . quickly, get me warm water." He had no idea what he was going to do with all of it, but something had to be done. Something . . . anything . . . they had to save him. It was his little boy, they had brought him home to die, and he wasn't going to let him slip away. He had to stop him before it was too late, and suddenly he felt a firm hand push him aside, and he saw his own mother cradle the boy's head in her hands and gently kiss his forehead as she crooned to him.

"It's all right, Nicolai, Grandmama is here . . . and your Mama and Papa. . . ." The three women had gone ahead with dinner without waiting for Konstantin, and Evgenia had instantly sensed what had happened as she heard the men come in. The rest of the Guards were standing awkwardly in the main hallway, and there was a terrifying scream as Natalya saw her son and fainted in the doorway. "Zoya!" Evgenia called out, and the young girl ran to her as Konstantin stood helplessly by watching his son's blood ooze across the marble floor and seep slowly into the rug. He could see Zoya tremble as she ran to her grandmother and knelt at her brother's side. Her face was white as chalk, and she gently took his hand.

"Nicolai . . ." she whispered. "I love you . . . it's Zoya. . . ."

"What are you doing here?" His voice was barely a whisper now and Evgenia could tell from looking at him that he no longer saw them.

"Zoya," she commanded, a general in

charge of her men, "tear my petticoat in strips . . . quickly . . . hurry. . . ."

With gentle hands at first Zoya began to tug beneath her grandmother's skirts, but at the sound of her grandmother's commands, she gave a fierce tug as her grandmother stepped out of her petticoat and Zoya tore it into strips and watched her grandmother tie them about his wounds. She was trying to stop the bleeding but it was almost too late as Konstantin wept and knelt to kiss him.

"Papa? . . . are you there, Papa? . . ." He sounded so young again. "Papa . . . I love you . . . Zoya . . . be a good girl. . . ." And then he smiled up at them, and was gone, their efforts too little, too late. He died in his father's arms. Konstantin kissed his eyes and gently closed them, sobbing uncontrollably as he held the son he had so dearly loved, his blood seeping into his father's vest while he held him close. Zoya stood crying beside him and Evgenia's hands shook terribly, as she stroked his hand, and then slowly turned away and signaled to the men to leave them alone with their pain. The doctor had arrived by then and was attempting to revive Natalya, still lying inert in the doorway. They carried her upstairs to her rooms, and Feodor stood weeping openly as a wail seemed to fill the entire hallway. All of the servants had come to stand there . . . too late . . . everyone too late to help him.

"Come, Konstantin. You must let them take him upstairs." She gently pulled her son away from him, and guiding him unseeing into the library, she pushed him gently into a chair and poured him a brandy. There was nothing she could say to ease the pain, and she didn't try. She signaled to Zoya to stand near, and when she saw how pale she was, she forced her to take a sip of brandy from the glass she poured herself.

"No, Grandmama . . . no . . . please. . . ." She choked on the fumes, but her grandmother forced her to drink it and then turned to Konstantin again.

"He was so young . . . my God . . . my God . . . they've killed him. . . ." She held him as he rocked mindlessly back and forth in his chair, keening for his only son, and then suddenly Zoya exploded into his arms, clinging to him as though he were the only rock left in the world, and all she could think of was that only that afternoon she had called him "stupid Nicolai" . . . stupid Nicolai . . . and now

he was dead . . . her brother was dead
. . . she stared at her father in horror.

"Papa, what's happening?"

"I don't know, little one . . . they've
killed my baby. . . ." He held her close
then as she sobbed in his arms, and a little
while later he stood and left her in her
grandmother's care. "Take her home with
you, Mama. I must go to Natalya."

"She's all right." Evgenia was far more
worried about her son than his foolish
wife. She feared that the loss of Nicolai
might break him. She reached out and
touched his hand again, and he saw her
eyes, they were the eyes of wisdom and
time and immeasurable sorrow.

"Oh, Mama," he cried, and held her
close to him for a long, long time, while
she held out a hand and drew Zoya to
them. And then slowly he pulled away
from them, and went up the stairs to his
wife's rooms, as Zoya stood in the hallway
and watched him. Nicolai's blood had
been washed away from the marble floor,
and the rug had been removed, and he
already lay silent and cold in the room he
had lived in since his boyhood. He had
been born there, and died there, in
twenty-three short years, and with him
went a world they all knew and loved. It

was as though none of them would ever be safe again. Evgenia knew it as she took Zoya back to her own pavilion with her, trembling violently beneath her cloak, her eyes filled with shock and horror.

"You must be strong, little one," her grandmother said to her as Sava ran up to them in her living room and Zoya began to cry again. "Your father will need you doubly now. And perhaps . . . perhaps . . . nothing will ever be quite the same again . . . for any of us. But whatever comes"—her voice quavered as she thought of her grandson dying in her arms, but as her thin hand trembled violently she took Zoya in her arms and kissed the smoothness of her cheek— "only remember, little one, how much he loved you. . . ."

Chapter 4

The following day was a nightmare. Nicolai lay washed and clean in his boyhood room, dressed in his uniform and surrounded by candles. The Volinsky Regiment mutinied, the Semonovsky, the Ismailovsky, the Litovsky, the Oranienbaum, and finally the proudest of all, Nicolai's own regiment, the Preobrajensky Guard. All of them defected to the revolution. Everywhere were red banners being carried high, and soldiers in tattered uniforms no longer the men they once were . . . St. Petersburg no longer the city it once was. Nothing was ever to be the same again as the revolutionaries set fire to the law courts early that morning. Soon the arsenal on the Liteiny was in flames and then the ministry of the interior, the military government building, the headquarters of the Okhrana, the secret police, and several police stations were destroyed. All of the prisoners had been let out of the jails, and by noon the Fortress of Peter and Paul was in rebel hands too. It was obvious that something desperate had to be done, and the Tsar had to return immediately to appoint a provisional government that would take control again. But even that seemed an unlikely scheme, and when Grand Duke Michael called him at headquarters in Mogilev that afternoon, he promised to come home immediately. It was impossible for him to absorb what had happened in St. Petersburg in the few days since he had left and he insisted on returning and seeing it all himself before appointing any new ministers to deal with the crisis at hand. Only when the chairman of the Duma sent him a message that night that his family's lives were in danger did he realize what was happening. The Empress herself didn't understand it. But by then it was too late. Much, much too late for all of them.

Lili Dehn had come to visit Alexandra at Tsarskoe Selo only that afternoon and found her totally occupied with caring for her sick children. The tales that Lili told were of disorders in the streets, and it still wasn't clear to her that this was more than

ordinary rioting, that it was in fact a
revolution.

In the midst of a blizzard General
Khabalov sent the Tsarina a message the
next morning. He insisted that she and the
children leave at once. He was holding
siege at the Winter Palace in St. Petersburg with fifteen hundred loyal men, but
by noon they had all deserted him. And
still the Empress did not understand it.
She refused to leave Tsarskoe Selo before
Nicholas returned. She felt safe with her
most loyal sailors, the Garde Equipage,
standing by, and besides, the children
were still far too ill to travel. By then
Marie had also developed pneumonia.

That same day, mansions around the
city were being looted and burned, and
Konstantin had all the servants burying
silver, and gold and icons in the garden.
Zoya was locked in her grandmother's pavilion with all the maids, and they were
frantically sewing jewels into the linings of
their heaviest winter clothing. Natalya
was running shrieking through the main
house, running frantically in and out of
Nicolai's room where his body remained.
Any attempts to bury him were impossible with revolution blazing everywhere
around them.

"Grandmama," Zoya whispered, as she forced a small diamond earring inside a button she was going to sew back on a dress, "Grandmama . . . what are we going to do now?" As she attempted to sew in spite of shaking fingers, her eyes were wide with terror and they could hear gunfire in the distance.

"We cannot do anything until we finish this . . . hurry, Zoya . . . there . . . sew the pearls into my blue jacket." The old woman was working furiously, strangely calm, and Konstantin was at the Winter Palace with Khabalov and the last of the loyal men. He had left them early that morning to go there.

"What will we do with . . ." She couldn't bring herself to say her brother's name, but it seemed so awful to leave him lying there as they sewed jewels into the hems of her grandmother's dresses.

"We will take care of everything in due time. Now be quiet, child. We must wait for word from your father." Sava lay whimpering at Zoya's feet as though she knew that even her life was in danger. Earlier that morning the old Countess had attempted to bring Natalya to the pavilion with her, but she refused to leave the main house. She seemed half mad as she kept speaking to her dead son and assuring him that everything was all right and his father would be home soon. Evgenia had left her there, and taken all of the servants to her own home to do as much as they could, before the rioters broke in and took everything. Evgenia had already heard that Kschessinska's mansion had been looted by the mobs, and she was going to save as much as she could before they came to them. And as she sewed, she wondered if they could reach Tsarskoe Selo.

At Tsarskoe Selo, the Empress had her own hands full. The children were still feverish, with Marie the worst of all, and Anna was still sick too. The mutinous soldiers arrived in the village by late that afternoon, but fearing the palace guard, they satisfied themselves with looting in the village, and shooting anyone and everyone at random.

The children could hear the shots from the sickroom, and Alexandra told them repeatedly that it was only their own soldiers on maneuvers. But that night, she sent word to Nicholas, begging him to come home. Still not understanding how truly desperate they all were, he chose to return by the longest route, not wishing to interfere with the routes used by the troop trains. It was inconceivable to him then that he no longer had a loyal army. Both the Garde Equipage and the Imperial guard, mostly composed of personal friends, whose mission had always been to guard the Tsar and Tsarina and their children, had left their posts. Even the soldiers from the garrison at Tsarskoe Selo had deserted and betrayed them. And St. Petersburg had fallen. It was Wednesday, March 14, and an entire world had changed overnight. It was almost impossible to conceive of the overall implications.

The ministers and generals were urging Nicholas to abdicate in favor of his son, keeping Grand Duke Michael as regent. But the frantic telegrams being sent to Nicholas on his way back from the front, explaining the situation to him, were getting no answer. And in the midst of his silence, Zoya and her grandmother were equally without news. Konstantin had not been home in two days and there was no way to get news of him. It was only when Feodor finally braved the streets, that he came home to tell them the dreadful news Evgenia had feared for days. Konstantin was dead. He had died at the Winter Palace with the last of the loyal troops, killed by his own men. There wasn't even a body to bring home to them. He had been disposed of along with countless others. Feodor returned with tears streaming down his face and sobbed openly as he told Evgenia what had happened to Konstantin. Zoya stared at him in horror, as they listened to him, and her grandmother spun around and ordered the maids to sew more quickly. All of her jewels had been hidden by then and Natalya's too, and the rest of it would have to be left behind, as she made another rapid decision. They were going to bury Nicolai in the garden. Evgenia and Feodor and three of the younger men went back to the main house, and stood silently in his room. He had been dead for three days and they could not wait any longer. Evgenia was solemn and dry-eyed as she stared at him, thinking of her own son now. It was too late for tears, she wanted to cry for all of them, but she had to think of Zoya now, and for Konstantin's sake, Natalya.

As they prepared to move the body, Natalya appeared like a ghost, drifting through the halls wearing a long white robe, with uncombed hair and mad eyes as she stared at them. "Where are you going with my baby?" She looked imperiously at her mother-in-law, and it was clear to all that she had lost her mind. She seemed not even to recognize Zoya. "What are you doing, you fool?" She reached out a clawlike hand to stop the men from taking him, but the old Countess held her back, and looked into her eyes.

"You must come with us, Natalya."

"But where are you taking my baby?"

Evgenia refused to answer her, it would only confuse her more or make her hysterical again. She had always had a weak mind, and without Konstantin to indulge her and shield her from the truth, she could no longer cope. She was totally mad, and Zoya knew it as she watched her.

"Put on your clothes, Natalya. We are going out."

"Where?"

Zoya was stunned when she heard the words. "To Tsarskoe Selo."

"But we can't possibly go there. It's summertime, and everyone is at Livadia."

"We'll go there eventually. But we must go to Tsarskoe Selo first. Now, we are going to get dressed, aren't we?" She grasped her firmly by the arm, and signaled to Zoya to take the other.

"Who are you?" She pulled her arm

away from the frightened girl, and only her grandmother's sharp eyes on her kept Zoya from fleeing in terror from the woman who had once been her mother. "Who *are* you?" she asked again and again of both of them, and the old woman answered her calmly. In four days she had lost both her son and grandson to a revolution none of them fully understood. But there was no time to question it now. She knew they had to leave St. Petersburg before it was too late. And if nowhere else, she knew they would be safe at Tsarskoe Selo. But Natalya was refusing to cooperate with them. She insisted that she was staying, her husband would be home at any time, and they were giving a party.

"Your husband is waiting for you at Tsarskoe Selo," Evgenia lied, and Zoya shuddered at all that was happening around them. With a force she never knew her grandmother had, she wrapped Natalya in a cloak and forced her down the stairs and out the back door into the garden, just as they heard a resounding crash. The looters had arrived, and were forcing their way into the Fontanka Palace. "Quickly," Evgenia whispered to the girl who had only yesterday been a child. "Find Feodor. Tell him to get the horses

ready . . . your father's old troika!" And
then the old woman ran toward her pavilion, panting heavily and clutching
Natalya's arm. She was shouting to her
maids, telling them to gather up all the
clothes in which the jewels were sewn,
and throw them into bags. They had no
time to pack anything. Everything they
could take would have to go in the troika.
And as she gave orders, she kept an eye on
the palace across the garden. She knew it
was only a matter of time before they
would abandon the palace and come to
the pavilion. But suddenly she realized
that Natalya was no longer beside her and
as she spun around she saw a white figure
racing across the garden. She began to run
after her daughter-in-law, but it was too
late. Natalya had gone back into the palace. Almost at the same time, the old
woman saw flames leaping from the upper
windows and heard Zoya gasp behind her.

"Grandmama!" And then they both saw
the figure in white racing from window to
window. Natalya was darting between the
flames screaming and laughing, and calling out as though to friends. It was a hid-
eous sight, as suddenly Zoya bolted toward the door and her grandmother
grabbed her.

"No! You cannot help her now! There are men in there with her. They will kill you, Zoya!"

"I can't let them kill her . . . I can't! . . . Grandmama! Please!" She was sobbing and fighting with a strength her grandmother could barely control, but at the same moment Feodor ran into the hallway.

"The troika is ready . . . behind the hedges . . ." He had wisely chosen to ease the troika into the side street, so that the looters would not see them from the palace.

"Grandmama!" Zoya was still fighting her, and suddenly her grandmother slapped her.

"Stop it! She is already dead . . . we must leave *now*!" There were no longer moments to spare. She had already seen a few faces looking out at the garden from the lower windows in the palace.

"I can't leave her there!" She was begging her grandmother to let her go, but the old woman wouldn't.

"You have to." And then her voice softened as she pulled her close for an instant. But as she did, there was a terrible sound, like an explosion. The whole upper floor was now in flames, and as they turned to look, they saw Natalya leap, with her white robe on fire, from the upper window. It would have been impossible for her to live, between the flames and the fall, Natalya's life had clearly ended, and it was a blessing to her. Her mind would never return after the double blow of losing both husband and son, and her entire world lay in broken shards around her.

"Come quickly!" Feodor was urging them, and with a swift move the old Countess swept Sava up off the floor, pushed her into Zoya's arms, and hurried her out the door to the waiting troika.

Chapter 5

As the troika began to move, Zoya turned
to see the flames leaping above the trees,
devouring what had once been her home
and was now only the shell of her former
life. But within moments, Feodor guided
them expertly into the back streets as the
two women huddled together, their bags
at their feet, filled with the clothes they
had taken with them, their jewels concealed in the linings, and little Sava trembling in the cold as Zoya held her. There
were soldiers in the streets, but no one
tried to stop them as they wended their
way through the back streets toward the
outskirts of the city. It was Thursday,
March 15, and far away in Pskov, Nicholas
was reading the telegrams sent to him by
his generals, telling him that he must abdicate. His face was deathly pale, as he saw
treason around him everywhere, but he
was no paler than Zoya, as she watched St.

Petersburg shrink behind them. It was more than two hours before they were on the back roads, on the way to Tsarskoe Selo, and it was a long time before they got there. They had no news as they moved along, and no clearer understanding of what had happened. All Zoya could think about was the vision of her mother, her robe in flames as she leapt to her death from the upstairs windows . . . and her brother as he must have been, as the flames enveloped him, lying dead in the room where she had so often visited him when she was a child . . . Nicolai . . . "stupid Nicolai" she had called him. She wondered if she would ever forgive herself . . . only yesterday . . . only yesterday when everything was all right and life was normal.

Her head was wrapped in an old shawl, and her ears ached from the cold, it made her think of Olga and Tatiana with their earaches from the measles. Such simple disasters had been their lot only days before . . . such small, stupid things like fevers, and earaches and measles. She could barely think as her grandmother held tightly to her hand, and they both silently wondered what they would find in Tsarskoe Selo. The village came into sight in the afternoon, and Feodor circled expertly around it. Wandering soldiers stopped him twice, and Feodor thought only for a moment about pressing the troika through. But he knew instinctively they might all be shot if he did, so he slowed carefully and said that he was carrying a sick old crone and her idiot granddaughter. Both women stared emptily at the men, as though they had nothing to hide, and the old Countess was grateful that Feodor had thought to take their oldest sled, with chipped paint but still useful runners. It was one they hadn't used in years, and although it had been handsome once, it no longer was. Only the extraordinarily fine horses he used suggested that they had great means, and the second group of soldiers laughingly relieved them of two of Konstantin's best black horses. They reached the gates of Tsarskoe Selo with only one horse prancing nervously as he pulled the old troika. The Cossack Guards were nowhere in sight, there were no guards anywhere, only a few uneasy-looking soldiers.

"Identify yourselves," one man shouted at them roughly and Zoya was terrified, but as Feodor began his tale, Evgenia stood up in the back of the troika. She was simply dressed, and, like Zoya, with only an old wool shawl covering her hair, but she was imperious as she stared him down, and pushed Zoya behind her.

"Evgenia Peterovna Ossupov. I am an old woman and a cousin of the Tsar. Do you wish to shoot me?" They had killed her grandson and her son, if they wished to shoot her now, they were welcome to it. But she was prepared to kill them first if they laid a hand on Zoya. Zoya was unaware of it, but her grandmother had a small pearl-handled pistol concealed in her sleeve and she was willing and ready to use it.

"There is no Tsar," he said fiercely, a red armband suddenly seeming more ominous than it had before, as the old woman's heart pounded and Zoya was seized with terror. What did he mean? Had they killed him? It was four o'clock in the afternoon . . . four o'clock and their entire world had come to an end . . . but Nicholas . . . had they killed him too? . . . like Konstantin and Nicolai . . .

"I must see my cousin Alexandra." Evgenia was imperious to the very tips of her fingers, as she stood staring at the soldier. "And her children." Or had they killed them too? Zoya's heart was racing as she sat frozen behind her grandmother's skirts, frightened to her very core, as Feodor stood tensed and silently watching. There was an endless pause as the soldier considered them and then suddenly stepped back, calling over his shoulder to his compatriots.

"Let them through. But remember, old woman," he turned to her with harsh words, "there is no more Tsar. He abdicated an hour ago, in Pskov. This is a new Russia." And with that he stepped aside, and hoping he had cut off his toes, Feodor whipped the troika past him. A new Russia . . . an end to an old life . . . all of the old and the new blending in terrifying confusion, as Evgenia sat white-faced beside her granddaughter. Zoya whispered to her as they passed the Feodorovsky Church, unable to believe what she had heard. Uncle Nicholas wouldn't do it. . . .

"Grandmama, do you think it's true?"

"Perhaps. Alix will tell us what has happened."

But the front doors to the Alexander Palace were strangely silent, there were no guards, no protection, no one anywhere, and as Feodor knocked loudly at the huge palace door, two nervous servants appeared and let them in. The halls seemed terrifyingly empty.

"Where is everyone?" the old Countess asked, and one of them pointed to the doorway Zoya knew so well, leading upstairs to the private apartments. There were tears on the woman's face as she wiped them away with her apron and finally answered.

"The Empress is upstairs with the children."

"And the Tsar?" Evgenia's eyes shot green fire at the woman crying helplessly.

"You've not heard?"

Oh, God, no . . . Zoya prayed . . .

"They say he has abdicated in favor of his brother. The soldiers came to tell us an hour ago. Her Highness doesn't believe it."

"But he's alive then?" Evgenia felt relief flood her body like new life.

"We believe so."

"Thank God." She swept her skirts around her, and glanced sharply at Zoya. "Tell Feodor to bring everything inside." She didn't want the soldiers touching their clothes with the jewels sewn into the linings. And as Zoya returned to her a moment later with Feodor at her side, her grandmother ordered the maid to take them upstairs to the Tsarina.

"I know the way, Grandmama. I will take you." And quietly she walked the halls she knew so well, the halls she had walked with her friend only days before.

The Alexander Palace was eerily quiet as she led her grandmother upstairs, and knocked gently on Marie's door, but there was no one there. She had been moved to one of her mother's sitting rooms, to be nursed with Anna Vyrubova and her sisters. Quietly, they moved along the hall, knocking on doors, until finally they heard voices. Zoya waited until someone bid them to come in, and slowly the door opened to reveal Alexandra, standing tall and thin, holding out a glass of tea to her two youngest daughters. Anastasia had tears on her cheeks as she turned to the door and Marie sat up in bed and began to cry when she saw Zoya.

Zoya was too overcome to speak as she rushed across the room and threw her arms about her friend, as Evgenia went to embrace her exhausted cousin.

"My God, Cousin Evgenia, how did you get here? Are you all right?"

Even the old woman had difficulty speaking, as she embraced the tall, elegant woman who looked so desperately tired. Her pale gray eyes seemed to be filled with a lifetime of sadness. "We came to help you, Alix. And we could not stay in St. Petersburg any longer. They set fire to the house this morning as we left. We left very quickly."

"I cannot believe it. . . ." Alexandra sank slowly into a chair. "And Konstantin?"

The old woman's face went pale and she could feel her heart pound beneath her heavy dress. She suddenly felt the weight of all she had lost and feared she would swoon at the younger woman's feet, but she would not allow herself that in the face of all Alix had to bear. "He is dead, Alix. . . ." Her voice cracked but she did not cry. "And Nicolai too . . . on Sunday . . . Natalya was killed as the house burned this morning." She did not tell her that her daughter-in-law had gone mad before leaping in flames from the window. "Is it true . . . about Nicky?" She was afraid to ask, but she had to. They had to know. It was so difficult to understand what had happened.

"About the abdication? It cannot be. They are saying it to frighten us . . . but I have heard nothing from Nicholas today."

She glanced at her two daughters embracing Zoya as the three girls cried. Zoya had just told them about Nicolai, and she sobbed openly as Marie held her. Even sick as she was, she offered solace to her friend, and none of them seemed to notice the two older women. "All our soldiers have deserted us . . . even . . ." The Empress seemed almost unable to say the words. "Even Derevenko has abandoned Baby." He was one of the two soldiers who had been with the Tsarevich since he was born. He had left them at dawn that morning without a word, or a look back over his shoulder. The other, Nagorny, had sworn to stay at Alexis's side until they killed him, and he was with him now in the next room, with Dr. Fedorov. Dr. Botkin had gone to try and find more medicines for the girls with Gibbes, one of their two tutors. "It is impossible to understand . . . our sailors . . . I can't believe it. If only Nicholas were here. . . ."

"He will come, Alix. We must remain calm. How are the children?"

"They are all ill. . . . I couldn't tell them at first, but they know now . . . there was no way I could conceal it from them any longer." She sighed and then added, "Count Benckendorff is here, he has vowed to protect us, and the Baroness Buxhoeveden arrived yesterday morning. Will you stay, Evgenia Peterovna?"

"If we may. We cannot go back to St. Petersburg now. . . ." She did not add "if ever." Surely the world would be set to rights again. Surely when Nicholas returned . . . surely the news of his abdication was a lie, spread by revolutionaries and traitors, to frighten and control them.

"You may have Mashka's room, if you like. And Zoya . . ."

"We shall sleep together. Now, what may I do to help you, Alix? Where are the others?" The Empress smiled gratefully as her husband's elderly cousin tossed off her cloak, and carefully turned back the cuffs of the simple dress she had worn.

"Go and rest. Zoya can keep the girls company while I see to the others."

"I'll come with you." And the old woman steadfastly followed her throughout the day, pouring tea, soothing fevered brows, and even helping Alix to change Alexis's sheets while Nagorny stood faithfully by. Like Alix, Evgenia found it difficult to believe that Derevenko had actually left him.

It was almost midnight that night, when Zoya and her grandmother slipped into their beds in Marie and Anastasia's room, and Zoya lay awake for hours, listening to her grandmother snore softly. It seemed impossible that less than three weeks ago she had visited Marie in this very room, and Marie had given her a bottle of her favorite perfume, long gone now, as everything lay shattered around them. She had realized also that none of the girls fully understood what had happened. She wasn't sure she understood it herself, even after seeing all she had in St. Petersburg. But they had been so ill, and they were so far removed from the disorder in the streets, the frantic riots, the murders, the looting. The vision of her home in flames never seemed to dim . . . nor the sight of her brother bleeding to death on the marble floor of the Fontanka Palace only four days before. It was morning before Zoya fell asleep, as a fresh blizzard raged outside and she wondered when the Tsar would come home and if life would ever return to normal.

But at five o'clock that afternoon, the possibility of that seemed even more unlikely. Grand Duke Paul, Nicholas's uncle, came to Tsarskoe Selo and gave Alexandra the news. Nicholas had abdicated the day before, passing the power on to his brother, Grand Duke Michael, who had been completely stunned and unprepared to take the throne. Only Alix and Dr. Fedorov truly understood why Nicholas had not abdicated in favor of his son, but rather his brother. The extent of Alexis's illness was a well-guarded secret. A Provisional Government was being formed as Alexandra heard the news in silence and desperately wished that she could talk to her husband.

Nicholas himself arrived at headquarters in Mogilev the following morning to say good-bye to his troops, and from there was finally able to call his wife. The call came as Alexandra was helping Dr. Botkin tend to Anastasia, and she flew from the room to talk to him, praying that he would tell her none of it was true, but at the sound of his voice she knew instantly that it was, beyond any hope. Their life and their dreams, along with his dynasty, were shattered. He promised to return as soon as possible, and as always, inquired lovingly about the children. And the following night, Sunday, General Kornilov came from St. Petersburg to see if she needed anything, medicines, or food, and her first thoughts were for the soldiers. She begged him to help supply the hospitals with med-

icine and food. After caring for them for so
long, she could not forget them now even
though they were no longer "her"
soldiers. He assured her that he would,
and something about his visit suggested to
her that there was worse to come. She
warned Nagorny that night not to leave
Baby's side, and she sat with her daughters long into the night. It was after midnight when she finally went to her own
room, and the old Countess knocked softly
at her door and brought her a glass of tea.
She saw that there were tears in the
younger woman's eyes and gently patted
her shoulder.

"Is there anything I can do for you,
Alix?"

She shook her head, still proud, still austere, and thanked her with her eyes. "I
only wish he would come home. Suddenly
. . . I'm afraid for the children here."
Evgenia was too, but she didn't want to
admit it to her young cousin.

"We are all standing by you." But the
"all" was such a precious few, a handful of
old women and loyal friends who could be
counted on one hand. They had been deserted by everyone, the blow was almost
too much to bear. But she knew she could
not break now. She had to remain strong

for her husband. "You must get some sleep now, Alix."

Alexandra looked around her famous mauve bedroom nervously and then glanced sadly at the old woman. "I have some things I want to do . . . I must . . ." She could hardly bare to say it. "I want to burn my diaries tonight . . . and my letters . . . who knows if in some way they will use them against him."

"Surely they can't . . ." But as Evgenia thought of it, she found that she agreed with Alexandra. "Would you like me to stay with you?" She didn't want to intrude, but the Empress looked so devastated and so lonely.

"I would like to be alone, if you don't mind."

"I understand." And she quietly left Alexandra to her unhappy task. She sat by the fire until morning, reading letters and journals, and burning even her letters from her grandmother Queen Victoria. She burned everything, except her correspondence with beloved Nicholas, and for two days she felt the pain of it, until Wednesday when General Kornilov returned and asked to speak with her alone. She met him downstairs in one of the rooms Nicholas often used. She stood tall and proud, and attempted to conceal her shock and pain as she listened to what he said. She was being put under house arrest, along with her family and her servants and her children. She wanted not to believe his words, but it was inevitable now. The end had come, and they all had to face it. He explained carefully that anyone who wished to remain with them could, but if they chose to leave, they would not be allowed to return to Tsarskoe Selo. It was staggering news, and it took all of her strength not to swoon as she listened.

"And my husband, General?"

"We believe he will be here by morning."

"And will you imprison him?" She felt physically ill as she asked, but she had to know now. She had to know all of it, what they could expect and what they were facing. And after the tales she had heard in the past few days, she supposed she should be grateful that they weren't all killed, but in the face of what was happening it was difficult to be grateful.

"Your husband will be under house arrest here at Tsarskoe Selo."

"And then?" She looked deathly pale as she asked, but the response was not as terrifying as she had feared. All she could think of now was her husband and her children, their safety and their lives. She would gladly have sacrificed herself for them. She would have done anything, as General Kornilov watched her in silent admiration.

"The Provisional Government wishes to escort you and your husband and your family to Murmansk. You will be able to travel from there. We will send you by steamer to England, to King George."

"I see. And when will that be?" Her face was as icy as granite.

"As soon as it can be arranged, madame."

"Very well. I shall wait until my husband returns to tell the children."

"And the others?"

"I shall tell everyone today that they are free to go, if they wish, but they cannot return. Is that right, General?"

"Exactly."

"And you will not harm them as they leave, our family and loyal friends, few as they are now?"

"I give you my word, madame." The word of a traitor, she wanted to spit at him, but she remained ladylike and calm as she watched him leave, and returned to tell the others. She told everyone that afternoon that they were free to go, and she urged them to do so if they wished to.

"We cannot expect you to stay here if you do not wish it. We shall be leaving for England in a few weeks, and it may be safer for you to leave us now . . ." perhaps even before Nicholas returned. She could not fully believe that they were being placed under house arrest for their own protection.

But the others refused to go, and the following day Nicholas finally returned, looking exhausted and pale on a freezing cold, dreary morning. He walked silently into the front hall and for a long moment he just stood there. The servants quickly brought word to Alix and she met him downstairs and faced him across the endless hall, her eyes filled with the words she could not say, her heart filled with compassion for the man she loved, and silently he came toward her and held her close to him. There was nothing left for either of them to say as they walked slowly upstairs to their children.

Chapter 6

The days following Nicholas's return were filled with fear and silent tension, and yet at the same time relief that he was safely home. He had lost everything, but at least they had not killed him. He sat quietly for hours with the Tsarevich, and Alexandra turned her attention to her daughters. It was Marie who was the sickest now, with pneumonia, which had resulted from the measles. She had a fearful cough that racked her body again and again, and a fever that would not seem to abate, as Zoya sat ever near her.

"Mashka . . . have a little drink . . . just for me . . ."

"I can't . . . my throat hurts so much." She could barely speak and her skin was hot and dry as Zoya touched her. She bathed her brow in lilac water, and spoke softly to her about their tennis games the previous summer at Livadia.

"Remember the silly picture your papa took of everyone hanging upside down. I brought it with me . . . Mashka, do you want to see it?"

"Later . . . my eyes hurt so much, Zoya . . . I feel awful."

"Shh . . . just try to sleep . . . I'll show you the picture when you wake up." She even brought little Sava in to cheer her, but Marie wasn't interested in anything. Zoya only hoped that she would be well enough to travel to Murmansk, and take the ship to England. They were leaving in three weeks, and Nicholas said everyone had to be well by then. He called it his final imperial order, which made everyone cry. He tried so hard to make everyone feel better about things, and keep the children happy. Both he and Alix looked more worn each day, but it was three days later that Zoya glimpsed him in the hall outside the mauve boudoir and his face was ghostly white. An hour later she knew why. His English cousin had refused to receive him, for reasons that were as yet unclear. But the imperial family would not be leaving for England. Originally he had asked Zoya and the old Countess to go with them, but now no one knew what would happen.

"What will happen, Grandmama?" Zoya asked her that night with terrified eyes. What if they were just going to keep them there at Tsarskoe Selo and then finally kill them.

"I don't know, little one. Nicholas will tell us when it is decided. They'll probably go to Livadia."

"Do you think they'll kill us?"

"Don't be stupid." But she feared the same thing. There were no easy answers now. Even the English had failed him. There was nowhere else for them to go, nowhere safe. The route to Livadia was perilous at best, she guessed. They were trapped now at Tsarskoe Selo. And Nicholas always seemed so calm, and he urged everyone not to worry, but how could they not?

It was the next morning when Zoya tiptoed silently from the room and looked down from the window to see Nicholas and her grandmother walking slowly in the snow-filled garden. There seemed to be no one else around, and as she stared at them, he with his straight, proud shoulders, and her grandmother so tiny, a figure in a stark black cloak against the snow, she thought that she saw her grandmother crying, and then gently he embraced her and they disappeared around the corner of the palace.

Zoya went to the room they shared and a little while later her grandmother returned, her heart heavy, her eyes sad, as she sank slowly into a chair and looked at her lovely granddaughter. Only weeks before she had seemed to be a child, and now suddenly she seemed so wise and sad. She was thinner and seemed more delicate to the eye, but her grandmother knew that the horrors of the past weeks would only help to make her stronger. She would need her strength now. They all would.

"Zoya . . ." She didn't know how to tell her, but she knew that Nicholas was right. And she had to think of Zoya's safety. She had a long life ahead of her, and her grandmother would gladly have given her own to protect it.

"Grandmother, is something wrong?" In the light of what had happened in the past two weeks, it seemed a ridiculous question, but she sensed further disaster was impending.

"I have just spoken to Nicholas, Zoya Konstantinovna . . . he wants us to leave now . . . while we still can. . . ."

Her eyes instantly filled with tears and

she leapt to her feet in terror. "Why? We said we would stay here with them, and they will all be leaving soon . . . won't they, Grandmama? . . . won't they? . . ." The old woman didn't answer, she weighed the balance between truth and lie and truth won, as it always did with her.

"I don't know. With the English refusing to take them in, Nicholas fears that things may not go well for them. He feels that they will be imprisoned here, perhaps for a long time, or even taken somewhere else. We might all be separated eventually . . . and he cannot offer us his protection, he has none to give. And I cannot keep you safe here from these savages. He's right, we must go . . . now . . . while we still can." She looked sadly at the girl who had only moments before been a child, but she was in no way prepared for the full measure of Zoya's fury.

"I won't go with you! I *won't!* I won't leave them!"

"You must! You could end in Siberia alone, you little fool . . . without them! We must leave in the next day or two. Nicholas fears that things could get much harsher. The revolutionaries don't want him around, and if the English won't take them in, who will? It is a very serious situation!"

"Then I'll die with them! You cannot make me go!"

"I can do anything I wish, and you must do as I say, Zoya. It is Nicholas's wish too. And you must not disobey his orders!" She was almost too tired to fight the girl, but she knew she had to use her last ounce of strength to convince her.

"I won't leave Marie here, Grandmama, she's so ill . . . and she's all I have left. . . ." Zoya began to sob, and like a little girl she laid her head down on her arms on the table. It was the same table where she had sat with Marie only a month before, as Marie had braided her hair and they giggled and chatted. Where had that world gone? What had happened to all of them? . . . and Nicolai . . . and her mother and father . . .

"You have me, little one. . . ." Her grandmother gently stroked her hair as Marie had once done. "You must be strong. They expect it of you. You must, Zoya. We must do what we have to do now."

"But where will we go?"

"I don't know yet. Nicholas says he will arrange it. Perhaps we can go to Finland.

And to France or Switzerland from there."

"But we don't know anyone there." She looked horrified as she turned her tear-stained face to Evgenia.

"That is how it is sometimes, my dear. We must trust in God and go when Nicholas tells us."

"Grandmama, I can't . . ." She wailed but her grandmother was firm. She was as strong as steel and twice as determined. And Zoya was no match for her, not yet in any case, and they both knew it.

"You can and you will, and you must not say anything to the children. They have their own worries just now. We must not burden them, it wouldn't be fair."

"What will I say to Mashka?"

Tears filled the old woman's eyes as she looked at the girl she loved so very dearly, and when she spoke it was in a hoarse whisper filled with her own grief for those they had lost and the others they would lose now. "Only tell her how very much you love her."

Chapter 7

Zoya tiptoed into the room where Marie slept, and stood for a long moment watching her. She hated to wake her up, but she couldn't leave without saying good-bye. She couldn't bear to leave her at all, but there was no turning back now. Her grandmother was waiting downstairs, and Nicholas had planned everything for them. They were to take the long Scandinavian route, through Finland and Sweden, and Denmark after that. He had given Evgenia the names of friends of his Danish aunt, and Feodor was coming with them to keep them safe. Everything had been decided. All that remained was a last farewell to her friend. She watched her stir feverishly beneath the sheets, and then Marie opened her eyes, and smiled at the familiar face, while Zoya tried valiantly not to cry.

"How do you feel?" she whispered in

the silent room. Although Anastasia was sleeping in another room with her two sisters, all of them were slowly improving. Only Marie remained very ill, but Zoya tried not to think of it now. She could not think of anything, couldn't allow herself to look back or even ahead, there was nothing to look forward to now. There was only this . . . one tiny last moment with her dearest friend as gently she reached out to her and touched her cheek. "Mashka . . ." Marie tried to sit up in bed and looked oddly at her friend.

"Is something wrong?"

"No . . . I . . . I'm going back to St. Petersburg with my grandmother." She had promised Alix that she wouldn't tell her the truth, it would be too much for her just then. But Marie looked worried anyway. She had always had a sixth sense about her friend, as she did now. She reached out and took Zoya's hand and held it tightly in her own much too warm one.

"Is it safe?"

"Of course," Zoya lied, and tossed back her red hair. "Your father wouldn't let us go if it weren't safe." . . . please God, don't let me cry now . . . please . . .

she handed her the water glass and Marie pushed it away, meeting her friend's eyes.

"Something's happening, isn't it? You're going somewhere."

"Just home for a few days . . . I'll be back soon." She leaned forward then and took Marie in her arms and held her close as tears filled her eyes. "You must get better now. You've been sick for far too long." They held each other close, and she was smiling brightly as she pulled away, knowing that they were waiting for her.

"Will you write to me?"

"Of course." She couldn't bring herself to leave, she just stood there staring at her, wanting to drink it all in, to hold on to all of it, the feel of her friend's hand, the smoothness of the sheets, the look in her huge blue eyes. "I love you, Mashka." Her words were whisper soft . . . "I love you so very much . . ."

"So do I." Marie lay back on her pillow then with a sigh. It was exhausting just to sit up and talk, and then she coughed horribly as Zoya held her.

"Please get well . . ." She bent one last time to kiss her cheek and felt the soft curls beneath her hand, and then quickly she turned away and walked to the door, turning for a last time with a silent wave, but Marie's eyes were closed again, and Zoya slowly closed the door, her heart tearing from her very soul as she bent her head and cried silently. She had bid the others good-bye half an hour before, and she stopped now for only an instant outside little Alexis's room. Nagorny was there with him, and Pierre Gilliard, and Dr. Fedorov was just leaving him.

"May I go in?" She wiped the tears from her cheeks and he touched her arm in silent sympathy.

"He's asleep." She only nodded then and hurried down the familiar stairs to her grandmother and the Tsar and Tsarina waiting in the main hall. Feodor was already outside, with two of the Tsar's best horses hitched to the old troika in which they had come. It was all almost more than she could bear as she walked toward them on leaden feet. She wanted everything to stop, wanted to turn back the clock . . . to run back upstairs to her friend . . . she felt as though she were deserting all of them, and yet she was being torn from them unwillingly.

"Is she all right?" Alexandra looked worriedly into Zoya's eyes, hoping that Marie hadn't been able to discern the raw agony there.

"I told her we were going back to St. Petersburg." Zoya was crying openly now, and even her grandmother had to fight back tears, as Nicholas kissed her on both cheeks and held her hands tightly in his, his eyes brutally sad but his lips still wearing a dignified smile. Although Evgenia had heard his sobs in his wife's rooms the night he returned, there was never any evidence of his grief to the rest of them. He staunchly encouraged everyone and was always charming and calm, as he was as he kissed her good-bye.

"Safe journey, Evgenia Peterovna. We shall look forward to seeing you sometime soon."

"We shall pray for you all every hour, Nicholas." The old woman gently kissed his cheek. "Godspeed to all of you." And then she turned to Alix as Zoya stood by with tears streaming down her cheeks. "Take care of yourself, don't exhaust yourself too much, my dear. I hope the children will all be well soon."

"Write to us," Alix said sadly, just as Marie had said to Zoya only moments before. "We will be anxious for news of you." She turned to Zoya then. She had known her since she was born, her baby and Natalya's born only days apart and such fast friends for all their eighteen years. "Be a good girl, listen to your grandmother, and take great good care of yourself." And then without a word, she held her close to her, feeling for an instant as though she were losing her own child.

"I love you, Aunt Alix . . . I love you all so much . . . I don't want to go . . ." She could barely speak through her sobs, and then she turned to Nicholas, and he held her close as her own father would have done, if he were still alive.

"We love you too, and we always shall. We shall be together again one day. Be certain of it. And God's blessings on both of you until then, little one." He pulled her gently away then, with a small smile. "You must go now." He led her solemnly outside as his wife took her grandmother's arm and they helped them into their sled as Zoya cried. The last of the servants had come to say good-bye to them and they were crying too. They had known Zoya since she was a child, and now she was leaving them, and soon others would be leaving too. And it was frightening to think of never coming back. It was all Zoya could think of now, while Feodor slowly lifted his whip and touched the Tsar's horses for the first time. The troika sprang to life and in the gray gloom they suddenly pulled away from Alexandra and Nicholas, who stood waving at them. Zoya turned, clutching little Sava close to her. The puppy suddenly whined as though she also knew that she was leaving home never to return again, and suddenly Zoya buried her face in her grandmother's arms. She couldn't bear seeing it anymore, those two with their brave faces standing there, waving at them, the Alexander Palace seen for the last time, and suddenly Tsarskoe Selo itself disappearing in a distant haze of snow as Zoya wailed in agony, thinking of Mashka . . . Mashka . . . her best and only dearest friend . . . her brother . . . her parents . . . everyone gone . . . She clung to her grandmother and cried as the old woman sat stoically in the sleigh, her eyes closed as icy tears rolled down her cheeks, a lifetime left behind, all she had ever known, a world they had all loved . . . gone like the snows, as Feodor drove them on, and Nicholas's horses carried them far, far from home, and away from everything and everyone they had known and loved.

"*Adieu, chers amis* . . ." Evgenia whispered into the falling snow . . . Goodbye, dearest friends . . . They had only each other now, a very old woman and a very young girl, fleeing from a lost world and the people they had loved there. Nicholas and his family were history now, never to be forgotten, always beloved, and never to be seen again by any of them.

PARIS

Chapter 8

The journey from Tsarskoe Selo to Beloostrov on the Finnish border took seven
hours, although it was not far from St. Petersburg, but Feodor was being careful to
travel by all the back roads. Nicholas had
warned him that it was safer to travel that
way, even if it took them longer. And
much to Evgenia's surprise, they crossed
the border easily. There were some questions, but suddenly Evgenia seemed to
sink into herself and look like a crone, and
bundled up and cold, Zoya looked more
like a child than she had for a long time. It
was Sava who saved them in the end. The
soldiers at the border were enchanted
with her and after an anxious moment,
waved them on, and the three refugees
heaved a sigh of relief as the troika moved
on behind Nicholas's horses. Feodor had
been careful to use the old harness he had
brought from St. Petersburg, and had pur-

posely not used any of the equipment from the Tsar's stable with the easily recognizable double-headed eagle.

The trip from Beloostrov across Finland to Turku took two full days, and by the time they arrived in Turku late at night, Zoya felt as though she would be numb for the rest of her life. Her whole body seemed to be frozen into the position she'd been in, in the troika. Her grandmother could barely walk when they helped her out, and even Feodor seemed exhausted. They found a small inn where they took two rooms, and in the morning Feodor sold the horses for a ridiculously small sum before the three of them boarded an icebreaker to Stockholm. It was another endless day on the ship, moving slowly amidst the ice between Finland and Sweden, and the three companions barely spoke, all were lost in their own thoughts.

They arrived in Stockholm late in the afternoon, just in time to catch the night train to Malmö. And once in Malmö, they took the railroad ferry the next morning to Copenhagen, and there they went to a small hotel, and Evgenia called the Tsar's aunt's friends, but they were away, and the next morning they left Copenhagen for France on a British steamer. Zoya seemed to be almost in a daze by then, and she was desperately seasick the first day on the ship. Her grandmother thought she looked feverish, but it was difficult to tell if she was ill or just exhausted. They were all exhausted after the six-day journey. It had been grueling to travel on day after day, by ship and by train and by troika. Even Feodor looked as though he had aged ten years in the single week, but they were also suffering from the sorrow of leaving their homeland. They spoke little, rarely slept, and none of them ever seemed to be hungry. It was as though their very bodies were filled with grief, and they couldn't have borne any more. They had left everything behind them, a way of life, a thousand years of history, the people they had loved and lost. It was almost too much to bear, and Zoya found herself hoping the ship would be sunk by German U-boats on the way to France. Far from Russia, it was the Great War and not the revolution people were afraid of. But Zoya found herself thinking that dying at anyone's hands would have been easier than facing a new world she didn't want to know. She thought of how often she and Marie had talked dreamily about going to

Paris. It had all sounded so romantic then, so exciting with all the elegant women and the beautiful gowns they would buy. Now there would be none of that. They had only the small amount of money her grandmother had borrowed from the Tsar before they left, and the jewels sewn into their clothing. Evgenia had already made up her mind to sell as many of them as she had to once they reached Paris. And they had to think of Feodor as well. He had promised to look for work as soon as they arrived, he had vowed to do everything he could to help them, but he had refused to let them make the trip alone. He had nothing left in Russia anymore, and he couldn't imagine a life without serving the Ossupovs. It would have killed him if they'd left him. He was as ill as Zoya was on the trip to France, he had never been on a boat before, and he was terrified as he clung miserably to the railing.

"What are we going to do, Grandmama?" Zoya sat watching her grandmother unhappily in the tiny cabin. Gone the grandeur of the imperial yachts, the palaces, the princes, the parties. Gone the warmth and love of family. Gone the people they had known, their way of life, even the security of knowing they would have enough to eat the next day. All they had were their lives, and Zoya wasn't even sure she wanted hers. All she wanted was to go home to Mashka, and Russia, to turn back the clock and return to a lost world, full of people who no longer existed. Her father, her brother, her mother. And Zoya wondered, as they pressed on, if Marie was getting better.

"We will have to find a small apartment," her grandmother answered her. She hadn't been to Paris in years. She had traveled very little since the death of her husband. But now she had Zoya to think about. She had to be strong for the girl's sake. She had to see her safely settled. She prayed that she would live long enough to take care of her, but it wasn't Evgenia who seemed in danger now, but Zoya. The girl looked very ill, and her eyes seemed larger than ever in her pale face, and when the old Countess touched her, she knew instantly that she was blazing with fever. She began coughing late that night, and the Countess began to fear pneumonia. By the next morning, her cough was even worse, and as they boarded the train to Paris in Boulogne, it became obvious what she was suffering from. The spots began appearing on her

face and hands, and when her grandmother forced her to pull up her wool
shirt, it was clear to both of them that
Zoya had the measles. Evgenia was less
than pleased, and now even more anxious
to get the girl to Paris. It was a ten-hour
trip to Paris by train, and they arrived just
before midnight. There were half a dozen
taxis outside the Gare du Nord, and
Evgenia sent Feodor in search of one, as
she helped Zoya down from the train. She
could hardly walk as she leaned heavily
against her grandmother, her face suddenly as flushed as her bright red hair. She
was coughing horribly and almost inco-
herent with fever.

"I want to go home," she whimpered as
she clutched the little dog. Sava was bigger now, and Zoya could hardly carry her
as she followed her grandmother out of
the station.

"We're going home, my love. Feodor is
finding us a taxi."

But Zoya only began to cry, the woman
she had become seeming to melt away, as
she looked up at her grandmother like a
lost child. "I want to go back to Tsarskoe
Selo."

"Never mind, Zoya . . . never mind.
. . ." Feodor was signaling frantically as

he juggled their bags, and Evgenia gently led Zoya from the station and helped her into the ancient taxi. Everything they still owned was piled in beside Feodor and the driver, as Zoya and her grandmother slid onto the backseat with tired sighs. They had no reservations anywhere, no idea where to go, and the driver was deaf and ancient. All the young men had long since gone to war, only the old and the infirm were still in Paris.

"Alors? . . . On y va, mesdames?" He smiled into the backseat and looked surprised when he saw that Zoya was crying. *"Elle est malade?"* Is she sick? Evgenia was quick to reassure him that she was only very tired, as they all were. "Where have you come from?" he chatted amiably as Evgenia tried to remember the hotel where she'd stayed with her husband years before, but suddenly she could remember nothing at all. She was eighty-two years old and utterly and completely exhausted. And they had to get Zoya to a hotel and call a doctor.

"Can you recommend a hotel to us? Something small and clean and not very expensive." He pursed his lips for a moment as he thought about it, and Evgenia instinctively pressed her bag close to her.

In it she carried her last and most important gift from the Empress. Alix had given her one of her very own imperial Easter eggs, made for her three years before by Carl Fabergé. It was an incredible piece of work in mauve enamel with diamond ribbons, and Evgenia knew it was the most important treasure she had. When all else failed, they could sell it and live on what it brought them.

"Do you care where it is, madame? . . . the hotel. . . ."

"As long as it's in a decent neighborhood." They could always look for something better afterward, tonight all she needed were rooms where they could sleep. The niceties, if any were still possible, would come later.

"There's a small hotel off the Champs-Élysées, madame. The night porter is my cousin."

"Is it expensive?" she asked sharply, and he shrugged. He could see that they were not well off, their clothes were simple, and the old man looked like a peasant. At least the woman spoke French, and he thought the girl did, too, although she cried most of the time, and she had a fearful cough. He only hoped she didn't have tuberculosis, which was currently rampant in Paris.

"It's not too bad. I'll have my cousin speak to the desk clerk."

"Very well. That will do," she said imperiously, and sat back in the ancient cab. She was a spunky old thing and he liked her.

The hotel was on the rue Marbeuf, and it was indeed very small, but it looked decent and clean as they walked into the lobby. There were only a dozen rooms, but the night clerk assured them two of them were vacant. They had to use a common bathroom down the hall, which was something of a shock to Evgenia, but even that didn't matter now. She pulled the sheets back in the bed she and Zoya would share, and they were clean. She pulled Zoya's clothes off, after concealing her bag under the mattress, and Feodor had brought in the rest of their things. He had agreed to keep Sava with him. And the Countess went back downstairs as soon as Zoya was in bed, and asked the desk clerk to send for the doctor.

"For yourself, madame?" he asked. He wasn't surprised, they all looked tired and pale, and she was obviously very old.

"For my granddaughter." She didn't tell him that Zoya had the measles, but two hours later when the doctor finally came, he confirmed it.

"She is very ill, madame. You must tend her carefully. Do you have any idea how she caught it?"

It would have been ridiculous to tell him that she caught them from the children of the Tsar of Russia. "From friends, I believe. We have made a very long journey." Her eyes were wise and sad as he looked at her and sensed that they had been through a great deal. But even he couldn't dream what misery they'd seen in the past three weeks, how little they had left, or how frightened they were of the future. "We have come from Russia . . . through Finland and Sweden and Denmark." He stared at her in amazement, and then suddenly he understood. Others had made similar journeys in the past weeks, fleeing from the revolution. And he guessed easily that there would be more in the ensuing months, if they were able to escape at all. The Russian nobility, or what was left of it, was fleeing in droves, and many of them were coming to Paris.

"I'm sorry . . . very sorry, madame."

"So are we." She smiled sadly. "She doesn't have pneumonia, does she?"

"Not yet."

"Her cousin has had it for several weeks, and they've been very close."

"I'll do my best, madame. I'll come back to see her in the morning." But when he did, she was worse, and by nightfall she was delirious with the fever. He prescribed some medicine for her and said it was her only hope. And the next morning, when the desk clerk told Evgenia that America had just entered the war, it seemed almost irrelevant. The war seemed so much less important now, in light of everything else that had happened.

She ate her meals in their simple room, and Feodor had gone out to buy medicine and fruit. They were rationing bread, and it was difficult to obtain anything, but he was ingenious at finding whatever the Countess needed. He was particularly pleased with himself, for having found a taxi driver who spoke Russian. Like them, he had only been in Paris for a few days, he was a prince from St. Petersburg, and Feodor thought he had been a friend of Konstantin's, but Evgenia had no time to listen to him. She was deeply concerned about Zoya.

It was several more days before the girl seemed to know where she was. She looked around the small, unadorned room, and looked into her grandmother's eyes, and then slowly she remembered that they were in Paris.

"How long have I been sick, Grandmama?" She tried to sit up but she was still too weak, at least her fearsome cough was finally a little better.

"Since we arrived, my love, almost a week ago. You had us all very worried. Feodor has been running all over Paris, trying to find fruit for you. The shortages here are almost as bad as they are in Russia."

Zoya nodded, her thoughts seeming to drift away as she stared out the room's only window. "Now I know how Mashka felt . . . and she was even sicker than I was. I wonder how she is now." She couldn't bring herself to think of the present.

"You mustn't think of it," her grandmother reproached gently as she watched the look of sadness in her eyes, "I'm sure she's well by now. We left two weeks ago."

"Is it only that?" She sighed as she looked into her grandmother's eyes. "It seems like a lifetime." It did to all of them, and her grandmother had barely slept since they left Russia. She had been sleeping sitting up in a chair for days, afraid to disturb Zoya's sleep by sharing the bed with her, and afraid she wouldn't be awake if the girl needed her, but now she could relax her vigil a little bit. That night she would sleep at the foot of the bed, and she needed the rest almost as badly as Zoya.

"Tomorrow we'll get you out of bed, but first you must rest and eat and get strong again." She patted Zoya's hand, and Zoya smiled weakly up at her.

"Thank you, Grandmama." Her eyes filled with tears as she pressed the once graceful gnarled hand to her cheek. Even that brought back painful memories of her childhood.

"For what, silly child? What have you to thank me for?"

"For bringing me here . . . for being so brave . . . and doing so much to save us." It had only just dawned on her how far they had come, and how extraordinary her grandmother had been. Her mother could certainly never have done it. Zoya would have had to carry Natalya all the way out of Russia.

"We'll make a new life here, Zoya. You'll see. One day we'll be able to look back, and everything won't be so painful."

"I can't imagine it . . . I can't imagine a time when the memories won't hurt like this." She felt as though she were dying.

"Time is very kind, my dear. And it will be kind to us. I promise you. We'll have a good life here." But not the life that they had known in Russia. Zoya tried not to think of it, but later that night as her grandmother slept, she crept softly out of bed and went to her own small bag and found the picture Nicholas had taken while they were clowning at Livadia the previous summer. She and Anastasia and Marie and Olga and Tatiana were leaning backward until they hung almost upside down, grinning after the game they'd played, while their father took the picture. It looked silly to her now . . . silly . . . and so sweet . . . even at that odd angle, they all looked so beautiful to her, even more so now . . . the girls she had grown up with and loved . . . Tatiana, Anastasia . . . Olga . . . and, of course, Mashka.

Chapter 9

The measles left Zoya painfully weak, but much to her grandmother's relief, she seemed to revive amidst the beauty of Paris in April. There was a seriousness about her now that hadn't been there before, and a slight cough that seemed to linger. But now and then there was laughter in her eyes almost the way there had been before, and it made her grandmother's heart a little lighter.

The hotel on the rue Marbeuf was becoming expensive for them, though, as simple as it was, and Evgenia knew they would soon have to find an apartment. They had already used a good part of the money Nicholas had given them, and she was anxious to safeguard their meager resources. It was clear to her by early May, that she was going to have to sell some of her jewelry.

On a sunny afternoon, she left Zoya

with Feodor and went to see a jeweler the hotel referred her to on the rue Cambon, after carefully cutting a ruby necklace out of the lining of one of her black dresses. She put the necklace in her handbag, and then took the matching earrings out of their hiding place in two carefully covered and rather large buttons. The hiding places had definitely served their purpose. She called for a taxi before leaving the hotel, and when she gave the driver the address, he slowly turned and stared at her. He was a tall, distinguished-looking man with silver hair, and a perfectly groomed white moustache.

"It's not possible . . . Countess, is it you?" She looked at him carefully then, and suddenly felt her heart beat a little faster. It was Prince Vladimir Markovsky. She recognized him with amazement, he had been one of Konstantin's friends, and his eldest son had even offered to marry the Grand Duchess Tatiana, and had been summarily refused. Tatiana thought him far too frivolous. But he was a charming boy, as was his father.

"How did you get here?"

She laughed, shaking her head at how strange their life was these days. She had seen other familiar faces in Paris since they'd been there, and on two other occasions she had called for taxis and discovered that she knew the drivers. The Russian nobility seemed to have no other way to earn a living, skilled at nothing at all, handsome, well born and extremely charming, there remained little that they could do, except drive a motorcar, like Prince Vladimir as he gazed happily at her. It brought bittersweet memories of better days back to her, and she sighed as she began to explain to him how they had left Russia. His own tale was much akin to hers, although far more dangerous when he crossed the border.

"Are you staying here?" He glanced at her hotel as he started the car, and headed toward the address she had given him of the jeweler in the rue Cambon.

"Yes, for the moment. But Zoya and I must look for an apartment."

"She's here with you then. She must be hardly more than a child. And Natalya?" He had always thought Konstantin's wife extremely beautiful, although nervous to be sure, and he had obviously not heard of her death when the revolutionaries stormed the Fontanka Palace.

"She was killed . . . only days after Konstantin . . . and Nicolai." Her voice was low as she spoke. It was still difficult to say their names, particularly to him, because he had known them. He nodded sadly from the front seat. He had lost both his sons too, and he had come to Paris with his unmarried daughter.

"I'm sorry."

"We are all sorry, Vladimir. And sorriest of all for Nicholas and Alexandra. Have you had any news of them?"

"Nothing. Only that they are still under house arrest at Tsarskoe Selo, God only knows how long they will keep them there. At least they're comfortable, if not safe." No one was safe anymore, anywhere in Russia. At least not the people they knew. "Will you stay in Paris?" They had nowhere else to go, any of them, and other Russians were filtering in day by day, with amazing tales of escape, and their terrible losses. To an already burdened city they were adding ever growing numbers.

"I think so. It seemed better to come here than anywhere else. At least here we're safe, and it's a decent place for Zoya."

He nodded in agreement and darted the taxi in and out of the traffic. "Shall I wait for you, Evgenia Peterovna?" It made her heart sing just to speak Russian again, and to speak to someone who knew her name. He had just pulled up in front of the jeweler's.

"Would you mind terribly?" It would be comforting to know he was there, and to return home again with him, particularly if the jeweler gave her a great deal of money.

"Of course not. I'll wait here." He helped her out of the car carefully and escorted her to the door of the jewelry store. It was easy to imagine what she was going to do there. It was the same thing all of them were doing, selling everything they could, all the same treasures they had smuggled out with them, which only weeks before were baubles they took for granted.

The Countess emerged half an hour later with a dignified air and Prince Markovsky asked her no questions as he drove her back to the hotel. She seemed more subdued, though, as he helped her out of the cab on the rue Marbeuf and he hoped that she had gotten what she needed. She was very old to be forced to survive by her wits and selling her jewelry in a strange country, with no one to care for her, and a very young girl to take care of. He wasn't sure how old Zoya was, but he was certain that she was considerably younger than his own daughter, who was almost thirty.

"Is everything all right?" He was worried as he escorted her to the door, and she turned to him with wounded eyes.

"I suppose so. These are not easy times." She glanced back at the waiting taxi and then into his eyes. He had been a handsome man in his youth and he still was, but like her, there was suddenly something different about him. It had changed all of them. The very face of the world was no longer the same since the revolution. "It's not easy for any of us, is it, Vladimir?" And when there was no jewelry left to sell, she wondered to herself, then what will we do? Neither she nor Zoya was able to drive a taxi, and Feodor spoke no English at all and wasn't likely to learn. He was almost more of a burden than a help, but he had been so faithful, and so loyal in helping them escape, she could not let him down. She had to be responsible for him, just as she was for Zoya. But two hotel rooms were twice as expensive as one, and with the insignificant amount of money she had gotten for her ruby necklace and earrings, she had little hope of their funds holding out for much longer. They would have to think of something very creative. Perhaps she could take in sewing, she thought to herself, as she bid Vladimir good-bye with a distracted air. And she suddenly looked older than she had an hour before when she left for the jeweler's. Prince Markovsky kissed her hand and absolutely refused to let her pay him. She wondered if she would ever see him again. She felt that way about everyone now, but two days later, she came downstairs with Zoya and Feodor to find him waiting for her in the lobby.

When he saw her he bowed low and kissed her hand again, glancing with kindly eyes beyond her at Zoya, and then with obvious surprise at how lovely she was, and how grown up. She had come to be a considerable beauty. "I must apologize for intruding upon you, Evgenia Peterovna, but I have just heard of an apartment . . . it's quite small, but near the Palais Royal. It is not . . . quite . . . the most ideal neighborhood for a young girl, but . . . perhaps . . . perhaps it might do. You mentioned the other day how anxious you were to find a place to live. It has two bedrooms." He glanced past her at old Feodor with sudden concern. "Perhaps that won't be large enough for all of you, though . . ."

"Not at all." She smiled up at him as though he had always been her dearest friend. It suddenly meant so much to see a familiar face, even one that she hadn't seen so very often before. It was at least a face from the not so distant past, a relic from home, and she introduced him quickly to Zoya. "Zoya and I can easily share a room. We are doing so here at the hotel, and she doesn't seem to mind it."

"Of course not, Grandmama." She smiled warmly at her and gazed with curiosity at the tall, distinguished Russian.

"Shall I arrange for you to see it, then?" He seemed very interested in Zoya, but her grandmother seemed not to notice.

"Could we see it now? We were just going out for a stroll." It was a lovely May afternoon, and it was difficult to believe that there was discord anywhere in the world, harder still to believe that all of Europe was at war, and America had finally joined too.

"I will show you where it is, and perhaps they will let you see it now." He drove them there as quickly as he could, as Feodor sat in the front seat with him, and Vladimir told the two ladies all the latest gossip. Several more of their acquaintances had arrived only days before, although none of them seemed to have fresh news from Tsarskoe Selo, and Zoya listened with interest as he reeled off the names. She recognized most of them, although none of them were close friends. He also mentioned that Diaghilev was there, and was planning an actual performance of the Ballet Russe. They were to perform at the Châtelet, and begin the following week with a full rehearsal. Zoya felt her heart beat faster as she listened, and she barely noticed the streets they drove through to reach the apartment.

The apartment itself was very small, but it looked out over someone else's very pleasant garden. There were two small bedrooms and a tiny sitting room, a small kitchen, and a bathroom down the hall, which they would have to share with four other apartments. The others had to come from other floors, so they were more fortunate than most. It was certainly a far cry from the palace on Fontanka, or even the hotel on the rue Marbeuf, but they had no choices left to them now. Zoya's grandmother had admitted to her what a paltry sum she had gotten for the ruby necklace. They had brought other jewels to sell as

well, but it did not bode well for their
future.

"Perhaps it is too small after all. . . ."
Prince Vladimir looked suddenly embarrassed, but it was no more embarrassing
than his having to drive a taxi.

"I think it will do very well," the Countess said matter-of-factly, but she had already seen the look of dismay in Zoya's
eyes. The hallway had an ugly smell, of
urine mixed with fetid cooking. Perhaps a
little perfume . . . the lilac smells that
Zoya was so fond of . . . and the windows
open onto the pretty garden. Anything
might help, and the rent was just what
they could afford. The Countess turned to
Vladimir with a warm smile and thanked
him profusely.

"We have to take care of our own." He
spoke warmly to her, but his eyes were
firmly on Zoya. "I'll drive you back to your
hotel." They had arranged to move in the
following week, and on the way back,
Evgenia began making a list of the furniture they would need. She was going to
buy as little as she could, she and Zoya
could make the curtains and the bedspreads, she was only planning to acquire
the essentials.

"You know, with a pretty rug on the

floor, it might make the room seem a little larger." She spoke cheerfully and forced herself not to think of the treasured Aubussons in the pavilion behind the Fontanka Palace. "Don't you think, my love?"

"Hm? . . . Sorry, Grandmama?" She had been frowning and staring out the window as they drove down the Champs-Elysées to the rue Marbeuf. She had been thinking of something far more important. Something they needed desperately. Something that would allow them to live decently again, perhaps not in a palace but in an apartment that was larger and more comfortable than a foul-smelling matchbox. She was anxious to get back to the hotel now and leave her grandmother to her lists and her plans, and her orders to Feodor to go in search of furniture and a pretty carpet.

They thanked Prince Markovsky again when he dropped them off, and Evgenia was startled when Zoya said that she was going out for a walk, but absolutely refused to let Feodor go with her.

"I'll be fine, Grandmama. I promise you. I won't go far. Just to the Champs-Élysées and back."

"Do you want me to come with you, my dear?"

"No." She smiled at the grandmother she so dearly loved, thinking of how much she owed her. "You rest for a little while. We'll have tea when I come back."

"Are you sure you'll be all right?"

"Absolutely certain."

Reluctantly, the Countess let her go, and walked slowly up the stairs, holding Feodor's arm. It was going to be good practice for the long hike up the stairs to the new apartment.

And as soon as Zoya left the hotel, she rounded a corner and hailed a taxi, praying that the driver would know where it was, and that when she got there, someone would know what she was speaking of. It was a wild, wild hope, but she knew she had to try it.

"The Châtelet, please," she said imperiously as though she knew what she was talking about, and prayed silently that the man knew its location. And after an instant's hesitation, she saw that her prayers were answered. She hardly dared to breathe as the taxi sped her there, and she gave the driver a handsome tip, because he had found it, and because she felt guiltily relieved that he wasn't Russian. It was depressing somehow to see members of the families she had known driving taxis and talking mournfully about the family at Tsarskoe Selo.

She hurried inside, and looked around, thinking back to her threats to run away to the Maryinsky Theatre, and she found herself thinking of Marie and how stunned she would have been at this. It made Zoya smile as she looked for someone, anyone, who could answer her questions. She found a woman finally, in ballet tenue, practicing quietly at the barre, and Zoya guessed correctly that she was a teacher.

"I am looking for Mr. Diaghilev," she announced, and the woman smiled.

"Are you now? Might I ask why?"

"I'm a dancer and I would like to audition for him." She put all her cards on the table at once, and she had never looked younger or prettier or more frightened.

"I see. And has he ever heard of you?" It seemed rather a cruel question, and the woman didn't even bother to wait for an answer. "I see you haven't brought anything to dance in, mademoiselle. That's hardly an outfit in which to audition." Zoya glanced down at her narrow navy blue serge skirt, her white sailor blouse, and the black leather street shoes she had worn every day during her last weeks at Tsarskoe Selo. She blushed furiously then and the woman smiled at her. She was so pretty and so young and so innocent. It seemed hard to believe that she would be much of a dancer.

"I'm sorry. Perhaps I could come back to see him tomorrow." And then in a hushed whisper, "Is he here?"

The older woman smiled. "No, but he will be soon. He is holding full rehearsal here on the eleventh."

"I know. I wanted to audition for him. I want to be in the performance, and join his troupe." She said it all at once and the woman laughed out loud.

"Do you now? And where have you been training?"

"At Madame Nastova's school in St. Petersburg . . . until two months ago." She only wished then that she could have lied and said "the Maryinsky," but he would have known the truth almost certainly. And Madame Nastova's school of ballet was also one of the most prestigious in Russia.

"If I get you a leotard and some shoes, will you dance for me now?" The woman looked amused, and Zoya hesitated only for a split second.

"Yes, if you like." Her heart was pounding like an entire orchestra, but she had to get a job and this was all she could do, and all she wanted to do. It seemed the very least she could do for Evgenia.

The shoes that the woman gave her hurt her terribly, and as she went to the piano, Zoya felt foolish to have even tried it. She would look stupid on the stage all alone, and perhaps Madame Nastova was only being kind when she had said she was very good. But as the music began, she slowly began to forget her fears, and slowly she began to dance, and do everything that Madame Nastova had taught her. She danced for almost an hour tirelessly, as the woman watched her critically with narrowed eyes, but nowhere on her face was either scorn or amusement. Zoya was drenched when the music stopped at last, and she made a graceful curtsy in the direction of the piano. And in the silence of the room, the two women's eyes met, and the woman at the piano slowly nodded.

"Can you come back in two days, mademoiselle?" Zoya's eyes widened into two huge green saucers as she ran toward the piano.

"Do I get a job?"

The older woman shook her head and laughed, "No, no . . . but he will be here then. We shall see what he says, as well as the other teachers."

"All right. I'll get some shoes."

"You don't have any?" The woman looked surprised and Zoya looked at her seriously.

"We left everything we had in Russia. My parents and brother were killed in the revolution, and I escaped with my grandmother a month ago. I must find a job. She's too old to work, and we have no money." It was a simple statement that spoke volumes and touched the other woman's heart to the core, although she didn't show it.

"How old are you?"

"Just eighteen. And I've studied for twelve years."

"You're very good. No matter what he says . . . or the others . . . don't let anyone frighten you. You're very good." Zoya laughed out loud then, it was just exactly what she had said to Marie, that afternoon at Tsarskoe Selo.

"Thank you! Thank you so much!" She wanted to throw her arms around her and kiss her, but she restrained herself. She

was afraid to lose the opportunity she had.
She would do anything to dance for
Diaghilev, and this woman was going to
let her do it. It was beyond anything she
had ever dreamed. Perhaps Paris wasn't
going to be so bad after all . . . not if she
could become a ballerina. "I'll be better
after I've danced again. I haven't danced
in two months. I'm a little rusty."

"Then you'll be even better than I
think." She smiled at the beautiful young
redhead standing so graceful and poised
beside the piano, and then suddenly Zoya
gave a gasp. She had promised her grandmother she'd be back in a little while, and
she'd been gone for almost two hours.

"I must go! My grandmother! . . . Oh
. . . I'm so sorry . . ." She dashed off to
change her clothes again, and returned in
her navy skirt and sailor blouse, a swan
having been changed back into a duck-
ling. "I'll be back in two days . . . and
thank you for the shoes! . . ." She started
to hurry off, and then suddenly turned
back again, and shouted to the woman
who watched her go. "Oh . . . what
time?"

"Two o'clock!" The woman called, and
then remembered something else.
"What's your name?"

"Zoya Ossupov!" she called back, and then was gone, as the woman at the piano sat down with a smile, remembering the first time she had danced for Diaghilev twenty years before . . . the girl was good, there was no denying that . . . Zoya . . . poor child, she had been through enough from what she'd said in her simple words . . . it was hard to imagine being eighteen again, and as exuberant as Zoya.

Chapter 10

At two o'clock on a Friday afternoon, Zoya arrived at the Châtelet with a small tapestry bag, a leotard, and a pair of brand-new ballet shoes. She had sold her watch to pay for them, and had told her grandmother nothing of where she was going. All Zoya could think of for two days was the extraordinary opportunity she was about to have, and she was praying to all her guardian angels and favorite saints that she wouldn't make a mess of it. What if she was awkward . . . if she fell . . . if he hated her style . . . if Madame Nastova had been lying to her all these years. She had been filled with dread, and by the time she reached the Châtelet again all she wanted to do was run away, but she saw the woman for whom she had danced two days before, and suddenly it was too late. Diaghilev himself arrived and Zoya was introduced to him. And the next thing she knew she was on the stage, dancing for all of them as they sat in the audience, and she even forgot they were there. She was more comfortable than she had been two days before, much to her own surprise, and the music seemed to lift her up and carry her away. And when she was finished, they asked her to dance again, this time with a man, and he was very good, as Zoya seemed to fly through the air on the wings of angels. All in all, she danced for an hour and a half, and once again she was drenched when she stopped, and the new shoes were killing her, but she felt as though she could have flown to the moon as she turned to them. They were nodding, there were unintelligible words. They seemed to confer for hours, and then one of the teachers turned summarily to her and called across the stage as though it were no very remarkable thing.

"Next Friday, four o'clock, *répétition générale*, right here. Thank you very much." And with that, they turned away from her, as she stood with tears rolling down her cheeks. Madame Nastova hadn't lied and the gods had been good to her. She didn't know if it meant she had a job, and she didn't dare to ask them. All she knew was that she was dancing in the re-

hearsal next Friday afternoon. And maybe
. . . maybe . . . if she was very, very
good . . . she didn't even dare think of it
as she changed her clothes and flew
through the doors. She wished she could
tell her grandmother, but she knew she
could not. The idea of Zoya becoming a
dancer would have driven her wild. It was
better not to say anything, at least not yet.
Perhaps if they actually let her dance with
the Ballet Russe . . . perhaps then . . .

But the following week, victorious, having landed a job, for the time being at
least, she had to share her good news.

"You did *what*?" Her grandmother
looked shocked, stunned beyond belief.

"I auditioned for Serge Diaghilev and
he is letting me perform with the Ballet
Russe. The first performance is next
week." She could feel her heart pound
and her grandmother did not look
pleased.

"Are you mad? A common dancer on
the stage? Can you imagine what your father would say to something like that?" It
was a blow below the belt and it hurt too
much as she wheeled on the grandmother
she loved with wounded eyes.

"Don't talk about him like that. He's
dead. He wouldn't like any of the things

that have happened to us, Grandmama. But they have, and we have to do something about it. We can't just sit here and starve."

"Is that it then? You're afraid we'll starve? I'll be sure to order an additional dinner for you tonight, but take my word for it, you are *not* going on the stage."

"I *am*." She looked at her defiantly for the first time. In the past she had only dared to fight with her mother this way, but she couldn't let her grandmother stop her now. It meant too much to her, and it was their only way out, the only one she could see anyway. She didn't want to work in a shop, or scrub floors, or sew tiny buttons onto men's shirts, or work for a milliner and sew plumes on a hat, and what else was there she could do? Nothing at all. And sooner or later it would come to that. And her grandmother knew it too. "Grandmama, be sensible. You got almost nothing for the ruby necklace you sold. And how much jewelry can we sell? Everyone else here is doing the same thing. Sooner or later one of us has to go to work, and this is the only thing I know how to do."

"That's ridiculous. First of all, our money has not run out yet, and when it does, we can both get respectable jobs. We both sew decently, I can knit, you can teach Russian or French, or German, or even English if you try a little bit." They had taught her all those things at the Smolny Institute, along with a great many other niceties that served no purpose whatsoever now. "There is absolutely no reason at all for you to become a dancer like . . . like . . ." She was so angry, she almost mentioned the woman Nicholas had been so involved with years before. "Never mind. In any case, Zoya, I shan't allow it."

"You have no choice, Grandmama." She spoke with quiet desperation and it was the first time her grandmother had ever seen her like that.

"Zoya, you must obey me."

"I won't. It's the only thing I want to do. And I want to do something to help you." Tears filled the older woman's eyes as she looked at her only granddaughter.

"Has it come to this?" In her eyes, it was only a little better than prostitution, but not much.

"What's so terrible about being a dancer? It doesn't shock you that Prince Vladimir drives a taxi. Is that so respectable? Is that so much better than what I want to do?"

"It's pathetic." Evgenia wheeled on her with broken eyes and a heart that was breaking. "He was an important man only three months ago, and long ago his father was a great one. He is the next best thing to a beggar now . . . but it's all he has left, Zoya . . . it's all he can do. It's all over for him, and at least he's alive. Your life is just beginning, and I can't let you begin it that way. You'll be ruined . . ." She covered her face with her hands and began to sob. "And there's so little I can do to help you." Zoya was stunned to see her grandmother cry, it was the first time she had ever seen her falter, and it touched her to the core, but she still knew she had to dance with the Ballet Russe, no matter what. She wasn't going to sew or knit or teach Russian.

She put her arms around her grandmother and pulled her close to her. "Please, don't, Grandmama . . . please don't . . . I love you so very much . . ."

"Then promise me you won't dance with them . . . please, Zoya . . . I'm begging you . . . you must not do it."

She looked at her grandmother sadly then, wise beyond her years. She had grown much too old far too quickly in the past months and there was no turning back now. They both knew that, no matter how hard Evgenia tried to fight it. "My life will never be the same as yours, Grandmama. never again. It's not something you and I can change, we must simply make the best of it. There's no turning back now. Just like Uncle Nicholas and Aunt Alix . . . they must do whatever they have to. I'm doing that now . . . please don't be angry. . . ."

The diminutive Countess sat down in a chair with a look of defeat and stared unhappily up at Zoya. "I'm not angry, I'm sad. And I feel very helpless."

"You saved my life. You got me out of St. Petersburg . . . and out of Russia. If it weren't for you, they'd have killed me when they burned the house, or perhaps worse than that . . . you cannot change history, Grandmama. We can only do our best . . . and mine is to dance . . . let me do it . . . please . . . please give me your blessing."

The old woman closed her eyes and thought of her only son and slowly shook her head as she looked at Zoya, but Zoya was right. Konstantin was gone. They all were. What did it matter now? But whatever happened, Evgenia knew that Zoya was going to do what she wanted, and for the first time ever that she could remember, she felt too old and tired to fight her.

"You have my blessing then. But you're a wicked, wicked girl!" She wagged a finger at her and tried to smile through her tears and then suddenly wondered how she could have managed the audition. "How did you ever get the shoes?" Zoya hadn't asked her for a penny since they'd arrived in Paris.

"I bought them." She grinned mischievously. She was ingenious at least. Her father would have liked that.

"With what?"

"I sold my watch. It was ugly anyway. One of my classmates gave it to me for my name day." And with that, Evgenia could only laugh at her. She was a remarkable girl, and the old woman loved her even more than she knew, outrageous though she was.

"I suppose I should be grateful you didn't sell mine."

"Grandmama! What a thing to say! I would never do a thing like that!" She tried to look hurt but they both knew she wasn't.

"God only knows what you would do . . . I shudder to think!"

"You sound like Nicolai. . . ." Zoya smiled sadly when she said the words, and their eyes met and held. It was a whole new world for them, filled with new principles, new ideas, new people . . . and a new life for Zoya.

Chapter 11

Her first rehearsal with the Ballet Russe on the eleventh of May was absolutely killing. It ended at ten o'clock that night, and Zoya came back to the apartment exhilarated but so tired, she could barely move. Her feet had actually bled as she went over the pas de deux and the tours jetés again and again and again. It made her years with Madame Nastova look like child's play.

Her grandmother was waiting up for her in the tiny living room. They had moved into the apartment two days before, and had bought a small couch, and several small tables. There were lamps with ugly fringes, and a green rug with gloomy purple flowers. Gone the Aubussons and the antiques and the pretty things they had once loved. But it was comfortable and Feodor kept it clean for them. He had gone out to the country with Prince Markovsky the day before and come home with the taxi filled with firewood. There was a warm fire blazing as her grandmother waited for her with a steaming pot of tea.

"Well, little one, how was it?" She was still hoping that Zoya would come to her senses, and abandon the idea of dancing with the Ballet Russe, but she could see in the girl's eyes that there was no hope of that now. She hadn't seen her so happy since the whole nightmare began exactly two months before, with the riots in the streets, and Nicolai's death. None of it was forgotten, but the memory of it seemed a little less acute as she fell into one of their uncomfortable chairs and smiled from ear to ear.

"Grandmama, it was wonderful . . . just wonderful . . . but I'm so tired I can hardly move." The long hours of rehearsal had been grueling beyond words, but in an odd way it was a dream come true for her, and all she could think of now was the performance in two weeks. Her grandmother had promised to come, and Prince Markovsky was coming with his daughter.

"You haven't changed your mind, little one?"

She shook her head with a tired smile,

and poured herself a glass of tea from the steaming pot. They had told her that night that she would dance in both parts of the performance, and she was so proud of the money they had given her. She slipped it quietly into her grandmother's hand with a shy look of pride as tears filled Evgenia's eyes. It had come to that then. She was to be supported by the child's dancing. It was almost beyond bearing.

"What's that for?"

"Grandmama, it's for you."

"We don't need it yet." But the bare walls around them and the ugly purple rug told another tale. Everything they had was threadbare and worn, and they both knew that the money from the ruby necklace would be gone soon. There were more jewels, of course, but not enough to support them forever. "Is this truly what you want to do?" Evgenia asked sadly, and Zoya gently touched her cheek, and then kissed it.

"Yes, Grandmama . . . it was beautiful today." It was just like her dream of dancing with the students at the Maryinsky, and she wrote to Marie that night, a long, brave letter that told her everything except about the small dreary apartment. She sat in the tiny sitting room long after her grandmother had gone to bed, and told her of the people they'd seen, and what Paris was like, and the excitement of dancing with the Ballet Russe. She could almost see Marie smile as she wrote it. She directed the letter to Dr. Botkin at Tsarskoe Selo and hoped that it would reach Marie before too long. It made her feel closer to her just to write it.

The following day she went back to rehearsal again, and that night there was an air raid. The three of them went to the cellar beneath the building, and then walked slowly back upstairs when it was over. It was a reminder of the war that raged nearby, but Zoya wasn't afraid. All she could think of now was her dancing.

Prince Markovsky was often there when Zoya got home. He always had stories to tell, and he frequently had brought her little cakes, and fresh fruit whenever he could find it. He even brought them one of the few treasures he still had, a priceless icon that her grandmother didn't want to accept, but he insisted. Evgenia knew only too well how desperately they all needed the things they could sell, but Markovsky only waved an elegantly veined hand with long graceful fingers and told them he had more than enough for the moment. His daughter already had a job teaching English.

And the night of her first performance they were all there, in the third row. Zoya had bought the tickets for them with her wages. Only Feodor didn't come. He was proud of her as well, but the ballet was beyond his ken, and Zoya brought him a program, with her name in tiny print near the bottom. Even her grandmother had been proud of her, though she had cried with bittersweet sorrow when she first saw her. She would have preferred anything than to see her own granddaughter on the stage like a common dancer.

"You were marvelous, Zoya Konstantinovna!" The Prince toasted her with champagne he had brought when they went back to the apartment. "We were all so proud of you!" He smiled happily at the young girl with the flaming hair, despite an austere glance and a sniff from his daughter. She thought it shocking that Zoya had become a dancer. The two had never met before, and she was a tall, spare girl with all the earmarks of a spinster. Life in Paris was excruciating for her. She hated the children she taught English to, and it was embarrassing beyond words to see her father drive a taxi. But Zoya shared none of her prim views. Her eyes seemed to blaze with excitement. There was a warm flush on her cheeks, as her fiery hair fell from the bun she had worn and cascaded like flames past her shoulders. She was a beautiful girl, and the excitement of the night seemed only to have enhanced her beauty.

"You must be tired, little one," the Prince said kindly as he poured the last of the champagne.

"Not at all." Zoya beamed and pranced around the room on feet that still wanted to dance. It was so much easier than rehearsal had been. It had been everything she'd always dreamed, and more. "I'm not even a little bit tired." She smiled and then giggled as she took another sip of the champagne he had brought, as Yelena, his daughter, looked on disapprovingly. Zoya wanted to stay up all night and tell them the tales of backstage. She needed to talk about it with people who cared.

"You were fabulous!" he said again, and Zoya grinned. He was so serious and so old, but he seemed to care about her. In a way she wished her father had been there, although it would have broken his heart to see her on the stage . . . but perhaps, secretly, he might have been proud of her

. . . and Nicolai . . . tears filled her eyes at the thought, and she set down her glass and turned away, to walk to the window and stare at the gardens outside. "You look lovely tonight," she heard Vladimir whisper at her side, and she turned to look up at him as he saw the tears shimmer in her eyes. Her lithe body was so young and strong. He ached with desire for her and it shone in his eyes, as she took a step away from him, suddenly aware of what she hadn't noticed before. He was even older than her father had been and she was shocked at what she thought she saw in his eyes now.

"Thank you, Prince Vladimir," she said quietly, suddenly sad at how desperate they all were, how hungry for love, and some shred of the past they could still share. In St. Petersburg, he would never have looked at her twice, she would have been nothing more than a pretty child to him, but now . . . now they were clinging to a lost world, and the people they had left behind there. She was nothing more than a way of continuing the past. She wanted to tell Yelena that as she stiffly said good night to them.

Zoya thought of Prince Vladimir again as she undressed and waited for her

grandmother to return from the bathroom down the hall.

"It was nice of him to bring us champagne," her grandmother said as she
brushed her hair, her lace nightgown
framing her face and making her seem
younger in the dim light. She had been
beautiful once, and the two women's eyes
were almost the same as they met and
held. Zoya wondered if she knew that Vladimir was attracted to her. His hand had
touched hers as they left, and he held her
too close when he kissed her on the cheek.

For a long moment, Zoya didn't answer
her. "Yelena seems so sad, doesn't she?"

Evgenia nodded and set her brush
down with a solemn air. "She was never a
happy child, as I recall. Her brothers were
far more interesting, more like Vladimir."
She remembered the handsome one who
had asked for Tatiana's hand. "He's a nice
man, don't you think?"

Zoya turned away for a moment and
then turned back to look at her honestly.
"I think he likes me, Grandmama . . .
too much . . ." She faltered on the words
and Evgenia frowned.

"What do you mean by that?"

"I mean that he . . ." Her face blushed
furiously in the soft light and she looked

like a child again. "That he . . . he touched my hand tonight. . . ." It seemed stupid to have to explain it now . . . maybe it didn't mean anything.

"You're a pretty girl, and perhaps you bring back memories for him. I think he was very fond of your Mama, and I know he was close to Konstantin when they were young. They hunted with Nicholas more than once . . . don't be too sensitive, Zoya. He means well. And it was nice of him to come to see you tonight. He's just being kind, little one."

"Perhaps," Zoya said noncommittally as they turned off the light and slipped into the narrow bed they shared. In the dark, Zoya could hear Feodor snoring in the next room, as she drifted off to sleep, thinking of how magical the performance had been.

But the next morning, she was sure that Vladimir wasn't just being kind. He was waiting for her downstairs, when she left for rehearsal again.

"Would you like a ride?" She was surprised to see him there, and he was carrying flowers for her.

"I don't want to put you out . . . it's all right." She would rather have walked to the Châtelet. He was suddenly making her uncomfortable the way he looked at her. "I like to walk." It was a beautiful day, and she was excited to be going to rehearsal again. The Ballet Russe was the happiest thing in her life these days, and she didn't want to share it with anyone, not even the handsome white-haired Prince who stood so gallantly holding white roses out to her. They only made her feel sad. Marie had always given her white roses in the spring, but he couldn't have known that. He knew nothing about her at all, he was her parents' friend, not hers, and it suddenly depressed her to see him standing there, his jacket worn, his collar frayed. Like everyone else, he had left everything behind, and escaped with his life, a few jewels, and the icon he had given them a few days before. "Perhaps it would be nice if you called on Grandmama." She smiled politely at him, and he looked hurt.

"Is that how you think of me? As your grandmother's friend?" She didn't want to say yes, but it was. He seemed a thousand years old as he stood looking at her. "Do I seem so old to you then?"

"Not at all . . . I'm sorry . . . I have to go. . . . I'll be late and they'll be very angry at me."

"Let me drive you then. We can talk on the way."

She hesitated, but she was going to be late. Reluctantly, she let him open the taxi door for her and she stepped in, leaving the white roses between them on the seat. It was nice of him to bring her gifts, but she knew that he could ill afford to bring her anything. No wonder Yelena was annoyed at them.

"How is Yelena?" she asked to pass the time as they drove, and she avoided his eyes, as she glanced at the other cars and then slowly back at him. "She seemed very quiet last night."

"She's not happy here." He sighed. "I don't suppose many of us are. It's such a sudden change, and no one was prepared. . . ." He said the words and then reached over and touched her hand, startling her with what he said next. "Zoya, do you think that I'm too old for you, my dear?"

Her voice caught in her throat and she gently took her hand away. "You're my father's friend." Her eyes were sad as she looked at him. "It's hard for all of us, we are all clinging to what we no longer have. Perhaps I am part of that for you."

He smiled. "Is that what you think it is? Do you know that you're very beautiful?"

She could feel herself blush and silently cursed the fair skin that went with her fiery hair. "Thank you very much. But I'm younger than Yelena . . . I'm sure she'd be very upset. . . ." It was all she could think of as she wished they would get to the Châtelet so she could escape him.

"She has her own life to live, Zoya. And I have mine. I would like to take you to dinner sometime. Perhaps at Maxim's." It was madness . . . the champagne . . . the roses . . . the idea of dinner at Maxim's. They were all starving, he was driving a cab, she was dancing with the Ballet Russe, and there was no point spending the little he had on her. He was far too old, but she didn't want to be rude.

"I don't think Grandmama . . ." She turned unhappy eyes to his, and he looked hurt.

"You'd be better off with one of us, Zoya Konstantinovna, someone who knows your world, than with some young fool."

"I don't have time for any of that, Vladimir. If they keep me on at the ballet, I'll have to work day and night to keep up."

"We can find the time. I can pick you up at night . . ." His voice drifted off as he looked at her hopefully, and she shook her head with an unhappy look.

"I can't . . . truly . . . I can't." She saw with relief that they had arrived, and she turned to look at him for a last time. "Please don't wait for me now. All I want is to forget . . . what was . . . we can't bring it back. It wouldn't be right for us . . . please . . ." He said nothing as she slipped out of the car and hurried away, leaving the white roses on the seat beside him.

Chapter 12

"Did Vladimir bring you home?" Her grandmother smiled at her as she came in, and Zoya noticed with a sinking heart the white roses in a vase next to her on the table.

"No. One of the others gave me a ride." She sat down with a smile and rubbed her legs. "It was hard today." But she didn't mind. Dancing with the Ballet Russe made her feel alive again.

"He said he'd bring you home." Evgenia frowned. He had brought her fresh bread, and a jar of jam. He was such a kind man, and he was being so good to them. And in an odd way, it comforted Evgenia to think of him taking care of Zoya.

"Grandmama . . ." Zoya looked at her, struggling for the words. "I don't want him to."

"Why not? You're far safer with him

than with someone you don't know." He had said as much to her himself that afternoon, when he came to the apartment to drop off Zoya's roses, and the pain of Zoya dancing with the Ballet Russe struck her again like a knife to her heart, but she knew there was no stopping her now. And she had to admit that one of them had to work, and Zoya was the only one who could. She just wished she would find something else, like Yelena's teaching. And perhaps, if Vladimir took her under his wing, Zoya might even stop dancing. He had suggested it only that afternoon, and it made Evgenia see him in a different light. That of hero and savior.

"Grandmama . . . I think Prince Vladimir . . . I think he has something more in mind."

"He's a decent man. Well mannered, wellborn. He was a friend of Konstantin's." Evgenia didn't want to show her hand too soon, although Vladimir had convinced her.

"But that's just what I mean. He was Papa's friend. Not mine. He must be sixty years old."

"He's a Russian prince, and a cousin of the Tsar."

"Does that make everything all right?"

Zoya asked angrily as she sprang to her feet. "Don't you care that he's old enough to be my grandfather?"

"He means you no harm, Zoya . . . someone has to take care of you. I'm eighty-two years old . . . I will not always be here for you . . . you must think of that." And secretly, she would have been relieved to know that she was leaving Zoya in Vladimir's hands. At least he was someone she knew, someone who understood the life they had led before. No one in Paris could possibly understand that, except one of their own, and she looked imploringly at Zoya, begging her with her eyes to think of that, but Zoya looked horrified.

"Would you have me marry him, then? Is that what you want?" Tears sprang to her eyes at the thought of it. "He's an old man."

"He would take care of you. Think of how kind he's been to us since we arrived."

"I don't want to hear about it anymore!" She ran into the bedroom and slammed the door, and then threw herself on the bed crying hopelessly. Was that all that was left? The prospect of marriage to a man three times her age, only because he was a Russian prince. The very thought sickened her, and it made her long more than ever for her lost life and friends.

"Zoya . . . don't . . . darling, please . . ." Her grandmother came to sit on the edge of her bed, and gently stroked her hair. "I'm not trying to force you to do anything you don't want. But I worry about you so much. Feodor and I are so old . . . you must find someone who can take care of you."

"I'm eighteen years old," she sobbed into the bed, "I don't want to marry anyone . . . and not him. . . ." Nothing about him appealed to her, and she hated Yelena. The thought of being doomed to live with them made her hysterical. All she wanted to do was dance, she would make enough money doing that to support herself, and Feodor and her grandmother. She vowed to herself then that she would do anything rather than marry a man she didn't love. She'd work day and night . . . she'd do anything. . . .

"All right . . . all right . . . please don't cry like this . . . please . . ." Her own eyes were filled with tears, thinking of the cruelty of their fate. Perhaps the child was right. It had only been a thought. He was of course too old, but he was one of them, and that mattered to her a great deal. But there were others who had survived, there were younger men too. Perhaps Zoya would meet one of them and fall in love. It was her fondest hope now. It was the only hope she had left . . . that and the little bit of jewelry concealed in the bed where they slept. There was nothing else left . . . except a few diamonds and emeralds, a long rope of exquisite pearls, and the Fabergé egg Nicholas had given her . . . and a lifetime of broken dreams. "Come, Zoya . . . dry your tears. Let's go for a walk."

"No," Zoya pouted unhappily, turning her face into the bed again, "he'll be waiting for us downstairs."

"Don't be ridiculous." Evgenia smiled at her. She was still such a child, although she'd grown up rapidly in the past two months. "His manners are impeccable. He's not a hoodlum lurking in the streets. Don't be foolish about this."

Zoya rolled slowly onto her back, looking incredibly beautiful. "I'm sorry, Grandmama. I don't want to make you unhappy. I promise I'll take care of us."

"That's not what I want for you, child. I want someone to take care of you. That's how it should have been."

"But everything's different now. Nothing is the way it was." She sat up with a shy smile. "Perhaps I'll be a famous dancer one day." She looked excited at the thought and Evgenia laughed.

"God help me, I almost think you're enjoying this."

Zoya smiled openly then. "I love the Ballet Russe, Grandmama."

"I know you do. And you're very good. But you must never think of this as something you will do for the rest of your life. Do it now, if you must. But one day things will change again." It was not a promise, but a prayer, but as Zoya swung her legs off the bed, and went to get her coat, she realized that she wasn't sure she wanted them to. She loved dancing with the Ballet Russe . . . far more than her grandmother understood.

And as they walked slowly toward the Palais Royal, and glanced at the arcades and their many wares, Zoya felt a thrill fill her soul. Paris was beautiful and she liked the people there. It wasn't such a bad life. She suddenly felt happy and young. Far too young to waste her life with Prince Vladimir. Ever.

Chapter 13

Zoya danced with the Ballet Russe all through June, and she was so totally involved in her work that she scarcely knew what was happening in the world. It came as an enormous surprise to her when General Pershing and his troops arrived on June 13. The city went wild, as they marched to the Place de la Concorde and the facade of the Hotel Crillon. People shouted and waved, and women threw flowers at the men, screaming *"Vive l'Amérique!"* Zoya could hardly get back to the Palais Royal to tell her grandmother what she'd seen.

"Grandmama, there are thousands of them!"

"Then perhaps they will end the war for us soon." She was exhausted by the nightly air raids, and some secret part of her thought that if the war came to an end, perhaps things would change in Russia again and they could go home. But most people knew there was no hope of it.

"Do you want to take a walk and see?" Zoya's eyes were bright. There was something wonderful about the hopeful look of the French, and the fresh-faced men in their khaki uniforms. They looked so wholesome and alive. Everywhere, there seemed to be hope again, but her grandmother only shook her head.

"I have no desire to see soldiers in the streets, little one." She had ugly memories of that, and she was safe at home and urged Zoya to stay there too. "Stay away from them. Crowds can quickly become dangerous." But there was no sign of that here. It was a happy day for everyone, and rehearsals had been curtailed for the remainder of the week. For the first time in a month, Zoya had some time to herself, to lie in bed, to go for walks, to sit by the fire and read. She felt carefree and young, and she appreciated the time now. That night, she sat in the living room and wrote a long letter to Marie, telling her of Pershing's march, and her work at the ballet. There seemed to be more to tell her now, although she didn't mention Prince Vladimir. She knew her friend would have been shocked at her grandmother's encouraging his pursuit, but it didn't matter to her now. He had understood, and although he still brought the Countess fresh bread while Zoya was at work, she herself hadn't run into him in weeks.

As she wrote to Marie that night, little Sava sat cozily in her lap, snoring happily. ". . . She looks so exactly like Joy, she makes me think of you the moment she bounds into the room. Although I don't need any reminders of you. It seems incredible to me still that we are in Paris, and you are there . . . and we won't be joining you in Livadia this summer. The funny photograph of all of us is next to my bed . . ." Zoya looked at it every night before she slept. She had also brought a photograph of Olga with Alexis on her lap when he was three or four . . . and a beautiful one of Nicky and Alix. Only memories now, but writing to her friend kept them alive in her heart. Dr. Botkin had sent her a letter from Marie only the week before, in which she told Zoya that all was well, although they were still under house arrest, but they'd been told that they would be going to Livadia in September. And she was all well again. She apologized to Zoya for giving her the measles, and said she would have liked to see her all covered with spots. Reading the letters made Zoya smile through her tears.

She was rereading her letter, when a message came. She was to dance *Petrouchka* at the Opéra with the Ballet Russe for General Pershing and his troops. Her grandmother, as usual, was less than happy at the news. Dancing for soldiers seemed even worse than the performance at the Châtelet, but she didn't even try to dissuade Zoya this time, knowing full well that there was no hope of it.

By then, Pershing and his staff were well ensconced in their headquarters on the rue Constantine, across from the Invalides, and he was living on the Left Bank, near the rue de Varennes, in a beautiful *hôtel particulier* loaned to him by a fellow American, Ogden Mills, who was serving elsewhere in the infantry.

"I want Feodor to go with you tonight," her grandmother said darkly as she left for the Opéra.

"Don't be silly, Grandmama, I'll be fine. They can't be any different from Russian generals. I'm sure they're quite well behaved. They're not going to storm the stage and carry us off with them." Nijinsky was dancing with them that night and Zoya could hardly wait. Just being on the same stage with him was almost more than she could bear. "I'll be fine. I promise you."

"You're not going alone. Either Feodor, or Prince Vladimir. Take your choice." She knew easily which one it would be, although she secretly regretted it, but she hadn't pressed Zoya about the Prince again. In a way, she knew Zoya was right, Vladimir was a great deal too old for her.

"All right." Zoya laughed. "I'll take Feodor. But he'll be miserable waiting backstage."

"Not if he's waiting for you, my love." The old servant served them with a devotion that bordered on the fanatical, and Evgenia knew that Zoya would be safe if he was standing by her. And Zoya only agreed to it to put her grandmother's mind at rest.

"At least tell him he mustn't get in the way."

"He wouldn't think of it."

Together they took a taxi to the Opéra, and within moments Zoya was swallowed up by preparations for the performance for Pershing and his men. She knew there were other festivities planned for them as well, at the Opéra Comique, the Comédie-Française, and in other theaters

around town. Paris was opening its arms
to them.

And when the curtain went up that
night, she danced as she never had before.
Just knowing that Nijinsky was there
spurred her on, and Diaghilev spoke to
her himself at the end of the first act. She
felt as though she could fly after hearing
his kind words, and she put even more of
herself into it, and was stunned to realize
that the performance had flown by as the
final curtain fell. She wanted the evening
never to end. She took her bows with the
rest of the troupe, and retreated with the
others to their common dressing room.
The primas had their own of course, but it
would be years before she could look forward to that, but she didn't really care. All
she wanted was to dance, and she was. She
had danced well, and she was filled with
pride as she slowly untied her shoes. Her
toes were sore from the blocks, but even
that didn't seem to matter now. It was a
small price to pay for so much joy. She had
even forgotten the General and his staff.
All she could think of that night was the
ballet as she danced and danced and
danced . . . and she looked up in surprise as one of the teachers entered the
room.

"You are all invited to a reception at the General's home," she announced. "Two military trucks will take you there." She looked at them with pride. They had done well, each and every one of them. "Champagne for all!" she added with a smile as everyone began to talk and laugh. Paris seemed to be coming alive again with the Americans at hand. There were parties and performances everywhere, and Zoya suddenly thought of Feodor waiting for her outside. She wanted desperately to go with them, to be like everyone else, in spite of her grandmother's fears. She slipped quietly outside and went to look for Feodor, and found him standing near the stage door, looking as miserable as she had told her grandmother he would. He felt ridiculous there, surrounded by women in leotards and tulle, and men striding past him less than half dressed. The obvious immorality of it horrified him.

"Yes, mademoiselle?"

"I must go to a reception with the rest of the troupe," she explained, "and I can't bring you, Feodor. Go home to Grandmama, and I'll come home as soon as I can."

"No." He shook his head solemnly. "I

promised Evgenia Peterovna, I told her I would bring you home."

"But you can't come with us. I promise you I'll be safe."

"She'll be very angry with me."

"No, she won't. I'll explain it to her myself when I come home."

"I will wait for you." He looked at her stolidly and she wanted to scream. She didn't want a chaperone. She wanted to be just like the rest of them. She wasn't a baby anymore after all. She was a grown woman, of eighteen. And perhaps, if she was very, very lucky, Nijinsky might speak to her . . . or Mr. Diaghilev again. She was far more interested in them than in any of Pershing's men. But first she had to convince Feodor to go home, and finally, after what seemed like endless arguments, he agreed to go, although he was certain the Countess would be furious at him.

"I promise you, I'll explain everything to her."

"Very well, mademoiselle." He touched his brow, bowed, and left via the stage door, as Zoya gave a sigh of relief.

"What was that all about?" one of the other dancers asked as she walked past her.

"Just a friend of the family." She smiled. No one knew her circumstances here, and no one cared. All they cared about was the ballet, not maudlin tales of how she had come to join the troupe, and having the old servant standing by like a Cossack Guard embarrassed her. She was relieved when he left, and she could return to the dressing room to change for the reception at General Pershing's house. Everyone was in high spirits, and someone had already begun pouring them champagne.

They piled into the military trucks happily, and crossed the Pont Alexandre III as they sang old Russian songs, and had to be reminded more than once to behave themselves as they reached General Pershing's house. But he seemed like a kindly man as he welcomed them, standing tall and slender in his full dress uniform, circulating in the elegant marble hall. And for an instant, Zoya felt her heart catch as she looked around. It reminded her of the palaces of St. Petersburg, although smaller of course. But the marble floors and the columns and the sweeping staircases were all too familiar to her, and all too sharp a memory of the world she had only recently left behind.

They were escorted into a large ball-

room with mirrored walls and gold columns and marble fireplaces, all of it beautifully authentic Louis XV. And Zoya
suddenly felt very young again, as the
dancers cavorted and laughed, and a military band that had appeared began playing a slow waltz, as others drank champagne. She felt an overwhelming urge to
cry as she listened to the music, and feeling breathless, she walked out into the
garden beyond.

She stood silently, staring at a statue by
Rodin, wishing that she hadn't come,
when a voice directly behind where she
stood spoke softly in the warm night.

"May I get you something, mademoiselle?" The voice was distinctly American,
yet he spoke perfect French. She turned
to see a tall, attractive man with gray hair
and brilliant blue eyes looking at her, and
the first thing she noticed about him was
that he looked kind. He seemed to sense
that something was wrong, and his eyes
gently probed hers as she shook her head,
the tears still glistening on her cheeks.
"Are you all right?"

She nodded silently and then turned in
embarrassment to wipe her tears. She was
wearing a simple white dress Alix had
given her the year before. It was one of

the few nice ones she had managed to bring from St. Petersburg, and she looked lovely as she stood looking up at him. "I'm sorry . . . I . . ." How could she begin to tell him all that she felt? She wished only that he would leave her to her memories, but he made no move to go as he watched her eyes. "It's so beautiful here." It was all she could say, but it brought the squalid apartment near the Palais Royal to mind, and reminded her again of how much their lives had changed, in sharp contrast to the elegant garden where she stood now.

"Are you with the Ballet Russe?"

"I am." She smiled, hoping he would forget her tears, as she listened to the distant strains of another waltz. She said the words with pride, thinking again how lucky she was. "Wasn't Nijinsky marvelous tonight?"

He laughed in embarrassment and came a little closer to her as she noticed again how tall and handsome he was. "I'm afraid I'm not a great devotee of the ballet, it was a command performance for some of us tonight."

"Aha!" She laughed. "And did you suffer terribly?"

"Yes." His eyes laughed back into hers.

"Until just now. Would you like a glass of champagne?"

"In a minute perhaps. It's so lovely out here." The garden was so peaceful, as everyone danced and laughed and cavorted inside. "Do you live here too?"

He smiled and shook his head. "They have us billeted in a house on the rue du Bac. It's not quite as palatial as this, but it's very nice, and it's quite nearby." He was watching her as she moved. She was quiet and elegant, and there was more than just the grace of a dancer as she walked closer to him. There was an aura of almost regal dignity as she moved her head, and a look of immeasurable sadness that belied her smile.

"Are you on the General's staff?"

"I am." He was one of his aides-de-camp, but he spared her the details. "Have you been with the Ballet Russe for long?" It couldn't have been very long, he suspected that she was a very young girl, although she had a great deal of poise as they switched from French to English finally. She spoke it very well, after her studies at the Smolny Institute.

"I've been with them for a month." She smiled at him. "Much to my grandmother's chagrin." She laughed and looked suddenly even younger.

"Your parents must be very proud of you." But he instantly regretted the remark as he saw the sadness in her eyes.

"My parents were killed in St. Petersburg . . . in March. . . ." She almost whispered the words and suddenly he understood. "I live with my grandmother."

"I'm sorry . . . about your parents, I mean . . ." The flash of blue eyes nearly made her cry again. It was the first time she had said the words to anyone. Her fellow dancers knew little about her, but for some reason she felt she could say anything to him. He reminded her in an odd way of Konstantin, the same elegance, the graceful way he moved, the dark hair shot with gray, and the brilliant eyes. "You came here with your grandmother?" He didn't know why, but he was fascinated by her. She was so young and so beautiful, with those big sad green eyes.

"Yes, we came two months ago . . . from . . . after . . ." But she couldn't go on, and he came and gently tucked her hand into his arm.

"Let's go for a walk, shall we, mademoiselle?" She felt safe with her hand in his arm. "And then perhaps a glass of champagne." They wandered to the Rodin statue and back, talking about Paris, the war, subjects that were less painful to her, and then with a smile she looked up at him.

"And where are you from?"

"New York." She had never thought too much about the United States. It all seemed terribly far away.

"What's it like?"

He laughed as he looked down at her. "Big, busy. Not as pretty as this, I'm afraid. But I like it there." He wanted to ask her about St. Petersburg, but sensed that this wasn't the time or the place. "Do you dance every day?"

"Almost." And then she laughed up at him. "Until tonight's performance, I was enjoying a week off."

"And what do you do then . . . in your spare time?"

"I go for walks with my grandmother, I write to friends, read . . . sleep . . . play with my dog."

"It sounds like a pleasant life. What kind of dog do you have?" They were silly questions, but he wanted to keep her close to him, and he wasn't sure why. She was clearly half his age, but so beautiful, it tore at his heart.

"A cocker spaniel." She smiled. "She was a gift from a very dear friend."

"A gentleman?" He looked intrigued and she laughed.

"No, no! A girl! My cousin, in fact."

"Did you bring the dog from Russia with you?" He was fascinated by her as she bent her head, the cascade of fiery red hair hiding her eyes.

"Yes, I did. I'm afraid she made the journey rather better than I did. I arrived in Paris with measles." She looked up at him again and grinned, looking once again like a child. "Stupid of me, wasn't it?" But nothing about her seemed that to him, and then he suddenly realized he didn't even know her name.

"Not at all. Do you suppose we ought to introduce ourselves?"

"Zoya Ossupov." She curtsied prettily, and looked up at him.

"Clayton Andrews. Captain Clayton Andrews, I suppose I should have said."

"My brother was a captain too . . . with the Preobrajensky Guard. I don't suppose you've ever heard of them." She looked up at him expectantly, and once again he saw her eyes grow sad. Her moods seemed to change with lightning speed, and as he looked at her for the first time he understood why people said the eyes were the windows of the soul. Hers seemed to lead one into a magic world of diamonds and emeralds and unshed tears, and he wanted to make her happy again, to make her dance and laugh and smile.

"I don't know very much about Russia, I'm afraid, Miss Ossupov."

"Then we're even." She smiled again. "I don't know anything about New York."

He walked her back inside the main ballroom then and brought her a glass of champagne as the others danced the waltz.

"Would you like to dance?"

She seemed to hesitate, and then nodded. He set her glass down on a table nearby, and led her onto the floor in a slow and dignified waltz, and once again she felt as though she were dancing in her father's arms. If she closed her eyes, she would be back in St. Petersburg . . . but his voice broke into her thoughts.

"Do you always dance with your eyes closed, mademoiselle?" He was teasing her and she smiled up at him. It felt good to be in his arms, good to be dancing with a tall, powerful man . . . on a magical night . . . in a beautiful house . . .

"It's just so lovely here . . . isn't it?"

"It is now." But he had enjoyed his time in the garden with her. It was easier talking to her there than with the music and the crowd. And at the end of the dance, General Pershing signaled him so he left her, and when he came back to look for her, she was gone. He looked everywhere, and walked out to the garden again, but she was nowhere in sight, and when he inquired, he was told that the first truckload of the Ballet Russe had left the party. He walked back to his own quarters thoughtfully, as he meandered down the rue du Bac, remembering her name, thinking of her big green eyes, and he found himself wondering who she really was. There was something deeply intriguing about her.

Chapter 14

"The next time I send Feodor somewhere with you, Zoya Konstantinovna, you will please have the goodness not to send him home." The old Countess was furious as they shared breakfast the next day. Feodor had come sheepishly back to her, and explained that the soldiers had invited the corps de ballet to go out somewhere, and he wasn't included. Her grandmother had been waiting for her when she got back, almost too angry to speak to her, and by morning, her fury was still white-hot, as she glared at Zoya.

"I'm sorry, Grandmama. I couldn't take Feodor with me. It was a beautiful reception at General Pershing's quarters." She remembered instantly the gardens and the Captain she had met, but she said nothing to her grandmother about any of it.

"Ah! So it's come to that, has it? Enter-

taining the troops? And what is next? This
is precisely why proper young ladies don't
run away to join the ballet. It is not suit-
able, absolutely not. And I won't tolerate
this. I want you to leave the ballet at
once!"

"Grandmama . . . please . . . you
know I can't!"

"You can if I tell you to!"

"Grandmama . . . please don't . . ."
She was in no mood to argue with her. She
had had such a nice time the night before
. . . and the handsome Captain had been
such a nice man, or at least he seemed like
it. But still, she said nothing about him to
her grandmother. It didn't seem appropriate, and she knew their paths would
not cross again. "I'm sorry. I won't do it
again." Not that she'd have the opportunity anyway. General Pershing was hardly
likely to give parties for the Ballet Russe
after every performance.

She stood up as her grandmother glared
at her. "Where are you going now?"

"I have a rehearsal today."

"I'm so tired of this!" She stood up and
paced around the room as best she could,
but she was still very spry. "Ballet, ballet,
ballet! Enough!"

"Yes, Grandmama."

She was going to sell a necklace again, an emerald one this time. Maybe Zoya would give up this nonsense then for a while. She had had enough of it. She was not a dancer. She was a child.

"What time will you be home tonight?"

"I should be back at four o'clock. Rehearsal starts at nine, and I don't have a performance tonight."

"I want you to think about leaving them." But Zoya enjoyed it too much, they both knew that, and the money did help, much as the Countess hated to think about it. She had bought her grandmother a pretty dress and a warm shawl the week before. And her wages helped pay for their food as well, although there were no little extra treats, except those Vladimir still brought in the hopes of catching a glimpse of Zoya.

"We'll go for a walk this afternoon when I come home."

"What makes you think I'd be willing to go for a walk with you?" her grandmother growled, and Zoya laughed.

"Because you love me so much. And I love you too." She kissed her cheek, and hurried out the door, like a schoolgirl late for class.

The old woman sighed and cleared

away the breakfast plates. It was so difficult having her here. Things were so different, and the hardest part was that
much as the old woman hated to admit it
to herself, Zoya was no longer a child, and
it wasn't easy to control her.

Zoya's rehearsal was at the Opéra again
that day, in preparation for another performance the following night, and she
danced and rehearsed and practiced at
the barre for hours and when she finished
shortly before four o'clock, she was tired
after the late night at General Pershing's
house. It was a sunny afternoon in the last
week of June, and she walked out into the
sunlight with a contented sigh.

"You sound tired, Miss Ossupov." She
wheeled in surprise at the sound of her
name, and saw Clayton Andrews standing
next to one of General Pershing's staff
cars.

"Hello . . . you startled me."

"I wish I could say the same. I've been
waiting here for two hours." He laughed
and she looked at him with wide eyes.

"Have you been waiting for me all this
time?"

"I have. I never got a chance to say
good-bye to you last night."

"I think you were busy when I left."

"I know. You must have gone back on the first truck." She nodded in answer, surprised that he had taken the trouble to find out. She hadn't thought she would see him again, but she was happy seeing him now. He was as handsome as she had thought him the night before, as tall and lean and graceful as he had seemed when they danced the waltz. "I was hoping you'd have lunch with me. But it's a little late now."

"I have to go back to my grandmother anyway." She smiled up at him, dallying like a schoolgirl just released from class. "She's dreadfully cross at me after last night."

He looked puzzled by the remark. "Did you go home very late? I didn't notice the time when you left." Then she was as young as he'd thought. She had the looks of a very young girl, the innocence . . . and yet, there was such wisdom in her eyes.

But Zoya laughed at the memory of sending Feodor away from the opera house. "My grandmother sent someone to chaperone me, and I sent him home. I suspect he was quite glad of it, though, and so was I." She blushed slightly then and he laughed.

"In that case, mademoiselle, may I offer you my escort now? I could drive you home." She hesitated, but he was so obviously a gentleman, there could be no harm in it, and who would know? She could leave him a block or two before the Palais Royal.

"Thank you very much." He opened the door for her and she slid into the car. She told him where she lived, and he seemed perfectly at ease as he drove her home. She had him stop a block away and he looked around.

"Is this where you live?"

"Not quite." She smiled and blushed again. "I thought I'd spare my grandmother the agony of getting angry at me again so soon after last night."

He laughed at her, his handsome face looking very young despite the silver hair. "Aren't you a naughty child! And if I ask you to join me for dinner tonight, mademoiselle? What then?"

She knit her brows as she thought of it, and then looked at him. "I'm not sure. Grandmama knows there is no performance tonight." It would be the first time she had ever been dishonest with her and she herself wasn't sure why she felt she had to be now. But she knew how Evgenia felt about soldiers.

"Won't she let you go out with anyone?" He seemed both amused and surprised.

"I'm not sure," Zoya confessed. "I never have."

"Oh, dear . . . am I allowed to ask how old you are in that case?" Perhaps she was even younger than he thought, but he hoped not.

"Eighteen." She said it almost defiantly, and once again he laughed.

"Does that seem very old to you?"

"Old enough." He didn't dare ask for what. "Not long ago, she was encouraging me toward a friend of the family." And when she said it, she blushed. It seemed stupid to tell him about Vladimir, but he didn't seem to mind.

"And how old is he? Twenty-one?"

"Oh, no!" Zoya was laughing now. "Much, much older than that. He's at least sixty years old!" This time, Clayton Andrews looked both amused and startled.

"Is he? And what does your grandmother think of that?"

"It's too complicated to explain, besides, I don't like him anyway . . . he's an old man."

He looked at her seriously for a moment

as they sat in the car. "So am I. I'm forty-five years old." He wanted to be honest with her, right from the start.

"And you're not married?" She seemed surprised, and then realized that perhaps he was.

"I'm divorced." He had been married to one of the Vanderbilts, but it had ended ten years before. In New York, he was thought to be an enviable catch, but in the ten years since his divorce, and among the flocks of women he'd taken out, none of them had snagged his heart. "Are you shocked?"

"No." She thought about it and then looked him in the eye, convinced more than ever that he was a decent man. "Why did you get divorced?"

"We fell out of love, I suppose . . . we were very different from the start. She's remarried and we're good friends, though I don't see her very often anymore. She lives in Washington now."

"Where's that?" It all sounded far away and mysterious to her.

"It's near New York but not near enough. Rather like Paris and Bordeaux. Or Paris and London perhaps." She nodded. That much made sense. But he glanced at his watch. He had spent hours waiting for her and now he had to get back. "What about dinner tonight?"

"I don't think I can." She looked sadly up at him, and he smiled.

"Tomorrow then?"

"I have to dance tomorrow night."

"What about afterward?" He was persistent in any case, but having found her again, he was not going to let her slip past him.

"I'll try."

"Good enough. Till tomorrow night then." He sprang from the car and helped her out. She thanked him politely for the ride, and he waved at her as he drove back toward the rue Constantine with a song in his heart as he thought of Zoya.

Chapter 15

For the first time in her life, she lied to her grandmother. It was the following day when she left for the Opéra again. She felt guilty about it, but by the time she left the house, she had forgiven herself for what seemed like a harmless lie. She was sparing her worry about something that wasn't worth worrying about, she told herself. After all, what harm was there in one dinner with a nice man? She had told her that Diaghilev was giving a supper for them, and it was an obligation for the entire ballet troupe.

"Don't wait up for me!" she had called over her shoulder so Evgenia could not see her eyes.

"Are you sure you must go?"

"Absolutely, Grandmama!" And then she had hurried out the door for rehearsal.

And after the performance, Clayton was waiting for her, with another of General Pershing's cars. "All set?" He smiled at her and slid behind the wheel as he watched her eyes. They spoke volumes, far more than her words, and they were the color of emeralds full of fire. "How was it tonight?"

"It was all right. But Nijinsky didn't dance tonight. He's remarkable, don't you think?" And then with a giggle, she remembered that he didn't like the ballet. "Never mind, I forgot you don't like ballet."

"Perhaps I can be taught." They drove straight to Maxim's, and Zoya's eyes grew wide as they walked in the door. The rich velvet decor and crowds of elegant people and men in dress uniforms dining there made her catch her breath as she looked up at him. It all seemed so grown-up, and a little startling, and she thought instantly of how to describe her surroundings in her next letter to Marie. But Clayton Andrews was going to be difficult to explain, even to her closest friend. She herself wasn't quite sure why she was dining with him, except that he'd been so kind to her, and he seemed so happy and at ease. She found herself wanting to talk to him, just this once . . . or perhaps one more time after that. There was no harm in it. He was respectable, and there was a certain excitement to it. She tried not to act like an excited child as they sat down at the table. "Hungry?" He eyed her happily as he ordered champagne for them, but she just wanted to look around.

"Have you ever been here before?"

She shook her head, thinking of the apartment where they lived, and the hotel where they had stayed before that. They hadn't been to any restaurants at all since they'd arrived. She and her grandmother cooked simple meals at home, and Feodor sat down to dinner with them every evening.

"No." She didn't explain. It would have been difficult to explain it all to him.

"It's pretty, isn't it? I used to come here before the war."

"Do you travel a great deal? Usually, I mean."

"Enough. Had you ever been to Paris before . . . I mean before you came here three months ago?" He had remembered that and she was touched.

"No. But my parents used to come here a lot. My mother was actually German, but she'd lived in St. Petersburg most of her life." He found himself suddenly wanting to ask her what the revolution had been like, but sensed wisely how painful it had been for her, and refrained. And then, just to make conversation with her, he casually asked a question which made her laugh.

"Zoya, did you ever see the Tsar?" And at the look of amusement on her face, he began to laugh too. "Is there something funny about that?"

"Perhaps." She felt so comfortable with him, she decided to open up a little bit. "We're cousins." But her face grew serious then, remembering her last morning at Tsarskoe Selo. Clayton patted her hand, and poured her champagne.

"Never mind . . . we can talk about something else." But as she looked at him, her eyes reached into his.

"It's all right . . . I just . . ." She fought back tears as she looked at him. "I just miss them so much. Sometimes I wonder if we'll ever see them again. They're still under house arrest now, at Tsarskoe Selo."

"Do you hear from them?" He looked surprised.

"I get letters sometimes from the Grand Duchess Marie . . . she's my very dearest friend. She was very ill when we left." And then she smiled sadly at the memory. "I caught the measles from her. They all had them before we left." It all seemed remarkable to him as he listened to her. The Tsar of Russia was a figure in history, not merely a cousin of this pretty young girl.

"And you grew up with all of them?"

She nodded and he smiled. He had been right after all. There was a great deal more to her than one would have thought at first sight. She wasn't just a pretty little ballerina. She was a girl from a fine family, a girl with a remarkable past. She began to tell him about it then, about the house where she'd grown up, about Nicolai . . . and the night he'd been shot, and staying at Tsarskoe Selo before they left Russia.

"I have such wonderful photographs of them. I'll show you sometime. We went to Livadia together in August every year. They're going this year again, or so Marie said when she last wrote. We always celebrated Alexis's birthday there, or on the yacht."

Clayton Andrews watched her with fascinated eyes as they talked. She spoke of a magical world, at a rare time in history, and to her it was commonplace, cousins and friends, and children and tennis, and dogs. And now she was dancing with the

Ballet Russe. No wonder her grandmother sent a chaperone with her. She even explained Feodor to him. And by the end of the evening, he felt as though he knew them all, and his heart ached for the life she had lost in Russia.

"What will you do now?"

"I don't know." She was honest with him. "When there is no more jewelry left to sell, I suppose I'll just go on dancing and we'll live on that. Grandmama is too old to work, and Feodor doesn't speak enough French to get a job, and he's also quite old." And when they died? He didn't even dare think of it. She was so open and innocent and fresh, and yet she had seen so much.

"Your father sounds like a nice man, Zoya."

"He was."

"It's hard to imagine losing all that. Harder still to imagine never going back."

"Grandmama thinks things might change after the war. Uncle Nicky said as much before we left." Uncle Nicky . . . the Tsar Nicholas . . . it still amazed him as he listened to her talk. "At least, for now, I can dance. I used to want to run away to the Maryinsky School when I was a little girl"—she laughed at the memory now—"this isn't so bad. I'd rather dance than teach English, or sew, or make hats." He laughed at the look on her face as she listed the alternatives.

"I'd have to admit, I can't quite imagine you making hats."

"I'd rather starve. But we won't. The Ballet Russe has been very good to me." She told him about her first audition, and he silently marveled at her courage and ingenuity. Even having dinner with him was rather brave. And he had no intention of taking advantage of her. He liked her, even though she was barely more than a child. But he also saw her differently now than he had the other evening. She wasn't just a pretty face, or a member of the corps de ballet. She was a girl from a family even more illustrious than his own, and even though she had nothing left, she had breeding and dignity, and he had no desire to violate that. "I wish you could meet Grandmama," she said as though reading his thoughts.

"Perhaps I shall sometime."

"She'd be shocked that we haven't been properly introduced. I'm not sure I could explain that to her."

"Could we say I'm a friend of

Diaghilev's?" he asked hopefully, and she laughed.

"That would be even worse! She hates all of it! She'd far rather I marry Prince Markovsky with his taxi than work at the ballet." But as he watched her, he understood why. It was frightening to think of her out in the world, unprotected, unknown, an easy prey for anyone, even himself.

He paid for their midnight supper then and she looked sad as he took her home. "I'd like to see you again sometime, Zoya." It seemed such a trite thing to say to her, but he was suddenly uncomfortable about making their outings clandestine. She was so young, and he didn't want to hurt her in any way. "What if I come to tea sometime with your grandmother?"

Zoya looked terrified at the thought. "What will I say to her?"

"I'll think of something. What about Sunday afternoon?"

"We usually go for a walk in the Bois de Boulogne."

"Perhaps we could take a drive. Say four o'clock?"

Zoya nodded, wondering what she would say to her grandmother, but his suggestion was simpler than all her schemes.

"You might just tell her that I'm General Pershing's aide, and we met at the reception last night. It's generally easier to tell the truth than a lie." He sounded just like Konstantin again, as he had several times that night, and she smiled happily up at him.

"My father would have said something like that." And as they pulled up in front of her address, she glanced at him, looking handsome and dignified in his uniform. He was a wonderful-looking man. "I had a lovely time tonight."

"So did I, Zoya . . . so did I." He gently touched the long red hair, and wanted to pull her close to him, but he didn't dare.

He walked her to her door and saw her safely inside, as she waved for a last time, and darted up the stairs to the apartment.

Chapter 16

Clayton's introduction to her grandmother went far more easily than either of
them had dared to hope. Zoya explained
breezily that she had met him at General
Pershing's soirée for the Ballet Russe, and
she had invited him to tea. Evgenia was
hesitant at first, it was one thing to enter-
tain Prince Vladimir, whose circumstances were as restrained as theirs, but
not someone they scarcely knew. But
Zoya bought half a dozen little cakes for
them, a much sought after loaf of bread,
and her grandmother brewed a pot of
steaming tea. They had no other niceties
to offer him, no silver tray, no lace napkins
or cloth, no samovar, but Evgenia was far
more concerned about why he wanted to
visit them than she was about the elegance of what they could offer him. But as
Feodor opened the door to him promptly
at four o'clock, Clayton Andrews himself

dispelled almost all her fears. He brought them both flowers, and a lovely apple tart, and he was every inch a gentleman as he greeted them both, Zoya quite formally, and her grandmother with respectable warmth. He seemed almost not to notice Zoya at all that day as he chatted comfortably about his travels, his small knowledge of Russian history, and his own youth in New York. And like Zoya, Evgenia found herself frequently reminded of Konstantin, with his warmth, his wit, his charm. And when at last she sent Zoya out of the room to make another pot of tea, she sat quietly watching him, knowing full well why he had come to visit her. He was too old to dally with the child, and yet she could not bring herself to disapprove of him. He was a fine and worthy man.

"What do you want with her?" The old woman asked in a soft voice, unexpectedly, while Zoya was still out of the room, and he met the old woman's eyes with honesty and kindness.

"I'm not sure. I've never even talked to a girl her age before, but she's quite remarkable in many ways. Perhaps I can be a friend to her . . . to both of you? . . ."

"Don't play with her, Captain Andrews. She has her whole life ahead of her, and it could be changed unpleasantly by what you do now. She seems to be very fond of you. Perhaps that will be enough." But neither of them thought it was. The old woman knew even better than he that once he brought her close to him, Zoya's life would never be quite the same again. "She is still very, very young."

He nodded quietly, thinking of the wisdom of her words. More than once in the past week he had told himself that he was foolish to pursue a girl so young. And when he left Paris afterward, then what? It wouldn't be fair to take advantage of her and then move on.

"In another world, another life, this wouldn't even have been possible."

"I'm well aware of that, Countess. But on the other hand"—he made a quiet case for himself—"times have changed, haven't they?"

"Indeed they have." And with that, Zoya came back to them, and poured each of them a cup of tea. She showed him her photographs then, of the previous summer in Livadia, with Joy gamboling at her feet, the Tsarevich sitting next to her on the yacht, and others with Olga and Marie, Tatiana, Anastasia, Aunt Alix, and the Tsar himself. It was almost like a lesson

in modern history, and more than once
Zoya looked up at him with a happy smile,
remembering, explaining it all to him as
he listened to her, and he knew the answer then to Evgenia's questions. He felt
far more than friendship for this girl. Even
though she was barely more than a child,
there was something remarkable in her
soul, something that reached out and
touched him to the core, something he
had never felt before, for anyone. And yet,
how could he possibly offer her anything?
He was forty-five years old, divorced, and
he had come to France to fight a war.
There was nothing he could offer her just
then, if he ever could. She deserved a
younger man, someone to grow up with
and laugh with, and share all her memories with. And yet, he wanted to put his
arms around her and promise that nothing
would ever hurt her again.

He took them for a drive when she put
her photographs away, and when they
stopped to walk in the park, he watched
her playing with Sava on the grass, as the
puppy leapt and barked, while Zoya ran
laughing and almost collided with him.
Without thinking, he put his arms around
her and held her close to him, and she

looked up at him, laughing like the child he'd seen in the photographs. Evgenia watched them both, and feared what was to come.

When he brought them home again, Evgenia thanked him and looked at him quietly as Zoya went to give Sava to Feodor. "Think carefully, Captain. What for you may be only an interlude could change my granddaughter's life. Be wise, I beg of you . . . and above all . . . be kind."

"What did you say to him just then, Grandmama?" Zoya asked when he had left them.

"I thanked him for the apple tart, and invited him to visit us again," Evgenia said calmly as she put their cups away.

"That's all? He looked so serious, as though you'd said something important to him. And he didn't smile when he said good-bye."

"Perhaps he's thinking about all this, little one." And then, carefully, "He's really far too old for you."

"It doesn't matter to me. He's such a nice man."

"Yes, he is." Evgenia nodded quietly, hoping silently that he would be nice enough not to call again. Zoya was too much at risk with him, and if she fell in love with him, what then? It could prove to be disastrous.

Chapter 17

Evgenia's prayers that Clayton Andrews would not return were not destined to be answered. After trying to stay away from her for a week, he found himself constantly thinking of her, obsessed with her eyes . . . her hair . . . the way she laughed . . . the way he had watched her play with Sava . . . even the photographs she had shown him of the family of the Tsar seemed to haunt him. She had made them real to him, and now instead of a tragic figure of history the Tsar had become a man, with a wife, a family, and three dogs, and Clayton found himself mourning the enormity of his losses as he sat imprisoned in his home in Tsarskoe Selo.

And as he thought of her all week, Zoya also found herself constantly thinking of Clayton.

He reappeared at Zoya's home this

time, and not the ballet, and with her grandmother's permission, took her to see *The Merry Widow*. She returned to excitedly tell her grandmother all of it, barely stopping for breath, as Clayton laughed and poured champagne. He had brought them a bottle of Cristal which he poured into crystal glasses. Without wanting to offend them, he found himself constantly wanting to make things easier for them, and bring them the little niceties he knew they missed and no longer had, warm blankets which he insisted had been "given" to him, a set of glasses, a lace tablecloth, and even a pretty little bed for Sava.

Evgenia knew by then that Clayton was badly smitten, as was Zoya. They went for long walks in the park, had lunch at little cafés, as Clayton explained the passing uniforms to her, the Zouaves, the English and Americans in khaki, the "poilus" in their pale blue coats, and even the Chasseurs d'Afrique. They talked of everything from ballet to babies. Zoya still insisted that one day she wanted six children, the thought of which made him laugh.

"Why six?"

"I don't know." She shrugged with a happy smile. "I prefer even numbers."

She shared her last letter from Marie, it spoke of Tatiana falling ill again, though not seriously this time, and Nagorny being so faithful and kind to Alexis. He never left his side now. ". . . And Papa is so good to all of us. He keeps everyone feeling strong and happy and cheerful . . ." It was difficult to imagine and it tore at Clayton's heart as he listened. But they spoke of far more than the Tsar's family when they met, they spoke of all their passions and interests and dreams.

It was a magical and lovely summer for Zoya. Whenever Zoya wasn't dancing, Clayton seemed to be there, amusing her, taking her out, and bringing them both small gifts and thoughtful little treasures. And then in September, all the innocent pleasures ended all too quickly. General Pershing announced to his aides that he was moving General Headquarters to Chaumont, on the Marne, and in a matter of days Clayton was to leave Paris. At the same time, Diaghilev was making plans to take the Ballet Russe to Portugal and Spain, and Zoya was faced with a painful decision. She couldn't leave her grandmother alone, and she had to abandon the troupe, which almost killed her.

"You can dance with one of the other

ballets here. It's not the end of the world,"
Clayton encouraged, but it was to her. No
other company was the Ballet Russe, and
it broke her heart to leave them. The
worst news of all came two weeks after
Alexis's birthday. Zoya received a letter
from Marie, sent to her, as always, by Dr.
Botkin. On August 14, the entire Romanov family had been removed from house
arrest at the Alexander Palace in Tsarskoe
Selo to Tobolsk in Siberia. The letter had
been written the day before they left, and
Zoya had no idea how they were, only that
they had gone. The thought was almost
more than she could bear. She had imagined that at any moment they would go to
Livadia and be safe there. But now everything had changed, and a sense of terror
clutched her heart as she read the letter.
She showed it to Clayton before he left,
and he tried vainly to reassure her.

"You'll hear from her again soon. I'm
sure of it, Zoya. You mustn't be so frightened." But how could she not, he asked
himself. She had lost everything only
months before, she had seen all too clearly
the terrors of the revolution, and the truth
was that her friends and relatives were
still in danger. It frightened him too to
think of it now, but there was nothing any-

one could do to help them. The American government had recognized the Provisional Government long since, and everyone was afraid to offer the Tsar and his family asylum. There was no wresting him from the revolutionaries now. All one could do was pray and believe that one day they'd be free. It was the only hope he could offer to Zoya. And worst of all, he himself was leaving.

"It's not very far. I'll come up to Paris whenever I can. I promise." She looked up at him with tragic eyes . . . her friend . . . the Ballet Russe . . . and now he had to leave her. He had been courting her for almost three months, and she gave him constant delight and innocent amusement. Much to Evgenia's relief, she rightly suspected that he had not done anything she would consider foolish. He simply enjoyed her company, and saw her whenever he could, for walks, an evening at the theater, dinner at Maxim's, or at some little bistro. And she seemed to flourish with his affectionate interest and protection. It was almost like having a family again, and now she was losing him as well, and at the same time she had to find a job with a lesser troupe. Much as she hated the thought, Evgenia knew that they were becoming dependent on Zoya's income.

By September 10, she had found another job, but with a ballet company she abhorred, they had no precision, no style, and none of the brutal discipline of the Ballet Russe that Zoya was used to, and the pay was much less as well. But at least she, Feodor, and her grandmother were still eating. The war news was not good and the air raids continued, and finally, she had a letter from Marie. They were living in the Governor's house in Tobolsk, and Gibbes, their tutor, was continuing their lessons. ". . . Papa reads us history almost every day, and he built us a platform on the greenhouse so we can take a little sun, but it will be too cold for that soon. They say the winters here seem endless. . . ." Olga had had her twenty-second birthday, and Pierre Gilliard was there too. ". . . He and Papa saw wood, almost every day, but at least while they're busy, we can escape some of our lessons. Mama looks very tired, but Baby worries her so much. He was feeling so ill after the trip, but I'm happy to tell you that now he is much better. The four of us sleep in one room here, and the house is very small, but at the same time cozy. Perhaps a bit like your apartment with Aunt Evgenia. Give her my love, dearest, dearest one, and write to me when you can. Your dancing sounds fascinating, when I told Mama she was shocked, and then she laughed and said how very like you to go all the way to Paris to run off to the ballet! We all send you our love, and I most especially . . ." And this time, she signed her letter as she hadn't in a very long time, "OTMA." It was a code they had devised as children for letters sent from all of them, signifying Olga, Tatiana, Marie, Anastasia. And it made Zoya's heart long for them all.

With Clayton gone, she was even more lonely. There was nothing to do but work and come home to Grandmama after each performance. She realized then the extent to which Clayton had spoiled her. When he was around, there were always outings, presents, surprises, plans. And now, suddenly, there was nothing. She wrote to him even more often than she wrote to Marie in Tobolsk, but his answers were brief and hurried. He had a great deal of work to do in Chaumont for General Pershing.

October was even worse, Feodor caught the Spanish flu, and Zoya and her grandmother took turns nursing him for weeks, but finally, unable to eat or drink, or even see anymore, he succumbed, as both women sat crying silently at his bedside. He had been so loyal and kind to them, but like an animal taken too far from his home, he was unable to survive in a different world. He smiled gently at them before he died, and said softly, ". . . Now I can go back to Russia. . . ."

They buried him in a little cemetery outside Neuilly, Vladimir had driven them there, and Zoya cried all the way home, feeling as though she had lost her only remaining friend. Everything seemed suddenly so grim, even the weather. Without Feodor there was never enough firewood and both Evgenia and Zoya couldn't bring themselves to use his room.

It was as though the pain of their losses was never going to end. Clayton hadn't been to Paris in almost two months, and when Zoya came home from work late one night, she got a dreadful shock as she opened the door and saw a man standing in their living room in his shirt sleeves. And for a moment, Zoya's heart stopped because she thought he was a doctor.

"Is something wrong?"

He looked at her in equal amazement, as he stared at her with wide eyes, momentarily silenced by her unexpected beauty. "I'm sorry, mademoiselle . . . I . . . your grandmother . . ."

"Is she all right?"

"Yes, of course. I believe she is in her room."

"And who are you?" Zoya couldn't understand what he was doing there in his shirt sleeves, and she almost reeled from his next words.

"Didn't she tell you? . . . I live here. I moved in this morning." He was a pale, thin, youngish man in his early thirties, with thin hair and a crippled leg. He walked with a marked limp as he went back to Feodor's room and closed the door, as Zoya flew into hers in a fury.

"What have you done? I can't believe it!" Zoya stared at her angrily as she sat in the bedroom's only chair, and then Zoya noticed that Evgenia had moved a few more things into their room for their private comfort. "Who is that man?" She offered no preamble, she couldn't believe what her grandmother had done, as Evgenia looked up quietly from her knitting.

"I've taken in a boarder. We had no

choice. The jeweler offered me absolutely
nothing for my pearls, and there's very
little left to sell. Sooner or later we would
have had to do it." Her face was filled with
quiet resignation.

"Couldn't you have at least asked, or
even warned me? I'm not a child, and I
live here too. That man is a total stranger!
What if he kills us in our sleep, or steals the
last of your jewels? What if he gets drunk
. . . or brings in awful women?"

"Then we'll ask him to leave, but calm
yourself, Zoya, he seems perfectly nice,
and very shy. He was wounded at Verdun
last year, and he's a teacher."

"I don't care what he is. This apartment
is too small to take in a stranger, and we
get enough money from my dancing. Why
this?" She felt as though she'd lost her
home to him, and she just wanted to sit
down and cry at the indignity of it. For
her, it was the final blow. But to Evgenia,
it had seemed the only way out. And she
hadn't told Zoya because she had suspected how she'd react. And Zoya's out-
rage only confirmed it. "I can't believe
you would do this!"

"We had no choice, little one. Perhaps
later we can do something different. But
not for the moment."

"I can't even make a cup of tea now in my nightgown." Her eyes were filled with tears of rage and sorrow.

"Think of your cousins and what their life must be like in Tobolsk. Can't you be as brave as they are?" The words made Zoya feel instantly guilty, as she slowly deflated and sank into the chair her grandmother had vacated to go and stand by the window.

"I'm sorry, Grandmama . . . I just . . . I was so shocked . . ." She smiled then, looking almost mischievous but not quite. "I think I frightened him to death. He ran into his room and bolted the door after I shouted at him."

"He's a perfectly nice young man. You should apologize to him in the morning." But Zoya didn't answer her as she contemplated the extremes they had come to. Everything seemed so constantly dreary. Even Clayton seemed to have let her down. He had promised to come to Paris as soon as he could, but there seemed to be no hope of it for the moment.

She wrote to him the next day, but she was too embarrassed to mention their boarder. His name was Antoine Vallet, and he looked terrified when he saw her in the morning. He apologized profusely, knocked over a lamp, almost broke a vase, and stumbled as he made every effort to get out of her way in the kitchen. She noticed he had sad eyes, and she almost felt sorry for him, but not quite. he had invaded the last bastion they had, and she wasn't anxious to share it.

"Good morning, mademoiselle. Would you like some coffee?" he offered, and the aroma was pleasant in the kitchen, but she shook her head and growled at him.

"I drink tea, thank you very much."

"I'm sorry." He stared at her in terrified admiration, and left the kitchen as quickly as he could. And shortly after that, he left to teach his classes. But when she returned from rehearsal that afternoon, he was back again, sitting in the living room, at the desk, correcting papers. Zoya slammed into her room and paced nervously as she glanced at her grandmother.

"I suppose this means I can't ever use the desk again." She wanted to write a letter to Clayton.

"I'm sure he won't be there all night, Zoya." But even her grandmother seemed to be confined to their room. There was nowhere she could go to be alone, no way she could collect her own thoughts, or get away from any of them. It seemed unbearable suddenly, and she was sorry she hadn't gone to Portugal with the Ballet Russe, but as she wheeled around and saw tears in Evgenia's eyes, she felt a knife of guilt pierce her heart as she dropped to her knees and put her arms around her.

"I'm so sorry . . . I don't know what's wrong with me. I'm just tired and nervous."

But Evgenia knew all too well what was troubling her. It was Clayton. And just as had been foreseen, he had left to fight the war, and Zoya had to go back to a life without him. It was just as well that nothing more had happened, and that he was an honorable man, or it would have been even more difficult for her. She didn't ask Zoya if she'd heard from him. She almost hoped that he wouldn't write her.

Zoya went to the kitchen and cooked dinner for her grandmother and herself, and as the young teacher kept looking up, in the direction of the good smells, Zoya relented, and invited him to join them for dinner.

"What do you teach?" she asked politely without really caring. She saw that his hands shook very badly, he seemed constantly frightened and very nervous, and it seemed to her that his war wounds had left him far more than a limp. He seemed perpetually shaken.

"I teach history, mademoiselle. And I understand that you dance in the ballet."

"Yes," she conceded, but barely. She wasn't proud of the troupe she danced with now, not like when she was with the Ballet Russe, however briefly.

"I'm very fond of the ballet. Perhaps I could come to see you sometime."

She knew he expected her to say that she would like that, but she couldn't bring herself to do it. She wouldn't.

"I like the room very much," he announced to no one in particular, and Evgenia smiled graciously.

"We are very happy to have you."

"The dinner is very good."

"Thank you," Zoya said, without raising her eyes. He spoke in a series of irrelevant non sequiturs and Zoya disliked him more than ever. He limped around the kitchen trying to help her clean up, and afterward he lit a fire in the living room, annoying her again by wasting the little firewood they had, but as long as he had lit it, she stayed to warm her hands. It was freezing in the small apartment.

"I visited Saint Petersburg once." He spoke softly from the desk, hardly daring to look up at her, she was so beautiful and so full of fire. "It was very lovely." She nodded and turned her back to him, staring into the fire with tears in her eyes as he watched her slim back with silent longing. He had been married before the war, but his wife had left with his best friend, and their only child had died of pneumonia. He had his own sorrows too, but Zoya did not ask to hear them. To her he was a man who had lived through great danger and barely survived it. And rather than strengthening him, it had broken his spirit. She turned slowly to look at him then, wondering again why her grandmother had taken him in. She couldn't bear to think that their situation was that desperate, but she knew it was, or Evgenia wouldn't have done it.

"It's so cold in here." It was just a statement, but he rose quickly and put another log on the fire.

"I'll get some more firewood tomorrow, mademoiselle. That will help. Would you like another glass of tea? I could make it for you."

"No, thank you." She wondered how

old he was, he looked to be somewhere in his mid-thirties. In fact, he was thirty-one, but his life had been far from easy.

And then, shyly, "Is it your room I have taken?" It would have explained her obvious displeasure at his presence, but she only shook her head, and then sighed.

"One of our servants came with us from Russia. He died in October." He nodded quietly as he listened.

"I'm sorry. It's been a hard time for all of us. How long have you been in Paris?"

"Since last April. We left right after the revolution."

He nodded again. "I've met several Russians here lately. They're brave, good people." He wanted to say "and you too," but he didn't dare. Her eyes were so big and bright and fierce, and as she tossed her head, her hair flew around her like sacred fire. "Is there anything you'd like me to do, since I'm here? I'd be happy to help in any way I can. I can do errands for your grandmother, if you like. I enjoy cooking as well. Perhaps we can take turns cooking dinner."

She nodded in silent resignation. Perhaps he wasn't so bad. But he was there. And she didn't want him. He gathered his papers up then and went back to his room, closing the door behind him, as Zoya stood alone, staring into the fire, and thinking of Clayton.

Chapter 18

As the winter wore on, people seemed hungrier and poorer as the weather got worse, and with more and more émigrés turning up in Paris, the jewelers were paying ever smaller prices. Evgenia sold her last pair of earrings on December first, and she was horrified at how little they gave her. All they had were Zoya's wages now, and they were barely enough to feed them and pay for the apartment. Prince Markovsky had his own troubles too. His car kept breaking down, and he seemed thinner and hungrier each time they saw him. He still spoke valiantly of better times, and reported on all the new arrivals.

In the face of such poverty, and the bitter cold and lack of food, Evgenia was even more grateful for the presence of their boarder. His own meager salary barely allowed him to pay the cost of the room, but nonetheless he always managed to bring home something extra, half a loaf of bread, or a log for the fire, or even a few books for Evgenia to read. He even managed to find some for her in Russian, some poor émigrés must have even sold their books for a meager loaf of stale bread. But he always seemed to think of Zoya and Evgenia, and more often than not, he brought some small offering home to Zoya. Once he had even heard her say how much she loved chocolates, and somewhere, by some miracle, he had managed to buy a tiny bar of chocolate.

As the weeks wore on, she was kinder to him, grateful for his gifts, but more grateful for the kindness he showed the Countess. She was beginning to suffer from rheumatism in her knees and just getting up and down the stairs was suddenly agony for her. Zoya came home one afternoon from a rehearsal at the ballet, and found him carrying her grandmother up the stairs, which, with his wounded leg, was a painful task for him, but he never complained. He was always anxious to do more, and Evgenia had grown very fond of him. She was also not unaware of the enormous crush he had on Zoya. She men-

tioned it more than once to the girl, but
Zoya insisted that she hadn't noticed.

"I don't know how you can't see how
much he likes you, little one." But Zoya
was more concerned by the terrible cough
that racked her grandmother as she said
it. She had had a cold for weeks, and Zoya
feared the Spanish flu that had killed Feodor, or the dreaded tuberculosis that
seemed to be devouring Paris. Even her
own health was not as strong as it had once
been. With so little food, and such hard
work, she had gotten desperately thin,
and her girlish face seemed suddenly
much older.

"How's your grandmother tonight?" he
asked quietly one night as they were cooking together in the kitchen. It was a
nightly ritual between them now. They no
longer took turns on her nights off, but
instead they cooked together, and when
she had to work, he cooked for Evgenia
himself, more often than not supplying
the food himself, buying it on the way
home with the pennies he earned from his
teaching. Like everyone else in Paris
these days, his small funds seemed to be
dwindling. "She was so pale this afternoon." Antoine looked at Zoya with worried eyes, as she sliced two ancient-look-

ing carrots to divide among the three of them. She was sick to death of stew, but it seemed to be what they ate almost every night, it was the easiest way to conceal the inferior quality of the meat and the near absence of vegetables.

"I'm worried about her cough, Antoine." Zoya glanced at him from across the kitchen. "I think it's worse, don't you?" He nodded unhappily and added two small cubes of meat to the pot where Zoya was boiling the carrots in a watery broth. There wasn't even any bread tonight. It was fortunate that none of them were very hungry. "I think tomorrow I'll take her to the doctor." But even that was more than they could afford, and there was nothing left to sell, only her father's last cigarette case, and three silver souvenir boxes that had been her brother's, but Evgenia had promised her that she wouldn't try to sell them.

"I know a doctor on the rue Godot-de-Mauroy, if you want his name. He's cheap." He did abortions for the prostitutes, but he was better than most in that milieu. Antoine had gone to him for his leg several times, and had found him skilled and sympathetic. It pained him terribly now in the bitter cold and damp of winter.

Zoya had noticed that his limp seemed to be getting worse, but he looked happier than he had when he'd first come to live with them. It seemed to do him good to have decent people to come home to, and her grandmother to worry about. It never occurred to her that his feelings for her kept him alive, and that at night he lay in bed and dreamed of her in the next room, sleeping huddled with Evgenia.

"How was school today?" she asked as she waited for the pot to boil. Her eyes were kinder now when she looked at him. He even dared to tease her now once in a while, and the exchanges vaguely reminded her of her brother. He was not a handsome man, but he was bright, and well read, and he had a good sense of humor. It helped during the air raids and the cold nights. It was what got them by in place of food and warmth and life's little pleasures.

"It was all right. I'm looking forward to the holidays, though. It will give me a chance to catch up on my reading. Do you want to go to the theater sometime? I know someone who might let us in at the Opéra Comique, if you want to try it." The mention of it reminded her of Clayton and the gentler days of summer. She hadn't heard from him in a while, and assumed he was busy with General Pershing, who was designing the entire French campaign, and Zoya knew it was very secret. God only knew when she would see him again, if ever. But she was used to that now. She had seen the last of so many people she had once loved. It was difficult to imagine loving anyone without losing them. She forced her mind away from Clayton and back to Antoine and his offer to go to the theater.

"I'd love to go to a museum sometime." He was actually good company, and very cultured, though not in the polished sense of her lost Russian friends. But in a quiet way all his own, which was equally pleasant.

"As soon as school is out, we'll go. How's the stew?" he inquired, and she laughed.

"As rotten as ever."

"I wish we could get some decent spices."

"I wish we could get some real vegetables and fruit. If I see another old carrot, I think I may scream. When I think of the food we used to eat in St. Petersburg, I could cry. I never even thought of it then. You know, I even had a dream about food last night."

He had dreamed of his wife the night before, but he didn't tell her that, he only nodded and helped her to set the table.

"How's your leg, by the way?" She knew he didn't like to talk about it, but more than once she had wrapped a hot water bottle for him and he'd taken it to bed and said it had helped him.

"The cold doesn't help much. Just be glad you're young. Your grandmother and I aren't as lucky." He smiled at her and watched her ladle out the thin stew into three chipped ugly bowls. It would have made her cry if she had let herself think of the beautiful china they'd dined on every night at the Fontanka Palace. There was so much they had taken for granted that they would never see again. It was horrifying to think of it now, as Antoine went to knock on her bedroom door to bring Evgenia to dinner. But he looked worried when he returned alone and eyed Zoya over the small kitchen table. "She says she's not hungry. Do you think I should get the doctor for her tonight?" Zoya hesitated for a long moment, weighing the decision. A night call to the house would be even more expensive than a visit to his office.

"Let's see how she is after dinner. She

may just be tired. I'll bring her some tea in a little while. Is she in bed?"

He shook his head with a look of concern. "She's dozing in the chair, with her knitting." She had been working on the same tiny square of wool for months, promising that one day it would become a sweater for Zoya.

The two of them sat down to dinner then, and by silent agreement did not touch the third bowl, no matter how hungry they were. There was still a chance that Evgenia might decide she wanted her dinner.

"How was rehearsal?" He was always interested in what she did, and although he wasn't handsome, there was a boyish look about his eyes. He had thinning blond hair, which he parted carefully in the middle, and nice hands, which she had noticed long since. They no longer shook, and though he was constantly in pain from his leg, he no longer seemed as nervous.

"It was all right. I wish the Ballet Russe would come back. I miss dancing with them. These people don't know what they're doing." But at least it was money for food. A job was too precious to lose in the winter of 1917 in Paris.

"I ran into some people in a café today

who were talking about the coup d'état in
Russia last month. It was an endless discussion about Trotsky and Lenin and the Bolsheviks with two pacifists who got so mad,
they threatened to punch the other two."
He grinned impishly. "It was pacifism at
its best. I actually enjoyed the discussion."
There was a great deal of hostile feeling
against the Bolsheviks at the time, and Antoine shared the pacifist view like so many
others.

"I wonder what effect that will have on
the Romanovs," Zoya voiced quietly. "I
haven't had a letter from Siberia in a long
time." It worried her, but perhaps Dr.
Botkin hadn't been able to get her letters
to Mashka. One had to consider that, and
be patient in waiting for an answer. Everything seemed to require patience
these days. Everyone was waiting for better times. She only hoped that they all
lived to see them. There was even talk of
the possibility of Paris being attacked,
which seemed hard to believe with English and American troops swarming all
over France. But after what she'd seen in
Russia only nine months before, she knew
that anything was possible.

She stood up then, and took the remaining bowl of stew to her grandmother's

room, but she came back with it a few minutes later, and spoke softly to Antoine in the kitchen. "She's asleep. Maybe we should just let her sleep. I put a blanket over her to keep her warm." It was one of the blankets Clayton had given them the previous summer. "Don't forget to give me that doctor's name tomorrow before you go to school."

He nodded and then looked at her questioningly. "Do you want me to go with you?" But she only shook her head, she still had a strong streak of independence. She hadn't come this far, almost on her own, in order to depend on anyone now, even someone as unassuming as their boarder.

She finished the dishes and sat down in the living room, as close to the fire as she could, and warmed her hands as he quietly watched her. The fire shot gold lights into her hair, and her green eyes seemed to dance. And unable to resist the lure of her, he found himself standing nearby, partially to keep warm, and partially just to be near her.

"You've got such pretty hair. . . ." He said it without thinking, and then blushed as she looked up at him in surprise.

"So do you," she teased, thinking of the

insulting exchanges with Nicolai they had so loved. "I'm sorry . . . I didn't mean to be rude . . . I was thinking of my brother." She stared into the fire pensively, as Antoine watched her.

"What was he like?" His voice was gentle, and he thought his heart would break in half, he was so hungry to reach out and touch her.

"He was wonderful . . . thoughtful and funny and daring and brave, and very, very handsome. He had dark hair like my father, and green eyes." And then suddenly she laughed, remembering. "He had a great fondness for dancers." Most of the imperial family had and Nicholas among them. "But he'd be so angry at me now." She looked up at Antoine with a sad smile. "He'd be furious at my dancing now . . ." Her thoughts drifted off again as Antoine watched her.

"I'm sure he'd understand. We all have to do what we must to survive. There aren't many choices. You must have been very close."

"We were." And then, out of nowhere, "My mother went mad when they killed him." Her eyes filled with tears as she thought of him bleeding to death in the front hall, and her grandmother tying her petticoats over his wounds to no avail to try and save him. It was almost more than she could bear thinking about it, as Sava came quietly to her chair and licked her hand, and forced her mind back to the present.

They sat quietly for a long time. He had pulled up the room's only other chair, and they sat by the fire, lost in their own thoughts, until Antoine dared to be a little braver. "What do you want to do with your life? Have you ever thought about it?"

She looked surprised at the question. "Dance, I suppose."

"And after that?" He was curious about her, and it was a rare opportunity to find her alone without Evgenia.

"I used to want to marry and have children."

"And now? Don't you think about that anymore?"

"Not very often. Most dancers never get married. They dance until they drop, or teach, whichever comes first." Most of the great dancers she knew had never married, and she wasn't sure she cared. There was no one she knew that she could imagine marrying. Clayton was only a friend, Prince Markovsky was too old, and the men in her troupe were beyond hope, and she certainly couldn't imagine herself married to Antoine. And there was no one else. Besides, she had to take care of Evgenia.

"You'd make a wonderful wife." He said it so seriously that she laughed.

"My brother would have said you were crazy. I'm a terrible cook, I hate to sew. I can't do watercolors or knit. I'm not sure I can run a house, not that that matters now . . ." She smiled at the thought as he watched her.

"There's more to marriage than cooking and sewing."

"Well, I certainly don't know if I'm good at *that*!" She blushed and laughed and he blushed too. He was easily shocked and she had shocked him.

"Zoya!"

"Sorry." But she looked more amused than contrite as she stroked little Sava. Even Sava had grown thin from the meager remains from their table.

"Perhaps one day someone will make you want to give up dancing." He had misunderstood, it wasn't that her passion for the ballet was so great. It was only that she had no choice. She had to work to support herself and Evgenia, and it was all she knew how to do. At least it was something.

"I'd better get Grandmama into bed, or her knees will be killing her tomorrow." She stood up and stretched and Sava followed her into the bedroom. Evgenia had already woken up and was changing into her nightgown. "Do you want your stew, Grandmama?" It was still waiting for her in the kitchen, but she shook her head with a tired smile.

"No, darling. I'm too tired to eat. Why don't you save it for tomorrow?" With all of Paris starving, it would have been a crime to waste it. "What have you been doing in the other room?"

"Talking to Antoine."

"He's a good man." She said it looking pointedly at Zoya, who seemed not to notice.

"He gave me the name of a doctor on the rue Godot-de-Mauroy. I want to take you there tomorrow before rehearsal."

"I don't need a doctor." She was braiding her hair and a moment later she climbed painfully into bed. The room was cold, and the pain in her knees was brutal.

"I don't like the sound of your cough."

"At my age, even having a cough is a blessing. At least I'm still alive."

"Don't talk like that." She had only been saying things like that since Feodor died. His death had depressed her deeply, that and the fact that she knew they were almost at the end of their money.

Zoya put her own nightgown on, and turned off the light, and she held her grandmother close to keep her warm as they huddled through the December night together.

Chapter 19

The doctor Zoya took her grandmother to said that it was only a cough and not tuberculosis. It was worth paying the price for the good news, but Zoya had had to give him almost the last of their money. Even his small fee was too much for their empty pockets. But she said nothing to Evgenia as Prince Markovsky drove them back to their apartment. He cast several meaningful glances at Zoya, which she ignored, and she left him chatting with her grandmother at the apartment when she went to rehearsal. And when she came back that night, she thought her grandmother looked a little better. The doctor had given her some cough medicine, and it seemed to be helping.

Antoine was already in the kitchen, cooking dinner. He had brought home a chicken that night, which was a rare treat. It meant they would not only have dinner

out of it, but soup for the next day. And as
she set the table for the three of them, she
found herself wondering if Mashka now
had the same considerations. Perhaps a
chicken looked luxurious to her now too.
If they had been together they could have
laughed about it. But now there was no
one to laugh with.

"Hello, Antoine." She smiled at him and
thanked him for the name of the doctor.

"You shouldn't have wasted the
money," Evgenia reproached from a chair
near the fire. Vladimir had brought them
firewood. It was suddenly a day of unexpected riches.

"Grandmama, don't be foolish."

The three of them enjoyed the chicken,
which he served swimming in its own
broth, and afterward Zoya sipped tea with
them by the fire. And when her grandmother went to bed, Antoine stayed to
talk to her again. They seemed to be doing
a lot of that, but at least he was someone to
talk to. He was talking about his Christmases as a child, and his eyes shone as they
talked. He loved being near her.

"Our Christmas is later than yours. It's
on January sixth."

"The Feast of Kings."

"There are beautiful processions all

over Russia. Or there were. I suppose we'll
be going to the Russian church here." In a
way, she was looking forward to it, and in
another way she knew it would be depressing. All those lost souls, standing together in the candlelight, remembering a
lost world. She wasn't sure she could bear
it, but she knew that her grandmother
would insist that they go. There would
certainly be no gifts this year. There
wasn't a spare penny with which to buy
them.

But when Christmas actually came, Antoine surprised her. He had bought her a
warm scarf and a pair of warm gloves, and
a tiny, tiny bottle of the perfume she had
casually mentioned to him once. It was
the perfume that touched her heart and
brought tears to her eyes. It was "Lilas,"
which Mashka had so loved and had given
her months before. She took the top off
the flacon, and the sweet smell brought
back the touch and feel and smell of all
that she loved, and her beloved Mashka.
There were tears rolling slowly down her
cheeks as she looked at him, and without
thinking, with childlike grace, she threw
her arms around his neck and kissed him.
It was a sisterly kiss, but his whole body
trembled to feel her near him. And

Evgenia looked on with tears in her own eyes. He was not what she would have wished for Zoya once upon a time, but he was a decent, hardworking man, and she knew he would take good care of Zoya. He had spoken to her only the day before, and she had given him her blessing. She was feeling weaker day by day, and she was terrified that if she died there would be no one to take care of Zoya. She had to marry him now, for her grandmother's peace of mind. But Zoya had no idea what they had planned, as she thanked him warmly for the perfume. He had given her grand-mother an embroidered shawl and a book of Russian poems. And Zoya was embar-rassed that all they had bought him was a clean notebook and a book about Russia.

She had found it at a bookseller's on the Quai d'Orsay, at an ugly little stand, but it was in French, and she thought he might like it. But not nearly as much as she liked the perfume.

Her grandmother quietly slipped away with her gifts, and softly closed her bed-room door, silently wishing him success, and praying that Zoya would be wise and accept him.

"You must have spent every penny you had," she chided him as she prodded the fire with a long metal poker and Sava wagged her tail as she watched her. "That was foolish, but kind, Antoine. Thank you so much. I will use the perfume for special occasions." She had already decided to wear it two weeks later on Russian Christmas. She didn't want to waste it before that.

He sat down in the chair across from hers and took a breath, trying to muster up his courage. He was thirteen years older than she, but he had never been so frightened in his life. Even Verdun had been less terrifying than facing Zoya.

"I wanted to talk to you about a special occasion, Zoya. Now that you mention it." He could feel his palms grow damp as she watched him strangely.

"What does that mean?"

"It means . . ." He could feel his heart pound. "It means . . . I love you." She could hardly hear the words, but she stared at him in amazement.

"You *what*?"

"I love you. I've loved you since the day I arrived here. Somehow, I thought that you suspected."

"Why would I ever suspect that?" She looked both startled and angry. He had spoiled everything. How could they be friends now if he was going to be so stupid. "You don't even know me!"

"We've lived together for two months. That's long enough. It wouldn't even have to be any different than this. We could stay here, except that you would sleep in my room."

"How lovely." She stood up and paced the room. "A mere change of rooms, and we go on just as we are. How can you even *suggest* it? We're all starving, none of us has a sou, and you want to get married. Why? *Why?* I don't love you, I don't even know you, nor you me. . . . Antoine, we are strangers!"

"We're not strangers, we're friends. And some of the best marriages start that way."

"I don't believe that. I want to be in love with the man I marry, madly, passionately, totally. I want it to be wonderful and romantic."

He looked so sad as she shouted at him, but she was shouting more at the fates that had put them there, than at the man who had bought her her favorite perfume.

"Your grandmother thinks we could be very happy." But it was the worst thing he could have said, as she strode around the room again in barely controllable fury.

"Marry my grandmother then! I don't want to get married! Not now! Everything around us is sick and cold and dying. Everyone is starving and poor and miserable. What a way to start a life!"

"What you're really saying is that you don't love me." He sat down quietly, willing to accept even that. And suddenly his own quiet actions subdued her. She sat down facing him and took his hands in her own warm ones.

"No, I don't. But I like you. I thought you were my friend. I really never thought there was anything else behind it. Not seriously anyway. You never said . . ." Her eyes filled with tears.

"I was afraid to. Will you think about it, Zoya?"

But she shook her head sadly. "Antoine, I couldn't do it. It wouldn't be fair to either of us. We both deserve more than this." She glanced around them, and then back into his eyes. "And if we loved each other, even this wouldn't matter. But it does. I just don't love you."

"You could try." He looked so young, despite his injuries and his losses.

"No, I couldn't. I'm so sorry . . ." She left the room then, and quietly closed the door to her own room, leaving the perfume and the scarf and gloves on the table. He looked around him then, and turned off the lights and went back to his bedroom. Perhaps she would change her mind. Perhaps her grandmother could convince her. She had thought it such a sensible plan. But he knew it was born not of love, but desperation.

"Zoya?" Her grandmother was watching her from their bed, as she undressed, facing the garden. Evgenia couldn't see her face, but she suspected instinctively that she was crying. And as Zoya turned around in her nightgown, her green eyes were blazing. "Why did you do it, Grandmama? Why did you encourage him to do that? It was cruel to both of us." She thought of the pain in Antoine's eyes and she felt terrible. But not terrible enough to marry him out of pity. She had to think of herself too. And she knew she didn't love him.

"It's not cruel. It's sensible. You must marry someone, and he'll take care of you. He's a teacher, he's respectable, and he loves you."

"I don't love him."

"You're a child. You don't know what you want." She suspected also that Zoya was still dreaming of Clayton, a man more than twice her age, from whom she hadn't heard since November.

"I want to love the man I marry, Grandmama. Is that so much to ask?" Tears rolled down her cheeks, as she sank into the room's only chair and clutched Sava.

"Normally, no, it's not. But in these circumstances, it is. You have to be sensible. I'm old, I'm sick. What are you going to do when I die? Stay here alone and go on dancing? You'll become old and hard and bitter. Stop this nonsense now. Accept him, and make yourself learn to love him."

"Grandmama! How can you say that!"

"Because I've lived a long time. Long enough to know when to fight and when to give in, and when to make compromises with my heart. Don't you think I would like to see you married to a handsome prince, back in St. Petersburg, in a house like Fontanka? But there are no princes anymore, they're all driving taxis. Fontanka is gone, Russia is gone. This is all there is, Zoya, perhaps forever. You must make adjustments. I won't leave you alone. I want to know you'll be well cared for."

"Don't you care that I don't love him?" Evgenia shook her head sadly. "It doesn't matter, Zoya. Not now. Marry him. I don't think you'll regret it." But he's ugly, she wanted to scream . . . he's crippled and lame . . . but in her heart of hearts, she knew that none of those things would matter to her if she loved him. Life with Antoine would always be sad, it would always be less than she had wanted. And the thought of having children with him made her want to cry even harder. She didn't want his babies, didn't want him. She just couldn't.

"I can't." She felt as though she were choking.

"You can. And you must. For me, Zoya . . . do it for me, before I die. Let me know that you are safe with a man who will protect you."

"Protect me from what? From starvation? We're all starving here together. He can't change any of that. And I don't care. I would rather starve here alone than be married to a man I don't love."

"Don't make up your mind, little one. Think about it. Give it a little time. Please . . . for me . . ." Her eyes begged and Zoya's streamed with tears as though her heart were broken. But the next morning, there were no tears. She spoke with Antoine first thing the next morning.

"I want you to know, without any doubt in your mind, that I won't marry you, Antoine. I want to forget this ever happened."

"I can't do that. I can't live here with you like this, knowing how badly I want you."

"You did before." She was suddenly terrified they'd lose their boarder.

"That was different. You didn't know then, now you do."

"I'll pretend you never said it." She looked frightened and childlike again, and he smiled sadly at her.

"That doesn't work. Are you sure, Zoya? Can't you think about it for a while?"

"No. And I don't want to give you false hopes. I can't marry you. I won't. Ever."

"Is there someone else?" He knew she had an American friend, but he had never thought it was serious between them.

"No, not like that. There is only a dream. But if I give up my dreams now, I'll have nothing. They're all I have left."

"Perhaps things will be better after the war. Perhaps we could even get our own apartment." His dreams were so small, and hers were still so much larger, as she shook her head, and this time he believed her.

"Antoine, I can't. You must believe me."

"Then I'll have to move out."

"Don't . . . please . . . I swear I'll stay out of your way. Grandmama will be heartbroken if you go."

"And you, Zoya?" She stood watching him in silence. "Will you miss me?"

"I thought you were my friend, Antoine," she said sadly.

"I am. I will always be. But I cannot stay here." He had some pride left, but as he packed his things that afternoon, Zoya panicked. She begged him to stay, promising him almost anything but marriage. Without his contribution to the rent, and the food, they'd be even more desperate. "I can't help that" was his only answer. Evgenia even talked to him, assuring him that she would talk some sense into Zoya, but he knew better. He had seen Zoya's eyes and heard her words. And she was right. She couldn't marry a man she didn't love. She wasn't that kind of woman. "It's better that I go. I will look for another room tomorrow."

"She's a foolish girl." And Evgenia told her as much again that night. She was wasting her only chance at marriage.

"I don't care if I never get married," Zoya answered with fresh tears. And in the morning when she got up, Antoine had left her a letter and taken his things and gone. There were three crisp bills on the table and the letter wished her a happy life, and anchoring it down was the bottle of perfume he had given her for Christmas.

Evgenia sobbed when she saw it, and Zoya quietly put the three crisp bills in her pocket.

Chapter 20

The next two weeks were bleak in the apartment near the Palais Royal. The ballet was closed for three weeks, and despite their putting out the word through Vladimir, no new boarder appeared. Filled with grief over what Zoya had done, Evgenia seemed to have aged almost overnight, and although her cough was better, she seemed to be failing. She reproached Zoya almost daily about Antoine, and their financial situation became so desperate that shortly after the New Year, Evgenia struggled down the stairs and had Vladimir drive her to the jeweler in the rue Cambon.

It was hardly worth the trip, but she felt she had no choice. She carefully unwrapped the package she had brought and revealed Konstantin's gold cigarette case, and three of Nicolai's silver souvenir boxes. They were covered with enamel replicas of his military insignia, engraved with amusing slogans and his friends' names, one of them bore a tiny frog, and another a string of white enamel elephants. They represented all the things he held dear or that meant something to him, and had each been gifts from friends. She had promised herself and Zoya long before that she would never sell them.

The jeweler recognized them instantly as pieces by Fabergé, but he had already seen more than a dozen more like them.

"I can't offer you very much," he apologized, and the sum he wrote down brought tears to her eyes, but they had to eat. And she had so hoped they could keep them. "I'm sorry, madame." She inclined her head in silent dignity, bereft of words, and accepted the small sum he offered. It would keep them for less than a week, if they didn't buy anything too extravagant.

Prince Vladimir noticed that the old woman looked pale when she emerged, but as always, he asked no vulgar questions. He simply drove her home, after stopping to buy a loaf of bread and a very thin chicken. Zoya was waiting for them when they returned, looking subdued, but extremely pretty.

"Where were you?" she asked as she settled her grandmother into a chair, and Vladimir went downstairs to bring up some more firewood.

"Vladimir took me out for a drive." But Zoya suspected more than that.

"Is that all?"

She started to say yes but tears filled her eyes, and she began to cry, feeling tired and old, and as though life had finally betrayed her. She couldn't even allow herself to die. She still had Zoya to think of.

"Grandmama, what have you done?" Zoya was suddenly frightened, but the old woman blew her nose on the lace handkerchief she still carried.

"Nothing, my darling. Vladimir had very kindly offered to drive us to St. Alexander Nevsky tonight." It was Christmas Eve for them, and Zoya knew every Russian in Paris would be there, but she wasn't sure it was wise for her grandmother to go to church for the midnight mass. Perhaps they were better off at home. She wasn't in the mood for it anyway, but her grandmother looked stern as she straightened her back, and smiled at Vladimir as he returned with the firewood.

"Are you sure you feel up to it, Grandmama?"

"Of course." And what did it matter now? "I have never missed midnight mass on Christmas in my life." But they both knew it would be a hard year for them. With so many lost, the service could only remind them of the previous year, when they had celebrated Christmas with their loved ones all around them. And Zoya had been thinking all day of Mashka and the others, spending Christmas in Tobolsk.

"I'll be back at eleven o'clock," Vladimir promised as he left. Zoya was planning to wear her best dress, and her grandmother had washed and ironed her only decent lace collar to wear on the black dress Zoya had bought her.

It was a lonely Christmas Eve in the quiet apartment, with Antoine's empty room staring at them like a reproach. Evgenia had offered it to Zoya a few days before, but she found that she couldn't bring herself to move in. After Feodor, and Antoine, she didn't want the room, and preferred to continue sleeping with her grandmother until they found a new boarder.

She cooked the chicken for her that night, roasting it carefully in their tiny oven. It was a luxury not to make soup of it, but it was the only gift they shared, and both of them concentrated desperately on trying not to remember years past in their days of grandeur. They had always stayed at home on Christmas Eve, then gone to church with the family at midnight, and then to Tsarskoe Selo the next day to celebrate there with Nicholas and the others. Now instead, they commented on the chicken, talked about the war, mentioned Vladimir, anything to avoid their own thoughts. When Zoya heard a soft knock on the door, she rose to see who it was, brushing away Sava, who was hoping for some of their chicken.

"Yes?" Zoya wondered if it would be the answer to their prayers, and a new boarder was about to appear, directed to them by Vladimir or one of his friends. But it was an odd time to come, and Zoya looked stunned when she heard a familiar voice . . . it couldn't be . . . but it was. She pulled the door open, and stood staring at him, as she took him in in his full uniform, his epaulets and his cap shining with his brass insignia, his face serious, but his blue eyes filled with warmth.

"Merry Christmas, Zoya." It was Clayton, standing there. She hadn't seen him in four months, but he knew the importance of the date for them, and he had moved heaven and earth to leave Chaumont in time to share it with them. He had a four-day leave, and he wanted to spend it with Zoya. "May I come in?" She was standing there, stunned, unable to say a word, as she stared at him in mute amazement.

"I . . . my God . . . is it really you?"

"I believe so." He smiled, and gently bent to kiss her cheek. Their flirtation of the summer before had gone no further than that, but he longed to take her in his arms now. He had almost forgotten how beautiful she was, as she stood lithe and graceful before him.

She followed him inside, gazing happily at his broad shoulders and straight back, and her heart flooded with joy, as he greeted her grandmother, and she noticed that he was carrying a bag, from which he took out incredible treasures for them. There were freshly baked cookies from headquarters, a bar of chocolate, three big fat sausages, a head of fresh lettuce, some apples, and a bottle of wine from General Pershing's own cellars. They were riches beyond words, beyond anything they'd seen in months. But Zoya was looking at him, with round, happy eyes, and an expression of adoration.

"Merry Christmas, Countess," he said quietly. "I've missed you both." But not half as much as Zoya had missed him. She realized it even more now as he stood before them.

"Thank you, Captain. How is the war?" Evgenia asked quietly, watching her granddaughter, and what she saw warmed her heart, and brightened her all at once. This was the man Zoya had wanted, whether she knew it or not. It was plainly apparent.

He was handsome and proud, as he stood virile and tall in their tiny living room, dwarfing everything around him. "Unfortunately, it's not over yet, but we're working on it. We should have things in control in a few months, though."

The remains of their dinner sat on the table, looking paltry now, as Zoya glanced hungrily at the chocolates. She laughed as she offered her grandmother one, and then gobbled two, like a hungry child, and Clayton laughed. He was so happy to see her.

"I'll have to remember how much you like those," he teased, gently taking her hand in his own.

"Mmm? . . . wonderful! . . . thank you

very much . . ." Evgenia laughed, watching her, she seemed so young and happy again as the Captain looked over her head and met the old woman's eyes. She had aged in the past four months, and they both looked thinner to him now, thinner and tired and more worn, but Zoya looked so beautiful to him. He longed to take her in his arms and just hold her.

"Please sit down, Captain," Evgenia invited, looking elegant and proud, despite her age and her pains and her constant sacrifices for Zoya.

"Thank you. Are you ladies going to church tonight?" He knew it was a ritual for them. Zoya had told him all about the candle-lit processions on Christmas Eve, and he wanted to go with them. He had done everything possible to be there on that night with them, as Zoya nodded emphatically, questioning her grandmother with her eyes.

"Would you care to join us, sir?" Evgenia invited.

"I'd like that very much." He opened the wine for them, and Zoya got out the glasses he'd given them the summer before, and silently watched him pour. It was like a dream seeing him standing there in his uniform, like a vision, and she

remembered suddenly what she had said
to Antoine. She couldn't marry a man she
didn't love. And she knew she loved this
man. She could have married him, no matter how old he was, or where he had been,
or what happened to them . . . but they
were foolish thoughts. She hadn't even
heard from him in two months. She had
no idea how he felt about her, if he cared
about her at all. All she knew was that he
was generous and kind, and he had
walked back into her life on Christmas
Eve. She knew nothing more than that.
But as Evgenia watched them both, she
knew more than that, even more than
Clayton knew himself as he stood there.

Vladimir arrived shortly after eleven
o'clock. He had promised to drive them to
church, and he looked startled when he
saw Clayton. The Countess introduced
the two men, and Vladimir searched his
face, wondering who he was and what he
was doing there, but the light in Zoya's
eyes told its own tale. It was as though she
had survived the past months only to live
for this moment.

Clayton followed her to the kitchen
briefly as Evgenia poured the Prince some
wine, and gently he touched her arm and
pulled her slowly toward him. His lips

softly touched her silky hair, and his eyes closed as he held her.

"I've missed you terribly, little one. . . . I wanted to write to you, but I couldn't. Everything is top secret now. It's a miracle they even let me come here." He was intimately involved with all of Pershing's plans for the American Expeditionary Force. He pulled away from her then, and looked down at her with his warm blue eyes. "Did you miss me at all?"

She couldn't speak, and tears filled her eyes in answer. Everything had been so difficult for them, their poverty, the lack of food, the cold winter, the war. It was all a nightmare, and now suddenly here he was, with his cakes, and his wine, and his strong arms held fast around her. "I missed you very much." She spoke in a hoarse whisper and averted her eyes. She was afraid to even look at him, he would see too much there. But she felt so safe with him, as though she had waited for him for a lifetime. She heard a polite cough then in the kitchen doorway and they both turned. It was Prince Vladimir, watching them with quiet envy.

"We should go to church soon, Zoya Konstantinovna." He spoke to her in Russian, and for a moment his eyes met

Clayton's. "Will you be coming with us, sir? The ladies are going to a midnight service."

"I'd like to very much." He looked down at Zoya. "Do you think your grandmother would mind?"

"Of course not." Zoya spoke for them both, especially for herself, as she found herself wondering where he was staying. She thought of offering him Antoine's room, but suspected correctly that her grandmother wouldn't think it proper. Not that it mattered anymore. What did propriety mean when you had no food, no money, no warmth, and the world you had lived in was gone? Who was there to even care about what was proper? It all seemed so foolish to her now, as Clayton gently took her hand and led her out of the kitchen. Sava followed them closely as they went, looking up at them, hoping for a scrap of food. She quietly reached down and fed her one of the treasured cookies.

Her grandmother went to get her hat and coat, and she took her own worn coat from a peg near the door, as the two men waited, chatting politely about the war, the weather, and the prospects for peace in the coming months. Vladimir seemed to be looking him over critically, but in spite of himself he couldn't dislike him. The American was too old for Zoya, of course, and Evgenia would be foolish if she let anything happen between them. When the war was over, he would go back to New York and forget the pretty girl he had toyed with in Paris. But Vladimir couldn't blame him for wanting her, of course. He still longed for her himself, although he had been courting one of his daughter's friends for over a month now. She was a hearty Russian girl from a good family, who had come to Paris the previous spring, like the rest of them, and was eking out a small living by taking in sewing. She and his daughter were meeting him at the church.

Clayton helped the old Countess downstairs, as Zoya watched, and Vladimir led the way to his waiting taxi. And they drove slowly through the quiet streets, as Clayton looked around him and especially at Zoya. She looked as though she needed some fun, and some good meals. She needed a new coat, too, her old one looked almost threadbare as the wind whistled past them in front of St. Alexander Nevsky.

It was a beautiful old church, and there were crowds of people already inside

when they got there. They could hear the
organ music from the front steps as they
went in, and all around them was the soft
hubbub of voices. The incense smelled
sweet, and it was warm inside, and suddenly tears filled Zoya's eyes as she looked
around her at the familiar faces, and heard
the sounds of everyone speaking Russian.
It was almost like going home again, their
faces alive and warm as they each held a
tall candle. Vladimir handed one to
Evgenia and another to Clayton, and Zoya
took one from a little boy. He looked up at
her with a shy smile and wished her a
Merry Christmas. And all she could think
of now were other Christmases, other
days . . . Mashka and Olga and Tatiana
and Anastasia . . . Aunt Alix and Uncle
Nicky . . . and tiny Alexis . . . they
went to Easter services together each
year, much like these . . . and as she
fought back the memories, Clayton gently
took her hand and held it, as though he
could look into her mind and feel what she
saw there. He put an arm around her as
they sang the first hymn, and he was over-
whelmed by the beauty of their powerful
voices lifted in Russian. Tears rolled slowly
down the men's cheeks, and many of the
women cried, as they remembered the

life they had shared in a place they would always remember. It was almost more than Zoya could bear, the smells and the sounds and the feelings were so agonizingly familiar. With her eyes closed, she could imagine Nicolai standing there, and her mother and father. It was almost like being a child again as she stood close to Clayton, and tried to pretend they were still in Russia.

And after the service, countless people they knew approached them. The men bowed and kissed Evgenia's hand, the ones who had been servants knelt briefly at her feet, and people cried openly and embraced, as Clayton watched them. Zoya introduced him to as many as she knew. There were so many faces that looked familiar to her, although she didn't know them all. But they seemed to know her and Evgenia. Grand Duke Cyril was there, and some other cousins of the Romanovs too, all wearing old clothes, worn-out shoes, and faces that scarcely concealed their troubles. It was painful just being there, and yet it was heart-warming too, like a brief trip into a past they all wanted to retrieve and would spend a lifetime reliving.

Evgenia looked exhausted as she stood

beside Vladimir. She stood tall and proud
and greeted everyone who came to see
her, and there was a terrible moment
when Grand Duke Cyril came to her and
sobbed like a child. Neither of them could
speak, and Evgenia touched him in silent
blessing. Zoya gently took her arm then,
and with a look at Vladimir, led her quietly outside to his taxi. It had been a hard
night for all of them, but it meant a great
deal to them just to be there. And she
settled back against the seat with a tired
sigh and eyes that spoke volumes.

"It was a beautiful service." Clayton
spoke quietly, moved beyond words. One
could sense their love, their pride, their
faith, and their sorrow. And it was almost
as though, in silent unison, they had been
praying for their Tsar, and his wife and
children. Clayton wondered if Zoya had
heard from Marie again, but he didn't
want to ask her in front of Evgenia. It was
all much too painful. "Thank you for letting me come."

Clayton escorted them back upstairs
when they got back to the apartment, and
Vladimir poured the last of the wine. Seeing Evgenia's sad eyes and worn face,
Clayton was sorry he hadn't brought them
brandy. He stoked the fire again, and ab-

sentmindedly patted Sava, as Zoya quietly munched another cookie.

"You should go to bed, Grandmama."

"I will in a minute." She wanted to sit there for a moment and remember, and then she looked tenderly at all of them. "Merry Christmas, children. God's blessings on us all." She took a sip of wine then and slowly stood up. "I will leave you now. I'm very tired." Clayton saw that she could hardly walk as Zoya helped her to their room, and returned a few minutes later. Vladimir left shortly after that, with a last look of envy at Clayton. But he smiled at him. He was a lucky man to have Zoya look at him the way she did. She was so young and so alive and so pretty.

"Merry Christmas, Zoya." His eyes were sad, still touched by the midnight service.

"Merry Christmas to you, Prince Vladimir." He kissed her cheeks and hurried back down the stairs to his taxi. His daughter and her friend were waiting for him at home. And as the door closed, Zoya turned quietly to Clayton. It was all so bittersweet, the old and the new, the happy and the sad. The memories and the real . . . Konstantin, Nicolai . . . Vladimir . . . Feodor . . . Antoine . . . and now

Clayton. . . . As she looked at him, she remembered them all, and her hair shone like gold in the light from the fire. He walked quietly to her and took her hands in his own, and without a word he took her in his arms and kissed her.

"Merry Christmas." He said it in Russian, as he had heard again and again at St. Alexander Nevsky.

She repeated it back to him, and for a long quiet moment he stood and held her. He gently stroked her hair, and listened to the fire crackle as Sava slept beside them.

"I love you . . . Zoya . . ." He hadn't wanted to say it to her yet, he had wanted to be sure, and yet he was. He had known it since September when he left her.

"I love you too." She whispered the words that were so easy to say to him. "Oh, Clayton . . . I love you . . ." But then what, there was the war, and eventually he would have to leave Paris and go back to New York. She wouldn't let herself think of it now. She just couldn't.

He pulled her gently onto the couch, and they sat holding hands, like two happy children. "I've worried about you so much. I wish I could have stayed here for all these months." And now they only had four days, a tiny island of moments in a troubled sea that might drown them at any moment.

"I knew you'd come back." She smiled. "At least I hoped so." And she was more than ever grateful that she hadn't allowed her grandmother to force her to marry Antoine. If she had listened, she might have been married to him, or even Vladimir, by the time Clayton returned to see her.

"I tried to fight this, you know." He sighed and stretched his long legs out on the ugly purple rug. It had grown even more threadbare in the past months. Everything in the apartment looked dingy and old and shabby, except the beautiful girl at his side, with the green eyes and red hair, the sharply etched face like a perfect cameo, the face he had dreamed of for months, in spite of all the reasons he gave himself to forget her. "I'm too old for you, Zoya. You need someone young, to discover life with you, and make you happy." But who was there? The son of some Russian prince, a boy who had as little as she did? The truth was that she needed someone to take care of her, and he wanted to be the one to do it.

"You make me happy, Clayton. Happier than I've ever been . . ." she smiled honestly, "in a long, long time anyway." She turned to him with serious eyes, "I don't want anyone younger. It doesn't matter how old or young you are. It only matters what we feel. I wouldn't care if you were rich or poor, or a hundred years old, or ten. If you love someone, none of those things should matter."

"But sometimes they do, little one." He was older and wiser than she was. "This is a strange time, you have lost everything, and you're trapped here, in a war, in a strange land. We're both strangers here . . . but later, when things quiet down, you might look at me and ask yourself what am I doing with him?" He smiled at her, afraid it might happen just as he predicted. "War does funny things." He had seen it happen to others.

"For me, this war is forever. I can't go home again. Oh . . . some of them think we will go back one day . . . but now there has been another revolution. Everything will always be different. And we're here now. This is our life now, this is real . . ." She looked at him seriously, suddenly no longer a child no matter how young she was in actual years. "All I know is how much I love you."

"You make me feel so young, little

Zoya." He held her close again, as she felt his warmth and his strength, all the good things she had felt long before when her father held her. "You make me so very happy." This time she kissed him and suddenly he pulled her more tightly into his arms and had to fight his own passion for her. He had dreamed of her for far too long, ached for her, needed her, and now he could barely fight his own feelings and desire. He stood up and went to look out the window into the garden, and then slowly he turned to her, wondering which path their lives would take now. He had come back to Paris to see her, and yet suddenly he was afraid of what might happen. Only Zoya seemed sure and calm, certain that she was doing the right thing being there with him. Her eyes were peaceful as she looked at him. "I don't want to do anything you'll regret, little one." And then, "Are you dancing this week?" She shook her head and he smiled. "Good, then we'll have time before I have to go back to Chaumont. I suppose I should leave you now." It was three o'clock in the morning, but she wasn't tired as she walked him to the door and Sava followed.

"Where are you staying?"

"The General very kindly let me use Ogden Mills's house this time." It was where they had met, the beautiful *hôtel particulier* on the rue de Varennes, on the Left Bank, where they had walked in the garden the night of the reception for the Ballet Russe. "May I come to get you tomorrow morning?"

She nodded happily. "I'd like that."

"I'll come at ten." He kissed her again in the doorway, uncertain of where they were going, but aware to his very core that there was no turning back now.

"Good night, Captain," she teased, her eyes dancing as they never had before. "Good night, my love," she called softly as he hurried down the stairs on feet that wanted to dance. He couldn't help smiling to himself, thinking that never in his life had he been this happy.

Chapter 21

"You must have gone to bed very late last night." Her grandmother spoke quietly over breakfast. Zoya had sliced some of the apples for her, and made a precious piece of toast from the bread that Clayton had brought them.

"Not very." She averted her eyes as she sipped at her tea, and then stealthily gobbled a chocolate.

"You're still a child, little one." Her grandmother said it almost sadly as she watched her. She knew what was coming and she was afraid for her. He was a good man, but it was not a desirable situation. Vladimir had said as much to her the night before and she couldn't disagree with him, but she also knew that she couldn't stop Zoya. Perhaps the Captain would be wiser than the child, but having come all the way from Chaumont to see her, she thought it unlikely. And it was obvious to everyone who saw him, that he was desperately in love with Zoya.

"I'm eighteen, Grandmama."

"And what does that mean?" The old woman smiled sadly.

"It means that I'm not as silly as you think."

"You're silly enough to fall in love with a man old enough to be your father. A man who is in a foreign land, with an army at war, a man who will go home someday and leave you here. You must think of that before you do anything foolish."

"I'm not going to do anything foolish."

"See that you don't." But she was already in love with him, and that was enough to cause her pain when he left. And he would leave, when the war was over, if not sooner. "He won't marry you. You must know that."

"I don't want to marry him anyway." But that was a lie, and they both knew it.

When Clayton arrived at the apartment shortly after breakfast, he saw the guarded look in the old woman's eyes. He brought her flowers this time, three fresh eggs, and another loaf of bread.

"I shall grow fat while you visit us, Captain." She smiled graciously at him. He

was a charming man. But she was still very
much afraid for Zoya.

"There's no danger of that, madame.
Would you like to take a walk in the Tuileries with us?"

"I would." She smiled, almost feeling
young again herself. He seemed to bring
sunlight and happiness with him everywhere, with his thoughtful gifts and gentle ways, so much like her own son, with
his warm eyes and quick laughter. "But
I'm afraid that my knees won't agree. I
seem to have a touch of rheumatism this
winter." The "touch" she referred to
would have crippled a lesser woman. Only
Zoya suspected how much pain she was in.

"Will you allow me to take Zoya for a
walk then?" He was proper and well bred,
and she liked him immensely.

"You're very kind to ask me, young
man. I don't think there would be any
stopping Zoya." They both laughed while
Zoya went to get her things with a happy
blush that outshone her worn clothes, and
tired dresses. For the first time in months,
she longed for something pretty to wear
again. She had had so many lovely dresses
in St. Petersburg, all of them burned and
gone now, but not yet forgotten.

Zoya kissed her grandmother good-bye,

and the old woman watched them go, feeling happy for them, as Clayton took Zoya's hand. One couldn't feel anything less for them. They seemed to light up the room with their excitement. Zoya was chatting happily as they left, and she could hear them as they hurried down the stairs. He had one of the staff cars outside, that had been commandeered for the army.

"Well, where would you like to go?" He smiled at her from behind the wheel. "I'm entirely at your service." And she was free too. There were no rehearsals or performances to worry about. She could spend every minute with Clayton.

"Let's go to the Faubourg St. Honoré. I want to look in all the shops. I never have time to do things like that, and besides there isn't much point anyway." She told him, as they drove, how much she and Mashka had loved clothes, and how beautiful Aunt Alix's dresses had been. "My mother was always beautifully dressed too. But she was never a very happy person." It was an odd thing to admit to him, but it seemed so natural to tell him everything, she wanted to share her every thought, every wish, every dream, every memory, so he would know her better. "Mama was very nervous. Grandmama says Papa spoiled her." Zoya suddenly giggled, feeling young again.

"You should be spoiled too. Maybe you will one day, just like your mother."

She laughed openly at him as they parked the car and got out to walk. "I don't think it would make me nervous."

He laughed back at her, and tucked her hand into his arm as they strolled along, and the hours seemed to fly past them like moments.

They had lunch at the Café de Flore, and he thought she seemed happier than she had been the previous summer. She was still in shock then, but now at least some of the pain had dimmed. It had been nine months since she'd come to Paris. It was still hard to believe that only a year before she had been in St. Petersburg and life was still normal. "Have you heard from Marie lately?"

"Yes, finally. She seems to like it in Tobolsk, but she's such a good sport, she would. She said the house she lives in is tiny, she and her sisters all share one room, and Uncle Nicky reads history to them all the time. She says that even in Siberia, they're still having lessons. They think they might be able to come out of Russia soon. Uncle Nicky says the revolutionaries won't harm them, they just want to keep them there for the time being. But it seems so cruel of them, and so stupid." And Zoya was still furious at the English for not granting them asylum the previous March. If they had, they could all have been together by then, in London or Paris. "I'm sure Grandmama would have gone to London, if they were there."

"Then I wouldn't have met you, would I? And that would have been terrible. Maybe it's just as well you had to come to Paris, while you wait for them to leave Russia." He didn't want to alarm her, but he had never felt as confident as some that the Tsar and his family would ultimately be safe in Russia. But it was only a feeling he had, and he didn't want to say anything to worry her as they finished lunch and walked down the Boulevard St. Germain in the winter sunshine. Lunch at the Café de Flore had been pleasant, and she felt as though she had nothing but free time on her hands, with no performances and no rehearsals.

They wandered aimlessly for a while, and eventually wound up at the rue de Varennes, as they both realized they were near the house where he was staying.

"Do you want to come to the house for a while?"

She still had happy memories of it from the night they'd met, and she nodded happily as they walked along. He told her about New York, his boyhood, and his years at Princeton. He said he lived in a house, on Fifth Avenue, and she thought it sounded very pretty.

"Why did you never have children when you were married? Didn't you want them?" She had the innocence of youth, the fearlessness about treading on delicate ground that one suppressed when one was older. It never occurred to her that perhaps he couldn't have them.

"I would have liked to have children, but my wife didn't want them. She was a very beautiful, selfish girl and she was far more interested in her horses. She has a beautiful farm in Virginia now, and she has a hunt there. Did you ride much when you were in Russia?"

"Yes," she smiled, "in the summer at Livadia, and sometimes at Tsarskoe Selo. My brother taught me to ride when I was four. He was dreadfully mean about it, and whenever I fell off he said I was stupid." But Clayton could tell just from the

way she spoke how much she had loved
him.

They had reached the Mills house by
then, and Clayton used his key to let them
in. There was no one else staying there at
the time. All of the General's staff were in
Chaumont. "Would you like a cup of tea?"
he asked, as their footsteps echoed in the
marble halls.

"I'd like that." It was cold outside, and
she had forgotten her gloves at the apartment. And suddenly, for no reason at all,
she remembered the sable hat she had left
in Russia. They had worn heavy shawls
over their heads while they were escap-
ing. Her grandmother had wisely thought
that elaborate fur hats would catch too
much attention.

She followed him into the kitchen, and a
moment later the kettle was steaming. He
poured out two cups of tea and they sat
and talked, as the sun set quietly over the
garden. She felt as though she could have
sat and talked to him for hours, but suddenly their voices grew quiet, and she
sensed Clayton watching her strangely.

"I should take you home. Your grandmother will be worried." It was after four
o'clock and they'd been gone all day, but
Zoya had wisely warned her grandmother

that she might not be home for dinner. With only four days of his leave to share, they wanted to spend every moment possible together.

"I told her we might not come back till later." And then she had a thought. "Do you want me to make dinner here?" It seemed a cozy idea, not having to go out, they could sit and talk for several more hours as they had done all day. "Is there any food here?"

"I don't know," he smiled. She looked so young and beautiful as she sat there. "I should take you somewhere. Maybe Maxim's. Wouldn't you like that?"

"It doesn't matter," she said honestly. She just wanted to be with him.

"Oh, Zoya . . ." He came around the kitchen table to hold her close to him. He wanted to get her out of the house before something happened that she'd regret. The pull of her was so great, it was almost painful. "I don't think we should stay here," he said quietly, far wiser than she was.

"Would the General be angry that I'm here?" Her innocence touched his heart, as he looked down at her and laughed softly.

"No, my love, the General would not be

angry. But I'm not sure I can control myself for much longer. You're far too beautiful for me to be trusted with you alone.
You don't know how lucky you are that I
haven't just leapt across the table and
grabbed you." She laughed at the picture
he painted and leaned her head happily
against him.

"Is that what you've been planning to
do, Captain?"

"No. But I'd like to." They were both
perfectly relaxed as he stroked her long
red hair. "I'd like to do a lot of things with
you . . . go to the south of France after
the war . . . and Italy . . . have you
ever been there?" She shook her head and
closed her eyes. It was all so dreamlike just
being with him.

"I think we should go," he repeated
softly, and the room seemed very still. "I'll
go change. I won't be a minute." But he
seemed to take forever, as she strolled quietly through the elegant rooms on the
main floor, and then suddenly, feeling
mischievous, she decided to wander up
the marble staircase and see if she could
find him.

There were several more sitting rooms
on the second floor, a handsome library
filled with books in both French and En-

glish, several closed doors, and then in the distance she heard him. He was singing to himself as he changed, and she smiled, unable to keep away from him, even for a few minutes.

"Hello? . . ." she called out, but he didn't hear her, there was water running in the bathroom, and when he went back to the bedroom she was standing there, like a fawn standing very still in the forest. He was wearing his trousers and his chest was bare. He had decided to shave again quickly before taking her out to dinner. He had a towel in his hands and his face was still damp, as he looked at her in sudden amazement.

"What are you doing up here?" He seemed almost afraid, of himself, but not of lovely Zoya.

"I was lonely downstairs without you." She walked slowly toward him, feeling a magnetic force she had never felt before. It was as though without any will of her own, she was irreversibly pulled to him. He dropped the towel at his feet and pulled her close to him, kissing her face and her eyes and her lips, tasting the sweetness of her skin until it made him dizzy.

"Go downstairs, Zoya." His voice was

hoarse and he wanted to pull her away but he couldn't make himself do it. "Please. . . ." She looked up at him so sadly, almost hurt, but not afraid.

"I don't want to . . ."

"Zoya, please . . ." But he only kissed her again and again, as he felt her heart next to his chest beating wildly.

"Clayton, I love you. . . ."

"I love you too." And finally, painfully, he peeled himself from her. "You shouldn't have come up here, silly girl." He tried to make light of it as he pulled away, and turned to get a shirt out of the closet, but when he turned, she was still standing there, and the shirt dropped from his hands as he came toward her. "I can't stand this for much longer, little one." She was driving him mad with her youth and her sensual beauty. "Zoya, I would never forgive myself if . . ."

"If what?" The girl was gone, and she stood before him, fully a woman. "If you loved me? What difference does it make, Clayton? There is no future anymore . . . there is only now. There is no tomorrow." It was the hardest lesson she had learned in the past year. And she knew how much she loved him. "I love you." She was so small and proud and strong, it tore at his heart seeing the look in her eyes that told him she did not fear him, she only loved him.

"You don't know what you're doing." He had his arms around her again and was cradling her like a child. "I don't want to hurt you."

"You couldn't . . . I love you too much . . . you will never hurt me."

And then he could no longer find the words to convince her to go away. He wanted her too much, had ached for her for too long. His mouth overcame hers, and without thinking he let his hands peel away her clothes and he gently carried her to the bed and held her and stroked her and kissed her as she kissed him and wept softly. His own clothes seemed to come away from him, and they slipped into the enormous bed with the canopy hanging over them like a blessing. It was dark in the room as they made love, but in the light from the bathroom beyond he could see her face as he made love to her, kissing her and holding her and loving her as he had never loved any woman before her.

It seemed hours before they lay silent side by side, and she sighed happily as she nestled close to him like a tiny animal seeking its mother. His eyes were serious then and he was thinking of what they had done, praying that she wouldn't get pregnant. He rolled over on his side and rested on one elbow as he looked at her.

"I don't know if I should be furious with myself, or just let myself be as happy as I feel right now. Zoya . . . darling, are you sorry?" He was terrified of that, but she smiled a womanly smile, and reached her arms out to him, as he felt desire for her flood him again. They lay in bed and talked and made love until almost midnight, when he glanced at the clock on the bed table with sudden horror.

"Oh my God, Zoya! Your grandmother will kill me!" She laughed at him as he leapt out of bed and pulled her out with him. "Get dressed . . . and I didn't even feed you!"

"I didn't notice." She was giggling like a schoolgirl and suddenly he turned and put his arms around her again.

"I love you, you crazy girl. Do you know that? Old as I am, I happen to adore you."

"Good. Because I love you too, and you're not old, you're mine!" She pulled his silver hair gently and brought his face close to hers. "Remember that, no matter what happens to either of us, remember

how much I love you!" It was a lesson she
had learned early in life, that one never
knew what grief could come on the morrow. The thought of it touched him deeply
and he held her tightly.

"Nothing is going to happen, little one,
you're safe now."

He ran a bath for her in the enormous
tub, and the sheer luxury of it was too
much for her. For a minute, she could tell
herself that she was back in the Fontanka
Palace, but as she dressed in her ugly gray
wool dress again and slipped on her worn
black shoes, she knew she wasn't. She
wore black wool stockings to keep her legs
warm, and when she saw herself in the
mirror, she looked like an orphan.

"My God, I look awful, Clayton. How
can you love me like this?"

"You're beautiful, silly one. Every inch
of you, every bright red hair . . . everything about you," he whispered into her
hair, and it was like breathing summer
flowers. "I adore you."

They could hardly force themselves to
leave, but he knew he had to take her
home to the apartment at the Palais Royal.
There was no way at all she could stay out
with him all night, and as he followed her
up the stairs to the fourth floor, he kissed

her one last time in the dingy, dark halls, and she opened the door with her key, as they saw Evgenia asleep in a chair, waiting for them. Their eyes met for a last time, as Zoya bent to kiss her cheek gently.

"Grandmama? . . . I'm sorry I'm late, you shouldn't have waited up. . . ."

The old woman stirred and smiled up at them both, even in her half sleep she could see how happy they both were. It was like a breath of spring in the ugly room, and she found that she couldn't be angry.

"I wanted to be sure you were all right. Did you have a nice time?" She looked at them both, searching Clayton's eyes, but all she saw there was kindness and his love for Zoya.

"We had a lovely time," Zoya answered without guilt. She belonged to him now, and nothing could change that. "Did you have dinner?"

"I had some of yesterday's chicken, and one of the eggs the Captain brought. Thank you," she turned to him as she struggled to stand up, "it was lovely, Captain." He was embarrassed not to have brought her more, but he had been in a hurry that morning. And he realized again suddenly that he had never fed Zoya that night, and wondered if she was as hungry as he was. They had been distracted for long, happy hours but now he was starving. And as though she read his mind, she glanced at him with an ill-concealed smile and handed him the chocolates. He swallowed one guiltily and put one in her mouth as she smiled and then went to help her grandmother into their bedroom.

She came back for a moment afterward and they kissed again. He hated to leave her and go home, but he knew he had to.

"I love you," she whispered happily before he left.

"Only half as much as I love you," he whispered back.

"How can you say that?"

"Because I'm older and wiser," he teased, and then quietly closed the door behind him, as Zoya stood there, young again and happy and free, as she quietly turned off the lights in the apartment.

Chapter 22

Clayton returned the next morning looking impeccably groomed, and carrying an enormous basket of food for them. This time he had taken the time to go shopping.

"Good morning, ladies!" He seemed in exceptionally good humor, Evgenia noticed with a worried glance, but she knew that there was nothing she could do to stop them. He had brought meat and fruit, and two different kinds of cheese, cookies, and more chocolates for Zoya. He kissed her lightly on the cheek and squeezed her hand, and insisted that the Countess come out for a drive with them. They drove happily through the Bois de Boulogne, talking and laughing, and even Evgenia felt young again just being with them.

Clayton took her out to lunch with them, to the Closerie des Lilas this time, and then they took her home. She was so tired, she almost couldn't make it up the stairs, and Clayton half carried her, as she smiled gratefully at him. She had had a wonderful time, and for a little while, their poverty and the war and their sorrows were forgotten.

They sat drinking tea in the living room for a long time, and then Zoya went out with Clayton again. They went back to the Mills house on the rue de Varennes, and they made passionate love for hours. But this time, he insisted on taking her out to dinner. He took her to Maxim's and then regretfully home, and Evgenia was asleep in bed when they got there. The two lovers tiptoed soundlessly around the living room, eating chocolates and whispering, as they kissed in the firelight, and shared their dreams with each other. She wished she could stay with him all night, but there was no way imaginable that she could do that, and when he left, feeling like a boy again, he promised to return in the morning.

The next day he was later than he had been the day before, and by eleven o'clock, Zoya was getting worried. They had no phone, so she couldn't call, but at eleven-thirty he appeared, struggling with an enormous bundle wrapped in brown paper. He set it heavily on the kitchen table with a look of mysterious delight and told Zoya it was for her grandmother. The old Countess came to join them then, and he stood back as he watched her pull the paper off to reveal an extraordinarily beautiful silver samovar, engraved with the crest of the Russian family that had brought it to Paris and been forced to sell it. He couldn't even imagine how they'd gotten it there, but when he'd seen it that morning in a shop on the Left Bank, he had known instantly that he had to buy it for Evgenia.

She caught her breath as she stood back, staring at it, in wonder, and for a moment she felt a sharp pain of sadness, knowing how dear her own treasures had been and how much it hurt when she had to sell them. She was still grieving over the cigarette cases she had been forced to sell just before Christmas. But now she could only stare at the samovar and at the kind benefactor who had brought it to them.

"Captain . . . you are far too good to us . . ." Tears filled her eyes, and she gently kissed him, the faded satin of her cheek touching his male flesh, reminding her of her own son, and her husband. "You are so very kind."

"I only wish I could do more." He had brought Zoya a white silk dress, and her eyes opened wide with amazed delight as she peeled away the wrappings. It was designed by a little dressmaker he had found on the Left Bank, a woman named Gabrielle Chanel. She had a small shop, and she seemed amazingly gifted. She had showed the dress to him herself and she seemed lively and amusing, which was unusual these days for the war-worn people of Paris.

"Do you like it?" She ran to her room to try it on, and emerged looking absolutely splendid. The dress looked pure and simple, and the creamy white set off the fire of her hair wonderfully. She only wished she had pretty shoes to wear with it, and the pearl necklace Papa had given her that had burned with Fontanka.

"I love it, Clayton!" She wore it to lunch with him that day, and it lay on his bedroom floor later that afternoon.

The next day was his last, he was leaving at four o'clock that afternoon, and she couldn't bear the thought of it as they made love for the last time, and she clung to him like a drowning child, as he kissed her. When he took her back to the apartment, even Evgenia looked sad to see him go. The farewells in their lives had already been far too painful.

"Be careful, Captain . . . we will pray for you each day," as they did now for so many others. She thanked him for his great kindness to them both, and he seemed to linger, not wanting to go, unable to leave Zoya for a moment, let alone for months. He had no idea when he would be able to get back to Paris.

Evgenia left them discreetly alone, as tears filled Zoya's eyes and she looked at him in the tiny living room, the silver samovar dwarfing everything in sight, but she saw only him as she flew into his arms with a sob, and he held her to him.

"I love you so much, little one . . . please, please be careful." He knew how potentially dangerous it was for her in Paris. There was still a possibility that Paris could be attacked, and he prayed for her safety as he held her. "I'll come back the minute I can."

"Swear to me you'll be careful. Swear!" she commanded through her tears, she couldn't bear the thought of losing anyone else she loved, and not someone as dear to her as he was.

"Promise me you won't regret what we've done." He still worried about that and he was still desperately afraid she might have gotten pregnant the first time they made love. He'd been careful after that, but not careful enough the first time. She'd taken him too much by surprise and his own desire for her had been too over-whelming.

"I will never regret anything. I love you too much." She followed him down the stairs to his car, and stood waving until he was out of sight, the tears rolling down her cheeks as she watched him disappear, per-haps forever.

Chapter 23

Contrary to what he promised her, she did not hear from him again. Their strategies and maneuvers were too top secret now, and they were virtually cut off from everyone as they sat by the Marne, trying to protect Paris.

In March, the last great German offensive began, as they sat waiting to pounce just outside the city. There was shelling in the streets, and Evgenia was afraid to go out now.

The statue of Saint Luke was beheaded by shells at the Madeleine. And everywhere, people were hungry and cold and frightened. Diaghilev gave Zoya an opportunity to escape. On March 3, he left for another tour in Spain with the ballet, but Zoya insisted she couldn't leave Evgenia alone in Paris. Instead she stayed in Paris, but most of their performances were curtailed. It was almost too dangerous to move through the streets now. And only by a miracle did she manage to survive the destruction of the church of St.-Gervais-St.-Protais near the Hôtel de Ville on Good Friday. She had decided to go there instead of St. Alexander Nevsky, and she left only moments before shells hit the roof and it collapsed, killing seventy-five souls and wounding nearly a hundred.

Trains for Lyon and the south were filled with people panicking, fleeing Paris. But when Zoya suggested to her grandmother that they leave, the old woman became enraged.

"And just how many times do you think I will do this? No! No, Zoya! Let them kill me here! Let them dare! I have run all the way from Russia, and I will not run anymore!" It was the first time Zoya had seen her cry in helpless rage. It was almost exactly a year since they had left everything behind them and fled Russia. And this time there was no Feodor, there was nothing left to sell, there was nowhere to go. It was totally hopeless.

The French government itself was preparing to flee, if necessary. They had made plans to move to Bordeaux, but Foch himself had vowed to defend Paris till the end, in the streets, and on the rooftops. All of Zoya's performances and re-hearsals were canceled in May. And by then, the Allies were losing on the Marne. With Pershing there, all Zoya could think of was Clayton. She was terrified he would be killed, and she had had no news of him since he left Paris.

The only news she had was a letter from Marie that Dr. Botkin had managed to send to her, and she was surprised to learn that they had been moved to Ekaterin-burg in the Urals from Tobolsk the month before. And she could tell from what Marie said that things had gotten much harder. They were no longer allowed to lock their doors, and the soldiers even fol-lowed them to the bathroom. Zoya shud-dered to herself as she read the words, aching for her childhood friend, and espe-cially Tatiana, who was so prim and shy. The thought of them in such grim circum-stances was almost beyond bearing.

". . . There is nothing but for us to en-dure it here. Mama makes us sing hymns whenever the soldiers chant their awful songs just downstairs. They are very harsh with us now. Papa says we must do noth-ing to make them angry. They allow us out for a little while in the afternoon, and the rest of the time we read, or do needlework . . ." Zoya's eyes spilled tears onto her cheeks at the next words, ". . . and you know how I hate sewing, darling Zoya. I've been writing poetry to pass the time. I shall show it all to you when we are finally together again. It seems hard to imagine that we are both nineteen now. I used to think nineteen was so old, but now it seems too young to die. Only to you, can I say things like that, beloved cousin and friend. I pray that you are happy and safe in Paris. I must go for our exercise now. We all send you our love, and please give ours to Aunt Evgenia." She had signed it not with OTMA this time, their familiar code, but simply "your loving Mashka." Zoya sat in her room for a long time and cried, reading the words over and over again, touching the letter to her cheek, as though touching her paper would bring her friend's touch back to her again. She suddenly feared terribly for them. Everything seemed to be getting worse everywhere, but at least the ballet in which she danced went back to work in June. She and Evgenia were both desperate for the income, and they had never found another boarder. People were leaving Paris, not coming to it anymore. Even some of the Russian émigrés had gone south, but

Evgenia still refused to leave. She had gone as far as she was going to.

By mid-July, the city was warm, but still hungry. Zoya was horrified to hear from Vladimir that he and Yelena had been catching pigeons in the park, to eat them. He pronounced them surprisingly tasty and offered to bring them one, but Zoya declined, feeling ill at the thought. And two days afterward, as she began to despair that the war would ever end, Clayton reappeared like a vision in a dream. Zoya almost fainted when she first saw him. It was on the eve of Bastille Day and together they watched the parades from the Arc de Triomphe to the Place de la Concorde, the uniforms looked incredibly beautiful in the bright sun, the Chasseurs Alpins in their berets and black tunics, the British Life Guards, the Italian Bersaglieri in rooster-tail hats, even an anti-Bolshevik unit of Cossacks in fur hats, but all she really saw that day was Clayton. When they returned to the house on the rue de Varennes, as deeply in love as ever, there was a fierce pounding on the door at midnight. The M.P.'s were rounding everyone up, all leaves were canceled, the German offensive had begun in earnest.

German troops were only fifty miles away
and the Allies had to stop them.

"But you can't go now . . ." Zoya cried.
Tears filled her eyes in spite of her attempts to be brave. "You just got here!"
He had only arrived that morning, and
after six months without him, she couldn't
bear to see him go so soon. But there was
no choice. He had half an hour to report to
the headquarters of the military police on
the rue St. Anne. He barely had time to
take her home, before they escorted him
back to General Pershing. But to Zoya, it
seemed cruel beyond words to have had
so little time together before he went
back to the front to risk his life again. And
like a small child abandoned, she sat in her
living room and cried late that night, as
her grandmother brought her a cup of tea
to console her.

But the tears she shed for Clayton were
nothing to the tears she shed a few days
later. On the twentieth of July, Vladimir
appeared at the apartment with a solemn
face, and a copy of *Izvestia*, the Russian
newspaper. Zoya sensed instantly when
she opened the door that something terrible had happened, and she felt almost ill as
she escorted him inside and assisted her
grandmother from the bedroom.

He began to cry as he held the newspaper out to her. He looked like a heartbroken child, his white hair almost the same color as his face, and repeating the same words again and again. ". . . They have killed him . . . oh my God . . . they've killed him . . ." He had come directly to them, they had a right to know, after all they were Romanov cousins.

"What do you mean?" Evgenia looked at him with horror, and rose halfway in her chair, as he showed her the notice in the paper. On the sixteenth of July, the Tsar Nicholas had been executed, it said. He had been shot. And it said that his family had been moved to safety. Moved to where? Zoya wanted to scream . . . where is my beloved Mashka? . . . where *are* they? . . . almost as though she knew, Sava began to keen softly, as the three Russians sat and cried for the man who had been their father, their Tsar . . . and was the two women's much loved cousin.

There were the sounds of sorrow in the room for a long time, and at last Vladimir stood and walked to the window, his head bowed, his heart heavy almost beyond bearing. All over the world the Russians who had loved him would be crying, even the peasants in whose name the dreaded revolution had been mounted.

"What a terrible, terrible day," he said softly. "God rest his soul," he whispered, and turned to the women. Evgenia looked a hundred years old, and Zoya was deathly pale, the only color in her face the fierce green eyes, red-rimmed with tears, which still fell silently down her cheeks. All she could think of was that last morning in Tsarskoe Selo when he had kissed her good-bye and told her to be good . . . "I love you, Uncle Nicky," her own words echoed in her head . . . and then he had told her he loved her too. And now he was dead. Gone forever. And the others? . . . she read the words in *Izvestia* again . . . "The family has been moved to safety."

Chapter 24

July seemed to drag by like a nightmare. The fact that Nicholas had been killed seemed to weigh on them like an unbearable burden. Their gloom never seemed to lift anymore. All over Paris, Russians were grieving for him, as the war waged on around them.

Zoya was invited to a wedding celebration for one of the ballerinas she knew. Her name was Olga Khokhlova and she had married Pablo Picasso a few weeks before at St. Alexander Nevsky, but Zoya had no desire to go anywhere now. She wore the few black dresses she had, and was in deepest mourning for her cousin.

In August, Diaghilev cabled her once again, this time with an offer to join his troupe for a tour in London, but she still couldn't leave her grandmother, and she didn't want to see anyone. She could barely make herself go to work, which she did each day, just so they could put food on their table.

And in September, the Allies pressed ahead once more, and within a few weeks, the Germans were attempting to negotiate peace with them. But there was still no news of Clayton. Zoya barely dared to think of him now. If something happened to him too, she knew she couldn't go on living. It was all too much to bear, too much to think about, impossible to understand. Uncle Nicky was dead. The words rang again and again in her head. She had written three letters to Marie since she heard the news, but as yet there had been no answer. She was no longer clear about where Dr. Botkin was, and if the family had been moved, as the newspaper had said, it was impossible to say how long it would take for the letters to reach her.

But finally, after an endless October of silence from those she loved, November came, and with it peace at last.

They sat in their living room when they heard the news, listening to the shouting in the streets, the screams, the jubilation, the church bells, the cannons. It had finally come to an end. The whole world had shuddered from the blow of it, but now, at last, it was finished. The great war was over.

She quietly poured her grandmother a cup of tea, and without a word, she stood watching the celebrations in the street from the window. There were Allied troops everywhere, Americans, English, Italians, French, but she didn't even know if Clayton was still alive, and she hardly dared to hope. She turned to look at Evgenia, so old now, so frail, the cough that had plagued her the previous winter had returned, and her knees were so bad she could no longer leave the apartment.

"Things will be better now, little Zoya," she said softly, but she was racked by coughs as she said it. She knew what was on the girl's mind. She hadn't heard from Clayton since he left Paris at midnight on Bastille Day. "He'll come home to you, little one. Trust a little bit. You must have faith." She smiled at her gently, but there was no joy in Zoya's eyes anymore. She had lost too much. And she was worried about too many.

"How can you still say that? With so many people gone . . . how can you believe anyone will come home again?"

"The world goes on. People are born, and die, and others are born after them. It is only our own sadness that is so painful. Nicholas knows no pain now. He is at peace."

"And the others?" She had now written five letters to Marie, and all of them were still unanswered.

"We can only pray for their safety." Zoya nodded. She had heard it all before. She was angry now at the fates that had taken so much from them.

It was almost impossible to get through the streets during those first days after the armistice, and she only went out to bring back food for them. Once again, their supplies had dwindled to almost nothing. There were no performances of the ballet, and they had to get by on the tiny sum she had saved. It suddenly all seemed so exhausting.

"May I help you carry that, mademoiselle?" She felt someone tug at the baguette under her arm, and she turned with angry words on the tip of her tongue, ready to kill for the food she had, or to defend herself against an amorous soldier. Not everyone in Paris wanted to be kissed by an excited boy in uniform, she thought to herself as she swung around, her hands in fists, and gasped as she dropped the prized baguette and he pulled her to him.

"Oh . . . oh . . ." Tears sprang to her eyes instantly as she melted into his arms with relief. He was alive . . . oh, God . . . he was *alive* . . . it was as though they were the only two people left . . . the only survivors of a lost world, as she clung passionately to Clayton.

"Now that's better!" He looked down at her from his great height, his field uniform stained and wrinkled, his face rough from the beard stubble he hadn't been able to shave in days. He had just arrived in Paris and had come straight to find her. He had already seen Evgenia, and she had told him Zoya was out buying some food and he had rushed back down the stairs to meet her in the street.

"Are you all right?" She was laughing and crying all at once and he kissed her again and again, as relieved as she was that they had both survived.

It seemed miraculous now, in the face of everything, and he didn't tell her how close he had come more than once to being killed on the Marne. It didn't matter now. He was alive, and she was safe, and he silently thanked whatever guardian angels they had as they made their way through the crowds back to the apartment.

He was billeted in a small hotel on the Left Bank this time, along with dozens of other officers. Pershing was back in the Mills house himself, and it was difficult for them to be alone anywhere, but they stole what private moments they could, and one night they even dared to make love quietly in Antoine's old room, long after Evgenia had gone to sleep. She was so tired now, and she slept so much of the time. Zoya had been worried about her for months, but even those fears seemed to dim in the light of being reunited with Clayton.

They talked about Nicholas late one night, and he admitted to her that he had always feared it might come to that. And she shared her fears with him about the others.

"The Russian newspaper said they had been moved to safety . . . but where? I've written to Mashka five times, and I still have no answer."

"Botkin may not be able to get the letters out anymore. It may not mean anything, little one. You just have to have faith," he said quietly, hiding his own fears from her.

"You sound like Grandmama," she whispered to him in the dark room as they lay pressed close together.

"Sometimes I feel as old." He had noticed how frail the old woman had become since July. She didn't look well, and he sensed that Zoya knew it too. She was almost eighty-four years old now, and the past two years had been hard for all of them. It was remarkable that she had survived at all. But they both forgot their concerns for her as their bodies meshed again as one, and they made love until he tiptoed stealthily down the stairs before morning.

They spent as much time as possible together in the next few weeks, but on December 10, almost exactly a month after the end of the war, he came to her with a heavy heart. They were sending him back to the States at the end of the week, but more important than that, he had made a painful decision about her.

She heard him say he was leaving as though in a dream. It seemed impossible to believe. He couldn't be. The moment she had never faced, the day she had thought would never come, was finally upon them.

"When?" she asked, her heart like a stone in her chest.

"In two days." His eyes never left hers, there was still more to say. And he still wondered if he'd have the courage to say it.

"They don't give us much time for good-byes, do they?" Zoya said sadly. They were in her tiny, bleak living room, and it was a gray day, as Evgenia slept peacefully in their room, as she did most of the time now. Zoya was back at work again, but her grandmother didn't seem to notice.

"Will you be coming back to Paris again?" Zoya asked him as though he were a stranger, feeling separate from him now, preparing herself for what was to come. There had already been too many good-byes in her life, and she wasn't sure she would survive this one.

"I don't know."

"There's something you're not telling me." Maybe he was married and had ten children in New York. Anything was possible now. Life had already betrayed her too often, not that Clayton ever had. But she was even angry at him now.

"Zoya . . . I know it won't make sense to you, but I've been thinking a great deal . . . about us." She waited, blinded by pain. It was amazing that just when one

thought there couldn't be any more pain,
there was. It seemed to be endless. "I
want to set you free, to lead your own life
here. I thought about taking you to New
York with me . . . I wanted to very
badly. But I don't think the Countess
could make the trip, and . . . Zoya," he
seemed to choke on the words, he had
been thinking about it for days, "Zoya, I'm
too old for you. I've told you that before.
It's not fair. When you're thirty, I'll be
almost sixty."

"What difference does that make?" She
had never shared his fears about their
ages, and she looked at him angrily now,
her hurt at his going making her resentful
toward him, especially now. "What you're
saying is that you don't love me."

"I'm saying that I love you too much to
burden you with an old man. I'm forty-six
years old and you're nineteen. That's not
fair to you. You deserve someone young
and alive, and after everything settles
down here, you'll find someone else to
love. You've never had a chance. You were
a child when you left Russia two years ago,
you'd been protected there, and you came
here, during the war, with barely more
than the clothes on your back. One day,
life will be normal again, and you'll meet

someone more your age. Zoya," he sounded suddenly firm and almost like Konstantin, "it would be wrong to take you to New York. It would be selfish on my part. I'm thinking of you now, not myself." But she didn't understand that as she glared at him and tears sprang to her eyes.

"It was all a game for you, wasn't it?" She was being cruel but she wanted to be. She wanted to hurt him as much as he was hurting her. "That's all it was. A wartime romance. A little ballerina to play with while you were in Paris."

He wanted to slap her but he restrained himself. "Listen to me. It was never like that. Don't be a fool, Zoya. I'm more than twice your age. You deserve better than that."

"Ahh . . . I see," the green eyes flashed, "like the happy life I have here. I've waited out half of this war for you, barely breathing for fear you'd be killed, and now you get on a ship and go back to New York. It's easy for you, isn't it?"

"No, it's not." He turned so she wouldn't see the tears in his eyes. Maybe it was better this way. Maybe it was better if she was angry at him. She wouldn't pine for him when he was gone, as he would for her. "I love you very much." He turned to

face her quietly, as she strode purpose-
fully to the door and yanked it open.

"Get out." He looked stunned. "Why
wait two more days? Why not just end it
now?"

"I'd like to say good-bye to your grandmother."

"She's asleep, and I doubt if she'd want
to say good-bye to you. She never liked
you anyway." She just wanted him to
leave, so she could cry her heart out in
peace.

"Zoya, please . . ." He wanted to take
her in his arms again, but he knew it
wasn't fair. It was better to let her feel she
had ended it, to leave her with some
pride. Better if he was the one with a broken heart. He hated himself as he walked
slowly down the stairs, the sound of the
door slamming behind him ringing in his
ears. Hated himself for getting involved
with her. He had always known she would
get hurt, he just hadn't realized that it
would hurt him as much. But he was certain he was doing the right thing. There
was no turning back. He was too old for
her, and even if it hurt her now, she was
better off free of him, to find a man her
own age, and make a new life for herself.
He had a heavy heart for the next two

days, and the day before he left, he got a bank draft for five thousand dollars. He enclosed it in a letter to her grandmother, begging her to keep it, and to let him know if there was anything he could do for them later on. He assured her that he would always be their friend, and that he would love her granddaughter for the rest of his life.

"I have done this for her good, I can promise you that. And because I also suspect that it is what you want as well. She is younger than I. She will fall in love again. I am certain of it. And now, I bid you both adieu with a saddened, but loving heart." He had signed it and had it delivered the morning he left by a corporal on General Pershing's staff.

He left on the morning that President and Mrs. Wilson arrived. There was a parade on the Champs-Élysées for them as he steamed slowly out of Le Havre thinking of Zoya.

Chapter 25

For weeks after Clayton left Zoya, she sat in Antoine's old room and cried, and thought she would die of a broken heart. Nothing seemed to matter to her anymore. She didn't care if she starved. She made soup for her grandmother, and was surprised they even had enough money left to buy that. Evgenia had sent Prince Markovsky to the bank for her once, shortly after Clayton left, and afterward she had pressed some bills into Zoya's hands.

"I've been saving this. Use it to buy whatever you need." But there was nothing she needed or wanted anymore. He was gone. It felt like the end of her life. But the money her grandmother had apparently saved and gave to her to buy food allowed her to stay home from work. She told them she was ill, and didn't even care if they fired her. The Ballet Russe was back, and if she'd wanted to, she could have danced with them. But she didn't even want to do that, now. She didn't want anything now, no food, no friends, no job, and certainly no man. He was a fool to have told her she needed a younger man. She didn't need anyone. Except a doctor for Evgenia. She developed a terrible flu on Christmas night. She had insisted she wanted to go to church anyway. But she was too weak even to sit up, and Zoya insisted that she lie back quietly and when Prince Vladimir came she urged him to bring a doctor back with him at once, but it was hours before they came back to see her.

The doctor was a kindly old man, who had learned Russian as a child, and he spoke to Evgenia in her own tongue. Her flawless French seemed to have faded from her mind.

"She is very ill, mademoiselle," he whispered to Zoya in the living room. "She may not live the night."

"But that's ridiculous. She was fine this afternoon." As fine as she ever was now. He had to be wrong. Had to be. Zoya knew she would not survive another loss. She just couldn't face it.

"I'll do everything I can. You must call

me at once if she gets any worse. Monsieur can come to find me at my home." He was recently back from the front himself, and he was practicing medicine out of his home. He glanced at Prince Vladimir, who nodded unhappily, and then looked at Zoya with sad eyes.

"I'll stay with you." She nodded. She knew she had nothing to fear from him. He had been living with a woman for almost a year, and his daughter had been so furious, she had moved out and was living in a convent on the Left Bank.

"Thank you, Vladimir." She went to make her grandmother a cup of tea, and when she slipped back into her room she found her almost delirious. Her face was white-hot, and her whole body seemed to have shrunken in a matter of hours. Zoya realized suddenly how much weight she had lost recently. It wasn't as apparent when she was dressed, but now she looked desperately frail, and when she opened her eyes, she had to struggle to see who Zoya was.

"It's me, Grandmama . . . shh . . . don't talk." She tried to help her sip the tea, but Evgenia only pushed it away, muttered to herself, and then slept again. And it was daybreak, before she stirred and spoke. Zoya had been sitting in the chair, watching her, and she hurried to her side to hear the words. Her grandmother had been waving her hand, and Zoya approached quietly, gave her a sip of water for her parched lips, and gave her some of the medicine the doctor had left, but she could see that she was much worse.

". . . You must . . ."

"Grandmama . . . don't talk . . . you'll tire yourself."

The old woman shook her head. She knew better than that. It didn't matter now. ". . . You must thank the American for me . . . tell him I am very grateful to him . . . I was going to pay him back. . . ."

"For what?" Zoya looked confused. Why was she grateful to Clayton? For leaving them? For abandoning her and going back to New York? But Evgenia was waving weakly toward the tiny desk in the corner of the room.

". . . Look . . . in my red scarf. . . ."

Zoya opened the drawer, and found it there. She pulled it out, put it on the desk, untied it, and gasped. There was a fortune there. Almost five thousand dollars when she counted it out. "My God . . . Grand-

mama, when did he give this to you?" She
was stunned and she didn't understand.
Why would he do something like that?

"He sent it when he left . . . I was going to send it back . . . but I was afraid
. . . if you needed it . . . I knew he
meant well. We will return it to him when
we can. . . ." But she was fumbling behind her bed as she spoke, looking for
something she thought was concealed
there, and Zoya saw that she was becoming agitated and was afraid it would do her
more harm.

"Grandmama,   lie   down   . . .
please . . ." She was still stunned by the
veritable fortune Clayton had sent. It was
a grand gesture, but it made her angry at
him again. They didn't need his charity. It
was too easy to buy them off . . . but at
what price, and then suddenly she
frowned at the old wool scarf her grandmother held in her trembling hands, as
she seemed to pull it from behind her pillow. It was the scarf she had worn the day
they left St. Petersburg, she remembered
it well, and now her grandmother held it
out to her, a small smile on her pale lips.

"Nicholas . . ." she could scarcely
speak, as tears filled her eyes, ". . . you
must keep it safe, Zoya . . . take good

care of it . . . when there's nothing left,
sell it . . . but only when you are desperate . . . not before . . . there is nothing
else left."

"Papa's cigarette case, and Nicolai's . . . ?" she asked, but the old woman
shook her head.

". . . I sold them a year ago . . . we
had no choice," but Zoya heard the words
like a knife to her heart. There was nothing left of them now, no trinket, no souvenir, only memories, and whatever it was
that her grandmother now held in her
hands. Zoya took it from her carefully and
unwrapped the scarf on the bed, and as
she did, she gasped . . . she remembered it . . . it was the Easter egg Nicky
had given Alix when Zoya was seven years
old . . . it was incredible, made by
Fabergé, it was a veritable work of art.
The Easter egg itself was of a pale mauve
enamel, with diamond ribbons circling
the enamel gracefully, and a tiny spring
opened it revealing a miniature gold swan
on a lake of aquamarine, and crying softly,
she touched the lever she remembered
beneath the wing. The swan spread its
tiny golden wings, and walked slowly
across her palm. "Keep it safe, precious
one . . ." her grandmother whispered,

and closed her eyes as Zoya wrapped it in the scarf again, and then gently took her grandmother's hand.

"Grandmama . . ." Evgenia opened her eyes again, with a peaceful smile. "Stay with me . . . please don't go . . ." She sensed that the old woman was more comfortable, she seemed to breathe more easily.

"Be a good girl, little one . . . I have always been so proud of you . . ." She smiled again as Zoya began to sob.

"No, Grandmama . . ." The words were a farewell, and she wouldn't let her die. "Don't leave me alone, Grandmama . . . please . . ." But the old woman only smiled and closed her eyes for a last time. She had given her final gift to the child she had so loved, she had brought her safely to a new life, had watched over her, but now it was over.

"Grandmama . . ." Zoya whispered in the silent room, but Evgenia's eyes were closed. She was resting peacefully. Gone with the rest of them. Evgenia Peterovna Ossupov had gone home.

Chapter 26

They buried her in the Russian cemetery outside Paris, and Zoya stood silently beside Prince Vladimir, and a handful of people who had known Evgenia. She hadn't been close to any of them. Her years in Paris had been spent mostly with Zoya, and she had no patience with the complaints and depressing memories of the other émigrés. She was occupied with the present and not obsessed with the past.

She died on the sixth of January, 1919, in the tiny apartment, the same day Theodore Roosevelt died in his sleep, and Zoya sat staring out the window, stroking Sava.

It was impossible to absorb the events of the past few days, more incredible still to think of a life without her grandmother. She was still amazed by the imperial egg her grandmother had concealed for almost two years, and the money Clayton had given her when he left. It would be enough for her to live on for the next year, if she lived carefully, and for the first time in years, she had no desire to dance now. She never wanted to see the ballet again, never wanted to do anything again. She just wanted to sit there with her dog and die quietly. And then she thought guiltily of how angry her grandmother would be at her for those thoughts. Her grandmother had been committed not to death, but to life.

She lived quietly for a week without seeing anyone, and she looked thinner and very pale, when Vladimir knocked on her door. He looked quiet and strained, and he was obviously worried about her, and she was startled when she saw that there was someone standing just behind him in the dark hall when she opened the door. Perhaps he'd brought the doctor to check on her, but she didn't want to see anyone, and the doctor least of all. She was wearing black wool stockings and a black dress, her red hair pulled severely back in sharp contrast to her ivory face.

"Yes?" Vladimir hesitated as he spoke. He had almost been afraid to bring him there, afraid the shock would be too great for her, but he knew that they had to come. "Hello, Vladimir." Without saying a word, he stepped aside, and she gasped as she saw Pierre Gilliard behind him.

His eyes filled with tears as he looked at her, it seemed a thousand years since they'd last met on the day she left Tsarskoe Selo. He took a step toward her and she fell into his arms. And then she looked up at him, begging him, barely able to speak through her sobs.

"Have they come at last?" Gilliard was the tutor the imperial daughters had studied with all their lives, and Zoya knew he had gone to Siberia with them, but unable to speak, he only shook his head in answer.

"No . . ." he answered finally. "No . . . they have not . . ." She waited for more news from him, and feeling her body turn to stone, she walked inside to the ugly living room, as he followed her. He looked thin and worn, and desperately pale. Vladimir left them alone then. He closed the door softly as he went, and with head bowed, walked slowly down the stairs to his taxi.

"Are they all right?" Her heart pounded as she waited for Pierre Gilliard to speak, and as they faced each other in chairs, he reached out and took her hands in his own. Hers were like tiny icebergs, as Gilliard began speaking.

"I have only just now come from Siberia . . . I had to be certain before I came . . . We left them in Ekaterinburg in June. They told us we had to leave." It was as though he wanted to apologize, but all she wanted to hear was that Mashka and the others were all right. She sat in stunned silence, amazed just to see him there, as she clung to him with her icy hands trembling.

"You weren't there then when . . . when Nicholas . . ." She could not bring herself to say the words to him, but he understood and miserably shook his head.

"Gibbes and I had to leave . . . but we went back again, in August. They let us into the house, but there was no one there, mademoiselle." He couldn't bring himself to tell her what they'd found, the bullet holes, and the pale traces of washed blood. "They told us they had moved them somewhere else, but Gibbes and I feared the worst." She waited for the rest with a pounding heart, sure that there would be a happy end to it. After all this time, there had to be. Life surely couldn't be so cruel as to let the Bolsheviks kill the people she loved so much . . . one frail little boy, and four girls who had been her cousins and friends and their mother who loved them. It was bad enough that their father had died. It couldn't possibly get any worse than that. She watched his face as he went on, he closed his eyes, and fought back tears. He was still exhausted from the trip, and he had arrived in Paris only the night before, determined to see her.

"We arrived back in Ekaterinburg on Alexis's birthday, but they were gone by then," he sighed. "We've been there ever since. I was certain, even when I saw the bullet holes in the house, that they were still alive."

She felt her heart stop and stared at him. "Bullet holes. Did they shoot Nicky there in front of the children?"

"They killed Nagorny three days before . . . he tried to stop a soldier from stealing Alexis's medals. The Tsarevich must have been heartbroken, he'd been with him all his life." Faithful Nagorny, who had refused to abandon them. Was there no end to it?

"In the middle of July the Bolsheviks told them that their relatives were going to try and rescue them and they had to be moved before their whereabouts could be discovered." Zoya thought of Mashka's letters before that, telling her where they were. But who was it who tried to save them? "The bloody revolution had been raging since June, it was almost impossible to go anywhere. But they got them up at midnight and told them to dress." His voice caught and Zoya clutched his hands so tightly, they ached, as his eyes reached into hers, two people left on a deserted island, the others gone . . . but where? She waited for the rest without saying a word. Soon, soon he would tell her that they were on their way to Paris. "They went downstairs, the Empress, Nicholas, and the children . . . Anastasia still had Jimmy with her," Alexis's little spaniel, Pierre Gilliard began to cry again at the thought of it, ". . . and Joy . . ." Sava whined as though she knew her mother's name and he went on, ". . . The Tsarevich could no longer walk by then, he had been very ill. . . . They told them to dress and took them to the basement to wait for transportation . . . Nicholas had them bring chairs for Alexandra, and Alexis, and he was . . ." He could barely go on, ". . . he was holding him, Zoya, across his lap, when they came in . . . he was holding him when they opened fire."

She felt her heart turn to stone, it must have been the moment when they killed Nicholas, but Gilliard sobbed as he went on. "They shot them all, Zoya Konstantinovna . . . they opened fire on all of them, only Alexis lived a little longer than the rest of them, they beat his head in with rifle butts as he clutched his father . . . and then they murdered little Jimmy. Anastasia had fainted and when she screamed, they killed her with bayonets, and then," he went on as Zoya cried silently, unable to believe what he told her. "They put them all into a mine, and covered them with acid . . . they are gone, little Zoya . . . gone . . . all of them . . . even poor, sweet Baby." Zoya took him in her arms then and held him there as he cried. Even now, months later, he himself was unable to believe it. "We found Joy, one of the solders had taken her in, she was almost starved when they found her near the mine . . . crying for the children she loved. And oh, Zoya, no one will ever know how dear they were, or how much we loved them."

". . . Oh, God . . . oh, God . . . my poor little Mashka . . . murdered with rifles and bayonets . . . how frightened she must have been. . . ."

"Nicholas stood to stop them . . . but there was no stopping them. If only they had let us stay . . . but it would have made no difference." He didn't tell her the White Russians had come to liberate Ekaterinburg eight days later. Only eight days. It might as well have been eight lifetimes.

Zoya looked at him with empty eyes. Nothing mattered now. Nothing would ever matter again . . . not to her . . . or to them . . . she buried her face in her hands and cried as he held her.

"I had to tell you myself . . . I'm so sorry . . . so very sorry . . ." Such small words for the loss of such extraordinary people. How little they had understood on that last day at Tsarskoe Selo, and she knew then that she should have stayed with them, the Bolsheviks could have killed her too . . . should have . . . killed her with bayonets and bullets, as they had killed Mashka, and all of them . . . and Baby. . . .

He left her then, promising to return the next day after he had slept. He couldn't bear to look at her as he left, the broken eyes, the empty face. And when she was alone again, she clutched Sava to her, and rocked her back and forth in her arms as she cried, shouting into the emptiness, "Oh, Grandmama . . . they're gone . . . they've killed them all. . . ." And in the end only one whisper left in the silent room as she said her name for the last time. . . . She would never be able to bear saying it again . . . she whispered softly . . . "my Mashka . . ."

Chapter 27

Zoya felt as though she were in shock for several days after she heard the news from Pierre Gilliard. Added to the pain of her grandmother's death was the agony of the knowledge of the execution. Dr. Botkin had died with the rest of them, Pierre told her the next day when he returned, which explained why none of her letters had gotten through, but there was no one to answer them anyway. And she knew that Grand Duke Michael had been shot too, a week before the execution of Nicholas and Alexandra and the children. Four more grand dukes had been murdered after that. The list was seemingly endless. It was as though they wanted to destroy an entire race, a whole chapter in history. And the details were brutal beyond description.

In the face of what she now knew, it was understandable that the Versailles Peace

Conference meant little to her. For her, the war, and even its end, no longer held any meaning. She had lost her parents, her brother, her grandmother, her cousins, her friends, and her homeland, and even the man she loved had abandoned her. As she sat in the tiny apartment day after day, staring out the window, her life seemed like a wasteland. Pierre Gilliard came back to visit her several times before he left. He was going home to Switzerland for a rest, before returning to Siberia to help continue the investigation. But even that didn't seem important to her anymore. Nothing did. For Zoya, it was all over.

By the end of January, Paris was in high spirits again, and American soldiers seemed to fill the streets. There were parties and special performances and parades, all in honor of the dignitaries arriving from the States to confer at Versailles and celebrate the end of the Great Adventure, and usher in the new era of peace that was dawning.

But for Zoya, there were no celebrations. Vladimir came to visit her several times, after Pierre Gilliard left for Bern to join his wife, but Zoya barely talked as Vladimir sat watching her, afraid now for her sanity as well as her safety. The news had slowly spread to all of the émigrés, and there were endless tears, and silent mourning. The Romanovs would be sorely missed, and to those who had known them, never forgotten.

"Let me take you for a drive, little one. It would do you good to go somewhere."

"I have everything I need here, Vladimir." She looked at him sadly, and quietly stroked little Sava. He brought her food, as he had done when they first arrived. In desperation, he even brought her vodka. Perhaps, if nothing else, she could at least drown her sorrows. But the bottle remained unopened, the vodka untouched, like most of the food he brought her. She seemed to be wasting away, it was almost as though she was willing herself to die, anxious to join the others.

Several of the women he knew dropped in on her as well, but more often than not, she didn't answer when they knocked. She just quietly sat there, waiting for them to go away, and sitting alone in the dark apartment.

By late January, he was frightened, and had even spoken to a doctor. There seemed to be nothing for them to do, except wait for the tides to turn. But he was afraid she would do something drastic before that.

He was still thinking about her late one afternoon, as he drove his taxi to the Crillon, hoping for one of the important Americans to hail him. And then, as if it were an answer to a prayer, he looked across the street and saw him. He honked frantically, and waved, but the tall man in uniform disappeared into the hotel, and as Vladimir leapt out of his car, he prayed that it hadn't been an illusion. He dashed across the street and into the hotel, barely catching him as he stepped into an elevator. Clayton Andrews turned with a look of amazement as Vladimir called him. He stepped slowly off the elevator then, afraid that something terrible might have happened.

"Thank God it's you." Vladimir sighed with relief, hoping that he would still be willing to see the girl. He wasn't sure what had happened between the two, but he knew that there had been some kind of estrangement before Clayton had left Paris.

"Has something happened to her?" It was all Clayton could think of as he saw the look on Vladimir's face. He had arrived the day before, and had had to force himself not to go and see her. But he knew there was no point in torturing himself or Zoya. They were better off like this. He wanted her to have a new life, and hanging on to her wouldn't help her to find it, no matter how much he missed her. He had barely reached New York, when they asked him to return to Paris to assist with the many meetings associated with the treaty at Versailles before leaving the army forever. And he had come back with considerable trepidation. He didn't know if he was strong enough to go back to Paris and not see her. "Is it Zoya?" he asked the tall Prince, frightened by the look in his eyes. It spoke volumes.

"Can we go somewhere to talk?" Vladimir looked around the crowded lobby and back into Clayton's eyes. He had a great deal to tell him. Clayton looked at his watch. He had two hours before he had to be anywhere. He nodded and followed Vladimir outside to the conveniently waiting taxi.

"Just tell me, man, is she all right? Has anything happened to her?"

The Prince looked sorrowful as he started the car, his frayed cuffs and worn jacket looking worse than ever, but the clipped moustache was still impeccably neat, the snow white hair. Everything about him bespoke nobility and distinction. There were so many like him in Paris now. Counts and princes and dukes and just men of good families, driving taxis and sweeping streets and waiting on tables.

"Nothing has happened to her, Captain," he said, and Clayton heaved a sigh of relief. "At least not directly." They drove to the Deux-Magots, took a table in the back, and Clayton ordered two cups of coffee. "Her grandmother died three weeks ago."

"I was afraid of that." She had seemed so ill and so frail when he left Paris more than a month before.

"But worse than that, Pierre Gilliard came from Siberia to see her. The news was terrible. She hasn't left the apartment since he told her. I'm afraid she'll lose her mind, just sitting there, grieving for them. It's too much for her." There were tears in his eyes and he was sorry Andrews hadn't ordered something stronger. He could have used a stiff vodka. Just thinking about her broke his heart. Too much had happened to all of them, and now especially to Zoya.

"Was Gilliard there when they killed the Tsar?" He had a heavy heart himself, just thinking about it, although he had never known the man. But Zoya had brought him to life, with her tales of Livadia and the yacht and Tsarskoe Selo, and now he felt almost as though he knew him.

"Apparently the soldiers of the Soviet sent him and the English tutor away shortly before, but they came back two months later, and they've been speaking to soldiers and guards and local peasants in Ekaterinburg for months, helping with the White Army investigations. They know most of it and he wants to go back and talk to them some more. But it doesn't matter anymore." His eyes were old and sad as he looked at Clayton Andrews. "They're all dead . . . all of them . . . murdered at the same time as the Tsar . . . even the children." He was not ashamed of the tears that rolled down his cheeks. He cried every time he thought of it. He had lost so many good friends. They all had. But Clayton Andrews looked shocked, horrified, and he knew what it would do to Zoya.

"Marie as well?" It was a last hope . . . for Zoya's sake . . . but Vladimir only shook his head.

"All of them. Gone." He told Andrews

details that Gilliard hadn't even dared to tell Zoya, of acid and mutilation and burning. What she knew was bad enough. They had wanted to wipe them off the face of the earth, without a trace. But you cannot wipe out beauty and dignity and grace, kindness and compassion, and people who were so profoundly good and loving. In effect, they had not succeeded in destroying what they represented. Their bodies were gone but their spirit would live on forever.

"How did Zoya take the news?"

"I'm not sure she will survive it. She grows thinner day by day. She won't eat, she won't talk, she won't smile. It breaks my heart just to see her. Will you go to her?" He was ready to beg him. She must live on. Her grandmother had been old at least, but Zoya was young and alive, at nineteen her life was just beginning. He could not bear to see it end now. She had to live on, to carry with her the beauty they had all seen, into a new life, not bury it with her, as she was doing.

Clayton Andrews sighed, pensively stirring his coffee. What Vladimir had told him was shocking beyond belief, and more than that, it tore at his heart . . . even the boy . . . it was what Pierre Gilliard had said himself when he first heard the news, "The children! . . . not the children. . . ." But he looked sadly at the Prince, thinking of Zoya again. "I'm not sure she'll see me."

"You must try. For her sake." He didn't dare ask the man if he still loved her. He had always thought he was too old for her anyway, and he had said as much to Evgenia. But he was the only hope left, and he had seen the light in Clayton's eyes the year he'd gone to Christmas services with them. At least then, he had loved the girl deeply. "She doesn't answer the door most of the time. Sometimes I just leave some food outside for her, and eventually she takes it in, though I'm not sure that she eats it." But he did it for her grand-mother. He would have wanted someone to do as much for Yelena. And now he was begging Clayton Andrews to go and see her. He would have done anything to help her. He was almost sorry Gilliard had come, but they needed to know, they could not go on hoping forever.

"I'll do my best." He glanced at his watch. He had to get back to the hotel for one of the endless meetings. He stood up and paid for the coffee, and thanked Vla-dimir on the way back to the hotel, wondering if she would let him in. In her eyes, he had deserted her, and he knew that she had not understood his reasons. He thought she hated him now, and perhaps that was for the best, for her sake. But he couldn't let her just sit there and die. The picture Vladimir painted was a nightmare.

He sat impatiently through his meetings that night and at ten o'clock, he went outside and hailed a taxi, and gave the driver her address. It was a relief to discover that for once the driver was French, and not one of the noble Russians.

The building looked painfully familiar when he arrived, and for a moment he hesitated, before walking slowly up the stairs. He didn't know what to say, maybe there was nothing to say. Maybe all he could do was just be there. The walk to the fourth-floor apartment seemed interminable, and the halls were even colder and darker and more fetid than he remembered. He had left her six weeks before, but in that short time, so much had changed, so much had happened. He stood outside her door for a long time, listening, wondering if she was asleep, and then he jumped as he heard footsteps.

He knocked softly once, and the footsteps stopped. They stopped for a long time, and when she was satisfied he'd gone away, he heard them again, and this time he heard Sava bark. It made his heart beat faster just thinking of her so near, but he couldn't think of himself now, he had to think of her. He had come here to help her, not to help himself, and he had to force himself to think of that as he knocked again, and spoke through the door. *"Télégramme!"* he called out, *"télégramme!"* It was an awful trick, but he knew that otherwise she wouldn't open the door. The footsteps approached, and the door opened a crack, but from where he stood, she couldn't see him. And then with a single step and gentle push, he opened it wider and pushed her aside, speaking gently.

"You should be more careful, mademoiselle."

She gasped, and her face was deathly pale. He was shocked at how thin she was. The Prince was right. She looked terrible as she faced him with wide, frightened eyes. "What are you doing here?"

"I dropped by from New York to see how you are." He tried to sound flip, but the way she looked told its own tale. She

was beyond laughter, beyond love, beyond caring.

"Why did you come here?" She stood
looking angry and very small, and it almost broke his heart. He wanted to take
her in his arms again, but he didn't dare.
He was afraid he might break her.

"I wanted to see you. I'm here for the
peace treaty negotiations at Versailles."
They were still standing in the doorway,
and he looked at her questioningly as Sava
came to lick his hand. She hadn't forgotten, even if Zoya no longer cared to remember. "May I come in for a few minutes?"

"Why?" Her eyes were big and sad, but
more beautiful than ever.

And he couldn't lie to her anymore.
"Because I still love you, Zoya, that's
why." It wasn't what he had planned to
say, but he couldn't stop himself from saying the words to her.

"That's not important anymore."

"It is to me."

"It wasn't six weeks ago, when you left."

"It was very important to me then too. I
thought I was doing the right thing for
you. I thought you had a right to more
than I had to offer." He could offer her
everything materially, but he couldn't

give her youth or the years he had wasted before he met her. And that had seemed important at the time, now he wasn't so sure, in the face of everything Vladimir had told him. "I left you here because I love you, not because I didn't." But he knew, as he had then, that she hadn't understood it. "I didn't mean to abandon you. I had no idea that so much would happen after I left."

"What do you mean?" She looked up at him sadly, and sensed that he knew, but she was not sure how much.

"I saw Vladimir this afternoon."

"And what did he tell you?" She stood stiffly away from him, watching his eyes, as his heart went out to her. She had suffered so much. It wasn't fair. It should have happened to someone else. Not to her, or Evgenia, or the Romanovs . . . or even Vladimir. He felt sorry for all of them. But more than that, he loved her.

"He told me everything, little one." He took one step closer to her and pulled her gently into his arms, and much to his surprise, she didn't fight him. "He told me about your grandmother," he hesitated, but only for a moment, ". . . and your cousins . . . and poor little Mashka . . ." She gulped on a sob, and turned her face

away as he held her, and then as though
suddenly the dam had broken, she began
to sob in his arms, and he gently kicked
the door closed and carried her like a very
small child into the apartment and sat
down on the couch, still holding her while
she cried. She cried for a very long time,
shaking horribly, as she told him everything she'd heard from Gilliard, racked by
sobs, as she'd been then, and for a long,
long time, Clayton held her. And then at
last, the room was silent again, and there
was only the sound of an occasional sniff.
She turned broken green eyes up to his,
and he kissed her gently as he had longed
to do since he left her.

"I wish I'd been here when he came."

"So do I," she admitted, crying softly
again. "Everything's been so terrible since
you left . . . it's all been so awful . . .
and Mashka . . . oh, God, poor Mashka
. . . at least Pierre said that the bullets
killed her quickly. But the others . . ."

"Don't think about it anymore. You
must put it behind you."

"How can I?" She was still sitting on his
lap, and it reminded her of talks long ago
with her father.

"You have to, Zoya. Think of your
grandmother, think how brave she was.

She took you out of Russia in a troika, to freedom, to safety. She didn't bring you here for you to give up hope, to abandon everything, to sit in this apartment and starve to death. She brought you here for a better life, to *save* your life. Now you must never, never waste it. It would be an affront to her, to her memory, and to all that she tried to do for you. You must honor her and do everything you can to have a good life."

"I suppose you're right, but it's so hard now," and then she remembered and looked up at him shyly. "She told me about the money before she died. I was going to send it back to you, but I've been using it." She blushed and looked more like herself again.

"I should hope so." He looked pleased, at least, he had done something for her. "Vladimir says you haven't danced in months."

"Not since Grandmama got sick, and after she died, and Pierre was here. . . . I couldn't bring myself to go back."

"That's just as well." He looked over her shoulder and noticed the samovar with a nostalgic smile.

"What do you mean by that? You know, Diaghilev asked me to go on tour again with them. And I could now, if I wanted to." She sniffed again, but he smiled at her this time.

"No, you couldn't."

"Why not?"

"Because you're going to New York."

"I am?" She looked stunned. "Why?" She looked more than ever like a child as he smiled at her.

"To marry me, that's why. You've got exactly two weeks to sort out your things, and then we leave. How does that sound?" She looked up at him with wide eyes.

"Are you serious?"

"Yes, I am, if you'll have me." He realized with a start, that she was a countess now, but not for long. He was going to marry her before they left Paris. And then she would be Mrs. Clayton Andrews, for the rest of her life. "If you're foolish enough to saddle yourself with an old man, then that's your problem, Miss Ossupov. I'm not going to warn you anymore."

"Good." She clung to him like a lost child, crying again, but this time they were tears of joy and not sorrow.

"In fact," he said, setting her gently on her feet as he stood up, "take some things with you now. I'm going to get you a room at the hotel. I'm going to keep an eye on

you before we leave. I don't want to have
to be pounding on that door, shouting
'telegramme' for the next two weeks." She
laughed at him then and dried her eyes.

"That was very rude of you!"

"Not as rude as you, pretending not to
be in. Never mind, get your things. We
can come back here in a few days and get
what you want to take with you."

"I don't have very much." She looked
around the room, there was almost nothing she wanted to take with her, except
perhaps the samovar and some of her
grandmother's things. She wanted to
leave the past behind and start a new life
with him. And then suddenly in terror she
glanced up at him. "Are you really serious?" What if he changed his mind? What
if he left her again, or abandoned her in
New York? He saw the fear in her eyes and
his heart went out to her.

"Of course I am, little one. I should have
taken you with me when I left." But they
both knew she couldn't have left her
grandmother, and she hadn't been well
enough to travel then. "I'll help you
pack."

She packed a pathetically small bag, and
then remembered the dog. She couldn't
leave her behind, and she was the only

friend she had left, except Clayton, of course. "Can I take Sava to the hotel?"

"Obviously." He picked up the little dog, who tried frantically to lick his chin, and then he picked up Zoya's small bag, as she quietly turned out the lights. It was time to go home. She closed the door without looking back, and followed Clayton down the stairs, to a new life.

Chapter 28

It took less than a day to pack up her things. She packed the samovar, and her books, her grandmother's needlework, and her shawls, her own clothes, and their lace tablecloth, but there was very little else. She gave away the rest to Vladimir, a few friends, and the priest at St. Alexander Nevsky.

They said good-bye to Vladimir, and she promised to write. And then in a matter of days, she was standing next to Clayton at the ministry, and became his wife. It was all like a dream as she looked up at him, with tears rolling slowly down her cheeks. She had lost everything, and now even her own name was gone. But she clung to him for dear life, as they went back to the hotel. It was as though she were terrified that he might change his mind again.

They spent two more days in Paris, and then took the train to Switzerland. They had decided to spend their honeymoon there, and she admitted to Clayton that she wanted to see Pierre Gilliard again before she left.

It took two days to reach Bern, with the train stopping endlessly everywhere, but as she woke up on the last day, her heart skipped a beat. The snowcapped mountains greeted her, and for a moment, it looked as though she were back in Russia.

Gilliard met them at the train, and they went home to have lunch with his wife, who had been the Romanov children's nurse. She embraced Zoya as she cried and Clayton listened as they reminisced over lunch. It was all so painful, and yet they shared such tenderness, such happy memories.

"When will you go back?" Clayton asked quietly as Zoya went to look at photographs with Gilliard's wife.

"As soon as we feel strong again. Life in Siberia was very hard on my wife. I don't want to take her back with me. Gibbes and I have agreed to meet, and see if there is any more we can find out.

"Does it matter now?" Clayton was honest with him. It all seemed to be over now, and there was no point clinging to the painful past. He had told Zoya as much, but Gilliard seemed to be obsessed with it. It was even more real to him, but it was understandable, he had been with the Tsar's children for twenty years, and they were his entire life.

"It matters to me. I won't rest until I know everything, until I find any of them who survived." It was a new thought.

"Is there any chance of that?"

"I don't believe there is. But I must be certain of it, or I shall never rest."

"You loved them very much."

"We all did. They were an extraordinary family, even some of the guards in Siberia softened when they got to know them. They had to keep changing them in order to keep things rough. It frustrated the Bolsheviks no end. Nicholas was kind to everyone, even to those who had destroyed his empire. I don't think he ever forgave himself for abdicating to them. He was always reading history, and he told me that one day, the world would say of him that he had failed . . . that he had given up . . . I think it broke his heart." It was an insight into the man the others would never know. A glimpse back to a special time that would never come again, for any of them. The grandeur of what they had all known dwarfed even what he had to offer Zoya in New York. But he knew she'd be happy there. She would never be cold or hungry again. At least he had that to give. He had already thought of buying a house for her. His own brick mansion on lower Fifth Avenue suddenly seemed much too small.

They spent three days in Bern, and then he took her to Geneva and Lausanne.

They got back to Paris in late February, and they took the *Paris* to New York. She sailed from Le Havre on a beautiful day, her four smokestacks standing tall. She was a beautiful ship, the pride of the French Line, and she had sat idle for three years, since she was launched halfway through the war.

Zoya was like an excited child for most of the trip. She had gained back a little weight and her eyes had come alive again. They had dinner at the captain's table several times, and they danced late into the night. She almost felt guilty for having so much fun. She had left so many people behind in her lost world, but Clayton wouldn't let her think of it now. He only wanted her to look ahead, to the new life they would share. He talked of the house they would build, the people she would meet, the children they would have. She had her whole life ahead of her. She was not even twenty years old, and life had only just begun for her.

And the night before they reached New York, she gave him the wedding gift she had been saving for him. It was still wrapped in her grandmother's scarf. And he gasped when he saw the egg, and how intricately exquisite it was. She set the tiny gold swan on the table when he had opened it, and showed him how it worked.

"It's the most beautiful thing I've ever seen . . . no, the second most beautiful," he said, smiling at her.

She looked at him with disappointed eyes, she had so wanted him to love it as much as she did. It meant so much to her. It was the only relic she had of her past. "What was the first?"

"You, my love. You are the most beautiful and the best."

"Silly man." She laughed at him, and he made love to her all that night. They were both still awake when the Statue of Liberty came into sight, as they docked in New York the next morning.

NEW YORK

Chapter 29

Zoya stood on the deck and watched with awe as the *Paris* docked at the French Line pier on the Hudson. They boasted of having the longest gangplank in the world, and she was wearing a black Chanel suit that Clayton had bought her before they left Paris. Chanel had moved to the rue Cambon by then, and her designs seemed far more exciting than Poiret's, although she wasn't as famous. Zoya wore a matching cloche, with her hair pulled into a tight knot, and she had felt very chic when she had bought it, but now as she looked around, she felt suddenly dowdy. The women around her wore expensive dresses and furs, and she hadn't seen as many jewels since she'd left Russia. All she had was the narrow gold wedding band Clayton had slipped on her finger when they were married.

There was no evidence of champagne

anywhere, unlike their departure from Le Havre. The French ships had to respect a new prohibition on alcohol, and all evidence of liquor had to disappear once they were inside the three-mile limit. They could only serve alcohol in international waters, unlike American ships, which served none at all. It was making the French and British ships very popular.

The skyline of New York looked like nothing she had ever seen. Gone the churches, domes, and spires and ancient elegance of Russia, or the graceful splendor of Paris. This was modern and alive and exciting and she felt very young as he led her to his Hispano-Suiza, and his chauffeur ushered their trunks through customs.

"Well, little one, what do you think?" He was watching her with happy eyes as they drove to Fifth Avenue, and headed downtown to the mansion he had once shared with his wife. It was elegant and small and had been decorated by Elsie de Wolfe. The two women had been good friends, and she had decorated the homes of the Astors and the Vanderbilts in New York, as well as those of many of their friends in Boston.

"Clayton, this is wonderful!" It was a

lifetime from the snow-covered roads she had traveled by troika, going to Tsarskoe Selo. There were horses and cars in the streets, women in brightly colored coats trimmed in fur, and men hurrying along beside them. Everyone looked happy and excited, and Zoya's eyes danced as she stepped from the car and looked up at the brick mansion. It was smaller than Fontanka Palace certainly, but by American standards it was still very large, and as she stood in the marble hall, two gray-uniformed maids in proper aprons and caps took her coat, and she smiled at them shyly.

"This is Mrs. Andrews," Clayton announced quietly, introducing her to both of them, and the elderly cook who wandered in with two more maids, fresh from the kitchen. The butler was British and looked very serious, and the house bore all the earmarks that Mrs. de Wolfe was so fond of, French antiques mixed with "moderne," as she liked to call it. He had already told Zoya that she could change anything she wanted, he wanted her to feel at home, but she loved what she saw, and there were wide French windows looking out on a snow-covered garden. She clapped her hands like a child as he laughed, and walked her upstairs to their bedroom. There were pink satin bedspreads and curtains and a lovely chandelier, and there was a dressing room with pink satin walls just for her, with closets that reminded her of her mother's. And she laughed at the sight of her few dresses hanging there when the maid unpacked for her that afternoon.

"I'm afraid the servants will be very disappointed," she laughed as she stood naked in her dressing room before dinner. She had just had a bath in the sumptuous marble bathtub . . . gone the horrors of the tiny bathtub in the room at the end of the hall in the apartment near the Palais Royal. She would never again have to share her bathroom with her neighbors. It was all like a dream as she looked around her and at the man who had saved her from the agonies of her life in Paris. She had had no idea how wealthy he was, or how important in New York society. In his uniform, and with his unassuming ways, there had been no reason to suspect it. "Why didn't you tell me about all this?"

"It wouldn't have made any difference anyway." He knew that was not why she loved him, and that was refreshing too. It was a relief not to be hounded by aging debutantes, or the daughters of his late mother's friends, recently widowed or divorced, on the prowl for a prosperous wellborn husband. And he fitted the bill perfectly, but more important to Zoya, he was loving and kind, and he had saved her. "I was always so embarrassed talking to you about life in St. Petersburg . . . I was afraid you would think it all so excessive."

"I did," he laughed, "but also excessively charming . . . like my pretty bride." He watched her slip into her new satin underwear, and then decided just as quickly to remove it.

"Clayton!" But she didn't object as he carried her back to bed. They were late for dinner every night, and Zoya was embarrassed by the butler's obvious disapproval.

The servants were not warm to her, and she was aware of a certain amount of whispering whenever she walked through the house. They served her, but reluctantly, and whenever possible they mentioned his previous wife. The ex-Mrs. Andrews had apparently been the epitome of perfection. The maid even managed to leave a copy of *Vogue* in her dressing room, open to the pages where Cecil

Beaton raved about her latest gown, and a party she had given for her friends in Virginia.

"She was lovely, wasn't she?" Zoya asked quietly one night, as they sat by the fire, in their bedroom. But here, the fireplace only enhanced the decor, it was not a necessity for their very survival. She thought sadly more than once of Vladimir in his freezing apartment, and their other friends, literally starving in Paris. She felt guilty for all that Clayton gave her.

"Who was lovely?" He looked at her without understanding.

"Your wife." Her name was Margaret.

"She was very well dressed when she wanted to be. But so are you, little Zoya. We haven't even begun to go shopping yet."

"You spoil me too much." She smiled shyly at him, blushing in the way that touched his heart, as he reached out and pulled her to him.

"You deserve far more than I can ever give you."

He wanted to make up to her for all that she had lost, all that she had suffered in Paris after they left Russia. The imperial Easter egg was proudly displayed on the mantel in their bedroom, along with pho-

tographs of his parents in handsome silver
frames, and three tiny exquisite gold
sculptures that had been his mother's.

"Are you happy, little one?"

She beamed up at him in answer in the
quiet room. "How could I not be?"

He introduced her to his friends, and
took her everywhere with him, but they
were both aware of the quiet resentment
of the other women. She was pretty, she
was young, and she looked exquisite in the
expensive gowns he bought her.

"Why do they dislike me so much?" She
felt the pain of it more than once, as the
women stopped speaking when she arrived, and quietly shunned her.

"They don't dislike you, they're just
jealous."

He was right, but by late May, he was
furious at the rumors they had started.
Someone had begun saying that Clayton
Andrews had married a cheap little
dancer in Paris . . . there was vague
mention of the Folies-Bergère, a drunken
lout at his club had even asked him if she
did the cancan, and Clayton was hard
pressed not to strike him.

One woman at a party asked another as
they watched Zoya dance if it was true
that she had been a paid whore in Paris.

"She must have been. Just look at how she dances!"

She had mastered the steps of the new fox-trot to perfection, under Clayton's careful direction. And he stood handsome and proud as he whirled her around the floor, so obviously in love with his beautiful young wife that it made everyone hate her. She was twenty years old with a waist he could encircle with both hands, graceful legs, and the face of an angel. And when the waltz struck up, she felt tears sting her eyes, as they moved slowly around the floor, looking up at him with the memory of the night they'd met, and painful memories from long before that. If she closed her eyes, she was in St. Petersburg again . . . dancing with Konstantin, or handsome young Nicolai in the uniform of the Preobrajensky Guard . . . or even Nicholas at the Winter Palace. She remembered the coming-out ball she was to have, and never had, and now none of it seemed quite so painful. He had made it all up to her, and now she was even able to look at her photographs of Mashka, with a sad smile, but without tears. She would carry her friends and her loved ones with her in her heart forever.

"I love you so much, little one . . ." he

whispered as they danced at the Astors' ball in June, and then suddenly she stopped and stared, as though she had seen a ghost. Her feet were rooted to the floor, and her face went pale, as Clayton whispered to her, "Is something wrong?"

"It can't be . . ." She looked ill as he felt her hand go cold in his own. A tall, stunningly handsome man had just entered the room with a pretty woman in a shimmering blue gown.

"Do you know them?"

But she could not speak. It was Prince Obolensky, or someone who looked exactly like him, and the woman on his arm appeared to be the Grand Duchess Olga, the young Grand Duchesses' aunt who had brought them into town every Sunday for lunch with their grandmother, before stopping for tea at the Fontanka Palace with Zoya.

"Zoya! . . ." He was afraid she might faint, as the woman stared and gave a gasp of surprise as she hurried toward them. Zoya gave a little cry like a child, and flew into her arms.

"Darling . . . is it you? . . . oh, my little Zoya . . ." Lovely Olga folded her into her arms as they both cried tears of joy, filled with the tender memories of the loved ones they had lost, as Clayton and Prince Obolensky watched them. "But what are you doing here?"

Zoya curtsied low, and turned to introduce her handsome husband. "Olga Alexandrovna, may I present my husband, Clayton Andrews." He bowed and kissed the Grand Duchess's hand, and afterward Zoya explained that Olga was the Tsar's youngest sister.

"Where have you been since . . ." She had difficulty saying the words as their eyes met. She hadn't seen her since they both left Tsarskoe Selo.

"I was in Paris with Grandmama . . . she died after Christmas."

The Grand Duchess embraced the girl again, as everyone in the ballroom watched, and within hours it was everywhere. Clayton Andrews's new wife was a Russian countess. The tales of the Folies-Bergère faded on the wind, and Prince Obolensky told tales of glorious and exotic balls held at the Fontanka Palace.

"Her mother was the loveliest woman I've ever seen. Cold, of course, as Germans are, and rather high-strung, but incredibly pretty. And her father was a charming man. It was a terrible loss when he was killed. So many good men gone."

He said it with regret over a glass of champagne, but with less emotion than the women. Zoya never left Olga's side for the rest of the night. She was living in London, but had come to New York to visit friends. She was staying with Prince Obolensky and his wife, the former Alice Astor.

Word spread around New York like fire, about Zoya's origins, her noble family, her relationship to the Tsar, and within moments she was the darling of society. Cecil Beaton chronicled her every move, and they were invited everywhere. The people who had shunned her suddenly loved her.

Elsie de Wolfe wanted to redo the house, and then instead proposed a remarkable suggestion. She and her friends had bought a group of old farms on the East River, and were remodeling the old houses on a street called Sutton Place. It was not fashionable yet, but she knew that when it was finished it would be.

"Why don't you let me do one of them for you and Clayton?" She was decorating one of them for William May Wright, the stockbroker, and his wife, Cobina. But Zoya thought they were fine where they were in his comfortable brick mansion.

Zoya gave her first dinner party for Grand Duchess Olga, before she returned to London again, and her fate was sealed after that. She was destined to become the darling of New York, much to her husband's delight. He indulged her every whim, and secretly commissioned Elsie de Wolfe to remodel one of the houses on Sutton Place for them. It was an elegant gem, and when Zoya saw it, her eyes grew wide in amazement. It was not as excessive as the Wright's new home, where they had been the night before, and met Fred Astaire and Tallulah Bankhead. The most shocking thing of all had been the mink-lined bathroom, but there was none of that excess in the Andrews home. It was quietly elegant, with marble floors, lovely views, large, airy rooms, and filled with treasures de Wolfe had felt certain would please the young Russian countess. People had begun to address her as such, but she always insisted that she was now Mrs. Andrews. The thought of using the title seemed ridiculous to her, although Americans seemed to love it.

There were scores of other émigrés in New York by then, fresh from Paris and London, and some having come directly from Russia, with harrowing tales of their escape as civil war raged on, between Red and White forces trying to take control of the anguished nation. But the White Russians in New York more often than not amused her. There were, of course, the true nobles, many of whom she knew, but dozens of others now boasted titles they had never had in Russia. There were princes and princesses and countesses everywhere. She was even stunned to be introduced to an imperial princess one night, whom she recognized instantly as the woman who had made her mother's hats, but she said nothing to embarrass her when they were presented to each other. And later, the woman begged her not to expose her to the ever mourning Russians.

She herself entertained many of the nobles who had once been her parents' friends. But the past was gone, and no amount of talk and pretense, or painful memory, would ever revive it. She wanted to look ahead, to become an integral part of the life she was leading. And only on Christmas did she allow herself the luxury of remembering with fresh tears, as she stood beside Clayton, chanting the familiar Russian hymns and holding the candle which burned so brightly in memory of those she had loved and lost.

Christmas was a difficult time, but she had been in New York for nine months by then, and she had exciting news for Clayton.

She waited until they came home from church, and as they lay in their huge canopied bed on Sutton Place, she waited until after they'd made love, and then she told him.

"You're *what?*" He looked stunned, and was instantly terrified that he might have hurt her. "Why didn't you tell me?" His eyes glowed and there were tears of joy in her eyes.

"I only found out two days ago." She giggled, feeling as though she were the keeper of the world's most important secret. One couldn't see it yet, but she knew, and ever since the doctor had told her the news, she felt as though she knew life's true meaning. She had wanted Clayton's child more than anything, and she kissed him happily as he gazed at her in adoration. She was not yet twenty-one, and they were going to have a baby.

"When is it due?"

"Not for a long time, Clayton. Not until August."

He offered to move to another room, so

as not to disturb her sleep, and she only laughed at his concern. "Don't you dare! If you move to another room, I'll come with you!"

"That might be fun." He looked amused. Elsie de Wolfe had certainly given them enough bedrooms to choose from. And Zoya had her prepare a nursery in the spring. It was all done in pale blue, with sweet murals, and exquisite lace curtains. It was a new touch for Mrs. de Wolfe, who was amused by Cobina Wright Junior's miniature Rolls, but was pleased by Zoya's more restrained views of what was suit-able for children. Zoya always showed the dignity and good taste to which she'd been born, and added her own touches to the house on Sutton Place. It had an aura of quiet peace and exquisite beauty that everyone talked about. They had sold the brick mansion on Fifth Avenue long since, and for the most part, hired new servants.

And on the day Alexis Romanov, dear sweet Baby, would have become seventeen, their first child was born, a son. The delivery went easily and well, and he was a lusty eight-pound boy who sent up his first cry like a flare, as his father paced nervously outside their bedroom.

Zoya was almost asleep, with the tiny cherub in her arms, when Clayton finally saw her. The baby had his mother's red hair, and a round face, as he lay wrapped in lace, and tears of joy ran slowly down Clayton's cheeks as he saw him.

"Oh, he's so beautiful . . . he looks just like you . . ."

"Only the hair," she whispered sleepily. The doctor had given her something to make her drowsy, and she looked dreamily up at her husband, "He has your nose." It looked like a tiny rosebud in the angelic face as Clayton laughed, and stroked the silky red hair, and then Zoya looked up at him, her eyes pleading in silent question. "May we call him Nicholas?"

"If you like." He liked the name, and he knew how much it meant to her. It was both the Tsar's name, and her dead brother's.

"Nicholas Konstantin . . ." she whispered, looking down at him happily, and then she fell asleep, as her adoring husband watched her and then tiptoed from the room, grateful for all life's gifts. After all these years, he had a son . . . a son! Nicholas Konstantin Andrews. It had a nice ring to it, he laughed to himself, as he hurried downstairs to pour himself a glass of champagne.

"To Nicholas!" he toasted as he stood alone in the room, and then with a smile, ". . . to Zoya!"

Chapter 30

The next few years flew on angels' wings, filled with people and excitement and parties. Zoya bobbed her hair, which horrified him, she discovered cigarettes, and then decided they looked foolish. Cecil Beaton wrote about her constantly, and about their famous parties at the house they built for the summers on Long Island.

They saw Nijinsky's last performance in London, and Zoya grieved when she heard that he had gone mad and been committed to an institution in Vienna. But the ballet was no longer a part of her life, except for performances they occasionally attended with the Vanderbilts or the Astors. They attended polo matches, receptions, balls, and gave a number of their own, and the only time she slowed down at all was in 1924, when she again found out she was pregnant. The Prince of Wales had just been to Long Island to visit them, after attending the polo match there. She felt quite ill this time, and Clayton hoped that meant she was having a girl. At fifty-two, he yearned to have a daughter.

She was born in the spring of 1925, the same year that Josephine Baker became the rage in Paris.

And Clayton's heart leapt with joy when he first saw the baby. She had the same fiery red hair as her mother and brother Nicholas, and she made her presence known to her admirers at once. She cried the moment her commands weren't obeyed, and she was the apple of his eye from the moment she was born. Alexandra Marie Andrews was christened in the christening gown that had been in Clayton's family for four generations. It had been made in France during the War of 1812, and she looked like one of the imperial duchesses when she wore it.

Her hair was the color of her mother's, but her eyes were Clayton's, and her personality was her own. By the time she was two, she was in command of even her brother. Nicky, as he was called, had the gentleness of his father, and the lively humor that Zoya's own brother had had. He was a child everyone admired and loved, most especially his mother.

But Sasha, by the time she was four, had her father wrapped around the proverbial little finger. And even ancient Sava ran in terror when she was angry. The dog was twelve, and was still with them, ever at Zoya's heels when she was in the house, or with little Nicky, whom she had adopted.

"Sasha!" Her mother exclaimed in despair, as she came home to find her wearing her best pearls, or an entire bottle of "Lilas," which she still wore, and which Clayton always brought her. "You mustn't do things like that!" Even the nurse had a difficult time controlling her. She was a young French girl they had brought back with them from Paris, but no amount of rebukes or gentle reproaches ever impressed the tiny countess.

"She can't help it, Mama," Nicholas apologized for her from the door. He was eight years old by then, and as handsome as his father. "She's a girl. Girls like to wear pretty things." His eyes met Zoya's and she smiled. He was so kind, so forgiving, so much like Clayton. She loved them all, but it was Alexandra, Sasha, as she was called, who tried her patience.

At night, they were going to the Cotton

Club, to dance the night away in Harlem. And only months before they had gone to Condé Nast's incredible Park Avenue apartment for a fabulous party. Cole Porter was there, of course, and Elsie de Wolfe, who wanted to do a house for Zoya in Palm Beach, but with her fair skin she had no love for the sun, and was content only to visit there briefly each year, when they went to stay with the Whitneys.

Zoya was buying her clothes from Lelong that year, and was very fond of his charming wife, Princess Natalie, who was the daughter of Grand Duke Paul, and a Russian like Zoya. And Tallulah Bankhead had scolded Zoya more than once, telling her that she didn't use enough lip rouge.

Fancy-dress balls were the rage, and Clayton particularly enjoyed them. He was fifty-seven years old, and he was madly in love with his wife, although he teased her mercilessly that year, telling her that she was finally old enough to be married to him, now that she had turned thirty.

Hoover had been elected president, defeating Governor Al Smith of New York. Calvin Coolidge had decided not to run again. And the governor of New York was Franklin Roosevelt, an interesting man, with an intelligent wife, although she was not very pretty. But Zoya enjoyed her company, and the conversations they shared, and she was always pleased when the Roosevelts invited them to dinner. They saw the play *Caprice* with them, and although Clayton was bored, Zoya and Eleanor loved it. They saw *Street Scene* after that, which won the Pulitzer. But Clayton confessed he had a much better time at the movies. He was crazy about Colleen Moore and Clara Bow. And Zoya was equally fond of Greta Garbo.

"You just like those foreign types," he teased, but she didn't seem foreign to anyone anymore. Zoya had become totally integrated in the life of New York after ten years. She adored the theater and the ballet and the opera, and had taken little Nicky to see *Rosenkavalier* with them in January, but he was shocked to see a woman playing a man's role.

"But that's a *girl*!" he had whispered loudly as the people in the next box smiled. Zoya held his small hand gently in her own, and whispered a suitable explanation, that it had to do with the quality of their voices. "That's disgusting," he announced and sank into his seat as Clayton smiled, not sure he didn't agree with him.

Nicholas was far more interested in Lindbergh's flights. And Clayton and Zoya went to Lindbergh's wedding to Ambassador Morrow's daughter Anne, in June, shortly before they moved to Long Island for the summer.

The children were happy there, and Zoya herself loved to take long walks along the beach, talking to Clayton or their friends, or just being alone sometimes, thinking of the summers of her youth, at Livadia, on the Crimea.

She still thought about them sometimes, it would have been impossible not to. The figures of the past still lived on in her heart, but the memories were dimmer now, and sometimes she had to grope for their faces. There were framed photographs of Marie, and the other girls, in Fabergé frames on the mantel in their bedroom. The one where they all hung upside down was still the one she loved best, and little Nicholas knew their names and faces too. He loved to hear about what they had been like, what they had said and done, the mischief they'd gotten into as children, and it intrigued him that he and the Tsarevich shared the same birthday. He liked to hear about the "sad parts," too, as he called them . . . the parts about Grandfather, who must have been very good, and funny Nicolai after whom he was named. She told him about their arguments and their jokes and their disappointments, and she assured him that she and Nicolai had fought almost as much as he and Sasha. At four, he thought she was becoming a terrible nuisance. And there were others in the house who shared his view. She was spoiled by her father, beyond what even Zoya liked, but there was no scolding the child in his presence.

"She's a baby, darling. Don't upset her."

"Clayton, she'll be a monster when she's twelve if we don't discipline her now."

"Discipline is for boys," he told his wife, but he never had the heart to reprimand Nicholas either. He was kindhearted to all of them, and played with them endlessly on the beach that summer.

King George was healthy again in England by then and it always unnerved Zoya when she saw photographs of him. He looked so much like his first cousin, the Tsar, that it was always a shock to see his face gazing out from a picture. His own little granddaughter, Elizabeth, was only a year younger than Sasha.

The thing that impressed little Nicholas most that summer was a performance of

Yehudi Menuhin's in New York. The child was a prodigy on the violin, and only three years older than Nicholas, who was fascinated by the way he played. He talked about it for weeks, which pleased Zoya.

Clayton was reading *All Quiet on the Western Front* on the beach, and he was amusing himself that summer with the stock market. It had been dancing up and down since March, and people were making absolute fortunes. Clayton had bought Zoya two diamond necklaces in the past two months, with just a fraction of his profits. But she was distracted by the sad news that Diaghilev had died in Venice in August. It seemed to close another chapter of history for her, and she talked about him to Clayton as they walked on the beach after she had heard the news.

"If it hadn't been for him letting me dance, we would have truly starved. There was nothing else I knew how to do," she looked up at Clayton sadly, as he took her hand, remembering how hard her life had been then, the awful apartment near the Palais Royal, their almost nonexistent meals during the war, it had been a hard time, but it was long in the distant past, and she looked up at him with a smile.

"And then there was you, my love. . . ."
She never forgot how he had saved her.

"Someone else would have come along."

"Not someone I could have loved as I love you." She spoke gently. He bent to kiss her, and they stood for a long time in the last fiery sunset of the summer. They were moving back to New York the next day. Nicholas had to go to school, and Sasha was going to begin kindergarten. Zoya thought it would do her good to be with other children, although Clayton wasn't as sure. But he always deferred to Zoya on matters of that nature.

They had dinner with the Roosevelts again almost as soon as they got back. They had also just returned from their summer home in Campobello. And a week later, the Andrews gave a party to celebrate the onset of a new social season. Prince Obolensky came of course, as he always did, and a glittering cast of hundreds.

The month seemed to fly by with parties, theater, balls, and it was October before they knew it. Clayton was worried that his stocks weren't doing well, and he called John Rockefeller to have lunch with him, but he had gone to Chicago for a few

days, so he'd have to wait to see him. And
two weeks later, Clayton was too upset to
have lunch with anyone. His stocks were
plummeting and he didn't want to upset
Zoya by telling her, but he had put all
their assets into the stock market months
before. He had done so well, he was sure
that he could triple his family fortune.

By Thursday the twenty-fourth, everyone was dumping shares, and everyone
Clayton knew seemed to be in a panic. But
none more than he, as he went to the
stock market himself. He came home in
terror that afternoon, and things were
worse the next day. And Monday was a
day of fresh disaster. Over sixteen million
shares were dumped, and by nightfall,
Clayton knew he was ruined. The stock
market closed at one o'clock, in a vain effort to stop the frantic selling of shares, but
for Clayton it was too late. The Exchange
was to remain closed for the rest of the
week, but he had already lost everything
they had. All they had left were their
homes, and everything in them. The rest
was gone. Clayton walked all the way
home, and he felt a weight on his chest
like a stone. He could barely face Zoya as
he walked into their bedroom.

"Darling? . . . what is it? . . ." His

face was gray, as she turned to face him. She had been brushing her hair which she had grown long again because he hated the fashionable bobs so much, but he barely seemed to notice her as he walked into the room and stared into the fireplace with bleak eyes, and then slowly he turned to face her. "What's wrong?" Her brush clattered on the floor and she ran to his side. "Clayton . . . Clayton, what is it?"

His eyes reached into hers, and she was suddenly reminded of her father when Nicolai had been killed. "We've lost everything, Zoya . . . everything . . . I was a fool. . . ." He attempted to explain everything to her as she listened with wide eyes, and she put her arms around him and held him as he cried. "My God . . . how could I have been so stupid . . . what will we do now?"

Her heart almost stopped, it was like the revolution again. But she had survived it before, and this time they had each other. "We'll sell everything . . . we'll work . . . we'll survive, Clayton. It doesn't matter." But he wrenched himself from her arms and paced the room, frantic at the full realization that they were ruined, and his world had come crashing down around him.

"Are you crazy? I'm fifty-seven years old . . . what do you think I can do? Drive a taxi like Prince Vladimir? And you'll go back to the ballet? Don't be a fool, Zoya . . . we're ruined! *Ruined!* The children will starve. . . ." He was crying as she took his hands in her own, and his were icy.

"They will not starve. I can work, so can you. If we sell what we have, we can live on it for years." The diamond necklaces alone would keep them fed and housed for a long time, but he shook his head miserably, he understood the situation far better than she. He had already seen a man he knew leap from his office window. And she knew nothing of the enormous debts he had allowed to accrue, knowing he had the money to pay them whenever he wanted.

"And who will you sell it all to? All the others who've lost their shirts? It's all worthless, Zoya. . . ."

"No, it's not," she said quietly. "We have each other and the children. When I left Russia, we left on a troika with nothing, with rags, with two of Uncle Nicky's horses and what jewelry we could sew into the linings of our clothes, and we survived." They both thought at the same time of the misery of her Paris apartment, but they had lived through it, and now she had him and the children. "Think of what the others lost . . . think of Nicky and Aunt Alix . . . don't cry, Clayton . . . if they could be brave in the face of that, there is nothing we can't face . . . is there, my love. . . ." But he only cried in her arms unable to face it.

That night they went down to dinner, and he barely spoke. She was trying to think, to make plans, to decide what to sell and who to sell it to. They had two houses, all the antiques Elsie de Wolfe, now Lady Mendl, had helped them find, her jewelry, paintings, objects . . . it was endless. It was like planning an escape, as she made suggestions and tried to reassure him, but he walked upstairs with a heavy step, and as she talked to him from her dressing room while she undressed, she couldn't elicit an answer from him. She was desperately worried about him. It had been a terrible blow, but after surviving everything else that had happened in her life, she refused to be beaten now. She would help him fight, help him survive, she would scrub floors if she had to. She didn't care, and then as she listened, she wondered if he'd left the next room. He hadn't answered her in several minutes.

"Clayton?" She walked into the room in one of the lace nightgowns he'd bought her the year before in Paris. She gave a gasp as she saw him, slumped on the floor, as though he had fallen, and she ran to his side, and gently rolled him onto his back. But he stared at her with unseeing eyes. "Clayton! Clayton! . . ." She began to sob as she shouted his name, she slapped his face, she tried to pull him across the floor, as though anything she did might revive him. But he didn't move, he didn't see, and he could no longer hear her. Clayton Andrews had died of a heart attack, the shock of the crash too much, the prospect of losing everything more than he could bear, and as she sank to her knees and cried as she held his head on her lap, she looked down at him in disbelief. The man that she had loved was dead. He had left her. Desolate, and alone, and poor again, the dream that had become her life was suddenly a nightmare.

Chapter 31

"Mama, why did Papa die?" Sasha looked up at Zoya with her huge blue eyes, as they rode back from the cemetery in the Hispano-Suiza. Everyone in New York had come, but Zoya had scarcely seen them. She felt as though she were in a daze as she stared down at the child, her heavy black veil concealing her face, her hands in black gloves, with her children sitting in mute anguish beside her.

Nicholas had stood beside her at the funeral, a tiny man holding her arm, his own eyes filled with tears as the choir sang the agonizingly sweet "Ave Maria." But there were others like him who had died in the past week, most by their own hand, but a few, like him, felled by the blow they couldn't endure. It wasn't fear, it was grief, but whatever it was, she had lost him.

"I don't know, sweetheart . . . I don't

know why . . . he had a terrible shock, and . . . he went to be in heaven with God." She choked on the words, as Nicholas watched her.

"Will he be with Uncle Nicky and Aunt Alix?" Nicholas asked quietly, and she looked at him. She had kept them alive for him, but to what end? What did it matter now? Everyone she had ever loved was gone . . . except her children. She pulled them close to her as she left the car, and hurried into the house ahead of the chauffeur. She had invited no one to the house, she didn't want to see anyone, didn't want to have to explain, to tell them anything. It was going to be bad enough to have to tell the children. She had decided to wait a few days, she had already told most of the servants that they were free to go. She was keeping only one maid and the nurse, she could cook for them herself. And the chauffeur was going to leave as soon as she sold the cars. He had promised to do everything he could to help her. He knew several people who had liked Clayton's Alfa Romeo and the Mercedes she used, and the Hispano-Suiza had been coveted by all. She only wondered if there was anyone left to buy them.

Old Sava came to her and licked her

hand as though she knew, as Zoya sat next to the fire in their bedroom, staring at the spot where he had died only days before. It seemed incredible that he was gone . . . that Clayton was no more . . . and now there was so much for her to do. She had called their lawyers the day after he died, and they had promised to explain everything to her.

When they did, it was grim. It was as bad as Clayton had feared, and perhaps worse. His debts were absolutely enormous and there was no money left at all. The lawyers advised her to try to sell the house on Long Island at any price, with everything in it. She took their advice, and they put it on the market for her. She didn't even go back to get her things. She knew she couldn't have faced it. Everyone was doing much the same thing, the ones who weren't committing suicide, or abandoning their homes in the middle of the night, to avoid bills and mortgage payments.

And it was Saturday before she could bring herself to face the children. She had been taking her meals with them, but she had been moving like a machine, moving from room to room, and speaking only when she had to. But she could hardly

think. There was so much to do, so much
to pack, so much to sell, and nowhere to
go once they sold it. She knew she had to
get a job but she couldn't even think of
that yet. She couldn't think at all as she
looked at them with anguished eyes. She
knew Sasha was still too young to understand, but she had to tell Nicholas and she
could hardly face the pain in his eyes as
she tried. In the end all she could do was
hold him close to her as they both cried for
the husband and father they had loved.
But she knew she had to be strong, as
strong as her grandmother had been for
her, their circumstances had been even
worse. She even thought of going back to
Paris with them, life might have been
cheaper there, but people had their own
troubles there too, and Serge Obolensky
had told her that there were now four
thousand Russians driving taxis in Paris.
And it would all be too foreign to them.
They had to stay in New York, Zoya decided.

"Nicholas . . . my love . . . we're going to have to move." The words seemed
wooden and strange as he looked up at her
with confused eyes.

"Because Papa died?"

"Yes . . . no . . . well, actually, because . . ." Because now we're poor . . . because we can't afford to live here anymore . . . because . . . "because these are going to be difficult times for us. We can't stay here anymore." He looked at her seriously, trying to be brave, as Sasha played with the dog, and the nurse quietly left the room in tears. She knew she would have to leave them now too, and it broke her heart to leave the children she had cared for since they were born. But Zoya had told her the day before. There was no hiding from it now.

"Mama, are we going to be poor?"

"Yes," she was always honest with him, "in the way I think you mean. We're not going to have a big house or lots of cars. But we're going to have the important things . . . except Papa . . ." She felt a lump rise in her throat, ". . . but we have each other, sweetheart. And we always will. Do you remember what I told you about Uncle Nicholas and Aunt Alix and the children when they took them to Siberia? They were very brave and they made kind of a game of it. They always knew that the important thing was to be together, and to love each other, and to be strong . . . and that's what we have to do now," the tears were running down her cheeks as she spoke, but Nicholas was looking at her solemnly, trying desperately to understand.

"Are we going to Siberia?" He looked intrigued for the first time and she smiled.

"No, darling, we're not. We're going to stay here in New York."

"Where will we live?" Like all children, he was interested in the simpler realities.

"In an apartment. I'll have to find a place for us to live."

"Will it be nice?"

She thought instantly of Mashka's letters from Tobolsk and Ekaterinburg, "We'll make it nice, I promise you."

And then with sad eyes, he looked at her again, "Can we take the dog?"

Her eyes filled with tears again as she looked at Sava playing with Sasha on the floor, and then back at him. "Of course we can. She came all the way from St. Petersburg with me." She choked on the words but she looked into his eyes reassuringly, "we're not going to leave her now."

"May I take my toys?"

"Some of them . . . as many as we can fit into the apartment. I promise."

He smiled, a little mollified, "Good."

And then his eyes grew sad again, thinking of his father and the fact that he would never see him again. "Will we go soon?"

"I think so, Nicholas." He nodded, and with a last hug for her, he took Sasha and the dog and they left the room, as Zoya sat on the floor, watching them go, praying that she would be as strong as Evgenia had been for her, and as she thought of her, Nicholas tiptoed slowly back into the room and looked down at her where she sat.

"I love you, Mama."

She closed her arms around him and tried not to cry, "I love you too, Nicholas . . . I love you so very, very much. . . ."

He bent closer to her then and pressed something into her hand without a word.

"What's this?"

It was a gold coin, and she knew how proud of it he was. Clayton had given it to him only a few months before, and he had showed it to everyone for weeks. "You can sell it if you like. Then maybe we won't be quite so poor."

"No . . . no, my love . . . it's yours . . . Papa gave it to you."

He stood very tall then, fighting back his own tears. "Papa would want me to take care of you." Zoya only shook her head, unable to speak, as she pressed the coin back into his hand, and holding him close to her, walked him back to his room.

Chapter 32

The Wrights had lost their money too. Cobina and her daughter had formed a supper club singing act, wearing frontier garb and funny hats. She and Bill were getting a divorce and the house on Sutton Place had been sold for almost nothing. Other women were selling their fur coats in hotel lobbies, and polo ponies were being traded for quick cash. Everywhere, Zoya saw the same kind of panic there had been in St. Petersburg twelve years before, but without the physical threat of the revolution.

Their own house on Long Island sold for barely more than the price of the cars kept there, and Clayton's attorneys told her to grab it. "Cholly Knickerbocker" reported fresh outrages almost daily. The column was actually written by a man named Maury Paul, and the fates he described now were beyond belief, society

ladies becoming waitresses and shopgirls.
Some remained unaffected by the crash,
but as Zoya looked around Sutton Place
now, it seemed almost deserted. Her own
servants were all gone, save the nurse who
had looked after the children. Sasha still
didn't seem to understand why Clayton
was gone, but Nicholas had grown
thoughtful and quiet, and asked Zoya constant questions about where they would
live, and when they would sell the house.
It would have driven Zoya mad, except
that she was so sorry for him. She remembered her own fears in Russia during the
revolution. His eyes were bottomless
green pools of pain and worry. And he
stood looking like a sad little man, as he
watched her pack her more practical
dresses in her bedroom. There seemed to
be no point taking her elaborate evening
gowns, all the Poirets and Chanels and
Lanvins, and Schiaparellis. She wrapped
those in bundles and gave them to the
nurse to sell in the lobby of the Plaza. The
indignity of it would have been crushing,
but she was too worried to care. They
needed every penny they could get to live
on.

And in the end, she sold the house with
the furniture Elsie de Wolfe had bought

for them, the paintings, the Persian rugs, even the china and crystal. It barely managed to cover Clayton's debts, and gave them enough to live on for only a few months.

"Won't we keep anything, Mama?" Nicholas looked around so sadly.

"Only what we'll need in the new apartment." She pounded the pavements for days, in neighborhoods she'd never seen before, and finally she found two small rooms on West Seventeenth Street. It was a tiny walk-up apartment, with two windows looking into the back of another building. It was small and dark and there was an almost overwhelming smell of garbage. For three days, she moved things in herself, with the help of the nurse and an old black man she hired for a dollar. They brought in two beds, and a desk, the settee from her boudoir, one small rug, and some lamps. And she hung the Nattier painting Elsie de Wolfe had recently brought them back from Paris. She dreaded bringing the children there, but in late November, the house on Sutton Place sold, and two days later, they tearfully kissed the nurse good-bye, and standing in the marble hall, Zoya watched her kiss Sasha as they all cried.

"Will we ever come back here, Mama?"

Nicholas looked at her, trying to be brave, his chin trembling, his eyes full, as he looked around for a last time. She would gladly have tried to spare him the pain of it, but she took his small hand in her own, and pulled her warm coat tightly around her, as she answered.

"No, darling, we won't." She had packed almost all their toys, and a box of books for herself, not that she could concentrate on anything now. Someone had given her Hemingway's *A Farewell to Arms,* but it had sat on her night table, unread. She could barely think, let alone read, and she was going to be busy, looking for a job. The money she'd gotten from selling the house would only keep them going for a few months, if they were lucky. Nothing was worth anything now, everyone was selling houses and furs and antiques and treasures. None of it was worth more than someone else was able to pay, and the market was glutted with once expensive objects that were now worthless. It seemed remarkable that there were others who were virtually untouched by the crash, as Cholly Knickerbocker continued to report their weddings and parties and dances. There were still people dancing at the Embassy Club every night, or at the Central Park Casino, to the music of Eddy Duchin. But Zoya felt as though she would never dance again, as she and the children walked down their front steps for a last time with their suitcases, and Sasha's best doll tucked under her arm. And as though it had happened only the day before, she could think of nothing but the burning of the Fontanka Palace . . . her mother's nightgown in flames as she leapt from the window . . . and Evgenia hurrying her out the back door of the pavilion to Feodor and the waiting troika.

"Mama? . . ." Sasha had been talking to her as they got into the taxi, and Nicholas waved at the nurse who stood crying on the sidewalk. She was going to stay with friends, and had already had an offer of a job from the Van Alens in Newport. "Mama . . . answer me . . ." Sasha tugged at her sleeve insistently as Zoya gave the driver their new address, her eyes dull, her face wooden. She felt as though she were leaving Clayton again . . . the house they had shared . . . the life that had always been so easy. Ten years gone like the blink of an eye, an eye filled with tears now, as she longed for him again. She sat back against the seat and closed her eyes in pain, trying to concentrate on her children.

"I'm sorry, Sasha . . . what did you say?" Her voice was a whisper as they left Sutton Place for the last time. Gone the beauty and the easy life that had ended so abruptly on that fateful day in October.

"I said who is going to take care of us now?" She wasn't so much pained by the loss of her nurse, as she was curious about who would take care of her. It was all very strange and confusing, even for Nicholas, who was four years older.

"I am, sweetheart."

"You are?" Sasha looked amazed, and Nicholas looked at his mother with the gentle smile that always reminded her of Clayton. It was almost painful to see it now. Everything was a constant reminder of all they had lost, just as it had been in the days when they had first left Russia.

"I'll help you, Mama," Nicholas said proudly, holding his mother's hand and trying not to cry. "I'll take care of you and Sasha." He knew it was what his father would have wanted of him, and he wouldn't let him down now. He was the man of the family suddenly. In one short month, his whole safe, happy world had been turned upside down, but he was determined to rise to the occasion, as was Zoya. She refused to be beaten once again. She would fight for them . . . she would work . . . and one day . . . one day . . . they would be safe and warm again. She wouldn't let her life end in defeat, like so many others.

"Will you cook for us, Mama?" Sasha asked as she took her doll from her mother and smoothed the hair. Her name was Annabelle, and she looked well loved. Her other dolls were waiting in the new apartment. Zoya had done everything she could to make the place look cozy and familiar, but there was nothing familiar to them about the ugly surroundings as the taxi stopped on West Seventeenth Street. Zoya shuddered as she looked around again, struck more than ever by how dismal it was, and Nicholas's face registered shock as he followed his mother up the stairs, and tried not to feel sick from the awful smells.

"Eghh . . . this smells ugly," Sasha said as she walked up the stairs behind Zoya. The driver carried their bags for them, and Zoya paid him from their meager funds. She vowed to herself not to take any more taxis. They would travel on buses now, or walk. There would be no

more taxis, no more cars. She had sold the
Hispano-Suiza to the Astors.

Zoya showed them into the apartment's
single bedroom, and their two beds were
there, dwarfing everything else. Their
toys were arranged neatly beside them,
and the paintings from Sasha's nursery
had been carefully hung over her bed.
Next to Nicholas's she had put a picture of
Clayton, looking handsome in his uniform
during the war. She had brought a suitcase
filled with photographs of her own, of
Clayton, and the children, and others that
were yellowing and frayed, of Nicky and
Alix, and the children at Livadia and Tsarskoe Selo. She had also brought the treasured imperial egg, it was carefully rolled
into a pair of Clayton's socks. She had
brought a box of his cuff links and studs as
well, but her own jewelry was going to be
sold at auction. For those who still had
money, there were fantastic opportunities
everywhere, diamond necklaces and ti-
aras and incredible emerald rings, picked
up for pennies in auctions or at private
sales. One family's desperation would suddenly become another's good fortune.

"Where will you sleep, Mama?" Nicholas looked worried again as he walked
around the apartment, and realized there

was only one bedroom. He had never seen quarters so small, even their servants on Sutton Place had had nicer rooms than these. The whole place looked so tiny and so ugly.

"I'm going to sleep here on the settee, my love. It's very comfortable." She smiled at him, and bent to kiss his cheek as she saw tears come to his eyes. It wasn't fair, having to do this to the children, and she fought back a wave of the anger she had recently begun to feel for Clayton. Others had been wiser than he, less daring, and less foolish than he had been in risking all they had. And if only he had lived, they might have survived it differently . . . the two of them . . . they could at least have raged at the fates, side by side, but now she was alone as she had never been before. It all rested on her shoulders now, as she realized it must have rested on Evgenia's. And how brave she had been, how strong, it served as an example to Zoya now, as she looked at her son with a gentle smile, as he offered her his bed in the room he was to share with his sister.

"You can have my bed, Mama. I will sleep here."

"No, darling . . . I'll be fine." And then

with a brave smile, "We all will. Now, you must watch Sasha for me while I cook dinner."

She hung up their coats and her own, glad that she had brought warm clothes for them. The apartment was cold and there wasn't even a fireplace as there had been in the apartment in Paris.

"Why don't you take Sava for a walk?" The old dog was sitting quietly by the door, as though waiting to be taken home again, as they all were.

Nicholas put her on the leash, and told Sasha to be good while he went downstairs and their mother cooked them the chicken she had brought from the house on Sutton Place. But she knew only too well that the provisions they had brought wouldn't last long, nor would their money.

Christmas was a day like any other, except for the doll she bought Sasha and the pocket watch she'd saved from Clayton's things to give Nicholas. They huddled together as they bravely tried not to cry, and think of the enormity of their losses. The apartment was freezing cold, the cupboards were bare, and Zoya's jewelry had gone at auction for pennies. She was determined to keep the imperial egg, but other than that, there was almost nothing left, and she knew she had to find a job soon, but the question of where haunted her day and night. She thought of working in a shop, but she didn't want to leave the children alone all day long. Sasha wasn't in school, and she couldn't leave her alone when Nicholas went to the public school nearby with the neighborhood children, most of whom were dressed in rags, and some of whom lived in shanties along the Hudson River. Shantytowns were springing up everywhere, filled with people who had once been stockbrokers and businessmen and lawyers. They cooked their meals in cauldrons on open fires, and they prowled the neighborhood at night, looking for food, and discarded items they could use. It broke Zoya's heart to see the children there, with their big hungry eyes and thin faces, their cheeks red from the cold, as they huddled near the fire to keep warm outside their shanties. It made the apartment seem like a haven in comparison, and she reminded the children of how much they had to be grateful for, almost daily. But even she had a hard time remembering that sometimes, as she watched their money dwindle, and began looking for a job in earnest. It would have to be something she could do at night, when the children were asleep, or at least safely at home. She knew she could trust Nicholas to take care of Sasha once he was home from school. He was responsible, and always kind to his little sister, sharing his games with her, helping her fix her toys, and talking endlessly about their father. The subject was still too painful for her, as she watched them and went back to the living room to cry silently, as she stroked ancient Sava. The little dog was almost blind now, and Nicholas had to carry her down the stairs, when he took her out into the bitter cold to walk her.

It was January when Zoya walked from West Seventeenth Street all the way to Sixth Avenue at Forty-ninth Street, with a wild scheme. She knew it was crazy, but it was all she could think of. She had applied at several restaurants, but the proprietors had seen too many other women like her. What do you know about being a waitress? they asked, she would drop their trays, break their plates, and be too refined to work the long hours for tiny wages. She had insisted that she could do it, but they had turned her away, and there was nothing else she knew how to do, except dance, but not in the ballet, as she had in Paris.

More than once, in desperation, she had even considered prostitution, others had turned to that too, but she knew she couldn't do it. The memory of Clayton was too strong and pure, he was the only man she had ever loved, and she couldn't bear the thought of another man touching her, even to feed her children.

Dancing was the only thing she knew, but she knew just as clearly that at thirty, she could not return to the ballet, after more than eleven years without dancing. She was still supple and lithe, but she was too old, and she felt a thousand years old, as she walked into the theater she had heard of. She had already been to the Ziegfeld and they had told her she wasn't tall enough. So there was nothing left but to try the burlesque halls. It was five blocks south of the Ziegfeld Theater. Not surprisingly, when she walked through the stage door, the theater was filled with half-dressed women, whom she tried not to stare at while she looked for someone she could talk to.

"Yeah?" the woman in charge said, amused, "you a dancer?"

"I was."

"With who?"

She swallowed hard, knowing she

looked too prim in her simple black Chanel dress. She should have worn something brighter and more racy, but she had sold all her evening clothes long since, and all she had were the somber, warm dresses she had salvaged from her closets at Sutton Place, the ones she knew she might have use for in the freezing cold apartment.

"I danced with the Ballet Russe in Paris. I trained in Russia before that."

"A ballerina, eh?" The thought seemed to amuse her beyond words, as Zoya stood quietly, her red hair pulled tightly back, her face without makeup. "Listen, lady, this ain't a retirement home for old ballerinas. This is Fitzhugh's Dance Hall!" She said it with fierce pride, and Zoya felt a sudden surge of fury.

"I'm twenty-five," she lied, "and I used to be very good."

"Yeah? At what? You ain't done nothing like this before, I'll bet." That much was true, but she was willing to do anything to save her children. She remembered suddenly her audition for the Ballet Russe thirteen years before in Paris.

"Let me try . . . just once . . . I can learn . . . please . . ." Her eyes filled with tears in spite of herself, as a small round man with a cigar walked past, glancing at her only briefly and then shouting at two men carrying scenery between them.

"Stupid jerks! You're gonna break that thing!" And then, in obvious annoyance he waved the cigar at the woman talking to Zoya. "Goddamn girls got the measles . . . can you beat that? I've got myself a bunch of old hoofers on my hands and they get sick like a bunch of goddamn kids . . . three of them out last week . . . seven more now . . . shit, what am I supposed to tell people paying good money to see the show? That they can watch a bunch of broads with spots waving their asses at them. I'd even do that if they'd come to goddamn work." He waved the cigar at Zoya and then beyond her, as though she didn't exist, and to him, she didn't.

Without waiting for him to address her directly, she spoke up for herself, "I'd like to audition for a job as a dancer." Her accent was slight now but still obvious, but neither of them recognized her as Russian. The woman had thought she was French, in her expensively cut black dress and her elegant airs. That was one thing

they didn't need at Fitzhugh's Dance
Hall.

"You a hoofer?" He turned to look at her
appraisingly but he didn't seem impressed.

"Yes." She decided to spare him the explanation.

"A ballerina," the other woman spoke
up with obvious disdain.

"You had the measles?" he asked her.
That was far more important to him with
ten dancers out sick, and God only knew
how many exposed and due to come down
with it in the ensuing weeks.

"Yes, I have," she murmured as she
prayed that she could still dance. Maybe
she'd forgotten everything. Maybe . . .

He shrugged, and stuck the dead cigar
back into his face. "Let her show you her
stuff, Maggie. If she can stand up and do
anything, she can stay till the others come
back." He left them then and the woman
named Maggie looked annoyed. The last
thing they needed was some fancy-assed,
pale-faced broad who thought she was too
good for a burlesque show. But he had a
point, with the others sick, they were in
big trouble.

"Okay," she said reluctantly, and then
shouted backstage. "Jimmy! Get your ass

out here and play!" A black man with a broad smile appeared and looked at Zoya.

"Hi, baby, what you want me to play?" he asked her as he sat down at the piano. And she almost laughed in nervous terror. What could she say to him? Chopin? Debussy? Stravinsky?

"What do you usually play for an audition?" she asked him, and he smiled into her eyes. It was easy to see that she was high-class white folks fallen on bad times, and he felt sorry for her, with her big green eyes and wistful smile. She looked like a kid as she stood there, and he wondered if she'd ever danced before. He had heard of others like her who'd gone to work in nightclubs, doing acts they made up themselves, like Cobina Wright and Cobina Junior.

"Where you from?" Maggie was momentarily talking to someone else as they chatted. And Jimmy decided that he liked her.

She smiled openly at him, still praying that she wouldn't make a fool of herself, but even the risk of that was worth it. "From Russia, a long time ago. I came here after the war."

And then he lowered his voice and glanced nervously over his shoulder. "You

ever danced before, baby? Tell me the
truth, while Maggie ain't listenin'. You can
tell Jimmy. I cain't help you if I don't
know if you can dance."

"I was in the ballet when I was young. I
haven't danced in eleven years," she whispered back, grateful for his assistance.

"My, my, my . . ." He shook his head in
distress. "The Fitzhugh ain't no ballet . . ." That was surely the understatement of the year, as two half-naked chorus
girls wandered past them. "Look," he said
to her in conspiratorial tones, "I'm gonna
play real slow, you just roll your eyes and
smile, hop around a little bit, shake yo'
bum and show yo' legs, and you gonna be
just fine. You got a costume with you?" But
he knew from the look in her eyes, that
she didn't.

"I'm sorry, I . . ."

"Never mind." And with that Maggie
turned her attention to them again.

"You gonna sit on your fat black ass all
day, Jimmy, or are we going to do an audition? Personally, I don't give a damn, but
Charlie wants me to see her do her stuff."
She looked malevolently at Zoya, as she
prayed that she wouldn't fail dismally. But
she followed his suggestions as he played
and Charlie, the director, wandered past

again, muttering as he watched her. He wanted her to hurry up so he could audition two new comedians and a stripper.

"Shit. Just what I don't need here . . . a lady." He said it like the ultimate insult, ". . . Shake your ass . . . there, that's it . . . let's see those legs . . . more . . ." She hiked up her skirt as she blushed and continued to dance as Jimmy rooted for her. She had beautiful legs, and the grace that had come from thirteen years of dancing had never left her. "What are you for chrissake?" The short fat man bellowed at her as she blushed, "A virgin? People don't come here to pray. They come here to watch broads dance. You think you can do that without looking like you just been raped?"

"I'll try, sir . . . I'll do my best. . . ."

"Good. Then be back here tonight at eight o'clock." Maggie stalked off in obvious disgust as he left, and Jimmy gave a cheer, and jumped up to give Zoya a hug.

"Hey, Mama! We did it!"

"I can't thank you enough," she shook his hand and her eyes thanked him warmly. "I have two children, I . . . we . . ." She was suddenly fighting back tears, as the old black man watched her, "I need the job very badly . . ." The tears spilled onto her cheeks as she wiped them away with embarrassed relief, unable to speak for a moment.

"Don't you worry. You gonna do just fine. See you tonight." He smiled and went back to the card game he'd been losing when Maggie called him.

Zoya walked all the way home to the apartment, and thought about what she'd done. Unlike her audition with the Ballet Russe years before, there was no feeling of victory and achievement. Just relief that she had a job and an overwhelming sense of embarrassment and degradation, but it was the only thing she could do, and it was at night, she wouldn't have to leave Sasha with people she didn't know. For the moment, it seemed like the perfect job, except that it was so awful.

She explained to Nicholas that night that she had to go out. She didn't say why or where she was going. She didn't want to have to explain to him that she'd taken a job as a chorus girl. The echo of Charlie's words still rang in her ear . . . "shake your ass . . . let's see those legs . . . what are you? A virgin? . . ." To their way of thinking, she was. At almost thirty-one years of age, in spite of the hardships in her life, she had always been protected from people like him, and the people she was going to dance for.

"Where are you going, Mama?"

"Out for a little while." She had already put Sasha to bed. "Don't stay up too late," she admonished and kissed him, hugging him for a moment as though she were about to go to her own execution. "Go to bed in half an hour."

"When will you be back?" He eyed her suspiciously from his bedroom door.

"Later."

"Is something wrong, Mama?" He was a perceptive child, and he was learning early about the cruel turns of fate that could change the course of a lifetime in a single moment.

"No, nothing's wrong, sweetheart." She smiled at him then. "I promise." At least they would have a little money.

But she was in no way prepared for what it would be like, the crude jokes, the vulgar girls, the sleazy costumes, and the comedians who pinched her behind as she hurried past them. But when the music began, and the curtain went up, she did her best for the jeering, laughing, excited crowd, and no one complained when she was out of step more than once. Unlike the Ballet Russe of long ago, here no one knew the difference. All they wanted to see was a good show of gams, and a bunch of pretty girls with most of their clothes off. There were sequins and beads, little satin shorts, and matching hats, and countless feather boas and huge headdresses. It was a cheap imitation of what the Ziegfeld girls wore, and more than once she silently bemoaned her fate at having been too short to be hired by the kindly Florenz Ziegfeld. Zoya gave her costumes back to the girl who had lent them to her, and she walked slowly home, with her stage makeup still on. She was even more shocked when a man scurrying past, offered her a nickel for "the best she could do for him," in a nearby doorway. She ran the rest of the way home, with tears streaming down her face, thinking of the awful life that lay ahead of her at Fitzhugh's Dance Hall.

Nicholas was sound asleep when she got back and she kissed him gently, her lipstick smearing his cheek as she cried, thinking how sweet he looked as he slept, and how much like his father. It wasn't possible that he was gone . . . that he had left her to this . . . if only he had known . . . if only . . . but it was too late for that. She tiptoed back into the living room where she slept, took her makeup off and changed into her nightgown. Gone the silks and satins and laces. She had to wear heavy flannel gowns against the bitter cold of the barely heated apartment.

And in the morning, she made Nicholas breakfast before he left for school. There was a glass of milk, a slice of bread, and a single orange she had bought the day before, but he never complained. He only smiled at her and patted her hand, and hurried off to school, after kissing Sasha.

And that night she went back to the theater again, as she did for the next weeks until the dancers returned from their measles. But when they did, Charlie gruffly told her they'd keep her on, she had good legs, and she didn't give him any trouble. Jimmy bought her a beer to celebrate, purloined from his favorite speakeasy nearby. She thanked him and took a sip not to hurt his feelings. She didn't tell him that it was her thirty-first birthday.

He was always kind to her, the only friend she had there. The others had sensed instantly that she was "different." They never shared their jokes with her, in fact they barely talked to her, as they told tales of their boyfriends, and the men who

followed them backstage. More than one
of them ran off with men who offered
them a little money. It was what Charlie
liked about her. She wasn't much fun to
have around, but at least she was steady.
They gave her a raise after the first year.
She couldn't believe herself that she had
stayed that long, but there was no way out,
nowhere else to go, and no one who would
pay her. She told Nicholas that she danced
with a small ballet and she left the theater
number with him in case anything happened. But she thanked God he never
called her. And sensing that she was
ashamed of what she did, he never asked
to go to a performance. And for that, and
all his little tendernesses toward her, she
was always grateful. One night Sasha had
woken up with a cough, and a fever, and
Nicholas was waiting up for her, but he
hadn't wanted to call her at the theater
and worry her. In every way, he was a
help to her and an enormous comfort.

"Will we ever see our old friends
again?" he asked her quietly one afternoon, as she cut his hair, and Sasha played
with Sava.

"I don't know, sweetheart." She'd had a
letter from their nurse months before. She
was happy with the Van Alens, and she

had been full of tales of Barbara Hutton's debut the summer before, and Doris Duke's in Newport. It seemed ironic that she was still part of that world, and Zoya wasn't. But just as they had shunned her when she first arrived, convinced that she had been a dancer at the Folies-Bergère, now she shunned them, knowing that she was at last what they had first thought, a chorus girl. She knew also that, having lost everything like so many others of their milieu, she was no longer of interest to them. The countess she had been, who had so impressed them once, was no more. She was no one now. Just a common dancer. The waters had closed over her. She was gone. Just like Clayton, and so many others. The only one she missed from time to time, was Serge Obolensky, and his coterie of noble Russians. But they couldn't possibly have understood what had become of her life, or why she did what she did. He was still married to Alice Astor.

Elsa Maxwell was writing a society column by then, and occasionally when Zoya read the newspapers, she read Cholly Knickerbocker's tales of the people she had known while she was married to Clayton. They all seemed so unreal to her now, almost as though she had never known them. There were stories of financial ruin, suicides, marriages, divorces. She was only grateful not to be listed among them. She read also of Pavlova's death of pleurisy in The Hague. And in May, she took the children to see the opening of the Empire State Building. It was 1931 by then, and a beautiful May afternoon. Nicholas stared in awe at the imposing structure. They went up in the elevator and stood on the observation platform on the hundred and second floor, and even Zoya felt as though she were flying. It was the happiest afternoon they had spent in a long time, and they walked back to the apartment in the balmy spring air, as Sasha ran ahead of them laughing and playing. She was six years old by then, and had a beautiful head of strawberry-gold curls, and a face just like Clayton's.

People were selling apples on the street as they walked past, and more than one woman admired the two beautiful children. Nicholas was going to be ten in August, but long before that, the city lay crushed by the oppressive heat. And the second of July was the hottest day ever recorded. Both children were still awake when she left for work, in a white cotton

dress, embroidered with little blue flowers. Nicholas knew that she worked, but
he still didn't understand where, and
somehow it didn't seem important.

She left a pitcher of lemonade for them,
and reminded Nicholas to watch Sasha.
The windows were wide open in the hope
of bringing some air into the furnace-like
apartment.

"Don't let her sit too close to the windows," Zoya warned, and watched Nicholas pull the golden-haired child back into
their bedroom. She was wearing only a
slip and bare feet and looked angelic as
she waved good-bye to her mother. "You'll
be all right?" she asked, as she always did,
when she left them, her heart aching at
having to leave them at all, and her heart
heavy as she walked uptown to the theater. She could hardly move in the torrid
heat, even at night the street seemed to
steam beneath her feet, and the holes in
her shoes made it even more uncomfortable to walk. She wondered where it
would all end sometimes, how they would
survive, how long she could go prancing
around on the stage in her plumes and
ridiculous costumes.

The performance was poorly attended
that night, it was too hot to go anywhere.

The people who still could had retreated
to Newport and Long Island, and the others were languishing at home in the heat,
or sitting on stoops, hoping it would break
soon. She was exhausted when she finally
walked home again, and she thought nothing of it as she heard the sirens in the distance. It was only when she neared her
street that she smelled the acrid smoke,
and then her whole body shook as she saw
the fire engines and what looked like the
entire block in flames as she turned the
corner. She gasped in horror as she began
to run, and an icy hand seemed to clutch
her throat as she saw the fire engines outside their building.

"No! . . . no! . . ." She was crying as
she tried to force her way through the
crowds who stood in the street staring up
at the three buildings in flames. There was
smoke everywhere and she choked as she
pushed her way past, and was stopped by
the firemen at the door of her building.

"You can't go in there, lady! . . ." They
were calling to each other in the midst of
the fierce crackling sounds, punctuated by
terrifying crashing noises. There was glass
exploding everywhere, and her arm was
cut, and began to bleed on the white dress

as one of the men held her back forcefully. "I said you can't go in there!"

"My children!" she gasped . . . "My babies . . ." She was wrestling with him with strength she didn't know she had, and for a moment she escaped his grip and then he caught her again as she tried to run past him. "Let me go!" She swung at him, and he grasped her arms in his powerful hands, as the neighbors looked on in silent horror. "My children are in there . . . oh, God . . . please . . ." She was sobbing uncontrollably, almost overcome by the smoke that burned her eyes and her throat as he called to two of the men rushing back into the building. They had already brought out several old women, and a young man was unconscious on the street, while two firemen tried to revive him.

"Hey, Joe!" the fireman called to one of the others, and then turned quickly to Zoya. "Where are they, lady? Which apartment?"

"The top floor . . . a boy and a girl . . ." She choked in the smoke-filled air, she had already seen that their ladders didn't go past the third floor. ". . . Let me go . . . please . . . please . . ." She fell against him, as he relayed the information to the two men, and they hurried back into the building for what seemed like hours . . . as Zoya watched, knowing that if they died, her life would finally be over. They were all she had left in the world, all she cared about, all she had to live for. But the firemen did not emerge again, and three more went in, with axes and anxious faces. There was a terrifying crashing sound, and an explosion of sparks and flames as part of the roof caved in, and Zoya almost fainted as she watched it. Her eyes were filled with terror, and suddenly she darted forward, determined to find them, or die with them. She slipped past the firemen too quickly as she ran into the hall, but then, in answer to her prayers, she saw the firemen rushing toward her through the thick smoke, two of them with bundles in their arms, and she heard a child crying through the roar of the flames. She saw that it was Nicholas waving his arms, and crying out to her, as the third fireman swept her into his own arms, like a child, and the three men rushed from the building with their precious burdens, just as the fire reached out to engulf them. They barely reached the street before the whole building sounded as though it were caving in. There was a wall

of flames behind them as they ran, and
Nicholas clung to her, coughing and crying her name, as she kissed his face over
and over again and then she saw that
Sasha was unconscious. She knelt on the
sidewalk beside her child, moaning and
calling her name, as the firemen worked
desperately to save her, and then slowly,
with a small cry, she stirred, and Zoya lay
down beside her and cried as she stroked
her curls and held her.

"My baby . . . my baby . . ." She felt
it was her punishment for leaving them
alone every night. All she could think of
now was what it would have been like if
she had come home and . . . it was almost beyond thinking. She sat huddled on
the street, clutching her children, watching the building burn, as they cried and
watched everything they owned go with
it.

"All that matters is that you're alive,"
she said it again and again, remembering
the night her mother had died in the
burning of Fontanka Palace.

The firemen stayed until dawn, on another blistering hot day in July, and they
said it would be days before anyone could
go in. They would have to find somewhere
else to stay, and before even attempting to

go back to look in the ashes for whatever remained of their belongings. She thought of the photographs of Clayton that would be lost . . . the small mementos she had kept . . . the photographs of her parents, her grandparents, the Tsar . . . she thought of the imperial egg she had kept in case she ever needed to sell it, but she couldn't worry about any of it now. All that mattered was that Nicholas and Sasha were safe. And then suddenly, with a sharp pang of grief, she remembered Sava. The dog she had brought from St. Petersburg so long ago had died in the fire.

"I couldn't get her to come out, Mama . . . she was hiding under the couch when the men came in," Nicky sobbed. "I wanted to take her, Mama . . . but they wouldn't let me . . ."

"Shh . . . darling, don't cry . . ." Her long red hair had come loose from its knot as she fought the firemen to go in after her children, and it hung over her torn white dress with the blue flowers. There were streaks of ashes on her face, and Nicholas's nightshirt reeked of smoke. It was everywhere, but he had never smelled so sweet, or meant so much to her as he did then. "I love you so much . . . she was very old,

Nicky . . . shh . . . baby, don't cry . . ."
Sava had been almost fifteen, and she'd
come so far with them, but the only thing
Zoya could think of now was the children.

A neighbor took them in, and Zoya and
both children slept on the floor of their
living room, on blankets. No matter how
often they bathed or she washed their
hair, they still smelled of smoke, but each
time she looked outside and saw the
charred relic across the street, she knew
how lucky they had been. The sight of it
made her shudder.

She called the theater the next day, and
told them she wouldn't be coming to
work, and that night, she walked to the
theater to pick up her last paycheck. She
didn't care if they starved, she would
never leave them alone again . . . ever.

The paycheck would be just enough to
buy them some clothes and a little food,
but they had nowhere to stay, nowhere to
go, and with a look of total exhaustion, she
went looking for Jimmy to say good-bye to
him.

"You leavin' us?" He looked sad to see
her go, but he understood when she told
him what had happened.

"I can't do this anymore. If anything
had happened . . ." And it could happen

again. It was sinful to leave them alone. She'd have to find something else, but he only nodded. He wasn't surprised, and he thought it was just as well.

"You don't belong here anyway, Mama. You never did." He smiled. All of her breeding showed just in the way she moved, although she had never said anything to him about her past, but it always made his heart ache to see her doing high kicks with the others. "Get yo'seff something else. A good job with your own kind of folks. This ain't for you." But she had been there for a year and a half and it had paid the rent. "Don't you got no family or friends you can turn to?" She shook her head, thinking again how lucky she was to still have her children. "You got any place to go back to? Like Russia or something?" She smiled at how little he knew of the devastation they had left behind them.

"I'll work it out," she said, not really knowing what she was going to do.

"Where you stayin' now?"

"With a neighbor." He would have invited her to stay in Harlem, with him, but he knew that it wasn't right for her. Her kind of folks went to the Cotton Club to dance and raise hell, they didn't move into Harlem with an old piano player from a dance hall.

"Well, let me know how you're doin' sometime. Y'hear?" She leaned over and kissed his cheek and he beamed as she went to pick up her check, and he shook her hand warmly when she left, relieved at what she had done. It wasn't until late that night that she discovered it in her bag. Five crisp twenty-dollar bills he had slipped into her handbag when she went to get her check. He had won it in a hot card game only that afternoon, and he was just glad to have it to give to her. She knew it could only have been from him. She thought of hurrying back to the theater to give it back, but only she knew how desperately she needed it. Instead, she wrote him a grateful note, and promised to pay it back as soon as she could. But she knew she had to think fast. She had to get a job, and to find them someplace to live.

By the end of the week, their building had cooled sufficiently to allow the residents to go back in. There was precious little that anyone could save, and two apartments had been entirely destroyed, but as Zoya crawled slowly up the rickety stairs, she held her breath and wondered what she would find there. She opened the door gingerly, and tested the floor with a shovel as she moved around. The smell of smoke was still heavy in the air, and the entire living room had been destroyed. The children's toys were all gone, most of their clothes, and her own, but she knew that they would probably always smell of smoke. She packed their dishes in a box, charred black from the smoke, and she discovered with amazement that the suitcase of photographs was still there, untouched, it was something anyway. And holding her breath, she began digging in what had once been a chest, and suddenly there it was . . . the enamel was cracked, but it was otherwise intact. The imperial egg had survived, she looked at it in silent wonder, and began to cry . . . it was a relic of a lost life, several lifetimes ago. There was nothing else to save, she packed the remains of the children's things in a single box, her black Chanel dress, two suits, and a pink linen dress, and her only other pair of shoes. It took her only ten minutes to get it all downstairs, and then as she turned to look around for a last time, she saw Sava beneath the couch, lying there . . . quiet and still, as though she were asleep. Zoya stood silently, looking at her, and then softly, she closed the door, and hurried back down the stairs to take their boxes to the children waiting across the street for her.

Chapter 33

After thanking the neighbors profusely for their kindness, Zoya rented a small hotel room with some of the money Jimmy had given her. Less than half of it was left by the time she'd bought the children new clothes, and herself a decent dress that did not smell of smoke. And they had to eat in a restaurant every night. They talked about what they were going to do, as Nicholas looked expectantly at her, but as she read the newspaper one night, scanning it for jobs, she suddenly had an idea. It wasn't something she would have done if she had the choice, but she no longer had. She had to use the little available to her, even if it embarrassed her. The next day she put on her new dress, carefully combed her hair, and wished she had some of her jewelry left, but all she had was her wedding ring, and a certain regal air, as she stood quietly, looking at herself in the mirror.

"Where are you going, Mama?" Nicky asked as he watched her dress.

"I'm going out to get a job." She wasn't embarrassed this time, as both children stared at her.

"Can you do anything?" Sasha asked innocently, as Zoya laughed.

"Not much." But she knew clothes, she had worn the best for the past ten years, and even as a child, she and Marie had studied everything their mothers and other relatives had worn. She knew how to put herself together with style, and perhaps she could teach others to also. There were plenty of women who could afford that sort of thing. She took the bus uptown, after committing Sasha to her brother's care, and with a nervous heart, leaving them alone, she got off close to the address in the ad. It was on Fifty-first Street, just off Fifth Avenue. And when she reached the door, she saw that it was as stylish as she had hoped it would be. A liveried doorman stood by to assist ladies from their cars, and once inside she saw fashionable women and a few men gazing at the shop's expensive wares. There were dresses and hats, handbags and coats, and an incredibly beautiful line of handmade shoes. The salesgirls were well dressed,

and many had an aristocratic air. It was
what she should have done from the first,
she reproached herself, trying to block the
fire from her mind, and praying that the
children were all right. It was the first
time she had left them alone since that
night, and she would never again be sure
that they were safe if they were out of her
sight, but she knew that this was something she had to do. She had no choice
now.

"May I help you, mademoiselle?" a
gray-haired woman in a black dress asked
quietly, as Zoya looked around. "Is there
something you wished to see?" Her accent
was clearly French, and Zoya turned to
her with a dignified smile. She was trembling inside but she prayed it didn't show
as she answered in her own flawless
French, which she had spoken since her
childhood.

"May I see the manager, please?"

"Aha . . . how nice to hear someone
speak French." The older woman smiled.
She looked like a very well-dressed school-
mistress in a very elegant school for young
ladies. "I am she. Is there something you
wish?"

"Yes," Zoya spoke quietly, so no one else
would hear her. "I am Countess Ossupov,

and I am looking for a job." There was a long beat as the two women's eyes met, and then after an interminable wait, the Frenchwoman nodded.

"I see." She was wondering to herself if the girl was a fraud, but her air of quiet dignity suggested that she was what she claimed, and the Frenchwoman waved discreetly to a closed door just beyond her. "Would you care to come to my office, mademoiselle?" The title was unimportant to her, but she knew it might not be to the clients she served, Barbara Hutton, Eleanor Carson, Doris Duke, and their friends. She had an elite clientele, and titles meant a great deal to most of them. Many of them were marrying princes and counts, just so they could have titles too.

Zoya followed her into a beautifully appointed black and white sitting room. It was where she showed their most expensive gowns, and her only competition was Chanel, who had recently brought her wares to the States, but there was room for both of them in New York. The Frenchwoman's name was Axelle Dupuis, she had come from Paris years before, and had set up the elegant salon known only as "Axelle." But it had already been the rage in New York for several years. Zoya had even bought a gown there herself once but she had of course not used her Russian name, and mercifully Madame Dupuis seemed not to remember her.

"Have you any experience at this?" She looked Zoya over carefully. The dress she wore was cheap, and her shoes were worn, but the graceful hands, the way she moved, the way she wore her hair, all spoke of someone who had seen better times. She was articulate, and she spoke French, not that it mattered so much here. And she seemed to exude an innate sense of style, even in the inexpensive dress. Axelle was intrigued. "Have you worked in fashion before?"

"No," Zoya was honest with her as she shook her head. "I haven't. I moved to Paris from St. Petersburg after the revolution," she could say the words now, worse things had happened since, and she had Nicky and Sasha to think of. For them, she would crawl on her hands and knees for this job, and she could read nothing in the woman's face as she quietly poured herself and Zoya a cup of tea. The silver service she used was extremely beautiful, the china, French. She had ladylike airs, and she watched Zoya carefully as she took a sip of the tea. Things like that mattered to her, her clients were the most elegant, the most elite, the most demanding women in the world, she couldn't afford to have them served by people with bad manners, crude ways, and as she looked Zoya over with sharp gray eyes, she was pleased.

"When you went to Paris, did you work in fashion there?" Axelle was curious about this girl. There was something unmistakably aristocratic about her every move, as Zoya squarely met her eyes.

"I danced with the Ballet Russe. It was the only thing I knew how to do, and we were very poor." She had decided to be honest with her, to a point anyway.

"And then?"

Zoya smiled sadly, as she sat very straight in her chair. "I married an American and came here in 1919." Twelve years before, it was hard to believe now. Twelve years . . . "My husband died two years ago, he was older than I," she didn't tell the Frenchwoman about everything they'd lost. It was unimportant now, and she wanted to save Clayton's dignity, even in death. "I have two children to support, and we just lost everything we had in a fire . . . not that there was much . . ." Her voice drifted off, thinking of the tiny apartment where Sava had died. She looked back into Axelle's eyes. "I need a job. I'm too old to dance anymore," she forced the images of the dance hall from her mind, and went on, "and I know something about clothes. Before the war . . ." She hesitated but forced herself to go on, if she was going to trade on her title, she would have to say something about that. "In St. Petersburg, the women were elegant and beautiful. . . ." She smiled, as Axelle watched.

"Are you related to the Romanovs?" So many minor Russians had made that claim, but something about this girl told her it might be possible. She was prepared to believe anything, as Zoya's green eyes met her own, and she spoke in her gentle voice, primly holding the cup of tea like a lady.

"I am a cousin of the late Tsar, madame." She said nothing more, and for a long moment Axelle thought. She was worth a try. She might be just what her clients wanted, and how they loved countesses! The idea of a countess serving them would excite them beyond words, Axelle knew.

"I could give you a try, mademoiselle . . . Countess, I suppose I should say. You must use your title here."

"Of course." Zoya tried to look calm, but she wanted to shout with glee, like a child . . . she was going to have a job! At Axelle's! It was perfect. The children would both be in school in the fall, and she would be home by six o'clock every night. It was respectable . . . it was perfect . . . she couldn't repress a smile of relief as Axelle smiled at her. "Thank you, madame. Thank you so very much."

"Let's see how you do." She stood up to indicate that the audience had come to an end, and Zoya quickly followed suit, carefully setting the teacup down on the tray, as Axelle watched, extemely pleased.

"When would you like to start?"

"How would next week be?"

"Perfect. Nine o'clock. Sharp. And, Countess," she said the word with practiced ease as she looked at Zoya's dress, "perhaps you'd like to select a dress to wear before you go . . . something black or navy blue . . ." She thought of her beloved black Chanel which hadn't recovered from the fire. It still reeked of smoke, no matter what she did to it.

"Thank you very much, madame."

"Not at all." She inclined her head grandly, and swept back through the door into the main room of the shop, where a

woman in a huge white hat was ex-
claiming over the shoes. It reminded Zoya
that she would have to buy new shoes,
with the little money they had left, and
she suddenly realized that she had forgotten to inquire about the salary, but it
didn't matter now. She had a job, at any
price. It was a lot better than selling apples on the street.

She announced the news to the children
as soon as she got back, and they went for
a walk in the park, and then went back to
their hotel to escape the heat. Nicholas
was as excited as she, and Sasha inquired
with her big blue eyes if they had little
girls' dresses there too.

"No, my love, they don't. But I'll buy
you a new dress as soon as I can." She had
bought them the bare minimum after the
fire, just as she had for herself, but now a
new day had dawned. She had a respectable job, hopefully she'd earn a decent
wage. She would never have to dance
again. Life was looking up. And then suddenly, with a smile, she wondered if she
would see any of her old friends at Axelle's. Just as they had snubbed her, when
she'd first come from France, and then
fallen in love with her. They had forgotten
her completely when Clayton died, and

shunned her entirely when they lost everything. How fickle people were, not that she cared. She had her children, that was all she cared about. The rest had come and gone, and come again, and gone again. It didn't matter to her anymore. Just so they survived . . . life suddenly seemed infinitely precious to her again.

Chapter 34

Her days at the shop were tiring and long, the women she served demanded a great deal. They were impetuous and spoiled, some of them were unable to make up their minds, but she was always patient with them, and she found that she had a good eye for what suited them. She was able to take a gown, pull it there, tuck it here, and suddenly the woman seemed to bloom as she looked at herself in the mirror . . . she was able to pick the perfect hat to go with just the right suit . . . a bunch of flowers . . . a little fur . . . the exceptionally lovely shoes. She created images that became poetry, and her employer was more than pleased with her. By Christmas, Zoya had made a real niche for herself at Axelle's, she had outsold everyone, and everyone asked for the Countess when they came in. It was Countess this, Countess that . . . and don't you think, Countess . . . and oh, Countess, please . . . Axelle watched her perform, always with discretion and a dignified air, her own clothes put together perfectly with quiet elegance, her white gloves immaculate when she came to work, her hair impeccably done, her faint accent adding to her mystery. And Axelle let it be known early on that she was a cousin of the Tsar. It was exactly what she needed for the shop, and when Serge Obolensky came in to see this "Countess" everyone was talking about, he looked at her, stunned, as tears filled her eyes.

"Zoya! What are you doing here?"

"Keeping amused." She said nothing about the brutally hard two years she had survived.

"How silly of you! But rather fun perhaps, too, I suppose. You must come to dinner with us." But she always declined. She no longer had the clothes, or the time, or even the energy to run with his crowd. That was over for her. She went home to her children every night, waiting for her in the apartment on Thirty-ninth Street, near the East River, that she had been able to move into in time for Christmas. They were both in decent schools, and the regular raises and commissions Axelle had been giving her did not allow them room for luxuries, but it was enough to keep them comfortable, which was a vast improvement over the previous two years when she was dancing at Fitzhugh's Dance Hall.

She had been working for Axelle when the Lindbergh baby was found killed in May of 1932, and she read with surprise that Florenz Ziegfeld had died in July of the same year. She wondered what it would have been like to work for him and not Fitzhugh's Dance Hall. She wondered too what had happened to Jimmy by then. She had long since sent him the hundred dollars he had slipped into her bag when she was so desperate, but she had never heard from him again. He was part of another life, another chapter closed, as she went on working as the Countess at Axelle's. And she was particularly touched when Eleanor Roosevelt came to see her to buy some clothes during the campaign. She remembered Clayton's old friends with warmth, and sent them a telegram when Franklin won, and she sent Eleanor a lovely fur hat, which she said she would wear at the inauguration in January, and Axelle was thrilled with her.

"You certainly have a way with them,

ma chère." The elegant Frenchwoman
beamed at her. She was fond of the girl,
and she was enchanted by little Nicholas.
He had the gentle ways of a young prince,
and the stories Obolensky had told her
one afternoon, of Zoya and the daughters
of the Tsar were easy to believe now. She
was an unusual woman, born at an unfortunate time. Had things happened otherwise, she might have been married to a
prince of her own, and living in one of the
palaces she had frequented as a child. It
seemed so unfair, but no more so than the
crushing depression that raged on. All except Axelle's customers seemed to be
starving that year.

At Christmastime, Zoya took Nicholas
to see the movie *Tarzan,* and he was
thrilled, and afterward she took him out to
tea. He was going to the Trinity School
and doing well there. He was a good stu-
dent and a bright child, and at eleven
years of age, he said he wanted to be a
businessman one day, like his Daddy had
been. Sasha wanted to be a movie star.
Zoya had bought her a Shirley Temple
doll, and she always carried it with her,
along with Annabelle, who had survived
the fire. They were happy children, in
spite of the difficult times that had hap-

pened to them. In the spring, Zoya became the assistant manager of Axelle's. It
meant more money and more prestige,
and allowed Axelle herself a little more
leisure time. Zoya convinced Axelle to let
Elsie de Wolfe redesign the shop, and business seemed to boom.

"God bless the day you walked in the
door!" Axelle grinned at her over the
heads of their excited customers the first
day they reopened after it was redone.
Even the mayor, Fiorello La Guardia,
came and business was even better than
before. She gave Zoya a mink coat as a
gift, and Zoya gasped as she looked at it. It
was made of ranch mink, and was intricately made, and it only added to her remarkable elegance as she took the bus
home to her children every day, and by
the following year she was able to move
into a new apartment with them. It was
only three blocks from Axelle's, and it was
convenient for her, the children each had
their own rooms now, Nicholas was twelve
by then, almost thirteen, and he was relieved not to have Sasha constantly under-
foot.

And two years later, on Sasha's eleventh
birthday, Axelle invited Zoya to go to
Paris with her, for her first buying trip.

Nicholas went to stay with a friend, and she hired a baby-sitter to stay with Sasha for three weeks, and she and Axelle set sail on the *Queen Mary* in a flurry of excitement and champagne. As Zoya stood looking at the Statue of Liberty as they pulled slowly out of New York, she thought about how far she had come in the years since Clayton had died. It had been seven years. She was thirty-seven years old, and she felt as though she had already lived several lifetimes.

"What are you thinking about, Zoya?" Axelle had been watching her, standing quietly by the rail as they reached the open seas. She was beautifully dressed in an emerald-green suit, the color of her eyes, and a little fur hat set rakishly on her head, and as she turned to face her employer her eyes were almost the same color as the sea.

"I was thinking about the past."

"You do too much of that, I suspect," Axelle said quietly, she had great respect for her, and often wondered why she didn't go out more. She certainly had ample opportunity. Their clients were crazy about her, and there was always a stack of invitations on Zoya's desk, addressed simply to "Countess Zoya," but she seldom went out, and always said she had "done all that before." "Maybe Paris will put some new excitement in your life." Zoya only laughed, and shook her head.

"I've had enough excitement in my life, thank you very much." Revolutions and wars, and marriage to a man she had adored. She was still in love with Clayton after all those years, and she knew that seeing Paris again would be painful without him. He was the only man she had ever loved, and she knew there would never be another man like him . . . except her son perhaps . . . she smiled at the thought, and took a deep breath of the sea air. "I'm going to Paris to work," she announced briskly to Axelle, and then laughed at the older woman's words.

"Don't be so sure, my dear." They walked back to their stateroom then, as Zoya unpacked, and set the photographs of her children next to her bed. She didn't need anything more than that, and never would again. She went to bed with a new book that night, and made a list of the clothes they were going to order in Paris.

Chapter 35

Axelle had reserved rooms at the Ritz, conveniently located on the Place Vendôme, and resplendent with all the luxury Zoya had all but forgotten. It had been years since she had taken a bath in a deep marble tub, just like the one she'd had in the house on Sutton Place. She closed her eyes, and lay luxuriating in the deep bathtub full of warm water. They were to begin their shopping the following morning, but that first afternoon, Zoya quietly left the hotel by herself for a walk, and was overcome by the memories as she wandered the streets and the boulevards and the parks she had once shared with Clayton. She went for a drink at the Café de Flore, and then, unable to stop herself, she took a cab to the Palais Royal, and stood silently in front of the building where she had lived with Evgenia. It had been seventeen years since she died, seventeen

years of good times and bad ones, and
hard work, and her beloved children. The
tears rolled slowly down her cheeks as the
memories of her grandmother and her
late husband overtook her. It was almost
as though she was waiting for him to tap
her on the shoulder as he had the night
they met. She could still hear his voice as
though he had spoken to her hours before.
The memories were overwhelming as she
stood there, and then, turning slowly, she
walked to the Tuileries and sat on a bench,
lost in thought, watching the children
playing in the distance. She wondered
what it would have been like to bring
Nicholas and Sasha up here, easier in some
ways than it was in New York, but there
her life moved at a brisk pace, and her
work at Axelle's had given her life new
purpose. She had been with Axelle for five
years by then, and it was exciting to be on
the buying end, instead of just waiting on
endless hordes of spoiled, demanding
women. She knew the women so well.
They were women she handled well,
women she understood, and had known
all her life. More than once, she was reminded of her own mother. And the men
liked Zoya too, she was just as capable of
dressing their wives, as she was of dis-

creetly outfitting the mistresses they brought there. No word of gossip ever escaped her lips, no unkind critique, merely good taste and interesting suggestions. Without her, Axelle knew the success of her shop would never have been as great. "The Countess," as everyone called her, added an unmistakable air of aristocratic chic to the lives of wealthy New Yorkers. But now, suddenly, she felt far, far from there. She felt young again, and at the same time sad, thinking of the new life that had begun for her when last she was in Paris.

As she took a taxi back to the hotel, her heart gave a little leap as she wondered if she might meet Vladimir Markovsky. She looked for him in the phone book that night at the hotel, but his name wasn't there. She suspected that he might have died by then. He would have been almost eighty.

Axelle invited her to dinner at Maxim's that night, but with a nostalgic look in her eyes, she declined and said that she was tired and wanted to get a good rest before they began their tour of the collections. She didn't explain to Axelle that her memories of Clayton taking her to dinner there would be too painful. Here, she constantly had to close the doors to the past. It seemed only a step from St. Petersburg. All of it was so close now. She wasn't half a world away anymore. She was right there, in the places she had discovered with Evgenia and Vladimir, the places Clayton had taken her to. It was almost too painful to be there, and she longed to get to work, so that she could forget the past, and delve into the present.

She called Nicholas that night, at his friend's, and told him all about Paris. She promised to take him there one day. It was such a beautiful city, and it had played an important role in her life. He told her to take care of herself, and that he loved her. Even at fourteen, almost fifteen now, he wasn't afraid to show his emotions. "It's the Russian in you," Zoya teased him sometimes, lately thinking of how much like Nicolai he was at times, particularly when she heard him tease Sasha. Her call to her daughter was equally typical, Sasha had given her a shopping list of everything she wanted in Paris, which included a red dress and several pairs of French shoes. In her own way, she was as spoiled as Natalya had been, and almost as demanding. She wondered what Mashka would have thought of them, or what her own children would have been like, if she had lived to marry.

It was a relief to go to sleep that night, and escape the memories. The trip to Paris was far more difficult than she had thought it would be, and she dreamed of Alexis, and Marie, and Tatiana, and the others that night, waking at four in the morning, and unable to go back to sleep again until almost six. The next morning, she was tired when she ordered croissants and steaming black coffee.

"*Alors,* are we ready?" Axelle asked when she appeared at the door in a beautiful red Chanel suit, her white hair perfectly groomed, her Hermès bag over her shoulder. She looked suddenly very French again, and Zoya wore a blue silk dress and matching coat, made by Lanvin. It was the color of the sky, and her red hair was tied in a chic knot. They looked very Parisian, as the doorman assisted them into a cab, and Zoya smiled as she recognized the driver's accent. He was one of the countless elderly Russians who were still driving taxis in Paris, but when she asked him if he knew Vladimir, he only shook his head. He didn't remember hearing the name, or ever meeting him. It was the first time in years that Zoya had spoken Russian. Even with Serge Obolensky, she spoke French. And Axelle listened to the musical lilt of the words, as they drew up outside Schiaparelli's studios on the rue de la Paix. They had agreed to make it their first stop, and Zoya and Axelle went wild there. They ordered dozens of different sweaters for the shop, and had a long conversation with the designer herself, explaining the needs and preferences of their clientele. She was an interesting woman, and they were intrigued to find that she was only three years older than Zoya. She was enjoying a remarkable success at the time, almost as great as Gabrielle Chanel, still on the rue Cambon. They went there next, and later that day to the house of Balenciaga, where Zoya selected several evening gowns, and tried them on herself to see how they moved, how they worked, how they felt, as Axelle watched her.

"You should have been a designer yourself," Axelle smiled at her, "you have an amazing feeling for the clothes."

"I've always loved pretty clothes," she confessed as she whirled in the intricately made creations of the Spanish genius. "Even as children, Marie and I used to look at the clothes our mothers and their friends wore," she laughed at the memory, "we were very nasty about the ones we thought had awful taste."

Axelle had been looking at the faraway look in her eyes, and asked gently, "Was she your sister?"

"No," Zoya quickly turned away, it was rare that she opened the doors of the past to anyone, least of all Axelle, with whom she maintained an air of business almost always, but this was all so close to home for her, almost too much so. "She was my cousin."

"One of the Grand Duchesses?" Axelle looked instantly impressed, as Zoya nodded. "What a terrible thing all that." They went back to business then, and the next morning they went to see Dior's sketches after dining in their rooms that night, and poring over the lists of what they had ordered, what they had liked, and what they still thought they needed. Some of it Axelle wasn't going to buy, but only wanted to see so that she could draw sketches for the dressmaker they used occasionally to copy someone else's designs. She was very skillful, and it allowed Axelle greater profit.

They met Christian Dior himself, a charming man, and Axelle introduced

Zoya with her full title. Lady Mendl was there that day, previously Elsie de Wolfe, and after they had left, she filled Dior in on the details of Zoya's life with Clayton.

"It's a terrible shame, they lost everything in twenty-nine," she explained, as Wally Simpson came in. Dior was a great fan of hers, and she arrived with her two pug dogs.

That afternoon, Zoya and Axelle went back to see Elsa Schiaparelli again, this time at her more luxurious showroom, built two years before on the Place Vendôme, and Zoya laughed at the amusing couch Salvador Dali had designed for her in the shape of a pair of lips. They talked about the sweaters again, and several coats that Axelle wanted to order. But they were rapidly reaching the limits of their budget. It all went too quickly, Axelle complained, and it was all so lovely. It was an exciting time to be involved in fashion in Paris.

Schiaparelli left them then, she had an appointment with an American coat manufacturer. Like Axelle, he was one of her better foreign clients, she explained, as one of Schiaparelli's assistants came and whispered to her in Italian.

"Will you excuse me, ladies? My assistant will show you the fabrics the coat can be ordered in, Mr. Hirsch is waiting in my office." She said good-bye to Zoya too, and the two women conferred at length with the assistant, and ordered the coat in red, black, and a dove gray that Zoya particularly liked. She always seemed to favor the more muted colors, just as she did in her own clothes. She was wearing a delicate mauve dress designed by Madame Grès that Axelle had let her buy at an enormous discount.

As they left the shop an hour later, they were followed by a tall, rugged-looking man with a shock of dark hair, and a face that looked as though it had been carved from marble by a master. They saw him again in the elevator of their hotel.

"I'm not following you. I live here too," he said, smiling at Zoya with a boyish look on his face. Then he reached out and offered a hand to Axelle. "I think you've bought a few things from my line. I'm Simon Hirsch."

"Of course," she smiled, seeming very French again now that she was here. Her accent even seemed to have gotten thicker. "I'm Axelle Dupuis," and she quickly remembered Zoya. "May I introduce the Countess Ossupov, my assistant."

It was the first time in a long time that Zoya had been embarrassed by her title. He looked like such a straightforward, pleasant man that she felt foolish putting on airs as she shook his hand. He had the powerful handshake of a man who ran an empire of his own, and he looked straight into Zoya's green eyes with gentle brown ones.

"Are you Russian?" he inquired as the elevator stopped on their floor, and she nodded, blushing faintly, a failing she had decided was destined to plague her for a lifetime.

"Yes," she spoke in a soft voice, admiring the way he walked. His room seemed to be right next to theirs, and he strode along the ample corridors, suddenly making them seem too narrow. He had the shoulders of a football player, and the energy of a boy as he walked beside them.

"So am I. My family is anyway. I was born in New York." He smiled, and the two women stopped at Zoya's room. "Have a good time with your shopping. *Bonne chance!*" He spoke in heavily accented French as he disappeared into his own room.

Axelle commented as they walked into Zoya's room, and they took their shoes off,

"God, my feet hurt . . . I'm glad we met him. He has a good line. I wanted to take a look at it again when we go back. We need more coats for next fall, and if we don't get everything here, we can buy a few models from him, if he gives us a decent price." She smiled and Zoya ordered tea as, once again, they went over the day's orders. They only had four more days in town, before they sailed back to New York on the *Queen Mary.*

"We really ought to be thinking more about hats and shoes," Zoya said pensively, as she closed her eyes and thought for a moment. "We have to give them more than just dresses and evening gowns and suits . . . that's always been our strength. The whole look they love so much."

"That's what you're so good at." And then out of the blue, as she looked at the pretty woman in the mauve dress, her hair unleashed from its knot and cascading down her back like a child's, "Handsome, isn't he?"

"Who?" Zoya opened her eyes in obvious confusion. She had been trying to decide if they should order their hats from Chanel to go with the suits, and if they should order some of her fabulous costume jewelry. Their clients had so many jewels of their own, she wasn't sure they'd understand the chic of what Chanel was doing.

"The coat man from New York of course. If I were twenty years younger, I'd have grabbed him." Zoya laughed at the image of the ladylike Axelle grabbing anyone. She could almost see the man flying into the room, tackled by Axelle, and she laughed at the thought again.

"I'd like to see you do it."

"He's so rugged-looking, and he has a nice face. I like men like that." He had been almost as tall as Clayton but much broader, but Zoya hadn't given him a thought since they'd left him. "I'll take you with me when I go to his showroom. Maybe he'll invite you out to dinner, after all you're both Russian." She was teasing, but not entirely. She had seen the way he had looked at Zoya, and the interest on his face when he heard the title.

"Don't be silly, Axelle. The poor man was just being polite."

"*Mon oeil!* My eye," she said, as she wagged a finger at Zoya. "You're far too young to act like a nun. Do you ever go out with anyone?" It was the first time she had dared to ask her, but they were far from home, and it was easier to ask personal questions here, away from the shop, and their clients.

"Never," Zoya smiled, looking strangely peaceful. "Not since my husband died."

"But that's awful! How old are you now?" She had forgotten.

"Thirty-seven. That's rather too old to act like a debutante. We see enough of those at the shop." She laughed easily and Axelle narrowed her eyes in friendly disapproval, as Zoya poured her another cup of tea from the usual silver tray. The luxuries of the Ritz were becoming pleasantly addictive.

"Don't be ridiculous!" she scolded, "at your age I had two lovers." She looked mischievously at her young friend, "Unfortunately, both were married." But one of them had set her up with the shop. It was a rumor Zoya had heard before but had never lent much credence to. Perhaps it was true after all. "In fact," she went on to add, "I see a very nice man in New York now. You can't just spend the rest of your life between the shop and your children. They'll grow up one day, and then what will you do?"

Zoya laughed, but she appreciated Axelle's concern. "Work harder. There's no room in my life for a man, Axelle. I'm at the shop till six o'clock every night, and then I'm busy with Sasha and Nicky until nine or ten. By the time I bathe, read the newspapers, and an occasional book, it's all over. I'd fall asleep in my plate if anyone took me out." Axelle knew how hard she worked, but she was sorry for her. There was an aching void in the younger woman's life, and Axelle wasn't even sure Zoya knew it.

"Maybe I should fire you, for your own good," the older woman teased, but they both knew there was no danger of that. Zoya was too important to her now. At last, she had found a safe harbor.

But the next morning, when they went back to Dior again, to discuss shoes this time, they ran into Simon Hirsch getting out of a taxi at the same time they did.

"We meet again, I see. I'd better be careful or you'll be selling the same coats I am!" But he didn't look worried. He cast an eye over Zoya again, this time in a bright pink linen suit that made her look almost girlish.

"No danger of that, Mr. Hirsch," Axelle assured him, "we've come back to discuss shoes."

"Thank heaven." He followed them in, and they met again on the way out, and this time all three of them laughed. "Maybe we should combine our schedules, just to save time and money on taxis." He smiled at Zoya, and then glanced at his watch. He was well dressed, with obviously handmade English shoes, and a very good-looking suit, and the watch on his wrist was one he had just bought at Cartier. "Do you ladies have time for lunch, or are you too busy?"

Zoya had been about to decline, when Axelle startled her by accepting. And without halting for a beat, Simon Hirsch hailed a cab, and gave him the address of the new George V Hotel.

"They do a very nice lunch. I stayed there the last time I was in Paris." He looked serious then, as they approached the hotel just off the Champs-Élysées. "I went to Germany then, it was only a year ago, but I'm not going back this time. It was extremely unpleasant." He didn't elaborate as they got out, and when they reached the dining room, the headwaiter took them to an excellent table. They ordered lunch and he asked Axelle if they were going anywhere else, but she said they only had time for Paris.

"I bought some beautiful fabrics in England and Scotland before I came, for my men's line. Beautiful goods," he said, as he ordered wine, and Zoya sat back quietly in her chair and watched him. "I won't set foot back in Germany though," he mentioned again. "Not with all this business with Hitler."

"Do you think he's really doing the things they say?" Zoya had heard about his hostility to the Jews, but she wasn't quite sure she believed it.

"I don't think there's any doubt. The Nazis have created an atmosphere of anti-Semitism that permeates the whole country. They're almost afraid to talk to you these days. I think it's going to lead to some very serious trouble." His eyes were quiet but angry, as Zoya slowly nodded.

"It seems difficult to believe." But so was the revolution.

"That kind of insanity always is. My family left Russia because of the pogroms. And now it's starting here, in a subtler way, of course, but not much. There's nothing very subtle about going after Jews," his eyes burned with quiet fire, as the two women listened. And then, as though to change the subject, he turned to Zoya with a quiet smile of interest. "When did you leave Russia, Countess?"

"Please," she blushed in embarrassment, "call me Zoya. In 'real life,' my name is Zoya Andrews." Their eyes met and held, and she looked away for a moment before answering his question. "I left Russia in 1917. Just after the revolution."

"It must have been a painful time for you. Did your family go with you?"

"Only my grandmother." She was able to talk about it now. It had taken almost twenty years for her to do that. "The others were killed before we left, most of them. And some a year later." He didn't realize she was referring to the Tsar, it never occurred to him that she was that well connected.

"Did you go to New York then?"

"No," she smiled pleasantly as the waiter poured their wine. It was a fine 1926 wine, which Simon had ordered. "We came to Paris. I lived here for two years before I married and went to New York with my husband." His eyes searched for the wedding ring, and saw with dismay that it was still on her finger, but Axelle noticed it too, and knew Zoya well enough to foresee that she wouldn't explain any further.

"The Countess is a widow," she provided helpfully, and Zoya shot her a look of annoyance.

"I'm sorry," he offered politely, but it was obvious that he was interested in the information. "Do you have children?"

"Two, a son and a daughter." She looked proud as she said it, and he smiled. "And you, Mr. Hirsch?" She was merely being polite as they waited for lunch, but Axelle looked very satisfied at the conversation. She liked him, and it was obvious that he was very taken with Zoya. "Do you have children too?"

"No," he smiled and shook his head regretfully, "Never married, and no children. I haven't had time. I've been building a business for the past twenty years. Most of my relatives work for me. My father just retired last year, I think my mother has finally given up. I think she figures that if I haven't married at forty, there's not much hope left. She used to drive me crazy. I'm her only son, only child, and she wanted ten grandchildren or something like that." Zoya smiled wistfully, remembering her earlier conversations with Mashka, talking about how many children they wanted. She had wanted six, and Mashka four or five, but neither of their lives had happened as they had expected.

"You'll probably marry in a few years and surprise her with quintuplets."

Simon Hirsch pretended to choke on his wine, and then looked amused. "I'll have to tell her that, or maybe it'll just get her started again." And then their meal arrived, delicate quenelles for Axelle, and quail for Zoya. He had ordered a steak, and apologized for his American palate. "Am I allowed to ask you ladies about your buying trip, or is that all very hush-hush?" Zoya smiled and glanced at Axelle who seemed very relaxed, and answered for her.

"I don't think we need have too many secrets from you, Mr. Hirsch, except perhaps about our coats." They all laughed, and Zoya told him about some of what they'd bought, particularly the sweaters from Schiaparelli.

"That new pullover she's doing is sensational," Zoya said, looking pleased. "And the shoes we ordered today at Dior are just lovely."

"I'll have to come and see it all when it arrives. Did you buy any of Elsa's new

Shocking Pink?" He had liked the color a lot and was planning to duplicate it in his line, and he wondered what Zoya thought of it.

"I'm not sure what I think of that yet. It's a little strong for some of our clients."

"I think it's a great look."

Zoya smiled, it was so odd to think of this rugged man, who looked more like a football player, discussing Elsa Schiaparelli's Shocking Pink, but there was no doubt that his coats were the best made in the States, and it was obvious he had an eye for fashion and color and he knew what he was doing. "My father was a tailor," he explained, "and his father before him. And he started Hirsch and Co., with his two brothers on the Lower East Side. They made clothes and coats for the people they knew, and then someone on Seventh Avenue heard about them, and started ordering goods from them, and my father figured to hell with that," he glanced apologetically at Zoya, who was too intrigued by the tale to care about his language, "he moved to Seventh Avenue, and opened a workroom there himself, and when I came into it I turned everything upside down, with something called fashion. We had some terrific fights over it, and when my uncles retired, I really got my hand into it, with English wools, and some colors that almost made my father cry. We got into ladies' coats then, and well, for the last ten years we've done pretty much what I thought we should from the first. It's a good look, particularly now that Pop has retired and I'm bringing in new designs from Paris."

"It's an interesting history, Mr. Hirsch," Axelle said. It was the kind of story that had built the success of their adopted country. "Your coats are beautiful. We've done very well with them."

"I'm happy to hear it." He smiled, he was a man at ease in his own skin. He was enormously successful, and he had done it all almost single-handedly. "My father swore I'd ruin the business. It was a real vote of confidence when he retired last year, and now he pretends he's not interested anymore. But whenever I go out, my tailors and cutters tell me that he sneaks in and patrols the workrooms." Zoya laughed at the image he created, and he turned to her again. "And you, Countess . . . sorry, Zoya . . . how did you get to Axelle's?"

"Oh," she laughed, feeling oddly at ease with him, and closer to Axelle than she

had before, "by a long, hard road." Her
face grew serious then. "We lost everything in the crash," she said it honestly,
and Axelle knew that much anyway.
"Overnight, we were destitute, our two
homes had to be sold, our furniture, my
clothes and furs, even our china." It was
the first time she had actually spoken of it
to Axelle, and she seemed at ease as she
said it. "I had two children to support, and
virtually no skills. I danced with the Ballet
Russe here in Paris, during the war, and
with another ballet company as well, but
in 1929, I was thirty years old, and a little
too old to join the ballet again." She
looked at them both with an amused
smile, and Axelle was in no way prepared
for what she heard next. "I applied to the
Ziegfeld Follies, but I wasn't tall enough,
so I got a job dancing in a burlesque hall."
Axelle's jaw almost dropped, and Simon
Hirsch looked at her with intense respect.
Not many women would have gone from
riches to rags so courageously, or admitted
that they'd worked in a dance hall. "That
must surprise you, Axelle. No one knows
that, not even my children. It was awful. I
worked there for a year and a half, hating
every minute of it, and one night," her
eyes still filled with tears at the memory,

"there was a terrible fire when I was at work, and I almost lost my children. They are all that matters to me, and I knew I couldn't leave them alone at night anymore, so I packed up what was left in two boxes, moved to a hotel, borrowed a hundred dollars from a friend, and knocked on Axelle's door. I don't think she ever knew how desperate I was," she looked gratefully at her friend, as Axelle tried to absorb what she had just heard, she wanted to cry just hearing it, "and I was very lucky, she hired me. And there I have been ever since, and always will be, I hope." She smiled at the two listeners, unaware of how much she'd moved them both, especially Simon, "And they all lived happily ever after."

"That's quite a story." He stared at her in open amazement and Axelle delicately dabbed at her eyes with a lace hankie.

"Why didn't you tell me then?"

"I was afraid you wouldn't hire me. I would have done anything to get that job. I even came to you and flaunted my title, something I'd never done before." She laughed good-humoredly then, "If I had, I'm sure they would have had me bumping and grinding as someone shouted from backstage, 'And our very own *Countess*!'"

All three of them laughed, but Zoya more easily than the others. The others were too impressed by the tale to laugh at her, and only Axelle knew how unkind people would have been if they had known Countess Ossupov had danced in a burlesque hall. "You do what you have to do in life. During the war here, some of our friends actually caught pigeons in the park and ate them." Simon wondered at what else she had lived through. The revolution had to have been a brutal blow, with all of her family killed before she escaped. There was more to her than met the eye, in her pretty pink linen suit. A lot more. And he wanted to know all of it. He was sorry to see the lunch come to an end, and he dropped them off at the Ritz on his way to see the representative from a French mill, from whom he was ordering more fabric.

He shook hands with Zoya as she stood beside the cab, and he watched her long and hard as he drove away, thinking of what an incredible woman she was. He wanted to know everything about her now, how she had escaped, how she had survived, what her favorite color was, her dog's name, her worst fears when she'd been a child. It seemed crazy to him, but in the space of one short afternoon, he knew he had fallen in love with the woman of his dreams. It had taken him forty years, but on an afternoon in Paris, three thousand miles from home, he had found her.

Chapter 36

Zoya saw their trip come to an end with regret. They had had a good time, and on their last night, they had dinner at the Cordon Bleu, and strolled slowly back to the hotel, as Axelle urged her to get a good night's sleep, and thanked her for all her help in selecting the fall line for the shop. She was still stunned at the story Zoya had told at lunch at the George V with Simon Hirsch several days before. It gave her fresh respect for Zoya's courage.

They hadn't run into him again, and Zoya wondered if he was still there. She had dropped him a note, thanking him for lunch, and wishing him luck on the rest of his trip, and they had been busy finishing their own business after that. They had bought the rest of the hats, and finally some of the jewelry at Chanel, and on the last day, Zoya had gone shopping for the children. She had actually found the red dress Sasha wanted, and she bought Nicholas a beautiful jacket, and a coat, some books in French, which he spoke beautifully, and a little gold watch at Cartier, which had reminded her of Clayton's. And she bought Sasha a lovely French doll, and a pretty little gold bracelet. Her bags were laden down with the things she'd bought for them, and already packed, in preparation for the trip back to Le Havre the next morning. But there was something she was planning to do that night, which she didn't tell Axelle. The next day was Russian Easter, and she had decided, after much debate, to go to midnight mass at the Russian cathedral of St. Alexander Nevsky. It was a decision that had been painful to make. She had gone there in the past with Clayton and Vladimir, and Evgenia. But she knew she couldn't leave Paris without going back once more. It was as though part of her was still there, and she wouldn't be free until she went back and faced it. She would never go home again, St. Petersburg was long gone for her, but this last piece of what her life had been had to be touched, and held, and felt one last time, before she could go back to New York and her children.

She bid Axelle good night, and at eleven-thirty, she was downstairs, and hailed a taxi. She gave the driver the address on the rue Daru, and when she saw it, she caught her breath . . . it was still the same . . . nothing had changed since that Christmas Eve long ago when she had gone there with her grandmother and Clayton.

The service was as lovely as she remembered it, as she stood solemnly with the other Russians, singing and taking part in the service, holding her candle high as she cried silently, missing all of them again, yet feeling them close to her. She felt sad, but strangely at peace as she stood in the cathedral afterward, and watched the others, chatting quietly outside, and then suddenly she saw a familiar face, much aged, and worn, but she was sure it was Vladimir's daughter, Yelena. She didn't speak to her as she left, she only walked quietly down the steps, and looked up into the night sky with a smile, wishing them well, the souls who had once been part of her life. . . . She hailed a taxi, and went back to the hotel, feeling older than she had in a long time, and when she went to bed she cried, but they were the clean tears of grief that time had healed, and was now only sometimes remembered.

In the morning, she said nothing to Axelle, and they took the train to Le Havre, and boarded the *Queen Mary*. Their cabins were the same as when they'd come, and Zoya watched as they set sail, remembering when she had gone to the States on the *Paris*, with Clayton.

"You look so sad . . ." The voice just beside her made her jump, and she turned to see Simon looking down at her gently. Axelle had stayed downstairs to get unpacked, and she had gone upstairs alone with her own thoughts. She looked at him with a shy smile. His hair was blowing in the wind, and he looked more rugged than ever.

"Not sad, just remembering."

"You've had an interesting life, I suspect even more so than you told us at lunch."

"The rest doesn't matter anymore." She looked out to sea without looking at him, and he longed to touch her hand, to make her smile, to make her feel happy and young. She was so serious, and just then, almost solemn. "The past is only worth what it makes of us, Mr. Hirsch. It was difficult to come back here, but I'm glad I did it. Paris is full of memories for me." He nodded, wishing he knew more about her life than the little she had told him.

"It must have been rough here during the war. I wanted to go too, but my father wouldn't let me. I finally enlisted but it was too late. I never left the States. I wound up in a factory in Georgia. A textile mill, of course," he smiled ruefully, "I seem to be destined never to escape the rag trade." His eyes grew serious again then. "But it must have been hard for you here."

"It was. But our fate was easier than those who stayed in Russia." She was thinking of Mashka and the others, and he was afraid to pry. He didn't want to frighten her away, and she looked so beautiful as she stood lost in her own thoughts and then smiled up at him. "None of that is important now. Did you have a successful trip?"

"I did. And you?"

"Excellent. I think Axelle is pleased with everything we ordered." She made as though to leave him then, and he wanted to physically pull her back to him before she could run away again.

"Will you have dinner with me tonight?"

"I'll have to ask Axelle what she'd like to

do. But thank you very much, I'll extend your invitation to her." She wanted to make it clear to him that she was not available. She liked him very much but he made her vaguely uncomfortable. There was something so intense about his eyes, his handshake was so strong, even the arm with which he guided her as the ship began to roll seemed too powerful to resist, and she had every intention of resisting him. She was almost sorry they were on the same ship. She wasn't sure she wanted to see that much of him. But when she mentioned his invitation to Axelle, she seemed thrilled.

"By all means, accept. I'll drop him a note myself." She did, and then horrified Zoya by announcing at the last minute that she felt ill from the rolling ship, and left Zoya alone with him in the dining room, which was not what she wanted. But within minutes, she had forgotten her hesitation, and found herself enjoying him. He was describing his year in Georgia, in the textile mill, he claimed that he couldn't understand anything they said with their heavy southern drawl, and finally, in revenge, he spoke Yiddish to them. She laughed at the thought, and she listened as he told her about his family.

His mother sounded almost as tyrannical as her own, although they came from very different backgrounds.

"Maybe all Russian women are the same," she teased, "although actually my mother was German. And thank God my grandmother wasn't like that. She was incredibly kind and tolerant and strong. I owe my life to her, in a great many ways. I think you would have liked her very much," she said over dessert.

"I'm sure I would." And then, unable to restrain himself, "You're an amazing woman. I wish I'd met you a long time ago."

She laughed at the thought. "Perhaps you wouldn't have liked me as much. Adversity has a way of humbling one, maybe I was too spoiled then," she was thinking of her days of ease on Sutton Place, "the last seven years have taught me a great deal. I always thought, during the war, that if my life ever got comfortable again, I'd never take it for granted again, but I did. Now, I appreciate everything . . . the shop . . . my job . . . my children . . . all of it." He smiled, each moment more in love with her.

"I want to know about your life before that, in Russia." They were strolling outside on the deck by then. The gentle pitching of the ship didn't bother her at all, and the night air was cool as she pulled her wrap close to her. She was wearing a gray satin evening gown, copied from a design of Madame Grès, by Axelle's little dressmaker, and a silver fox jacket she'd borrowed from the shop, but borrowed finery or not, she looked extremely beautiful as he looked down at her.

"Why do you want to know about that?" Zoya was intrigued. What could it matter to him? Was it idle curiosity or something more? She wasn't sure what he wanted of her, yet oddly, she felt so safe with him.

"I want to know everything about you, you're so full of beauty and strength and mystery." He was so earnest as he looked down at her and she smiled. No one had ever said anything like that before, not even Clayton, but she'd been so much younger then, barely more than a child. And she was so much older now, so much wiser than the girl she'd been then.

"You already know a great deal more than anyone," she smiled. "I've never told anyone about being a chorus girl before," and then she laughed, feeling young and mischievous again, "poor Axelle almost fell out of her chair, didn't she?" He laughed too.

"So did I," he confessed. "I've never known a burlesque dancer before."

She couldn't stop laughing then, "Think how pleased your mother would be!" He chuckled at the thought, as Zoya grew serious again, "I don't suppose she'd be very fond of me, in any case. If your parents left Russia to escape the pogroms, I doubt if they feel very kindly about the Russians."

"Did you know the Imperial Family as a child?" He didn't want to embarrass her by agreeing with her, but of course she was right. His mother spoke of the Tsar now and then as a hated figure, responsible for all their ills, his father was gentler about it, but not much. But he noticed then that she was looking quietly at him, weighing something in her mind, and then she nodded almost imperceptibly.

"Yes, I did." She hesitated for only a beat, "The Tsar and my father were cousins. I grew up with his children much of the time." She told him about Mashka then, the summers at Livadia, and winters at the Alexander Palace with them. "She was like a sister to me. It almost killed me when I got the news, and then . . . Clayton came . . . we were married just after that . . ." Her eyes filled with tears and he took her hand, marveling at how strong she was, how brave she had been. It was like meeting someone from another world, a world that had always fascinated and mystified him. He had read books about the Tsar, as a young man, much to his mother's dismay, but he had always wanted to know more about the man that he had been. And Zoya told him now, bringing him to life with all his gentleness and charm. It made him see another side of the Tsar than the one he was familiar with.

"Do you think there will be another war?" It seemed incredible that in her lifetime there should be two great wars, yet something told her that it was not impossible, and Simon agreed with her.

"I think there could be. I hope not." He looked serious as he said it.

"So do I. It was so terrible, so many young men killed. Paris was devastated twenty years ago, everyone had gone off to war. I can't bear to think of it again." Particularly now that she had a son of her own, and she said as much to him.

"I'd like to meet your children sometime."

She smiled. "They're funny—Nicholas

is very serious. And Sasha is a little bit spoiled. She was the apple of her father's eye."

"Does she look like you?" He was intrigued by everything, but she shook her head. "Not really, she looks more like him." But she didn't invite him to come and meet them in New York. She still wanted to keep a certain distance from him. He was so easygoing and so nice, but the extent to which she felt at ease with him frightened her, she didn't want to start anything with him.

He walked her back to her cabin next to Axelle's, and he left her at the door with a longing look she ignored. And the next day, when she took a walk around the deck with Axelle, he seemed to be waiting for them. He invited Zoya to a game of shuffleboard, invited them to lunch, which Axelle accepted before Zoya could say a word, and the afternoon seemed to fly by. They dined with him again, and Simon took her dancing that night, but he sensed that she was withdrawn and he asked her why as they strolled on the deck again afterward.

She looked up at his handsome face in the dark, and decided to be honest with him. "Perhaps because I'm afraid."

"Of what?" He was hurt. He meant her no harm. On the contrary.

"Of you." She looked up at him and smiled. "I hope that doesn't sound rude."

"Not rude. But I'm confused. Do I frighten you?" No one had ever accused him of that before.

"A little bit. Perhaps I'm more afraid of myself than of you. It's been a long time since a man took me anywhere, let alone to lunch and dinner and dancing on a ship." She was reminded of her trip on the *Paris* with Clayton again, but that had been their honeymoon. "There's been no one since my husband. And I don't want to change that now."

He looked stunned. "Why not?"

"Oh . . ." She seemed to think about it as they talked. "Because I'm too old, because I have my children to think of now . . . because I loved my husband so much . . . all of that, I suppose."

"I can't argue with your love of your husband, but it's ridiculous that you think you're too old. What does that make me? I'm three years older than you are!"

She laughed. "Oh dear . . . well, it's different for you. You've never been married before. I have. All of that is behind me now." She seemed sure of it, and he looked annoyed.

"That's ridiculous! How can you say a thing like that at your age? People fall in love and get married every day, people who've been widowed and divorced . . . some of them are even married . . . and some of them are twice your age!"

"Perhaps I'm not as interesting as they are," she smiled, and he shook his head with a rueful look.

"I warn you, I'm not going to sit back and accept any of that. I like you very much," he looked down at her with his warm brown eyes and she felt something in her stir that had lain dormant for years. "I don't intend to give up now. Do you have any idea what's out there for a man like me? Twenty-two-year-old girls who giggle when they talk, twenty-five-year-olds who are hysterical they haven't gotten married yet, thirty-year-old divorcées who want someone to pay the rent, and forty-year-old women who are so desperate they scare me to death. I haven't met anyone I was this crazy about in the last twenty years, and I don't intend to sit here and let you tell me you're too old, is that clear, Countess Ossupov?" She smiled at his words, and laughed in spite of herself, as he went on. "And I warn you, I'm a very stubborn man. I intend to pursue you if I have to pitch a tent outside Axelle's shop. Does that sound reasonable to you?"

"Not in the least, Mr. Hirsch. It sounds totally absurd." But she smiled as she said it.

"Good. I'll order the tent as soon as I get back to New York. Unless, of course, you agree to have dinner with me the night we get back."

"I haven't seen my children in three weeks." She laughed at him again. But she had to admit, she liked him a great deal. Perhaps he'd agree to being friends eventually.

"All right then," he compromised, "the day after that. You can bring your children along too. Perhaps they're more sensible than you are." He tilted her chin up to him and looked into the green eyes that had stolen his heart from the first moment he'd seen her at Schiaparelli's.

"Don't be so sure," she was thinking of the children as he spoke, "they're very devoted to their father's memory."

"That's a good thing," he spoke quietly, "but you have a right to more than that in your life, and so do they. There's only so much you can do for them. Your son needs a man around, and your little girl probably does too."

"Perhaps." She would concede nothing as he walked her home, but he took her by surprise as he kissed her gently on the lips. "Please don't do that again," she whispered with no conviction whatsoever.

"I won't," he said as he did it again.

"Thank you." She smiled dreamily up at him, and a moment later closed the door in his face, as he walked upstairs to his own cabin, with a grin on his face, like a schoolboy.

Chapter 37

The romance flourished in spite of her, as they sailed toward New York. They dined and they danced, and they kissed and they talked. And she felt as though she had known him all her life. They had the same interests, the same likes, and even some of the same fears. Axelle left them alone, and chortled to herself as she watched from afar, and on the last night, they stood on the deck and Simon looked sadly down at her.

"I'm going to miss you terribly, Zoya."

"I'm going to miss you too," she confessed, "but it's just as well." She was enjoying herself too much with him and she knew it had to stop, but she no longer remembered exactly why. It had all made sense several days ago, but it no longer did. She wanted to be with him, as much as he wanted her, and now they were going back to New York to lead their own lives again. "We shouldn't have started this, Simon," she said as he looked at her and smiled.

"I'm in love with you, Zoya Ossupov." He loved the sound of her Russian name, and still teased her now and then about the title she hated to use, but did for work.

"Don't say things like that, Simon. It will only make things more difficult."

"I want to marry you." He said it quietly, without a shred of doubt in his voice, as she looked up at him unhappily.

"That's impossible."

"No, it's not. Let's go home and tell the children we're in love."

"That's crazy. We just met." And she hadn't even let him make love to her yet. She was still frightened, and too bound by her loyalties to her late husband.

"All right. Then let's wait a week."

She laughed at him and he kissed her again.

"Will you marry me?"

"No."

"Why?"

"Because you're crazy," she laughed between kisses on the deck. "You might even be dangerous for all I know."

"I'll be very dangerous if you don't marry me. Have you ever seen a crazed

Russian Jew go berserk on an English ship? It could cause an international incident! Think of the people you'll upset . . . I think you'd better say yes. . . ." He kissed her again.

"Simon, please . . . be sensible. . . . You might hate me when you see me again in New York."

"I'll let you know tomorrow night. If I don't, will you marry me?"

"No!" It was impossible to be serious with him at times, and at other times he seemed to be able to look into her very soul.

He took her hands firmly in his then and looked down into her eyes. "I have never in my life ever asked a woman to marry me. I'm in love with you. I'm a responsible man. I have a business. My family thinks I'm very intelligent. I am begging you, Zoya . . . please, darling . . . please marry me."

"Oh Simon, I can't." She looked at him unhappily. "What would my children think? They depend on me entirely, they're not ready for someone to walk into their lives, and neither am I. I've been alone for too long."

"Yes, you have," he said quietly. "Much

too long. But you don't have to stay that way. Will you think about it?"

She hesitated, and then melted as she looked up at him. "I will . . . but that doesn't mean anything will ever come of it." But that was enough for him, they sat for hours, talking on the deck, and the next morning he knocked on her cabin door at seven o'clock.

"Come and look at the Statue of Liberty with me."

"At this hour?" She was still in her nightgown, and her hair hung down her back in a long braid as she opened the door to him. "What time is it?"

He smiled as he saw the nightgown and the braid. "It's time to get up, lazy face. You can get dressed afterward. Just put on a coat and some shoes." She slipped into the mink Axelle had given her several years before, and laughed as she put on high heels, and followed him onto the deck in her outlandish outfit.

"If any of my clients see me, they'll never trust my judgment again."

"Good. Then maybe Axelle will fire you, and I can save you from a terrible fate." But they both fell silent as they saw the skyline of New York and the Statue of Liberty as they sailed slowly in. "It's beautiful, isn't it?"

"It is." She nodded happily. She had paid homage to the past, and now she was looking at the future again. Everything here seemed new and alive, and just looking at it made her feel good again. He turned then and took her in his arms, and held her close as they docked, and then she hurried downstairs to dress and close her trunks. And she didn't see him again until they were ready to leave the ship. He offered them a ride, but they had to decline as Axelle had a car waiting for them. But he followed them down the gangplank, carrying their small bags, and suddenly Zoya gave a small shout and surged ahead. Nicholas was waiting for her on the pier, scanning the crowd, looking so handsome and young. She ran to him, calling his name, and he flew into her arms and held her close. He had come alone, after taking Sasha to school, and it was obvious how much she loved the boy. Simon watched them enviously as he assisted Axelle, and then he went to where Zoya stood with her son, and solemnly shook her hand and smiled at the boy. He would have liked to have a son just like him, particularly when he saw how like Zoya he was.

"Hello, I'm Simon Hirsch." He introduced himself as the boy looked up at him. "You must be Nicholas." Nicky smiled shyly at the man, and then laughed.

"How did you know?"

"Your mother talks about you all the time."

"I talk about her too," he smiled, slipping an arm around her, as Zoya told him he had grown. He was almost fifteen years old, and he was already as tall as Clayton had been. "Did you have fun?" He asked as they waited for her trunks, so the customs officer could inspect them.

"I did. But I missed you too much." She said something to him in Russian then, and he laughed, and Simon laughed too, as Zoya realized he had understood her. "That's not fair!" She had told him that his hair was too long, and he looked like a large lovably shaggy dog. But Nicholas was suddenly interested in Simon as they stood on the dock together.

"So you speak Russian, sir?"

"A little bit. My parents are from Vladivostok. My mother used to say things like that to me in Russian too, sometimes she still does." They all laughed, and a mo-

ment later the bags were checked, and
Axelle and Zoya were free to go, and as
they drove away, Simon stood watching
them, waving for a long time, as in the car
Nicholas asked his mother, in Russian
again.

"Who was that?"

"A friend of Axelle's. He happened to
be on the ship with us."

"He seems like a nice man." Nicholas
looked unimpressed.

"He is," Zoya said noncommittally, and
asked him how Sasha was.

"As impossible as she always is. Now she
wants a dog. A wolfhound, if you please.
She says they're 'all the rage,' and she's
going to drive you crazy till she gets one. I
think they're horrible. If we get anything,
let's get a pug, or a boxer."

"Who said we were going to get a dog?"

"Sasha did, and what Sasha wants, she
gets." Axelle smiled. They had switched
from Russian to French, when Zoya told
him not to be rude to Axelle.

"Is that so?"

"Isn't it?" Nicholas accused with a grin.

"Not all the time," she blushed, but he
was right, she was a very persistent child,
and sometimes it was easier to give in to
her, just to keep the peace. "Other than

that, has she behaved?" He had stopped in
to see her every day, Zoya knew, although
he had been staying with a friend, and she
was at home with a baby-sitter.

Nicholas groaned in answer. "Yesterday
she had a fit when I said she couldn't go to
the movies with a friend. But she hadn't
done her homework yet, and it was too
late anyway. I'm sure she'll tell you about
that the minute you walk in."

"Welcome home," Axelle smiled, and
Zoya laughed. She had missed them a
great deal, but she knew she was going to
miss Simon now too, and he had been so
sweet to Nicholas when they met.

"Your friend seemed nice," he said politely to Axelle on the way home.

"I think so too." She looked pointedly at
Zoya as the boy chattered on, and she silently hoped that Zoya would see Simon
again once they were home.

Soon after she arrived home a huge bouquet of roses was delivered. The card said
only, "Don't forget, Love, S." and she
blushed as she tucked the card into her
desk, and turned her attention to her
daughter, who, as predicted, was com-
plaining furiously about her brother.

"I've just gotten home, give me a minute to adjust!" Zoya laughed.

"Can we get a dog?" Nicholas had been right. The demands were endless in the first two hours, and she was scarcely mollified by the new red dress. But Nicholas was thrilled with his watch, and the clothes and the new books. He threw his arms around her neck and kissed her warmly on the cheek.

"Welcome home, Mama."

"I love you, sweetheart . . . and you too," she pulled Sasha into the circle of her arms also.

"What about the dog?" Sasha inquired as her mother laughed.

"We'll see, Sasha . . . we'll see . . ." The phone spared her then, and she went to answer it. It was Simon, and she thanked him for the roses as she laughed at Nicholas and Sasha arguing about the mythical wolfhound.

"Do you miss me yet?"

"Very much. I think I need a referee here."

"Excellent. I'll apply for the job. How about dinner tomorrow night?"

"How about a dog?" she laughed and he sounded confused, he could hear the excitement at the other end.

"You want to eat a dog?"

"That's a nice thought," she laughed

again, suddenly missing him more than she thought she would.

"I'll pick you up at eight o'clock." But she panicked as she thought about it. What would the children say? What would Nicholas think? She wanted to call him back and tell him she'd changed her mind, but even after they went to bed, she couldn't bring herself to do it.

He appeared promptly at eight o'clock the following night, and rang the bell, just as Zoya came out of her room. The apartment was small, but simple and elegant. They had very few things, but nowadays what they had was good. He stood in the doorway looking larger than life, and as she ushered him inside, she saw Sasha staring at him.

"Who's that?" Sasha inquired, making her mother furious that she was so rude. Nicholas was right about her.

"This is Mr. Hirsch, may I present my daughter, Alexandra?"

"How do you do?" He shook her hand solemnly and with that Nicholas wandered in.

"Oh hello . . . how are you?" He smiled ingenuously, and was telling Sasha what a pest she was as they left. Zoya smiled as she closed the door, and they waited for the elevator to take them down. She was worried about the look she'd seen in Sasha's eyes. It was as though she knew why he was there, but Simon told her he had expected it and he had a very thick skin, so not to worry.

He took her to dinner at "21," and they talked for hours, as they had on the ship. And then slowly he walked her home, and kissed her gently as they stood a few feet from her house.

"I can't stand not seeing you. I was like a kid waiting for Christmas all day today. Why don't we take the children somewhere tomorrow afternoon?" It would be Sunday and she didn't have to work, and she liked the idea, but she was also nervous about what Sasha would say, or even gentle Nicholas.

"What will the children think?"

"They'll think that they have a new friend. Is that so terrible?"

"They might be very rude to you again."

"I can handle it. Zoya, I don't think you understand. This is everything I want. I meant what I told you on the ship. I love you."

"How do you know? How can you be so sure?" She was still afraid of what she felt for him, but she had missed him all day too, and she hated to leave him now, even until the next day. How was it possible? How had it happened to her after all these years? She knew she was in love with him too. But she didn't know what to do about it yet. She still wanted to run away, and she was no longer sure she could.

"Just give it a chance, my love." He kissed her again. "I'll come to pick you all up at noon."

"You're a very brave man."

He smiled at her happily. "Not as brave as you, my love. See you tomorrow. Maybe we'll take a drive somewhere."

"The children would love that."

And the next morning, when he arrived, in spite of Sasha's complaints that she wanted to play with her dolls, they drove to Long Island and loved it. Nicholas almost fainted when he saw the car, a brand-new Cadillac, in a distinguished shade of dark green, with white sidewall tires, and every possible new device. He had never seen anything so beautiful, and Simon invited him to sit next to him in the front seat.

"Would you like to drive it, son?" He waited until they were on a back road, and actually let Nicholas take the wheel. The boy felt as though he had died and gone to heaven, as Zoya watched him from where she sat in the backseat with Sasha. Simon was right, the boy needed a man in his life. He needed a friend. Even Sasha seemed to behave better than she had in months, and she flirted mercilessly with Simon as they drove home again. He had taken them to lunch at a little restaurant he knew. They ate oysters and shrimp, and for dessert they had ice cream.

"Well, Countess Ossupov," he teased, once the children had gone to bed, and he was sitting in the living room with her. "How did I do? Pass or fail?"

"What do you think? Nicholas was never so happy in his life, and I think Sasha is in love with you."

"And her mother?" He looked at her seriously, gazing into her eyes, as she avoided his, and then slowly she turned to him. "What do you say, Zoya . . . will you marry me?"

She felt as though she had swallowed her heart as she whispered to him, and held out a hand, "Yes . . . yes, Simon, I will." He looked as though he were going to faint, and she wondered if she'd gone mad. It was a crazy thing to do and she scarcely knew the man, but she knew she couldn't live without him.

"Do you mean it?" he asked quietly, afraid to believe his ears, as he pulled her into his arms and she looked up at him with a frightened smile.

"Yes, Simon, I mean it."

Chapter 38

Axelle was stunned when Zoya told her at work the next day that she was getting married. She had hoped that something would come of the relationship, but she had never imagined that it would happen so quickly.

"What do the children think?" she asked, as Zoya looked at her, still amazed herself at what she'd done, or what she'd agreed to. They had agreed to wait for a while, to let the children get used to him first. And Zoya wasn't ready to get married immediately either. After all her years alone, Simon knew she needed time to get used to the idea, and he was ready to give her all the time she needed, within reason.

"We haven't told them yet. But they seem to like him." She told her about the drive to Long Island. It had truly been a whirlwind romance. They had only

known each other for a few weeks, and yet
Zoya knew that he was a good man, and
she also knew that she loved him.

He stopped by at the shop that afternoon, and brought flowers to her, and to
Axelle. The older woman was touched
that he had thought of her, and he
thanked her for championing their romance.

"Just don't steal her from me too soon,
Mr. Hirsch." She already hated the
thought, but they both assured her that
they were going to proceed slowly. And
he still had to introduce her to his parents.
And there was more than that that
needed tending to. That weekend he
knew both children were staying with
friends, and without warning her, he
showed up at Zoya's apartment on Saturday morning. He was carrying a huge bouquet of white lilacs, and a mysterious
smile, which Zoya pretended not to notice.

"You're looking very pleased with yourself, Mr. Hirsch."

"Why shouldn't I? I happen to be engaged to a very beautiful, very wonderful
woman." He kissed her and she took the
lilacs to the kitchen to arrange them, and
he found her there, selecting a vase of

heavy cut crystal. She had bought it because it reminded her of one that her mother always used for flowers from their garden at the Fontanka Palace.

"They're lovely, aren't they?" She took a step back to admire them, and found herself in Simon's arms, as he gently turned her toward him and kissed her.

"Not as lovely as you are." She nestled in his arms silently for a moment, enjoying his gentleness and his warmth, and stroking her hair, he looked down at her and murmured. "Let's go for a drive somewhere. It's a beautiful day today." And he knew that she didn't have to rush back for the children.

"That's a lovely idea." She smiled happily at him, and he wandered back into the living room, while she went to change into white slacks and a white cashmere sweater. He glanced at the photographs in silver frames everywhere, and stopped in amazement in front of one of the Romanov children, seeming to hang upside down, while making funny faces at the person taking the picture. And as he looked at it carefully, he realized that one of the young girls in tennis garb was a much younger Zoya, and he correctly guessed that the girl next to her was

Marie, and the others were her sisters. It still amazed him to realize the history she had lived. But it was long in the distant past now. Even the photograph was fraying and faded. And there were others, of Sasha and Nicholas, and several of Clayton. He was a distinguished-looking man, and Zoya looked happy standing beside him.

"What are you doing in here so quietly?" She smiled as she walked back into the room, looking beautiful in the white slacks and sweater. There were times when she reminded him of Katharine Hepburn.

"I was looking at some of your photographs. Nicholas looks a lot like his father, doesn't he?"

"Sometimes." She smiled. "And a little bit like my father too." She picked up a large silver frame that held a photograph of her parents and handed it to Simon. "And a bit like my brother." She pointed to another on the table, as Simon nodded.

"They're a distinguished-looking group." As always, he was impressed by her aristocratic ancestors, but Zoya smiled sadly.

"That's all such a long time ago." It was hard to believe that it had been twenty years since she'd seen her parents. "Some-times I think one should only live in the present. The past is only a heavy burden to carry with you. And yet . . ." She looked up at him with wise eyes, "it's so hard to let them go . . . to forget . . . to move ahead . . ." It was why she had wanted to wait a little while until they married. She still had some letting-go to do. She still had a giant step to make, from the past to the present. But he understood that and he wasn't rushing her. He knew she needed time and he was willing to be patient. Especially now that she had agreed to marry him. With that promise made, he could wait for her, and help her to make the transition.

"I think we let go when we're ready to. Speaking of which, are you ready to go?"

"Yes, sir." She was carrying a dark blue flannel blazer, and a few minutes later they were in his car, driving to what he described as a "secret destination." "Does this mean I'm being abducted, Mr. Hirsch?" She was laughing, and she felt young as they drove along in the sunshine. It was a nice carefree feeling not having to worry about the children. It was different when she had to think of them, it made her feel more serious and less romantic.

But now all she had to think about was enjoying Simon.

And he laughed at her suggestion. "Abducting you is the best idea I've had since we met. Come to think of it, I should have done it in Paris." But he was willing to settle for Connecticut, as they drove along the Merritt Parkway. He was telling her about his business, and some of his thoughts about his fall collection. He loved talking to her, about anything and everything, and his hope that one day he would collect important paintings. He was particularly fond of the Impressionists, and Zoya told him of her parents' collection in Russia.

"I'm not sure 'things' are that important to me anymore. It's funny, I think I used to take all of the beautiful things around me for granted. But having lost everything once, and then sold everything I had with Clayton, it just doesn't mean that much to me anymore." She smiled slowly at him with loving eyes, "the people in my life are more important." He quietly reached out and touched her fingers across the table as they ate lunch, and their hands met and held, and a little while later, they left and talked quietly as they continued their drive through the country. It was late af-

ternoon by then, and Zoya was relaxed as
she leaned against him.

"Tired?"

She stifled a yawn and then laughed as
she shook her head. "No, just happy."

"We'll go back in a while. There's a
place I want to show you first."

"Where?" She loved being with him.
Everything about him made her feel safe
and loved and happy.

"It's a secret."

She giggled and half an hour later she
was amazed when she saw it. It was a little
English cottage on a back road Simon
knew, with a picket fence around it, huge
shade trees and a profusion of rose bushes
that let off a heady fragrance as they got
out of the car and looked around them.

"Whose house is this, Simon?"

"I wish I could say it was mine. It be-
longs to a wonderful English lady who
made an inn of it, in order to support it. I
found it years ago, and sometimes I just
come here to unwind from all the crazi-
ness in New York. Come inside, I want you
to meet her." He didn't tell Zoya, but he
had called Mrs. Whitman early that morning and warned her of their arrival. And
when they stepped into the cozy living
room, done in lovely English floral

chintzes, there was a proper English tea waiting for them. Her silver teapot gleamed invitingly and there were plates filled with delicate sandwiches and little cakes, and what Mrs. Whitman referred to as "biscuits." She was a tall, thin, white-haired woman, with a clipped accent, laughing eyes, and long, graceful hands roughened by her work in the garden. And it was obvious that she had been expecting Simon and Zoya.

"How good to see you again, Mr. Hirsch." She shook hands genially and looked appreciatively at Zoya, and she looked approving when Simon introduced her as his fiancée. "What good news! Are you recently engaged then?"

"Very." They answered in unison and then laughed, as Mrs. Whitman poured them each a cup of tea and invited them to sit down in her comfortable little parlor. There was a pretty fireplace, and handsome English antiques she had brought with her fifty years before. She had lived in London, and then New York, and when her husband died, she had retired to the country. She recognized Zoya's accent at once, and something about Zoya's bearing told her that there was a lot more to Zoya than met the eye.

She thought Simon had made a wise and interesting choice, and much to Zoya's amusement, she said so. And in celebration of their engagement, she brought out a bottle of her very best sherry.

The sun set over the garden as she toasted them, and a little while later, she quietly took her glass and left the room, with a discreet look at Simon. Her own quarters were at the back of the house, and when she had important guests, she let them use the parlor as well as the upstairs bedrooms. There were two, with a large Victorian bath connecting them, and beautiful canopied beds she had had sent over from England.

"Come and look." Simon was telling Zoya all about it, and Zoya looked hesitant.

"Won't she mind, Simon?" She was still trying to figure out where Mrs. Whitman had gone. She had been gone for ages, but it was so cozy sitting in the cheerful living room drinking sherry with him that Zoya didn't mind. But she felt strange going upstairs without an invitation.

"Don't be silly. I know this place like my own home." He took her hand, and led her upstairs to the pretty bedrooms, and Zoya smiled when she saw them. The

lights were turned on, and the beds were
turned down, as though she were expecting guests at any moment. But the rooms
were obviously unoccupied, and as Zoya
turned to go back downstairs, Simon
pulled her into his arms with a deep laugh,
and kissed her full on the lips. She was
breathless when he let go of her, and her
hair looked sexy and disheveled. And
then, with a teasing look, he pulled her
onto the bed with him, and Zoya gave a
gasp as she tried to escape his caresses.

"Simon! What will Mrs. Whitman think!
Stop that! . . . we'll get the bed all
messed up! . . . Simon! . . ."

But he was laughing at her as he sat
back under the huge canopy and laughed.
"I certainly hope so."

"Simon! Will you get up?" She was
laughing at him too. He looked perfectly
comfortable as he sat fully dressed on the
bed in one of Mrs. Whitman's two guest
rooms.

"I will not."

"You're drunk!" But he'd hardly had a
thing to drink all day, except for her very
proper little sherry, and he hadn't had
enough to make him drunk. But it was
obvious that he was enjoying himself im-

mensely. And then with a long arm, he reached out and pulled Zoya toward him.

"I'm not drunk. But you were right this morning, when you said you'd been abducted. I thought it might do you good to get away for a day or two, my love. So here we are, safely tucked into my secret hideaway." He planted a kiss on her open lips and then smiled at her as she stared at him. "Consider yourself abducted." He looked immensely pleased with himself as Zoya stared at him in amazement.

"Are you serious? We're staying here?"

"I am, and we are. In fact," he looked faintly embarrassed for the first time, "I took the liberty of bringing a few things I thought you might need." He looked sheepish and Zoya grinned at him in wonder.

"Simon, you are extraordinary!" She bounced onto the bed next to him like a child and threw her arms around his neck and kissed him. As it turned out, he had bought her a beautiful satin nightgown and peignoir, matching slippers, and had bought all sorts of creams and lotions and bath oils that he had thought might please her, along with two shades of lipstick, a new toothbrush, and the brand of toothpaste he had previously observed in her bathroom. He had packed it all in a small suitcase, which he brought upstairs to her a few moments later, and set it down in the bedroom next door to his own, as she proceeded to go through it with little gurgles of delight, and then she suddenly turned to him. "What will Mrs. Whitman think of our staying here, Simon? She knows we're not married." And she had seemed so terribly proper, although Simon knew she was far less stuffy than she looked, and had a terrific sense of humor. Besides which, it was difficult to resist two people as obviously in love as they were.

"What can she possibly think, Zoya? We have separate bedrooms." Zoya nodded, and went back to unpacking the treasures Simon had bought her, and was touched to discover a huge bottle of her favorite perfume.

"Good lord, Simon, is there anything you didn't think of?"

"I certainly hope not." He put his arms around her again, and then went to bring the rest of their sandwiches upstairs to their rooms with another glass of sherry. He had offered to take her out to dinner, but Zoya had insisted that she wasn't hungry.

"I'd love that." He lit a fire in his room,

and they sat cozily in front of it, eating watercress sandwiches and Mrs. Whitman's delicate little English biscuits, which she said were exactly like the ones her grandmother used to have for her when she was a child in Russia. "This is perfect, darling, isn't it?" She leaned over and kissed him again, and he looked at her contentedly. She was everything he had always wanted.

She left him around nine o'clock, and went to her own room to get ready for bed. They were both tired, and Simon sensed that she was nervous. He heard her running a bath, and it was a long time before he heard sounds in her room again. He wondered what she was doing and how she looked in the ivory satin nightgown. It was something to wear on a wedding night, which was precisely how he had pictured their secret weekend. He walked slowly to the door, and knocked softly, and when the door opened, his breath caught as he saw her. The satin gown molded her perfectly and her red hair flowed softly over her shoulders, as the creamy flesh of her neck beckoned him to touch her.

"My God . . . you look incredible . . ."

"This is beautiful, Simon . . . thank you . . ." She looked shy as she took a step back into the room and looked at him. He had never seen anyone lovelier. She managed to look both regal and inviting and it was all he could do to force himself not to reach out and grab her. But he didn't dare, she looked like fine porcelain as she stood there, like one of Mrs. Whitman's delicate English treasures in her parlor.

"Zoya . . ."

She smiled slowly at him, not a girl anymore, but a woman, a woman who had come to love him deeply, with all his gentleness, and his thoughtful gestures and kindness to her. She knew as she looked at him that she had been blessed the day she met him.

"Why don't you come in for a little while." She stepped aside, and her voice was husky as she invited him in. He stepped over the threshold feeling like a boy again, and then feeling the force of his manhood push aside his reserve, he took her in his arms, and the gown slipped slowly from her shoulders as he held her. It took the merest touch to drop it to her waist and then past her slim hips, and within moments she stood naked before him.

"I love you so much." He could barely speak as he kissed her lips and her neck, and her breasts, and then let his lips drift over her body, and then with a single powerful gesture he swept her into his arms and onto the bed, and a moment later, he lay there beside her. He made love to her as he had longed to since the day they met, and the room was quiet when they lay beside each other at last, sated, and happy and bonded for a lifetime. She was everything he had wanted her to be. She was more than he had ever dreamed of.

"I love you, Simon." And she knew as she said the words that she loved him as she had no other man before him. She was a woman now, and she was his woman, as she always would be. The present and the future were theirs, and the past was only a dim memory, as they went back to his room and turned off the lights, and lay in his bed, watching the fire turn to embers. And after they made love again, they drifted off to sleep in each other's arms, their dreams complete, their bodies one, their lives joined as surely as if they had been married that night at Mrs. Whitman's. It was the perfect wedding

night, and the next morning, their breakfast appeared mysteriously on trays in
Mrs. Whitman's parlor, as Zoya donned
the ivory satin peignoir over her bare flesh
and followed Simon downstairs with a
happy giggle.

"This feels absolutely sinful, doesn't it?"
she whispered over blueberry muffins.
She handed one to Simon and poured his
coffee. It was as though she had never belonged to any other man. It had been so
long since she had been Clayton's wife,
and she was someone else now. But Simon
only smiled at her and shook his head.

"I don't feel sinful at all. I feel married."

"So do I," she said softly, and looked at
him, her eyes filled with everything she
felt, and without another word, he took
her back upstairs, the muffins untouched,
the coffee forgotten.

Chapter 39

In the next two weeks, everything between them seemed to change. They belonged to each other and they knew it.
The only obstacle left to overcome was
the fact that Zoya hadn't met his parents.
She was nervous about meeting them, but
he reassured her as best he could after
surprising her one Friday night by telling
her he had told his mother he was bringing her to dinner.

"What did she say?" Zoya looked at him
worriedly, wearing a new black dress. He
hadn't warned her, so as not to frighten
her. He had just said they were going out.
And now, suddenly, despite all that had
happened between them at Mrs.
Whitman's two weeks before, she felt like
a young girl again, terrified at the prospect of meeting his mother.

"Do you really want to know?" He

laughed. "She asked me if you were Jewish."

"Oh no . . . and wait until she hears my accent. When she finds out I'm Russian, it's going to be awful."

"Don't be silly." But she was right. Simon had scarcely introduced them when his mother narrowed her eyes at Zoya.

"Zoya Andrews? What kind of a name is that? Is your family Russian?" She assumed she had been named for a grandmother, or some distant relative. She stood almost as tall as Simon, and looked down at Zoya.

"No, Mrs. Hirsch," Zoya looked at her with her big green eyes, praying that the storm wouldn't come. "*I* am."

"You are Russian?" She asked the question in her mother tongue, and Zoya almost smiled at the accent. It was the accent of the peasants she had known in her youth, and for an instant she was reminded of Feodor and his cozy wife, Ludmilla.

"I am Russian," she admitted again, but this time in her own language, which she spoke with the smooth diction and poise of the upper classes. She knew that the older woman would recognize it instantly, and more than likely hate her for it.

"From where?" The inquisition went on as Simon looked helplessly at his father, who was also intently watching Zoya. He liked what he saw, she was an attractive woman with obvious breeding and good manners. Simon had done well for himself, but he also knew that there was no stopping Sofia, Simon's mother.

"From St. Petersburg," Zoya answered with a quiet smile.

"St. Petersburg?" She was impressed, but she would rather have died than say it. "What was your family name?"

For the first time in her life, she was grateful that it wasn't Romanov, but her own name wasn't much better. She almost laughed as she faced the giant in the printed house dress. She had arms almost like a man's, which made Zoya feel all the more childlike. "Ossupov. Zoya Konstantinovna Ossupov."

"Why don't we sit down while we talk?" Simon suggested uncomfortably as his mother showed no sign of relenting, and made no move toward the room's straight-backed chairs in their small apartment on Houston Street.

"When did you come here?" She asked Zoya bluntly, as Simon groaned inwardly. He suspected what was coming.

"After the war, madame. I went to Paris in 1917, after the revolution." There was no point concealing what she was. She only felt sorry for Simon, who looked miserable as he listened to the exchange between his mother and the woman he wanted to marry. But after the bond of their lovemaking and the closeness that had been born of it, they both knew that nothing could keep them apart now.

"So, they threw you out after the revolution."

Zoya smiled at her. "I suppose you could call it that. I left with my grandmother," and then her eyes grew serious, "after my family was killed."

"So was mine," Sofia Hirsch said bluntly. Their name had previously been Hirschov, but the immigration officer at Ellis Island had been too lazy to write their full name, and without further ado they had become Hirsch instead of Hirschov. "My family was killed in the pogroms, by the Tsar's Cossacks." Zoya had heard tales of that as a child, but she had never realized that she would one day be put in a position to defend it.

"I'm very sorry."

"Mmm . . ." Simon's mother glowered and then stalked out to the kitchen to finish making dinner. And when it was ready, his mother lit the candles, and chanted the Sabbath prayer. His mother kept a kosher home, and had made the traditional challah, which they served with ceremonial wine. It was all a new experience for Zoya. "Do you know what kosher is?" halfway through dinner.

"No . . . I . . . yes . . . well, not really." They were still speaking Russian, and Zoya felt awkward about her lack of knowledge. "You don't drink milk with meat." It was the best she could do, as his mother glowered at him again and referred to him constantly as "Shimon," talking to him in Yiddish instead of Russian.

"Everything has to be kept separate. Dairy must never touch meat." They had separate plates, and with their new prosperity, she now had two ovens. It all sounded very complicated to Zoya as she explained, but she was fiercely proud of her devotion to Talmudic law, and then she looked proudly at her son as Zoya smiled. "He's so smart, he could have been a rabbi. But what does he do? He goes to Seventh Avenue and throws his family out of the business."

"Mama, that's not true," Simon smiled.

"Papa retired, and so did Uncle Joe and Uncle Isaac." Zoya realized as she listened that this was an aspect of his life she hadn't truly understood. It was one thing to hear him tell about it, and another to actually meet them. She felt suddenly terrified that she would never measure up in their eyes. She knew nothing of his religion, or how important it was to him. She didn't even know if he himself was religious, although somehow she suspected that he wasn't. Her own religion wasn't extremely important to her, although she believed in God. But she only went to the Orthodox church on Easter and Christmas.

"What did your father do?" Sofia Hirsch fired the question at her, after Zoya had helped her to clear the table. She already knew that Zoya worked in a shop, and that Simon had met her in Paris.

"My father was in the army." Zoya answered as the older woman almost shrieked.

"Not a *Cossack*?"

"No, Mama, of course not," Simon answered for her, he was obviously anxious to leave, and Zoya suddenly thought it all very funny. Their two lives, from such different beginnings had met in the middle somewhere, and after years of touting her title to some, she was now having to assure this woman that her father hadn't been a Cossack. And suddenly, she saw from the corner of her eye that Simon thought it was funny too. It was as though he knew exactly what she was thinking. And he decided to tease his mother a little. He knew she would be impressed, even though she might pretend to be horrified. He already sensed that his father approved, and even if his mother did, she wouldn't admit it. "Zoya is a countess, Mama. She's just too humble to use her title."

"A countess of what?" his mother asked, and Zoya laughed openly this time.

"Of absolutely nothing anymore. You're quite right. All of that is finished." The revolution had been nineteen years before, and although not forgotten, it seemed like part of another lifetime.

There was a long silence then, as Simon was thinking of how to make a graceful exit with Zoya, when his mother spoke in mournful tones, as though to whatever gods might be listening. "It's a shame she's not Jewish." Simon smiled. It was as close as Sofia would come to saying that she liked her. "Would she convert?" She asked Simon pointedly as though Zoya were not

in the room, and as Zoya sat looking startled, Simon answered for her.

"Of course not, Mama. Why should
she?"

His father offered her another glass of
wine, as Simon patted her hand, and his
mother looked at Zoya with continuing
interest.

"Simon says you have children." It was
more of an accusation than a question, but
Zoya smiled, always proud of them.

"Yes, I have two."

"You're divorced."

Simon groaned inwardly as Zoya smiled
at Sofia. "No, I'm a widow. My husband
died seven years ago, of a heart attack."
She decided to tell her just so she didn't
think she had killed him.

"That's too bad. How old are they?"

"My son, Nicholas, is almost fifteen, and
Alexandra is eleven." Sofia nodded, seemingly satisfied for once, and Simon took
the opportunity to stand up, and say they
had to go, as Zoya rose and thanked her
for dinner.

"It was nice to meet you," Sofia said
grudgingly, as her husband smiled. He
had barely spoken all evening, except occasionally, in a low voice to Simon. He was
a shy man, who had spent half a century in

the shadow of the far more talkative Sofia. "Come again sometime," she said politely as Zoya shook her hand, and thanked her again in her aristocratic Russian. And Simon knew that the next day, she would call him and he would get an earful.

He escorted Zoya to the waiting Cadillac parked downstairs and heaved a sigh of relief as he slid behind the wheel, and looked agonizingly at the woman he loved.

"I'm sorry. I shouldn't have brought you here."

Zoya laughed at the look on his face. "Don't be silly." She leaned over and kissed him. "My mother would have been *much* worse. Just be grateful you don't have to face her."

"I can't believe the questions she asks, and she wonders why I never bring anyone home. I would have to be crazy! *Meshugge!*" he added in Yiddish, tapping his head to explain it to Zoya as she laughed and he drove her slowly home.

"Listen, just wait till Sasha starts giving you a hard time. So far, she's been an angel."

"Then we're even. I swear, I'll never do that to you again."

"Yes, you will, and I don't mind. I was

just terrified she'd ask me something about the Tsar. I didn't want to lie to her, but I wasn't dying to tell her the truth," she smiled. "I'm just glad we're not Romanovs. She would have collapsed over the dinner." He laughed at the thought, and took her to the Copacabana for a while, to relax and drink champagne. As far as Simon was concerned, it had been a very rough evening. But Zoya was surprised at how smoothly it had gone. She had actually expected it to be worse, which horrified Simon.

"How could it have been worse?"

"She could have asked me to leave. At one point, I thought she would."

"She wouldn't dare. She's not as mean as she looks." He smiled sheepishly, "And she makes great chicken soup."

"I'll ask her to teach me," and then Zoya suddenly remembered something she had wondered. "Do we have to do kosher food?" But he couldn't stop laughing when she asked him. "Well, do we?"

"My mother would be thrilled if we did, but let me tell you, my love, I would refuse to eat at home. Just don't worry about that stuff. All right? Promise?" He leaned over and kissed her as the band started playing his favorite song, it was "I've Got You Under My Skin," by Cole Porter. "Would you like to dance, Mrs. Andrews, or should I call you Countess Ossupov?"

"How about just Zoya?" She laughed as she followed him onto the floor.

"How about Zoya Hirsch? How does that sound?"

She smiled up at him as they danced, and they both laughed, thinking the same thing again. It was certainly an odd name for the Tsar's cousin.

Chapter 40

They managed to keep it a secret from the children until June, when Sasha walked in on them one day, kissing passionately in their kitchen. She stared at them in mute horror, and then stalked off, locked herself in her room, and wouldn't come out until after dinner, when Nicholas threatened to knock the door down if she didn't come out and act like a human being. He was greatly offended by his sister. He liked Simon, and he was beginning to hope that he was serious about his mother. Simon had been nothing but kind to all of them, taking them for drives on Sunday afternoons, and out for dinner whenever possible, and bringing them thoughtful presents. He picked Nicholas up at school in his Cadillac more than once, and he had brought the children a radio, which they all loved dearly.

"Behave yourself!" Nicholas warned her angrily. "And go apologize to Mama!"

"I will *not*! She was kissing him in the kitchen."

"So what? She likes him."

"But not like that . . . that's *disgusting*!"

"You're disgusting. Now go tell them you're sorry."

She skulked off to the living room, and refused to look at Simon. And that night, after he left, Zoya finally told her.

"I'm very much in love with him, Sasha." The girl began to cry, as Nicholas listened from the doorway.

"What about Papa? Didn't you love him?"

"Of course I did . . . but, darling, he's gone now. He's been gone for a long time. It might be nice to have someone with us who loves us. Simon loves you and Nicholas very much."

"And I like him too," Nicholas staunchly defended Simon, which touched Zoya. "Are you going to get married?" he asked her gently, and looking from one to the other, she nodded, as Sasha burst into fresh hysterics.

"I hate you! You're ruining my life!"

"Why, Sasha?" The child's reaction

troubled her deeply. "Don't you like him? He's such a nice man, and he'll be so good to us." She tried to take her in her arms, but the overwrought child wouldn't let her.

"I hate you *both*!" Sasha wailed, not even sure why she was saying it, except perhaps to upset her mother. But Nicholas was instantly furious, leaping toward the sobbing figure on the bed.

"Apologize or I'll slap you!"

"Stop it! Both of you! This is no way to start a new life."

"When are you getting married?" Sasha stopped crying long enough to ask.

"We don't know yet. We wanted to give it a little time."

"Why don't you do it this summer, and then we can all go away together?" Nicholas offered, and Zoya smiled. It sounded like a good idea to her, and she knew Simon would be pleased, but the prospect obviously didn't appeal to Sasha.

"I won't go anywhere with you."

"Yes, you will, we'll just stuff you in a suitcase and go, and then at least we won't have to listen to you." She turned her fury on her brother then with an anguished look.

"I *hate* you! I'm not going anywhere

with them," she sniffed loudly and glared at her mother, but Nicholas had her pegged as he turned accusing eyes on her.

"You know what you are? You're jealous! You're jealous of Mama and Simon."

"I'm *not*!"

"You *are*!" They went on shouting and Zoya despaired of ever having peace again, but by the next day when she told Simon, Sasha had calmed down, although she was plainly not speaking to her brother.

"I like Nick's idea best," he said sympathetically. He knew how difficult Sasha was sometimes for Zoya to handle. He got along with her well enough, but she seemed to make constant demands on her mother, for her attention, her time, new dresses, new clothes, and she was constantly testing her limits. "Why don't we get married in July, and go to Sun Valley with the children?"

"Wouldn't you mind taking them on our honeymoon?" She was amazed at how kind he was, how willing to accept her children as his own, and it touched her deeply.

"Of course not. Would you like that?"

"I'd love it."

"Done," he said, and kissed her, before

going to look at a calendar. "How about July twelfth for our wedding?" He beamed at her as she put an arm around his waist. She hadn't been this happy in a long, long time. And it had actually become difficult, waiting to marry him. All she wanted now was to be his, for a lifetime.

"What will your mother say?"

He thought about it and then smiled. "We'll have her talk to Sasha. They were made for each other." Zoya laughed then as he kissed her.

Chapter 41

On the Twelfth of July, 1936, Simon Ishmael Hirsch and Zoya Alexandra Evgenia Ossupov Andrews were married by a judge in the garden of Axelle's pretty little brownstone on East Forty-ninth Street.

The bride wore a cream-colored Norell suit, and a tiny hat with a whisper of ivory veil, as she looked up into her husband's eyes and smiled, as he kissed her. His mother had opted not to come, just to let them know that she did not approve of Zoya's not being Jewish. But his father was there, and two of the girls from the shop. There were a handful of their friends, and of course both of Zoya's children. Nicholas was their best man, and Sasha stood beside them looking sullen. Zoya could have had a more elaborate wedding if she'd wanted to, and her more important clients, like Barbara Hutton and Doris Duke, would have loved to come, but although Zoya knew them well, she wasn't close to them. They were part of another life, and she wanted her wedding to be very small and private.

Axelle's butler poured the champagne, and at four o'clock, Simon drove them home in the Cadillac to Zoya's apartment. They had decided to stay there, until after their honeymoon, when they were going to look for a larger place. But they were going to spend three weeks in Sun Valley first. It had just opened that year, and they took the train to Idaho from Pennsylvania Station. Simon brought games for the children, and even Sasha was excited by the time they reached Chicago. They stayed at the Blackstone overnight, and continued on the next day, and all of them were in high spirits when they reached Ketcham, Simon and Zoya even more so after a night of unbridled passion. The physical relationship they shared was something neither of them had ever known before, and it brought them even closer together.

It was only three months since they'd met, but she felt as though she'd known Simon for a lifetime. He taught Nicholas how to fish, and they went swimming every day. And they returned brown and healthy and happy at the end of the month, to Zoya's apartment. And it was then that the reality of it really struck Zoya. She sat watching Simon shave on their first day back, and she felt a wave of happiness wash over her as she watched him lather his face, and she suddenly laughed, as she touched the smooth flesh she loved so much and kissed him.

"Something funny?" He turned to her with a smile and she shook her head.

"No, it just seems so real suddenly, doesn't it?"

"It sure does." He leaned over and kissed her and got soap all over her as she laughed, and he kissed her again, and a moment later, she locked the bedroom door, and they made love again before they both left for work. She had promised Axelle she would stay at the shop until the end of September. And the days seemed to fly by. Three weeks after their return, they found an apartment they loved on Park Avenue and Sixty-eighth Street. It had large, airy rooms, and their bedroom was at the opposite end from the two children's. Nicholas had a big, pleasant room, and Sasha insisted that her room be painted purple.

"I had a purple room when I was a little

girl too . . . when I was about your age."
She told her then about Alix's lovely
mauve boudoir. It brought back tender
memories as she described it and Sasha
listened in rapt fascination.

There was a photograph of Clayton in
Nicholas's room, and beside it he placed a
handsome picture of Simon. The two men
of the family went for long walks in the
late afternoon when Simon came home
from work, and the week after they
moved in, he brought them a little cocker
spaniel.

"Look, Mama!" Nicholas said excitedly,
"He looks just like Sava!" She was surprised that he still remembered her, and
Sasha sulked for a day because it wasn't a
Russian wolfhound. They were still all the
rage, though not quite as much as they
had been in the late twenties. But the dog
was very sweet and they named him Ja-
mie. Their life seemed idyllic as they settled into the new apartment. There was
even a guest room next to the library, and
Simon teased her that it was for their first
baby. But Zoya shook her head and
laughed.

"I had my babies a long time ago, Simon. I'm too old for that now." At thirty-
seven, she was long past wanting to have

more children. "I'll be a grandmother one of these days," she laughed, and he shook his head.

"Will you be wanting a cane too, Granny?" He put an arm around her shoulders as they sat in their bedroom and talked late into the night, the way she had with Clayton years before. But life was very different with Simon. They shared common interests, common friends, they were grown people who had come together in strength and not weakness. She had been barely more than a child when Clayton had saved her from the horrors of her life in Paris in 1919 and brought her to New York. This was all so very different, Zoya thought to herself as she went to work, enjoying her last days at Axelle's, and she looked at her friend mournfully on the last day.

"What am I going to do now?" She sat sadly at her Louis XV desk and looked over a last cup of tea at Axelle. "What will I do with myself every day?"

The older woman laughed. "Why don't you go home and have a baby?"

Zoya shook her head, wishing she could stay, but Simon wanted her to have the freedom she hadn't had in years. She had been working for seven years and there

was no need for her to now. She could
enjoy her children, her husband, their
home, and indulge herself, but Zoya
thought it all sounded very dull without
the shop to come to every day. "You sound
like my husband."

"He's right."

"I'll be so bored without work."

"I doubt that very much, my dear." But
there were tears in Axelle's eyes when Simon picked Zoya up that afternoon, and
the two women embraced. Zoya promised
to drop by the next day and take her to
lunch.

Simon laughed and warned the woman
who had championed their romance from
the first. "You're going to have to lock the
doors to keep her out of here. I keep telling her there's a whole world out there for
her to discover." But by October she
found that she had more free time on her
hands than she knew what to do with. She
visited Axelle almost every day, went to
museums, picked Sasha up at school. She
even dropped in on Simon at his office
frequently, and listened avidly to his plans
for his business. He had decided to add a
line of children's coats, and he was anxious
for her advice, which she gave him. Her
unfailing sense of style helped him make

interesting choices that otherwise he wouldn't have thought of.

"Simon, I miss it all so much," she confessed in December, as they took a taxi home from the theater. He had taken her to the opening of *You Can't Take It With You* with Frank Conlan and Josephine Hull at the Booth Theater. It had been an enjoyable evening, but she was restless and bored. She had discovered that she had worked for too many years to give it up and sit home and do nothing. "What if I go back to Axelle's for a little while?"

He thought about it, and then looked at her as they arrived at the apartment. "Sometimes it's hard to step back in time, sweetheart. Why don't you do something new?" Like what, she asked herself. All she knew was dancing and dresses, and dancing was certainly out of the question. She laughed to herself as they walked into the apartment, and he turned to look at her. She was so beautiful with her creamy skin and brilliant eyes and bright red hair. She still looked like a young girl and the sight of her always filled him with desire. She didn't look old enough to have a fifteen-year-old son, as she sat down in a chair and laughed as she looked up at him, handsome in the dinner jacket he wore.

He had had it made in London, much to his mother's disgust. "Your father could have made you one better."

"What's funny?"

"Just a crazy thought . . . I was remembering when I danced at Fitzhugh's. It was so awful, Simon. . . . I hated it so much."

"Somehow I can't quite see you, shaking your bottom and swinging your pearls," he laughed at the vision but his heart went out to her too. She had been so brave through all that she'd been through. He was only sorry he hadn't known her then. He would have married her and saved her from all that. She didn't need saving now, she was capable and strong. He was almost tempted to take her into his business with him, but knew his family would have been horrified. She didn't belong on Seventh Avenue. She belonged in a far more elite world, and then suddenly he had a thought. He poured himself a glass of cognac, and opened a bottle of champagne for her as they sat by the fire and talked. "Why don't you open your own shop?"

"Like Axelle's?" She looked intrigued, but she liked the idea, and then she thought of her friend and shook her head. "That wouldn't be fair to Axelle. I don't want to compete with her." Axelle had been too good to her to hurt her now, but Simon had other ideas in mind.

"Then do something different."

"Like what?"

"Do everything, women's wear, men's, maybe even some children's. But only the best, all that stuff you do so well. A whole look . . . shoes and bags and hats . . . teach people how to dress, not just the fancy ones like the women who go to Axelle's, but the others too, the ones with money who don't know how to put it all together." The women she had dressed at Axelle's were surely the best dressed in New York, but most of them also went to Paris for their clothes, like Lady Mendl, and Doris Duke, and Wallis Simpson. "You could start small, and then add to it as you go along. You could even sell my coats!" He laughed, and she looked up at him thoughtfully, sipping her champagne. She liked the idea, and then she glanced up at him with a serious question.

"Could we afford it?" She knew he did well, but she had no idea how much capital he had. It was something they never discussed. They had more than enough for the life they led, but his parents were still living on Houston Street, and she knew that he supported them, and all his father's brothers. He looked at her gently then, and sat down next to her.

"Maybe it's time we had a serious talk about all this."

She blushed as she shook her head. She didn't really want to know. But if she were to open a store of her own, perhaps she had to. "Simon, I don't want to pry. Your business is your own."

"No, my love. It's yours now too, and it does very well. Extremely well." He told her what he had made the previous year and she stared at him in amazement.

"Are you serious?"

"Well," he apologized, not understanding the look of shock in her eyes, "we could have done better if I'd ordered all the cashmeres I wanted in England. I don't know why I held back, next season I won't," he explained as she laughed openly at him.

"Are you crazy? I don't think the Bank of England handled that much money last year. Simon, that's incredible! But I thought . . . I mean, your parents . . ."
This time he laughed at her. "My mother wouldn't leave Houston Street if you took her out of there at gunpoint. She loves it."
All of Simon's attempts to move them to a

more luxurious apartment uptown had been unsucessful. His mother liked her friends, the shops where she did her marketing, and the neighborhood itself. She had moved to the Lower East Side when she had come to New York a generation before, and she was going to die there. "I think my father would get a kick out of moving uptown. But my mother won't let him." The woman still wore housedresses, and took pride in only having one "good" coat. But she could have bought every coat at Axelle's if she wanted.

"What are you doing with all that? Investing it?" She thought with a tremor of her late husband and his ventures on the stock market, but Simon was a great deal shrewder than Clayton. He had an instinctive sense for what worked, and in his case, what worked made a great deal of money.

"I've invested some of it, mostly in bonds, and I've put a lot of back in the business. I also bought two textile mills last year. I think if we start making our own goods, we'll do better than we do with some of our imports. besides which, I can control the quality better that way. Both of the mills are in Georgia, and labor is dirt cheap. It's going to take a few years, but I think it's going to make a big difference in our profits." She couldn't even begin to imagine it, the profits he had just mentioned to her were staggering already. He had built the business up from nothing in twenty years. At forty, he had already made a vast fortune. "So, my love, if you want to open your own store, get on with it. You're not going to take food out of anyone's mouth," he thought about it quietly for a minute as Zoya tried to absorb what she'd heard in the past half hour, "in fact, I think it might be a damn good investment."

"Simon," she set down her glass and looked at him earnestly, "will you help me?"

"You don't need my help, sweetheart, except maybe to sign the checks." He leaned over and kissed her. "You know more about this business than anyone I know, you have an innate sense of what's right and what's not. I should have listened to you about the Shocking Pink when we were in Paris." He laughed good-naturedly, he had eaten all his pink fabric, the orders for it just hadn't come in. New Yorkers weren't ready for it, except the handful who went straight to Schiaparelli and bought it in Paris.

"Where would I start?" Her mind was racing ahead, suddenly filled with excitement.

"You might look for a location over the next few months. And we could go to Paris in the spring so you could order some goods for a fall line. If you move now," he narrowed his eyes, calculating quietly, "you could open by September."

"That's awfully soon." It was only nine months away and there would be a great deal to do. "I could have Elsie decorate it for me, she has an unfailing sense of what people want, even when they don't know it."

But he smiled gently at his wife, sparked by her own excitement, "You could do it yourself just as well."

"No, I couldn't."

"Never mind, you may not have time anyway. Between finding the location, hiring staff, and buying for the store, you'd have too much to do anyway to worry about decorating it on top of it. Let me think about this. . . . I'll talk to some people I know about looking for a location."

"Do you mean it?" Her eyes danced with green fire, "Do you really think I should do it?"

"I sure do. Let's give it a whirl. If it

doesn't work, we'll close it and take a loss after the first year. It can't hurt." And she certainly knew now they could afford it.

She talked about nothing else for the next three weeks and when she took him for mass on Russian Christmas, she whispered to him for most of the service. One of his cronies in real estate had located what he thought was the perfect location, and she could hardly wait to see it.

"Your mother would faint if she saw you walking out of here," she laughed as she looked up at him happily. The services hadn't even made her sad this time, she was too excited about what they were trying to put together.

She had seen Serge Obolensky there for the first time in months, and he had bowed politely when she introduced him to Simon, speaking first in English for Simon's benefit, and then chatting with him in her elegant Russian.

"I'm surprised you didn't marry him," Simon said quietly, trying to hide the fact that he was jealous, but Zoya looked up at him and laughed as they drove home in the green Cadillac.

"Serge has never been interested in me, my love. He's too smart to marry poor old

Russian titles. He likes the American socialites much better."

Simon leaned over and kissed her as he
pulled her closer to him on the seat. "He
doesn't know what he's missing."

The next day Zoya took Axelle to lunch,
and talked excitedly about her plans. She
had told Axelle from the first, and had told
her nervously that she didn't want to compete with her directly.

"Why not?" Her friend looked at her in
surprise. "Doesn't Chanel compete with
Dior? And Elsa with all of them? Don't be
foolish. It will be terrific for business!"
Zoya hadn't thought of it that way, but she
was relieved to have Axelle's blessing.

And when she saw the location Simon's
friend had found, she fell in love with it on
the spot. It was perfect. It had previously
been a restaurant at Fifty-fourth and
Fifth, and it was only three blocks from
Axelle's. It was in terrible shape, but as she
squinted her eyes, she knew it was just
what she wanted, and better yet, the entire second floor was available just above
it.

"Take them both," Simon advised.

"You don't think it's too big?" It was
huge, which was why the restaurant had
failed. It had been too big for their small

clientele, but Simon shook his head with his instinctive sense for what worked in business.

"You can do women's wear on the main floor, and men's upstairs, and if it works," he winked at his friend, "we can buy the building. In fact, maybe we ought to do that right now, before they get smart and jack up the rent too high. He made a few calculations on a scratch pad and then nodded. "Go ahead, Zoya. Buy it."

"Buy it?" She almost choked on the words. "What'll I do with the other three floors?"

"Rent them out with one-year leases. If the store's a success, you can take back a floor every year. You might be damn glad to have five floors one day."

"Simon, this is crazy!" But she was so excited, she could hardly stand it. She had never even dreamed of owning her own store, and suddenly there she was, in the midst of it all. They hired architects and Elsie de Wolfe, and within weeks, she was surrounded by blueprints and renderings and drawings, there were samples of marble all over her library, fabrics, wood finishes for some paneling, the whole house was in a whirl as she made her plans, and Simon finally gave her a desk in his office and a secretary of her own to handle all the details for her. Cholly Knickerbocker even mentioned it in his column, and there was an article about it in *The New York Times*. "Watch out, New York!" the item said, "When Zoya Ossupov, the late great Countess of Axelle's, and Simon Hirsch, with his Seventh Avenue empire, joined forces last July, they might just have started something big!" And the words were prophetic.

They sailed for Paris in March on the *Normandie*, to buy for Simon's lines, and to select some of the mainstays of Zoya's first collection. And this time she picked all the things she loved, without having to defer to Axelle. She had never had as much fun in her life as shopping with him, and Simon gave her an unlimited budget. They stayed at the George V, and enjoyed a few rare moments alone which were like a honeymoon for them. They arrived back in New York a month after they'd sailed, happy and refreshed and more in love than ever. Their homecoming was marred only by the news that Sasha had been expelled from school. At twelve, she was becoming a little terror.

"How did that happen, Sasha?" She spoke to the child quietly on their first night home. As he had the year before, Nicholas had come to the ship to meet them but this time in the new Duesenberg Simon had ordered before they stopped making them the year before. Nicholas had been wildly excited to see them, and then he had told Zoya the news about his sister. She had worn lipstick and nail polish to school, and she had been caught kissing one of the teachers. He had been fired summarily, and Sasha had been expelled, without hope of being reinstated. "Why?" Zoya asked again, "what could have made you do it?"

"I was bored," Sasha shrugged, "and going to an all-girl school is stupid." Simon had paid the tuition at Marymount for her, and Zoya had been so pleased to see her in a better school than the one Zoya had been able to pay for. Nicholas had stayed on at Trinity, as he had before they were married, and he loved it there. He had two more years to finish before he went to Princeton, like his father before him. Sasha had lasted six months at Marymount and now she was out on her ear, and she didn't even have the grace to look embarrassed. There had been only two male teachers in the entire school, the music teacher and the dance master, the rest were nuns, and even then Sasha was able to make trouble. Zoya wondered if it was Sasha's way of punishing her for going away for so long, and being so excited about her new business. For the first time, she had second thoughts but it was too late now. She had ordered all her American lines before she left, and now she had bought and paid for the rest of it in Paris. She had to open, no matter what. And it was a hell of a time for Sasha to be making trouble. But Sasha wasn't the only thing on her mind now.

"Doesn't this embarrass you at all?" Zoya asked, "Think of how kind Simon was to send you there in the first place." But the girl only shrugged, and Zoya sensed that she hadn't gotten through to her, as she went back to their bedroom and found Simon unpacking. "I'm so sorry, Simon. It seems so incredibly ungrateful of her to have done this."

"What did she say?" Simon turned worried eyes to his wife. There was something in Sasha that had troubled him in the last few months. She had looked at him hungrily more than once, in a way that would have inspired a less decent man to treat her as a woman and not a child, but he never said anything about it to Zoya. He simply went on treating her like a little girl, which egged her on more. But she was only twelve years old after all, and incredibly pretty. She had her maternal grandmother's icy Germanic beauty, and her mother's Russian fire. Together, it was a fearsome combination. "Is she upset?" he asked, as Zoya shook her head in dismay.

"If only she were." She had seemed totally without contrition.

"What are you going to do now?"

"Look for another school, I guess. It's a little late in the year for that." It was already mid-April. "I could have her tutored until the fall, but I'm not sure that would be good for her."

But Simon liked the idea. "Maybe you should, for now. It would take the pressure off her." As long as the tutor was a woman. But the only one Zoya found was a nervous young man, who assured her that he could handle Sasha without any problem. He lasted exactly a month and then fled in terror, without explaining to Zoya that she had greeted him the previous day in a nightgown that was obviously her mother's, and after that had told him that she wanted him to kiss her.

"You're a brat," Nicholas still accused

her night and day. At nearly sixteen, he was a great deal more perceptive about her than her own mother. And she fought with Nicholas like a cat, scratching his face when she grew angry. Even Simon was concerned about the child, but just when he'd almost given up hope, she would become submissive and surprisingly charming.

The construction at the store was going unbelievably well, and by July it looked as though they would be open in September. They celebrated their anniversary at a rented house on Long Island that year, two days after Amelia Earhart disappeared over the Pacific. Nicholas was fascinated by her, and he told Simon secretly that one day he wanted to learn how to fly. Charles Lindbergh was his childhood hero. He had been equally fascinated by the *Hindenburg,* the dirigible that had exploded over New Jersey in early May. Fortunately, when he had tried to convince Zoya and Simon to travel to Europe on it, Zoya had been leery of it, and they had wanted to travel by ship anyway, in memory of their crossing the year before on the *Queen Mary.*

"Well, Mrs. Hirsch, what do you think of it?" Simon stood in the shoe department of the women's floor in her new store in early September. "Is it everything you wanted it to be?"

Tears filled her eyes as she looked around her in silent wonder. Elsie de Wolfe had created an atmosphere of beauty and elegance in pale gray silk with pink marble floors. There were soft lights, and vast arrangements of silk flowers on beautiful Louis XV tables. "It looks like a palace!"

"Nothing less than you deserve, my love." He kissed her and that night they celebrated with champagne. The shop was to open the following week with a glittering party attended by the cream of New York.

Zoya had bought her own dress for the opening at Axelle's. "This will be good for business! I might just have to say in my next ad that Countess Zoya shops here!" The two women had become fast friends, and they both knew now that nothing would change that.

Zoya and Simon had labored long and hard over the name for her store, and finally with a gleam in his eye Simon had chuckled. "I've got it!"

"So do I," Zoya smiled proudly, "Hirsch and Co."

"No," he groaned at the sound of the unromantic name. "I don't know why I didn't think of it before. 'Countess Zoya'!" It seemed too showy to her, but finally he had convinced her. It was what people wanted, to touch the mystery of the aristocracy, to have a title even if it meant buying one, or in this case, buying the clothes that a countess had selected for them. The items in the columns were endless about "Countess Zoya," and for the first time in years, Zoya went to the parties she was invited to. She was introduced as Countess Zoya, and her husband, Mr. Hirsch, but everywhere the socialites and the debs flocked around her. And she always looked exquisite in the simple gowns she wore, from Chanel or Madame Grès, or Lanvin. People could hardly wait to see the store, and women were convinced that they would emerge looking just like Zoya.

"You've done it, my friend," Simon whispered the night of her opening, the place was packed with every important name in New York. Axelle herself had sent her a tree six feet high of tiny white philanopsis orchids. *Bonne chance, mon amie, Affectueusement,* Axelle. the card had read as Zoya regarded it with tears in her eyes, and looked adoringly at Simon.

"It was all your idea."

"It's our dream." He smiled, in a sense, it was their baby. Even her children were there, Sasha in a beautiful white lace dress, that looked demure and was something the Tsar's children might have worn, or Zoya herself as a child, which was why she had bought it for her in Paris. And Nicholas, looking incredibly handsome at sixteen in his first dinner jacket and the studs Simon had given him, tiny sapphires set in white gold with a rim of diamonds around them. They were a handsome family as photographers snapped pictures of everyone, and Zoya posed again and again with the glittering women who were to become her clients.

And from that day on, the store was never empty. Women arrived in Cadillacs and Pierce-Arrows and Rollses. An occasional Packard or Lincoln drew up to the door, and Henry Ford came himself to buy a fur coat for his wife. Zoya had planned to sell only a few of them, she wanted most of the coats to be Simon's. But Barbara Hutton ordered an ermine wrap, and Mrs. Astor a full-length sable. The fate of Countess Zoya was sealed by the end of the year, and the sales at Christmastime were staggering. Even the men's department on the handsomely decorated second floor did well. The men did their shopping in wood-paneled rooms with handsome fireplaces, as their women spent their fortunes downstairs in the gray silk dressing rooms. It was everything Zoya had dreamed of and more, and on Park Avenue the Hirsches toasted each other happily with champagne on New Year's Eve.

"To us!" Zoya lifted her glass, wearing a black velvet evening gown, made for her by Dior.

But Simon only smiled as he lifted his glass again. "To Countess Zoya!"

Chapter 42

By the end of the following year, Zoya had to open another floor, and Simon's purchase of the building had proven to be prophetic. The men's department moved upstairs, and on the second floor, she sold her furs and most exclusive gowns, and there was a tiny boutique for her clients' children. Little girls were now being ushered in to buy party dresses and their first evening gowns. She even sold christening gowns, most of them French, and all of them as lovely as those she had seen as a child in Imperial Russia.

Her own daughter loved to come to the store, and pick out new dresses whenever she wanted, but Zoya curbed her finally. She seemed to have an insatiable appetite for expensive clothes, and Zoya didn't want her to overindulge it.

"Why not?" Sasha pouted angrily the

first time Zoya told her she couldn't go shopping on a whim.

"Because you have lots of pretty things in your closet already, and you outgrow some of them before you even have a chance to wear them." She was tall and lanky at thirteen, as Natalya had been. She was already almost a head taller than her mother. And Nicholas towered above them both at seventeen. He was in his last year of school before going to Princeton.

"I wish I could go into business now, like you," he had said admiringly to Simon more than once. Simon had been good to all three of them, and Nicholas adored him.

"You will one day, son. Don't be in such a big hurry. If I'd had the chance to go to college like you, I would have loved it."

"It seems like a waste of time sometimes," Nicholas confessed, but he knew that his mother expected him to go to Princeton. And it wasn't too far from home, he was planning to come into the city whenever possible. He had a busy social life, but he also managed to do well in school, unlike his sister. She was a beauty at thirteen, and she looked easily five years older than she was as she slinked around the room, in the dresses Zoya still bought her.

"That's too babyish!" she complained, eyeing the evening gowns at the store. She could hardly wait until she was old enough to wear them.

And when Simon offered to take her to the new Disney film *Snow White and the Seven Dwarfs,* she was highly insulted.

"I'm not a baby anymore!"

"Then don't act like one," Nicholas taunted. But she wanted to dance the samba and the conga instead, as Simon and Zoya did when they went to El Morocco. Nicholas wanted to go with them too, but Zoya insisted that he was too young. Instead, Simon took them all to "21," and they talked seriously about what was happening to the Jews in Europe. Simon was deeply worried about what Hitler was doing by the end of 1938 and he felt certain there was going to be a war. But no one else in New York seemed to be worried about it. They were going to parties and receptions and balls, and the dresses were flying out of Zoya's store. She was even thinking of opening another floor, but it seemed too soon. She was afraid business might slack off, but Simon only laughed at her worries.

"Face it, darling, you're a success! Business is never going to slack off. Once you've made it, as you have, that doesn't go away. You're backing up your name with quality and style. And as long as you have it to sell, your customers will be there." She was afraid to admit he was right, and she worked harder than ever, so much so that they had to call her at the store, when Sasha got suspended from school again, just before the Christmas vacation. They had gotten her into the Lycée Français, a tiny school run by a distinguished Frenchman, but he tolerated no nonsense there, and he called Zoya himself to complain about Mademoiselle. She took a taxi to Ninety-fifth Street to beg him not to expel the child. Apparently, she had been playing hooky, and she had smoked a cigarette in the town house's lovely ballroom.

"You must punish her, madame. And you must adhere to strict discipline, otherwise, madame, I fear we will all regret it some day." But after a lengthy conversation with Zoya, he agreed not to expel her. Instead she would be put on probation after the Christmas holiday. And Simon promised to drive her to school himself to make sure that she got there.

"Do you think I should leave the store every day when she gets home from school?" Zoya asked Simon that night. She was feeling guiltier than ever about the long hours she worked at the store.

"I don't think you should have to," Simon said honestly, angry at Sasha himself for the first time. "At almost fourteen, she should be able to behave herself until six o'clock when we both get home." Although he knew that sometimes Zoya didn't get home until after seven. There was always so much to do at the store, so many alterations she wanted to oversee herself, and special orders she wrote up herself so there would be no mistakes. And part of the success was her availability for clients who demanded Countess Zoya. "You can't do it all yourself," Simon had told her more than once, but she secretly thought she should, just as she thought she should also be at home with the children. But Nicholas was almost eighteen by then, and Sasha only four years younger, they were hardly children anymore. "She's just going to have to behave herself." And when he told her as much that night, she flounced out of the library and slammed her bedroom door, as Zoya cried.

"Sometimes I think she's paying the price of the life I led before," she blew her nose in Simon's handkerchief and looked up at him with unhappy eyes. Sasha was worrying Zoya terribly these days, and Simon was angry at her for it. "I was always at work when she was young, and now . . . it almost seems like it's too late to make it up to her."

"You have nothing to make up to her, Zoya. She has everything she could possibly want, including a mother who adores her." The trouble was that she was spoiled, and he didn't want to be the one to say it. Her father had indulged her as a small child, and Nicholas and Zoya had pampered her for all the years after that. Zoya had pampered Nicholas too, but he only seemed to grow kinder and more thoughtful as a result, appreciating everything Simon did for him, unlike Sasha, who only wanted more, and had tantrums almost every day. If she didn't want a new dress, it was a new pair of shoes, or a trip somewhere, or she lamented because they didn't go to St. Moritz, or didn't have a house in the country. But considering the fortune Simon had made, neither he nor Zoya had a taste for excessive luxuries. She had had all that before, and what she

shared with Simon now was more important.

Zoya's concerns about Sasha almost
spoiled their Christmas holidays, and after
Russian Christmas, she actually looked ill.
She was pale and she was working too
hard at the store, almost as though she
could drown her sorrows there. And to
cheer her up, Simon announced that he
was taking her to Sun Valley, without the
children, to go skiing. That infuriated
Sasha even more. She wanted to go with
them, and Simon told her firmly that she
couldn't. She had to stay in New York and
go to school, and she did everything she
could to spoil their trip. She called and
told them the dog was sick, and Nicholas
told them the following day that it was a
lie, she spilled ink on the rug in her room,
and she played hooky again, the school
called to say. All Zoya wanted to do was go
home, and get her back in control again.
But she was so worried, she was sick all the
way home on the train, and when they got
to New York, Simon insisted she go to the
doctor.

"Don't be stupid, Simon, I'm just tired,"
she snapped at him, which was unlike her.

"I don't care. You look like hell. My
mother even said she was worried about

you when she saw you yesterday." Zoya laughed at that, Sofia Hirsch usually lamented about her religion, not her health. But she finally agreed to go to the doctor the following week, feeling foolish. She knew she'd only been working too hard, and she was still worried about Sasha, although the child seemed more subdued now that they were back from Sun Valley.

But Zoya was in no way prepared for what the doctor told her after he had looked her over. "You're pregnant, Mrs. Hirsch," he smiled benignly at her from across the desk, "or should I call you Countess Zoya?"

"I'm *what*?" She stared at him in disbelief. She was forty years old, and the last thing she wanted was a baby, even Simon's. They had agreed two and a half years before when they were married that that was out of the question. She knew Simon regretted it, but now with the store, it would have been ridiculous anyway. It *was* ridiculous, she thought as she stared at the doctor in disbelief. "But I can't be!"

"Well, you are." He asked her some more questions, and calculated that the baby was due around the first of September. "Will your husband be pleased?"

"I . . . he . . ." Zoya could hardly speak, her eyes filled with tears, and promising to return in a month, she hurried out of the office.

She sat silently at dinner that night, looking as though someone had died, and Simon glanced at her worriedly several times. But he waited until they were alone in the library to ask what the doctor had said. "Was anything wrong?" He knew he couldn't live if anything happened to her, and he could see in her eyes that she was terribly upset about something.

"Simon . . ." She looked up at him with anguished eyes. "I'm pregnant."

He stared at her, and then suddenly he rushed toward her and took her in his arms with a shout of joy. "Oh darling . . . oh darling! . . . oh God, I love you! . . ." When she looked at him again, she saw that he was laughing and crying at the same time, and she didn't have the heart to tell him that all afternoon she had even thought of having an abortion. She knew they were dangerous to be sure, but she knew that several of her clients had had them and survived, and she was much too old to be having a baby. No one had a baby at forty! No one she knew anyway, no one in their right mind, tears filled her eyes again and she looked at her husband in irritation.

"How can you be so happy? I'm forty years old, I'm too old to have any more children."

He looked worried again as she cried, "Is that what the doctor said?"

"No," she said furiously, and blew her nose, "he said 'Congratulations!'" Simon could only laugh at her as she paced the room frantically. "What about the store? Simon, think of it. And what about the children?"

"It will be good for them," he sat down peacefully in a chair, looking as though he had conquered the world, "Nicholas will be in college next year, and I think he'll be pleased for us anyway. And it might do Sasha good not to be the baby anymore. In any case, she'll have to adjust to it. And the store will be fine. You can go in for a few hours every day, and you'll have a nurse afterward . . ." He already had it all planned as Zoya turned on him. She had worked so hard, and Sasha's moods were always so precarious, this was the one thing she didn't need in her life, a baby to upset the balance.

"A few hours? Do you think I can run

that place in a few hours? Simon, you're crazy!"

"No, I'm not," he said with a quiet smile, "I'm crazy about my wife though . . ." He beamed up at her, looking like a boy again. At forty-three, he was going to be a father. "I'm going to be a Daddy!" He looked so pleased that it took the wind out of her sails, as she sat down miserably on the couch and cried harder.

"Oh Simon . . . how could this happen?"

"Come here," he moved closer to her and put an arm around her shoulders, "I'll explain it . . ."

"Simon, stop that!"

"Why? You can't get pregnant now anyway." It amused him all the more because she was always so careful, but destiny dealt the cards differently sometimes, and he would not let her change that. She had already hinted darkly that things could be "changed," and he knew what she meant, but there was no question of it. He was not going to let her risk her life aborting the baby he had always wanted. "Zoya . . . sweetheart . . . calm down for a minute and think it out. You can work for as long as you can. You can probably sit in your office at the store every day until the baby comes, as long as you don't run around too much. And afterward, you can go back to work, and nothing will be changed, except that we'll have a beautiful little baby of our own to love for the rest of our lives. Is that so terrible, sweetheart?" It didn't seem it when he explained it that way, and he had been so good to her children that she knew she couldn't deny him his own. She sighed and blew her nose again.

"He'll laugh at me when he grows up, he'll think I'm his grandmother instead of his mother!"

"Not if you look anything like you do now, and why should that change?" She was still beautiful, and looked almost girlish at forty. Only the fact that she had a seventeen-year-old son ever gave her age away at all, and she was so proud of him that she talked about him all the time. But otherwise, no one would have guessed her to be more than in her late twenties, or at the very most thirty. "I love you so much," Simon reassured her again, and then Zoya's face paled as she thought of Sasha.

"What'll we tell her?"

"The good news," he smiled gently at his wife, "that we're having a baby."

"I think she'll be very upset." But that proved to be the understatement of the

century. Neither of them were prepared
for the hurricane that hit Park Avenue
when Zoya told her about the baby.

"You're *what*? That's the *most* disgusting thing I've *ever* heard! What am I going
to tell my friends for God's sake? They'll
laugh me right out of school, and it'll be *all
your fault*!" She raged as Zoya looked on
unhappily.

"Darling, it doesn't change how much I
love you. Don't you know that?" she said
helplessly.

"I don't care! And I don't want to live
here with you, if you have a baby!" She
had slammed her door and disappeared
later that afternoon, after school. It had
taken two full days to discover that she
was staying with a friend. Zoya and Simon
had called the police by then, and she met
them in the friend's living room with a
look of defiance that met their grief-
stricken faces. Zoya asked her quietly to
come home with them, and she refused
and suddenly, for the first time, Simon was
overcome with absolute fury.

"Get your things, *right now*! Do you understand?" He grabbed her arm and
shook her hard as she stared at him, he had
never done anything like it before, and
she had thought him possessed of unlim-

ited patience. But even Simon had his limits. "Now go get your hat and coat and whatever else you brought here, you're coming home with us whether you like it or not, and if you don't behave yourself, Sasha, I'm going to have you locked in a convent." And for a moment she believed him. But he didn't want his wife having a miscarriage, thanks to her spoiled brat of a daughter. Sasha came back into the room a moment later, with her things, looking somewhat subdued, and somewhat frightened of Simon. Zoya apologized profusely to the mother of Sasha's friend and they took her downstairs and drove her home, where Simon read her the riot act the moment they set foot in the apartment. "If you ever, ever dare, to give your mother any trouble again, Sasha Andrews, I'm going to beat you within an inch of your life, do you understand?" He roared, but Zoya smiled within herself. She knew he would never have laid a hand on the child, or anyone, but he was so angry his face was pale. And suddenly, she began worrying that he might have a heart attack like Clayton.

"Go to your room, Sasha," she said coldly, and the girl silently obeyed, for once amazed at their reactions, as Nicholas quietly walked in and looked at them.

"You should have done that a long time ago. I think that's what she needs. A good, swift kick in the behind." And then he laughed mischievously, as Simon relaxed again, "I'd be happy to deliver it for you, anytime you like." And then he turned to his mother with the smile that so often reminded her of her own brother's. "I just want you to know that I think it's wonderful, about the baby."

"Thank you, sweetheart," she went to him and put an arm around her tall, handsome son, looking up at him sheepishly. "You're not going to be too embarrassed that your old mother is having a baby?"

"If I had an old mother, maybe I might be." He smiled at her and a moment later his eyes met Simon's, and he saw the man's love for him there. He went to him and hugged him too.

"Congratulations, Dad," Nicholas said quietly, embracing him as tears leapt unrestrained to Simon's eyes. It was the first time the boy had called him that. A new life had begun, for all of them, not just for Simon and Zoya.

Chapter 43

In April of 1939, the World's Fair opened at Flushing Meadows, and Zoya was anxious to go, but Simon didn't think she should. It was terribly crowded, and she was four months pregnant. She was still working full-time at the store, though she was being a little more careful than before. And Simon took the children to the World's Fair instead, and they were both thrilled when they saw it. Even Sasha behaved, as she had much of the time since Simon's now famous explosion. But she was difficult with Zoya as often as she could get away with it, which was still far too often.

In June, the first transatlantic passenger flights were begun by Pan Am, and Nicholas was dying to go to Europe on the *Dixie Clipper*, but Simon wouldn't let him. He thought it was too dangerous, and more important than that, he was even more

worried than before by what was going on
in Europe. He and Zoya had gone over on
the *Normandie* again in the spring, to buy
for the store and fabric for his line of coats.
But he had felt the tension everywhere,
and he was far more aware of anti-Semitism than he had been before when he
was there. He felt certain now that there
was going to be a war, and he offered
Nicholas a graduation trip to California instead, which delighted Nicholas. He flew
to San Francisco and back, in love with
everything he'd seen there, and amused
by the size of his mother when he returned. In August, she finally stopped going to the store, and called them every
half hour instead. She didn't know what to
do with herself when she wasn't working.
Simon brought her candies and books and
the magazines she liked best, but all she
could think of by the end of August was
the nursery she'd made of the guest room
next to the library, and he found her there
every day folding tiny baby things. It was
a side of her he had never seen before. She
even reorganized his closets and changed
the furniture around in their bedroom.

"Take it easy, Zoya," he teased, "I'm
afraid to come home at night. I might sit
down in a chair that isn't there anymore."

She blushed, aware of it herself. "I don't know what's happening to me. I seem to have this constant need to get the house in order." She had redone Sasha's room too, she was away at a camp for young ladies in the Adirondacks, and it was a relief to Simon not to have to worry about her just then. And things seemed to be going well there, she had only escaped the counselors once, to go dancing with her friends in the nearby village. They had found her at the head of a conga line and summarily took her back with them, but at least they hadn't threatened to send her home. Simon wanted Zoya to be able to relax before she gave birth to their baby.

At the end of August, Germany and Russia stunned the world by signing a mutual nonaggression pact, but Zoya seemed uninterested in world news. She was too busy calling the store and changing the apartment around, and on the first of September, Simon came home and offered to take her to the movies. Sasha was due back the next night, and Nicholas was leaving the following week for Princeton, but he was out with some friends, showing off the car Simon had just given him to take to college. It was a brand-new Ford coupe, hot off the assembly line in Detroit,

with every possible extra feature they had
to offer.

"You're much too generous with him,"
Zoya had smiled, grateful as always for everything he did for them. He had stopped
by the store that night and gave her all the
news, as he noticed that she looked even
more uncomfortable than she had that
morning.

"Are you okay, sweetheart?"

"I'm fine." But she said she was too tired
to go to the movies. They went to bed at
ten o'clock that night, and an hour later,
he felt her stir, and then he heard a soft
moan, and he turned on the light. She was
lying beside him, her eyes closed, holding
her belly.

"Zoya?" He didn't know what to do, as
he leapt out of bed, rushing around the
room, looking for his clothes, and unable
to remember where he'd left them.
"Don't move. I'll call the doctor." He
couldn't even remember where the tele-
phone was as she laughed at him from the
bed.

"I think it's just indigestion." But the
indigestion got a lot worse in the next two
hours, and at three o'clock in the morning,
he called the doorman for a taxi. He
helped Zoya put on her clothes, and

helped her into the cab, waiting for them downstairs. She could hardly talk by then and she was having trouble walking, as terror enveloped him. He didn't even care about the baby suddenly, he just wanted her to be all right. He felt frantic as they wheeled her away at the hospital, and he paced the halls as the sun came up. He jumped a foot when an hour later, a nurse touched his shoulder.

"Is she all right?"

"Yes," the nurse smiled, "you have a beautiful little boy, Mr. Hirsch." He stared at her, and then began to cry, as she walked quietly away. And half an hour later, they let him see Zoya. She was dozing peacefully, with the baby in her arms, as he tiptoed into the room, and stopped in wonder as he saw his son for the first time. He had a shock of black hair like his own, and his tiny hand was curled around his mother's fingers.

"Zoya?" he whispered in the large sunny room at Doctors Hospital. "He's so beautiful," he whispered, as Zoya opened her eyes and smiled at him. It had been a difficult birth, the baby was big, but even then, right afterward, she knew it was worth it.

"He looks like you," she said, her voice still hoarse from the anesthetic.

"Poor kid." His eyes filled with tears again, and he bent to kiss her, he had never been happier in his life, and Zoya looked so happy and proud as she gently smoothed a hand over the silky black hair. "What'll we call him?"

"What about Matthew?" she whispered as Simon looked at his son.

"Matthew Hirsch."

"Matthew Simon Hirsch," she said, and then drifted off to sleep again, with her son in her arms, and her husband looking on, the tears of joy falling into her mane of red hair, as he kissed her.

Chapter 44

Matthew Simon Hirsch was still in the hospital and he was one day old on the day that war was declared in Europe. Britain and France had declared war on Germany, when their ally Poland was invaded by Germany. Simon came into Zoya's room with grim eyes and announced the news, but a moment later he had almost forgotten as he held Matthew, and watched the baby give a lusty cry for his mother.

When Zoya came home to the apartment on Park Avenue, Sasha was there to greet her. Even she couldn't resist the beautiful baby boy who looked so exactly like Simon.

"He has Mama's nose," she announced with amused delight, fascinated that everything was so perfect and so small as she held him for the first time. At fourteen, she was too young to visit at the hospital, but Nicholas had met his brother before leaving for Princeton. "And he has my ears!" Sasha giggled, "but the rest is Simon."

On September 27, after being brutally attacked, Warsaw surrendered, with enormous loss of life. Simon was heartbroken by the news, and he and Zoya talked long into the night, as she remembered the revolution. It was terrible, and Simon mourned the Jews being massacred all over Germany and Eastern Europe. He was doing everything he could for those who could get out. He had established a relief fund, and was trying to get papers for relatives he had never heard of. People in Europe would use phone books to call people in New York with similar names, and beg them for assistance, which he never refused. But those he could help were a precious few. The rest were being led to their death, locked up in detention camps, or slaughtered on the streets of Warsaw.

When Matthew was three months old, Zoya went back to work, on the day that Russia invaded Finland. Simon followed the news from Europe avidly, particularly Edward R. Murrow's broadcasts from London.

It was December first by then, and Zoya was excited to find Countess Zoya swarming. And they all went to see *The Wizard of Oz* when Sasha got out of school. Nicholas was home from Princeton and loving it, although he talked a great deal about the war with Simon, while he was home on vacation.

He liked it even more the second year, and before going back to Princeton again he went back to California for summer vacation. Zoya hadn't been able to go to Europe this year, with the war on, they had to use designers from the States. She was particularly fond of Norman Norell and Tony Traina. It was September 1941 and Simon was certain the country would go to war, but Roosevelt was still insisting they wouldn't. And the war certainly hadn't hurt the store, it was the best year Zoya had had. Four years after she had opened her doors, she was using all five floors of the building Simon had wisely bought. He had bought four more textile mills in the South, and his own business was doing extremely well. She had a whole department of his coats and she always teased him and called him her favorite supplier.

Little Matthew was two years old by

then, and the apple of everyone's eye, even Sasha's. She was a blossoming sixteen, and by everyone's standards, a raving beauty. She was tall and thin as Zoya's mother had been, but instead of Natalya's regal bearing, there was a sensual quality that drew men like bees to honey. Zoya was just grateful that she was still in school, and hadn't done anything outrageous in almost a year. As a reward, Simon had promised to take them all skiing in Sun Valley that winter, and Nicholas was anxious to join them.

They were sitting in the library discussing their plans on December 7, when Simon turned the radio on. He liked to listen to the news when he was at home, and he had Matthew on his knee as his face froze. He pushed him into Sasha's arms, and ran into the next room to find Zoya. His face was white as he found her in their bedroom.

"The Japanese have bombed Pearl Harbor, in Hawaii!"

"Oh my God . . ." He pulled her into the other room with him to listen to the news, as the announcer explained in staccato tones what had happened. They all stood rooted to where they stood, as Matthew tugged at Zoya's skirt and tried to get her attention, but she only picked him up and held him close. All she could think of was that Nicholas was twenty years old. She didn't want him to die as her brother had with the Preobrajensky. "Simon . . . what will happen now?" But she instinctively knew as they listened. Simon's predictions had finally come true. They were going to war. President Roosevelt announced it, with a voice filled with deep regret, but not as great as Zoya's. Simon enlisted in the army the following morning. He was forty-five years old, and Zoya begged him not to go, but he looked at her sadly when he came home.

"I have to, Zoya. I couldn't live with myself if I just sat here on my ass and did nothing to defend my country." And it wasn't just for his country, it was for the Jews in Europe that he did it. All over the world, the cause of freedom was being destroyed, he couldn't sit back quietly and let it happen.

"Please . . ." Zoya begged, "Please, Simon . . ." She was overcome with grief, "I couldn't live without you." She had lived through that before, losing the people she loved, and she knew she couldn't survive it again . . . not Simon, so gentle and so dear, and so loving. "I love you too much. Don't go. Please . . ." She was gripped with fear but he couldn't be dissuaded. "Zoya, I have to." They lay side by side in their bed that night, and he touched her gently with the big hands that held his son so lovingly, the same hands that touched her now and held her close to him as she cried, terrified of losing the man she loved so dearly. "Nothing's going to happen."

"You don't know that. We need you too much for you to go. Think of Matthew." She would have said anything to make him stay, but even that didn't persuade him.

"I am thinking of him. The world won't be worth living in when he grows up, if the rest of us don't stand up now, and fight for decency and what's right." He was still aching over what had happened in Poland two years before. But now that his own country had been attacked, there was clearly no choice. And even Zoya's passionate lovemaking that night and renewed pleas didn't sway him as much as he loved her, he knew he had to go. His love for Zoya was equaled only by his sense of duty to his country, no matter what it cost him.

He was sent to Fort Benning, Georgia,

to train, and three months later he came home for two days, before leaving for San Francisco. Zoya wanted to go back to Mrs. Whitman's little place in Connecticut to be alone with him, but Simon felt he should spend his last days at home with the children. Nicholas came home from Princeton to see him off, and the two men solemnly shook hands at Grand Central Station.

"Take care of your mother for me," Simon spoke quietly in the din around him, always gentle, always calm. Even Sasha was crying. Matthew was crying too, although he didn't understand what was happening. He only knew that his Daddy was going somewhere and his mother and sister were crying, and his big brother looked unhappy too.

Nicholas hugged the man who had been a father to him for the past five years, and there were tears in his eyes as Simon spoke to him. "Take care, son."

"I want to go too." He said it so low that his mother didn't hear him.

"Not yet," Simon answered. "Try to finish school. They may draft you anyway." But he didn't want to be drafted, he wanted to go to England and fly planes. He had been thinking about it for months, and by March he couldn't stand it any longer. Simon was in the Pacific by then, and Nicholas told them the day after Sasha's seventeenth birthday. Zoya didn't want to hear it, she raged at him and she cried.

"Isn't it enough that your father's gone, Nicholas?" She had come to refer to Simon as that and Nicholas didn't object. He loved him as a father.

"Mama, I have to. Can't you understand?"

"No, I can't. As long as they don't draft you, why can't you stay where you are? Simon wants you to finish school, he told you that himself." She tried desperately to reason with him, but she could always sense that he wouldn't be swayed as she sat with him in the living room and cried. She already missed Simon desperately and the prospect of having Nicholas go too was more than she could cope with.

"I can go back to Princeton after the war." But for years, he had thought that he was wasting his time. He enjoyed Princeton very much, but he wanted to enter the real world, to work as Simon did, and now to fight as he was doing in the Pacific. He wrote to them whenever he could, telling them as much as he was allowed to of what was going on around him. But Zoya wished now more than ever that he were at home to talk Nicholas into going back to school. After two days of arguments, she knew she had lost. And three weeks later, he was gone, to England to train. She sat in the apartment, alone, thinking bitterly of all she had lost and feared she might lose again . . . a father, a brother, a country in the end, and now her husband and son were gone. Sasha was out, and she sat staring into space. She didn't even hear the doorbell ring. It rang again and again, and she thought of not answering it at all, and then slowly she got up. There was no one she wanted to see. She just wanted the two of them to come home, before anything happened to them. She knew that if anything did happen, she couldn't bear it.

"Yes?" She had come home from the store an hour before, and even that didn't keep her mind full enough these days. Nothing did. She was constantly obsessed with thoughts of Simon, and now she would have Nicholas to worry about too, flying bombing raids over Europe.

The boy in uniform stood nervously outside. He had come to hate the job in the past few months. And he stared at Zoya now, wishing they had sent someone else. She looked like a nice woman, with her red hair intricately tied in a knot, and her smile as she looked at him, not understanding what was coming.

"Telegram for you, ma'am," and then with the sad eyes of a child, he muttered, "I'm sorry," as he handed it to her and turned away. He didn't want to see her eyes when she opened it and read the news. The black border said it all as she caught her breath and gasped, her hands shaking uncontrollably as she tore it open, and the elevator returned to rescue him. He was already gone as she read the words . . . Regret to inform you that your husband, Simon Ishmael Hirsch, was killed yesterday . . . the rest was a blur as she sank to her knees in the hall, sobbing his name . . . and suddenly remembering Nicolai as he bled to death on the marble floor of the Fontanka Palace. . . .

She lay there and sobbed for what seemed like hours, longing for his gentle touch again, for the sight of him, the smell of the cologne he used . . . the fresh smell of the soap he used to shave . . . anything . . . anything . . . he would never come home again. Simon was gone, like the others.

Chapter 45

When Sasha came home, she found her mother sitting in the dark. When she heard why, for once in her life she did the right thing. She called Axelle, who came to sit with her and make plans for a memorial service. The next day Countess Zoya was closed, its doors draped with black crepe. And Axelle stayed at the apartment with Zoya, as she sat woodenly, unable to think coherently, or do more than nod, as Axelle planned the memorial service for her. Zoya seemed unable to make any of the necessary decisions which was so unlike her.

Her final act of courage had been in going to see Simon's parents on Houston Street the night before, his mother had screamed and wailed in her husband's arms, and finally Zoya departed quietly, stumbling as she left, clutching Sasha's arm. She was blinded by grief and pain and the loss of the man she had loved more than any other.

The service itself was an agony, with its unfamiliar litany and his mother's wails, as Zoya clutched Axelle's and Sasha's hands, and then they had taken her back to cry endlessly at her apartment.

"You must go back to work as soon as you can," Axelle looked at her and said almost harshly. She knew how easy it would be to let go, to give up, she almost had when her own husband died. And Zoya couldn't allow herself that luxury now. She had three children to think of, and herself. And she had survived tragedy before. She had to do it again now, but she only shook her head, as the tears continued to stream down her face as she looked bleakly at Axelle. There seemed to be nothing left she wanted to live for.

"I can't even think about that now. I don't care about the store. I don't care about anything. Only Simon."

"Well, you have to. You have a responsibility to your children, yourself, your clients . . . and to Simon. You must continue in his memory, continue to build what he helped you start. You can't give up now. The store was his gift to you, Zoya."

It was true, but the store seemed so trivial now, so ridiculously unimportant, without Simon to share it with, what did any of it matter?

"You must be strong." She handed the beautiful redhead a glass of brandy from the bar, and insisted that she take a sip as she watched her. "Drink it all. It will do you good." Axelle was suddenly a martinet as Zoya smiled through her tears at her friend, and then only began to cry harder. "You didn't survive the revolution and everything that happened after that, only to give up now, Zoya Hirsch." But the sound of his name attached to her own only made her cry more, and Axelle returned every day until she convinced Zoya to go back to the store. It seemed a miracle when she finally agreed to go back, but only for a few minutes. She wore somber black, and sheer black stockings, but at least she was back in her office. And the minutes became hours after a few days. And eventually she went and sat at her desk, for most of the day, staring into space and remembering Simon. She went there like a robot every day and Sasha had begun giving her trouble again. Zoya knew she was losing control of her, but she couldn't deal with that just then either. All she could do was survive the days, hour by hour, hiding in her office, and then go home at night to dream of Simon. Even little Matthew broke her heart, just seeing him was a constant reminder of his father.

Simon's attorneys had been calling her for weeks, and she had avoided all their attempts to see her. Simon had left two loyal employees in charge of his mills and the factory where they made his coats. She knew everything was in control there, and she was having enough trouble running her own store without facing that as well. And talking to the attorneys about his estate would mean facing the fact that he was gone and she couldn't. She had been thinking of him, remembering their weekend in Connecticut when one of her assistants gently knocked on the door of her office.

"Countess Zoya?" The woman spoke through the door as Zoya dried her eyes again. She had been sitting at her desk, staring at a photograph of Simon. She'd had another argument with Sasha the night before, but now even that seemed unimportant.

"I'll be right out." She blew her nose again, and glanced in a mirror to patch up her makeup.

"There's someone here to see you."

"I don't want to see anyone," she spoke quietly as she opened the door a crack. "Tell them I'm not here." And then as an afterthought, "Who is it?"

"A Mr. Paul Kelly. He said it was important."

"I don't know him, Christine. Just tell him I'm out." The girl looked nervous, it was so upsetting to see Zoya as devastated as she had been since her husband was killed, but it was understandable. They were all worried these days about husbands, brothers, friends, and the dreaded black-bordered telegrams, like the one that had been delivered to Zoya.

Zoya closed the door again, praying that no one important would come in that day. She couldn't bear the sympathetic looks, the kind words. It just made it worse, and then there was a knock on the door again. It was Christine, nervous and flustered.

"He says he'll wait. What should I do now?"

Zoya sighed. She couldn't imagine who he was. Perhaps the husband of a customer, someone who was afraid she'd discuss a mistress with a wife. She got visits like that sometimes, and she always reassured them with polite restraint. But she hadn't dealt with anyone since Simon's death. She walked back to the door and opened it to her assistant again, looking gaunt in her black dress and black stockings. And her eyes told a tale of grief beyond measure. "All right. Show him in." She had nothing else to do anyway. She couldn't keep her mind on anything anymore. Not here, or at home, she was no good to anyone now. And she stood quietly, as Christine ushered in a tall, distinguished man in a dark blue suit, with white hair and blue eyes. He was struck by how beautiful she was, and how grim she looked, all dressed in black, with eyes that seemed to look right through him.

"Mrs. Hirsch?" It was unusual for people to call her that here, and she nodded unhappily, wondering who he was, but not really caring.

"Yes?"

"My name is Paul Kelly. Our firm is handling your husband's . . . er . . . ah . . . estate." She looked grief-stricken as she shook his hand, and invited him to sit down on one of the chairs near her desk. "We've been very anxious to get in touch with you." He looked at her with gentle reproach, and she noticed that he had interesting eyes. He had an Irish face and she correctly guessed that he had once had jet-black hair, now turned snowy white. "You haven't been answering our calls." But seeing her, he now understood why. The woman was devastated by grief, and he felt deeply sorry for her.

"I know." She looked away. And then with a sigh, she looked at him. "To tell you the truth, I didn't want to hear from you. It made it all much too real. It's . . ." Her voice dimmed to a whisper as she looked away again, ". . . it's been very difficult for me."

There was a long silence as he nodded, watching her. It was obvious how stricken she was, and yet beyond the pain, he sensed enormous strength, strength she herself had forgotten. "I understand. But we need to know your wishes on some of these matters. We were going to suggest a formal reading of the will, but perhaps under the circumstances at the present time . . ." His voice drifted off, as slowly her eyes met his again. "Perhaps all you need to know right now is that he left almost everything he had in trust for you, and his son. His parents and his two uncles have been left large bequests, as have your two children, Mrs. Hirsch." And then, sounding official, he went on, "Very generous bequests, I might add, of a million dollars each, in trust, of course. They can't touch any of the principal until they're twenty-one, and there are some other conditions in the trust, but very reasonable ones, I'm quite sure. Our trust department helped him with all that," but he stopped as he saw Zoya staring at him. "Is something wrong?" He was suddenly sorry he had come. She was really not up to listening to what he was saying.

"A million dollars each?" It was far more than she'd ever dreamed, and they were her children, not his. She was stunned. But it was so typical of Simon. Her love for him cut through her like a knife again.

"Yes, that's correct. In addition, he wanted to offer your son a position in his firm, when he's old enough, of course. It's a large company to run, with the factory, and all six textile mills, particularly now, with the war contracts that came in after he left . . ." He droned on as Zoya tried to absorb it. How like Simon to provide for all of them, and even plan on taking Nicholas into business with him. How like Simon . . . if only he had lived to be with them, instead of leaving them a fortune.

"What contracts?" Her mind was slowly

coming to life again, there was so much to think about, so much Simon had built, from nothing at all. And she owed it to him to try and understand it. "He didn't mention any war contracts to me."

"They were still uncertain when he left. The mills will be providing all the fabric for our military uniforms for the duration of the war." He glanced at her, unable to overlook how beautiful she was, and how elegant, as she sat there with quiet dignity, draped in grief and the pain of losing her husband.

"Oh my God . . . What does that mean in terms of sales?" For a moment, it was as though Simon were back. She knew how excited he would have been, and when the attorney gave her a rough idea of what it meant, she stared at him in disbelief. "But that's not possible . . . is it?" She wore the suggestion of a smile, and looked suddenly much younger, and certainly not forty-three years old, which he knew from the documents he had read. But that seemed difficult to believe now.

"I'm afraid it is possible. To be blunt, Mrs. Hirsch, you and your son are going to be very rich after the war. And if Nicholas joins the firm, Mr. Hirsch has provided a considerable percentage for him." He had

thought of everything, but it was small
consolation now. What would they do
with all of it without Simon? But as she
listened, she knew that Axelle had been
right. She owed it to Simon to continue
what he had built. It had been his final gift
to her, to all of them. And she had to continue for him, and their children.

"Are the men he left in charge capable
of handling this?" She narrowed her eyes
as she looked at him, as though seeing him
for the first time, and he smiled at her. She
was beautiful when she smiled, even more
beautiful than he had first thought her.

"Yes, I believe they are. They have to
answer to us, of course, and," he met her
eyes squarely with his own, "and to you.
Mr. Hirsch has made you a director of all
his companies. He had great respect for
your business sense." He looked away as
tears filled her eyes and she fought to
speak in a voice that was barely more than
a whisper. He had meant more to her than
all his companies, but this man could
never understand that.

"I loved him very much." She stood up
and walked away, looking out on Fifth Avenue. She couldn't give up now. She had
to go on . . . for the children . . . and
for him. She turned slowly to face Paul

Kelly again. "Thank you for coming here," she spoke through her tears and almost took his breath away with her beauty, "I might never have answered your calls." She hadn't wanted to. She hadn't wanted to face losing Simon, but now she knew she had to.

He laughed ruefully, "I was afraid of that. That's why I came. I hope you'll forgive me for intruding on you." And then, "It's a beautiful store. My wife shops here whenever she can." Zoya nodded, thinking of all the favored clients she had neglected and all but forgotten.

"Please tell her to ask for me when she comes in again. We can show her whatever she likes right here in my office."

"Perhaps it would be kinder to me if you just lock the doors, before she gets here." He smiled and Zoya smiled in answer. And then he asked her a few questions about Nicholas. She explained that he was in London, flying bombers with the American forces attached to the RAF. "You have a great deal on your plate, don't you, Mrs. Hirsch?" She nodded sadly, and he was touched by how vulnerable she was. She had built an empire of her own, with her husband's help of course, and yet she seemed as delicate as butterfly wings as she sat looking at him from across her desk. "Please let me know if there is anything I can do to help you." But what could he do? No one could bring Simon back to her, and that was all she wanted.

"I want to spend some time in my husband's offices," she said, frowning slightly. "If I'm going to be a director of his companies, I'll have to familiarize myself with all of it." And perhaps in work she would find blessed numbness.

"That might be wise." He was deeply impressed by her in every possible way. "I wanted to do that myself, and I'll be happy to share all of our information with you." He was a partner in one of New York's most important law firms on Wall Street, and she guessed that he was about ten years older than she was herself, but the way his eyes danced when he laughed made him look younger. In fact, he was fifty-three, and he looked it. They talked for a little while, and regretfully he stood up. "Shall we meet next week in Simon's office on Seventh Avenue, or would you like me to bring as much as I can here to your office?"

"I'll meet you there. I want them to know they're being watched . . . by both of us," she smiled and shook his hand, and then she spoke softly again, "Thank you, Mr. Kelly. Thank you for coming here."

He smiled again, his Irish charm evident in his eyes. "I'm looking forward to working with you." She thanked him again and he left, as she sat at her desk and stared. The numbers he had quoted to her from the war contracts were staggering. For the son of a tailor from the Lower East Side, he had done a hell of a job. He had built an empire. She smiled at the photograph of Simon again, and quietly left her office, looking like herself again for the first time since he'd died. The saleswomen noticed it too as they scurried past her to wait on their customers, and Zoya took the elevator that afternoon and stopped on each floor to look around at what they were doing. It was time they saw her again. Time for Countess Zoya to go on . . . with the memory of him close to her heart, as it always would be . . . like all the people she'd loved. But she couldn't think of them now. There was so much work left to do. For Simon.

Chapter 46

By the end of 1942, Zoya was spending one full day a week in Simon's offices on Seventh Avenue, and Paul Kelly was usually there with her. They had begun very formally, as Mr. Kelly and Mrs. Hirsch. She had worn simple black suits, and he had worn pinstripes or dark blue. But after several months, a touch of humor had crept in. He told her terrible jokes and she made him laugh with stories from Countess Zoya. She wore easier clothes to work in after that, and he took off his jacket and rolled up his sleeves. He was deeply impressed by her business acumen, Simon had been right to respect her as he had. At first Paul had thought he was crazy to make her a director, but he was crazy like a fox, and she was even smarter than that. And at the same time, she managed to remain feminine, and she never raised her voice, but it was clear to everyone that she would tolerate no nonsense from anyone. And she kept a sharp eye on the books. Always.

"How did you ever come to all this?" he asked her one day over lunch at Simon's desk. They ordered in sandwiches and were taking a welcome break. Atherton, Kelly, and Schwartz had replaced one of Simon's two top managers the previous day, and there was a lot of cleaning up to do now.

"By mistake," she laughed, she told him about her days in burlesque, and her job at Axelle's, and long before that dancing with the Ballet Russe. The success of her remarkable store was known to everyone by then. He himself had gone to Yale, and he had married a Boston debutante named Allison O'Keefe. They had had three children in four years, and he spoke of her with respect, but there was no spark in his eyes when he said her name, none of the laughter Zoya had so often shared with him. It came as no surprise to her when he admitted to her late one after-noon after a grueling day that he hated to go home.

"Allison and I have been strangers for years." She didn't envy him that. She and Simon had been best friends, aside from the physical passion they had shared, which she still remembered with longing.

"Why do you stay married to her?" The whole world seemed to be getting divorced, and then she remembered before he even answered her, with a look of regret.

"We're both Catholic, Zoya. She'd never agree to it. I tried about ten years ago. She had a nervous breakdown, or so she claimed, and she's never been the same since. I can't leave her now. And, well . . ." He hesitated, and then decided to be honest with her. She was a woman he could trust, in the past year they had become fast friends. "To be honest with you, she drinks. I couldn't live with myself if I were responsible for something happening to her."

"It doesn't sound like much fun for you," an icy Boston debutante who drank and wouldn't give him a divorce. Zoya almost shuddered at the thought, but she saw a lot of women like that at the store, women who shopped because they were bored, and never wore what they took home because they didn't really care how they looked. "It must be lonely for you," she looked at him with gentle eyes, and he reminded himself not to say too much.

They had to work together every week, and he had learned that lesson long since. There had been other women in his life, but they never meant very much to him. They were just someone to talk to once in a while, or to make love to occasionally, but he had never met anyone like Zoya before, and he hadn't felt this way about a woman in years, or perhaps ever.

"I have my work to keep me going," he smiled gently at her, "just like you." He knew how hard she worked. It was all she lived for now, that and the children she loved so dearly.

By 1943, they were having dinner together every Monday night, when they left Simon's offices. It became an opportunity to discuss at greater length whatever they had done that day, and they usually ate at the little restaurants just off Seventh Avenue.

"How's Matt?" He smiled at her one night that spring.

"Matthew? He's fine." He was three and a half, and the light of her life. "He makes me feel young again." It was ironic that she had thought she was too old to have a child when he was born, and yet he gave her the most joy of all now. Sasha was out so much, it was almost as though she were gone. She had just turned eighteen. He had seen Sasha once, and was stunned by how beautiful she was. But he suspected what a handful she was for Zoya too. More than once Zoya had said that she could barely keep her in school. And Nicholas was still in London, and she prayed for his safe return night and day.

"How are your children, Paul?" He didn't talk about them much. His daughters were both married, one in Chicago, and the other on the West Coast, and his son was somewhere around Guam. And he had two grandchildren in California he seldom saw. His wife didn't like to go to California and he was afraid to leave her alone at home.

"My kids are fine, I guess," he smiled, "they're so long gone from the nest, we don't hear from them much. Their childhoods weren't easy anyway, with Allison drinking so much. Something like that changes everything," and then he smiled at her, he always liked hearing her news. "What's new at the store?"

"Not much. I opened a new department, for men this time, and we're trying out some new lines. It's going to be nice to get to Europe again, after the war, so we can try new things." But there was no end in sight as it raged on across the Atlantic.

"I'd love to go back to Europe again sometime. By myself," he grinned at her honestly. Baby-sitting for his wife was no fun, as she made her way from bar to bar, or hid in her room, pretending to be tired instead of drunk. Zoya wondered why he put up with it. It seemed to be a terrible burden on him, and she said as much when he took her home and she invited him up for a drink. He had only been in her apartment once before, and he remembered only an impression that it was cozy and warm, the way she was when she looked at him. He went up happily in the elevator with her, and sat on the couch in the library as she poured him a drink. She had called out to Sasha when they arrived, but the maid was out and Sasha wasn't home yet. Only Matthew was there, asleep in his room with his nanny.

"You ought to take a holiday somewhere sometime, Paul. Go to California and see your children by yourself. Why should your life be crippled by what your wife does?"

"You're right, but it's not much fun alone." He was always comfortable and honest with her, as he was now as he sipped his drink, and watched Zoya where she sat. She was wearing a white dress and her hair was pulled back like a girl's.

"No, it's not much fun to do things alone." She smiled. "But I'm getting used to it." It had been brutal getting used to a life without Simon.

"Don't get used to it, Zoya. It's lousy." He said it with such vehemence, Zoya looked startled. "You deserve more than that." He had spent his life alone and he didn't want to see it happen to her. She was vibrant and beautiful and alive and she deserved more than the loneliness he knew too well.

But she only laughed and shook her head. "I'm forty-four years old, I'm too old to start again." And she knew that no one would ever measure up to Simon.

"Bullshit, I'm almost fifty-five, and if I had the chance to start again, I'd leap at it." It was the first time he had said that to her, as he stretched his long legs out before him, his shock of white hair smoothly combed, his eyes alive as he looked at her. He always loved being with her. He looked forward to their hardworking Mondays all week. They were what kept him going.

"I'm happy like this." She was lying to

herself more than to him. She wasn't happy, but it was all she had now.

"No, you're not. Why should you be?"

"Because it's all I have," she spoke quietly, wise enough to accept her life as it was, rather than longing for a past that was gone forever. She had done that before, and she wouldn't do it again. She had to be content with what she had, her children and her work, and once a week her talks with Paul Kelly.

He was looking hard at her then, and without saying a word he set his glass down, and went to sit next to her, staring at her intently with the blue eyes that bored into her. "I just want you to know something. I can't do a damn thing about it, and I can't offer you anything right now, but Zoya . . . I love you. I have since the day we met. You're the best thing that's ever happened to me." She looked stunned as he looked at her, and then without saying another word he took her in his arms and kissed her hard on the mouth, feeling his heart soar and his whole body ache for her. "You are so beautiful . . . and so strong . . ."

"Don't say that, Paul . . . don't . . ." She wanted to push him away, but she couldn't bring herself to. She felt so guilty

for wanting him, it seemed to deny
Simon's very memory, and yet she
couldn't stop herself as she kissed him
again, and clung to him as though she
were drowning.

"I love you so much," he whispered,
kissing her again, his powerful arms holding her close, feeling her heart beat
against his chest, and then he looked at
her and smiled. "Let's go somewhere . . .
away . . . anywhere . . . it would do us
both good."

"I can't."

"Yes, you can . . . *we* can." He held
tightly to her hand and felt himself come
alive again. The years seemed to fall away
from him as he looked at her. He was
young again and he wasn't going to let her
get away from him. If he had to live with
Allison for the rest of his life, then maybe
at least, for one shining moment, he could
have Zoya.

"Paul, this is crazy," she pulled away
from him, and walked around the room,
seeing Simon's face in their photographs,
glancing at his trophies, his treasures, his
art books. "We don't have a right to this."

But he wasn't going to let her go now. If
she had slapped his face, he would have
apologized and left, but he could see now

that she wanted him as badly as he wanted her. "Why not? Who makes those rules? You're not married. I am, but not in any way that means anything to anyone. I haven't been in years. I'm trapped in a marriage of form to a woman who doesn't even know I'm alive, and hasn't loved me in years, if she ever did . . . don't I have a right to more than that? I'm in love with you," his eyes fought for what he so desperately wanted, as she watched him.

"Why? Why do you love me, Paul?"

"Because you're exactly what and who I've always wanted."

"I can't give you very much." She was honest with him, as she had always been with Clayton and Simon. "Even a little of you will be enough, I understand that." And then, more quietly he kissed her, and much to her own amazement, she didn't fight him. They sat and talked for hours after that, kissing, holding hands, and it was after midnight when he left, promising to call her the next day, and she sat in the quiet apartment, feeling guilty when he left. It was wrong, it had to be . . . wasn't it? What would Simon think? But Simon wouldn't think anything, he was gone, and she was alive, and Paul Kelly meant something to her too. She valued his friendship, and he had stirred something in her she had all but forgotten. She was still sitting there, thinking about him, when she heard Sasha come in, and she walked quietly into her room. She was wearing a bright red dress and her makeup was smeared, and Zoya didn't like the look on her face. She suspected that she was drunk, and she had confronted her about it before. She faced her with tired eyes now. It was exhausting always fighting with her.

"Where have you been?" Her voice was calm, she was still thinking of Paul as she looked her daughter over.

"Out." She turned her back so her mother couldn't see her face. Zoya was right. She was drunk, but still beautiful.

"Doing what?"

"Having dinner with a friend."

"Sasha, you're only eighteen, you can't run around anywhere you like. What about school?"

"I graduate in two months, what difference does it make now?"

"It makes a big difference to me. You have to behave yourself. People will talk if you're too wild, they know who you are, who I am. You don't want all that, Sasha. Please be sensible." But there was no hope of that, and hadn't been long since. Since Simon had died and her brother had gone, Sasha had run wild, and Zoya had almost given up hope of controlling her, she was afraid to lose her entirely. More than once, she had threatened to move out, which would have been even worse. At least this way Zoya had some idea of what was going on and what she was doing.

"That's a lot of old-fashioned crap," Sasha said as she tossed her dress on the floor and stalked the room in her slip. "People don't believe in that garbage these days."

"People believe in the same things they always did. You're coming out this year. You don't want them saying ugly things about you, sweetheart." Sasha shrugged and didn't answer her, and with a sigh Zoya kissed her good night, smelling the liquor on her breath, the smoke in her hair, as she looked at her unhappily. "I don't want you to drink."

"Why not? I'm of age."

"That's not the point."

Sasha only shrugged again and turned her back until her mother left. It was pointless even talking to her. Zoya longed for Nicholas to come home, maybe he would still have some influence on her.

Surely no one else did. And now Zoya worried about what would happen when Sasha started coming into the money Simon had left. She would really go wild then, if someone didn't stop her before that. She was still thinking about it when the phone rang at one o'clock. Her heart stopped for an instant, fearing terrible news. But it was Paul. He was at home, but he had decided to call her. Allison slept locked in her own room, and after leaving Zoya's warmth, he was doubly lonely.

"I just wanted to tell you how much tonight meant to me. You've given me something very special."

"I don't know how, Paul," her voice was low and soft, and in her mind, she had given him very little. A few kisses and the warmth of a moment.

"You're making my life exciting again. Just our Monday nights make the rest of my life worth living."

She realized then how much she'd looked forward to them too, he was intelligent and kind and amusing.

"I'm going to miss you this week." And then he smiled, "do you suppose lightning would strike if we met on a Tuesday?"

"Do you suppose we should try it?" She

felt very bold as she said it. And they both laughed like happy children.

"Let's have lunch tomorrow and find out." He was smiling as he hadn't in years. She made him feel like a boy, and there was something about him that made her feel happy and peaceful.

"Do you suppose we should?" She wanted to feel guilty, but oddly enough she didn't. She had the odd feeling that Simon would have understood it.

"Tomorrow at one o'clock?"

"Make it noon." Her hand trembled as they hung up. It was a crazy thing to do . . . and yet, she didn't want to stop. She remembered the touch of his lips on hers in the library that night, and there was something innocent and sweet about it. He was her friend, no matter what happened now. He was someone she could work with and talk to, and spend time with, discussing his business and her children. He listened to her, and he seemed to care about what happened. She wondered if that was wrong but that night, when she slept, she dreamt of Simon, and he was standing next to Paul Kelly, and smiling.

Chapter 47

Paul arrived at the store shortly before noon the following day, and found her sitting in her office going over her work with a serious look and a pen stuck in her hair. He knocked softly on the door, and smiled as he opened it and saw her sitting at her desk.

"That's a familiar picture," he smiled as she looked up at him. "Too busy, Zoya? Should I come back later?"

"No, it's all right. It can wait," she smiled, enjoying the warmth of their friendship. He had been looking forward to seeing her all day, and he was struck again when she stood up and went to get her handbag by how lovely she was. She was still a remarkably beautiful woman.

"Rough day?" he asked, with his warm Irish smile.

"Not as rough as it could be." Her smile answered his, pleased that he had come to see her. It was easier meeting him here than in Simon's office. This was her turf, not his, and it allowed Paul to share her present more than her past, which suddenly seemed more important.

They walked to lunch at "21," and at three o'clock they were still talking and laughing. Spencer Tracy was at a table nearby, with a woman in a large hat and dark glasses, and Zoya wondered who she was, but Paul wasn't interested in her. He couldn't take his eyes off Zoya.

"Why are you doing this?" she asked finally, her eyes searching his, but comforted by what she saw there. There was only kindness and strength, and all the good feelings he had for Zoya.

"Because I love you," he said very softly. "I never intended to fall in love with you, but I did. Is that so wrong?" She couldn't tell him that it was, after all she knew of the emptiness of his life with Allison.

"It's not wrong. But, Paul . . ." She hesitated and then went on, ". . . what will we have if we indulge ourselves? A few stolen moments from time to time. Is that what you want?"

"If that's all there is, I'll be grateful. To me, they are treasured hours with you,

Zoya. The rest is . . . well, whatever it has to be." And he instinctively knew that she didn't want more than that from him. She had her children, the store, and her memories of Simon. "I won't ask you for more than that. I don't have a right to. I won't lie to you. Ever. You know that I can't leave Allison, and if what I can give you isn't enough, I'll understand it." He gently took her hand in his under the table. "Maybe I'm being very selfish." Zoya shook her head, as near them she saw Spencer Tracy laughing. She wondered again who the woman was and why he looked so happy.

"I'm not sure I'm ready for more than that anyway. I may never be. I loved Simon very much."

"I know that."

And then, in a small voice, "But I think I love you too . . ." It was so odd, she had never expected this, but she liked being with him. She had every Monday, and she had come to rely on him and respect him.

"I won't ask you for more than you want to give. I understand that." She couldn't ask any more of him. He seemed to understand everything she was feeling. And then, feeling braver, he smiled gently at her. "Will you go away with me one day, when you're ready?"

She looked at him for a long time, and then slowly nodded her head. "I don't know when that will be. I'm not ready yet." Although his kisses the night before had stirred her deeply. But she was not yet ready to be unfaithful to the memory of her husband.

"I'm not pressing you. I can wait. Maybe even for a lifetime." They both smiled. He was so different from Simon, with his buoyant impatience and excitement about life, and Clayton with his gentle, aristocratic ways. Paul Kelly was his own man, with his own style and situation.

"Thank you, Paul." She looked up at him gratefully, and without saying another word, he leaned over and kissed her.

"Let's have dinner whenever we can." He looked happy and hopeful.

"Won't Allison mind?"

He looked sad for a moment. "She won't even notice."

Zoya kissed him that time, a kiss to heal the hurt of years of loneliness. They were both lonely people now, yet their time together was always lively and happy. The decisions they made with Simon's business were important ones and she loved telling him about the store. Sometimes she made him laugh for hours, telling him about her more outrageous clients . . . or about little Matthew.

Paul walked her back to the store afterward, and they were both shocked to realize it was almost four o'clock, and more than ever, he didn't want to leave her.

"Can you make dinner Friday night, or shall we leave it till Monday?" He didn't press her as he looked down at her happily outside the store. She knew Sasha was going away for the weekend, and she suddenly wanted to see him before they met again in Simon's office.

"Dinner would be lovely." Her eyes touched his with green fire and he smiled.

"I must have done something right in my life to be so lucky now."

"Don't be silly." She laughed and then kissed his cheek as he promised to call her. She knew he would, and she would call him too, even if only on the pretext of business.

But the roses that arrived for her that afternoon were far from businesslike. They were two dozen white roses, because she had once told him that she loved them. And she'd long since known that he seldom forgot anything. The card read,

"Not stolen moments, darling Zoya, only borrowed. Thank you for the loan of you, for each precious moment. Love, P." She read the card, and smiled as she put it in her handbag, and left her office again to tend to her clients. But there was no denying Paul had added something to her life. He had added something very precious, something she had almost forgotten . . . the touch of a hand, the look of a man who cared about her and wanted to be there for her. There was no telling now where life would lead them one day. Perhaps nowhere. But in the meantime, she knew she needed him, just as he needed Zoya. And as she went back to work, she walked with a lighter step. She didn't even feel guilty about it.

"Who did you see at lunch today?" her assistant asked curiously as they got ready to close the store. It was rare for Zoya to leave the store for lunch. But she only laughed as her eyes danced as they hadn't in months.

"Spencer Tracy," she answered confidentially.

"Sure," the girl smiled in answer. But she had. It was true. She had seen Spencer Tracy . . . and Paul Kelly.

Chapter 48

Paul and Zoya continued to meet every Monday afternoon in Simon's offices after that. They worked hard, and dined late, and whenever they could both get away, they went away for a quiet weekend, to walk on the beach and talk about their lives, and make love, but their friendship was always more important to them than the lovemaking. And then they went back to New York, and their real lives, and the people they belonged to. She didn't let it interfere with the rest of her life. There was too much else they both had to do. And she never deluded herself about marrying him. There was no hope of that. He was her friend, a very special one, and as they sat through board meetings year after year, they prided themselves on the fact that no one ever knew about how much they meant to each other in private, not even her children. Matthew liked him very much, and Sasha tolerated him. She was too busy with her own life now to care much about what her mother did, and she never appeared to be aware of their involvement. And of course, Nicholas was still away, fighting with the RAF in Europe.

President Roosevelt died on April 12, 1945. And three weeks later the war ended in Europe, and Zoya rejoiced as tears streamed down her cheeks. Her son was still alive. He came home on the day he turned twenty-four, and two days later, the war ended in the Pacific as well. There were endless celebrations, and parades down Fifth Avenue. Zoya closed the store, and she went home to see Nicholas, standing at the window of their living room, watching people dance in the streets, with tears running down his face.

"If Dad had only lived to see this day," he whispered to her as he watched the jubilation in the streets, and Zoya looked up at her handsome son tenderly. He looked more than ever like Nicolai, particularly now in his uniform. He had become a man in his years away, and she wasn't surprised when he told her he wasn't going back to Princeton. He wanted to begin learning what he needed to of the empire

Simon had left behind him. Paul taught him all that he needed to know of it, and Nicholas was stunned by the money that had been left to him. Sasha knew also that she would be inheriting a great deal of money the following year, although she did not yet know how much. But Nicholas was aghast when he saw the way she behaved when he stayed with Zoya briefly. She was out until the early morning hours every night, came home drunk most of the time, and was rude to everyone who tried to talk to her about what she did, particularly Nicholas, but also Zoya. He was furious when he talked to his mother about it late one night. Sasha had come in early that night, and was already passed out cold in her room. A boy in uniform had dropped her off and he was so drunk he could hardly walk as Nicholas almost threw him out.

"Can't you do something about her, Mama? She's totally out of control."

"She's too old to spank, Nicholas, and I can't lock her in her room."

"I'd like to try it," he looked grim, but the next morning when he talked to his sister it was to no avail. She was gone again that night, and didn't return until well after four o'clock in the morning.

She was even more beautiful than she'd been before, she was too young for her excesses to hurt her looks, but Zoya knew that if she didn't stop, in time they would. And Zoya was less than pleased when, that December, she eloped. She had married a boy she had known for less than three weeks, and the fact that he was the son of a polo player in Palm Beach was small consolation to her. His life-style was as wild as her own, they drank and they danced and cavorted every night, and it was even more upsetting when Sasha blithely told her mother when she came to New York in March that she was expecting a baby sometime in September.

"On Matthew's birthday, I think." She was decidedly vague as he wandered into the room. He was six and a half years old, with Simon's big brown eyes and gentle ways. He adored Nicholas, but he had learned to keep out of his sister's way long since. She drank too much, and she was either indifferent or openly unpleasant. She was twenty-one by then, and the inheritance Simon had left only hurled her faster toward her own destruction.

In June, she came home again and announced that Freddy was cheating on her, and she instantly took revenge. She bought a new car, two diamond bracelets, slept with one of his friends, in spite of her delicate state, and went back to Palm Beach to find her husband. Zoya knew that there was nothing she could do. Even Nicholas didn't want to talk about it anymore. She was what she was, and none of it was pleasant. She talked about it often with Paul, and his gentle wisdom somewhat consoled her.

Nicholas took Matthew fishing on the weekends, and to the park to play ball, whenever he could. He had his hands full at work, but he always made time for the boy, which in turn, gave Zoya a few quiet moments with Paul Kelly. They continued to conduct their affair quietly, and Nicholas never knew, which was a tribute to Paul and Zoya's discretion.

In late August, Sasha's baby was born, a tiny baby girl with bright red hair. Zoya went to Florida to see her, and stood looking at her with awe. She was so small and so sweet, and her mother seemed to have no interest in her at all. Almost as soon as the child was born, Sasha was carousing and careening everywhere in her expensive cars, with or without the equally self-indulgent Freddy. Zoya never knew where they were, and the baby was always left with a nurse, much to Zoya's disapproval. She tried to talk to Sasha about her life-style during their rare conversations on the phone, but predictably Sasha didn't want to hear it. And Nicholas never heard from her anymore either. She almost seemed to have faded from their lives, and Zoya was especially sad not to see more of Sasha's baby, Marina. And when the phone rang on Christmas Eve, Zoya found herself hoping it was Sasha. Nicholas was having dinner with her, and Matthew had just gone to bed, after decorating the tree. He was seven years old, and still believed in Santa Claus almost, although Zoya suspected it would be the last year. He was still the joy in her life, and she was smiling happily as she picked up the receiver.

"Hello?" It was the Florida State Police. Her heart stopped, instantly fearing why they'd called her. They told her that Sasha and Freddy had been in an accident on their way home from a party somewhere, and as she held her breath, her worst fears came to fruition. She set the phone down, staring at Nicholas, unable to tell him. A moment later, the baby's nurse called them, hysterical to be left alone with the baby. And Nicholas talked to her and promised to fly down in the morning to pick up the child. The nurse explained everything to him, as he looked at his mother in silent horror. She blamed herself as she cried that night, she had done all the wrong things, she insisted, and now it was too late. She had failed her, and now she was dead. ". . . She was so sweet when she was small . . ." Zoya cried. But Nicholas had other memories of Sasha. He remembered only how spoiled she had been, how selfish, and how unkind to their mother. But to Zoya it didn't seem fair. She was only twenty-one, and now she was gone, like a fleeting, brilliant flash of falling star on a dark summer night. One moment alive and then suddenly gone forever.

Nicholas flew to Florida the next day, and brought back his sister's body, and her tiny baby, Marina. It was a somber Christmas for Zoya, as she opened presents with Matthew, fighting back tears, with trembling hands, and wondering if there were something she could have done and had failed to do for her daughter. Perhaps if she had never worked, if things had been easier, if Clayton hadn't died . . . or Simon . . . or perhaps . . . the agonies were endless, as she tried to concentrate on Matthew, who seemed not to understand what had happened to his sister, he was much too calm, which frightened Zoya. But she realized that he understood too well when he turned wide brown eyes up to Zoya's and inquired quietly, "Was she drunk again, Mom?"

She was shocked as she heard Matthew's words. But he was right. She had been. And Zoya didn't deny it, as she held Sasha's baby. And late that night, Zoya sat staring down at her, as she opened her eyes and yawned sleepily. She was four months old, and all she had was Zoya now, and Matthew and Nicholas, her uncles.

"I'm too old for this," Zoya sighed that night when Paul called, as he always did.

"No, you're not. She's better off with you than she would have been with them. She's a lucky child." And he was a lucky man to share his life with her. The blessings in Zoya's life touched everyone around her . . . except for Sasha, and she accused herself again that night, knowing how totally she had failed her. But could she have done otherwise? She knew, with searing pain, that she would never have the answer. All she could do now to make up for it was love Marina as though she were her own. She put the baby's crib next to her own bed, and sat for hours looking at the baby sleeping there, her eyes closed, her skin warm, her hair silky red, like Zoya's own, and she promised to keep her safe, and do the best she could this time. And then, as a sob caught in her throat, she remembered the night Sasha and Nicholas had almost died in the fire . . . little Sasha had lain on the pavement, the firemen fighting to revive her from the thick smoke, and then she had stirred, and Zoya had held her sobbing, as she did now, remembering her . . . how could things have gone so wrong. In the end, in spite of everything, at only twenty-one, she had lost her.

The funeral was two days afterward, attended by some of her friends from school, and the people she had known growing up in New York. Their faces registered silent shock, as Zoya left the church on Nicholas's arm, Matthew holding her hand, and she saw Paul standing solemnly in the back row, his white hair standing out above the crowd, his eyes offering her everything he felt for her. She looked at him for only a moment and then walked on, her sons on either side of her, and tiny Marina, her whole life about to begin, waiting for them at home, in the bed next to Zoya's.

Chapter 49

Nineteen forty-seven was the year of the New Look from Dior, and Zoya took Matthew and Marina to Paris with her, when she went to order her new lines. Matthew was almost eight years old by then, and Marina was still a baby. But she took him to the Eiffel Tower, walked along the Seine with him, and to the Tuileries, where she had gone with Evgenia so very long ago.

"Tell me again about your grandmother." She smiled as she told him all of it again, about the troikas in Russia when she was a child, and the games they had played, the people they had known. It was a way of sharing her history with him, and in effect his own. They went to the south of France afterward, and the following year, with both children again, Zoya went to Rome. She took Marina everywhere with her, as though in some way she could make up to her for the mother she had lost. Marina was like her own child now, and she looked so much like Zoya as she staggered happily around the ship on the way home, that people naturally assumed she was Zoya's child. At forty-nine, she still had an air of youth, and it wasn't incredible to anyone that she should still have young children around her.

"It keeps me young, I suppose," she told Paul more than once. And he agreed with her. She looked even lovelier than before. Nicholas was running the company by then, and by the spring of 1951, he had the textile mills well in hand. He was almost thirty years old, and when Zoya came back from Europe with the little ones, he came to see them to hear all about the trip. Matthew was eleven, and Marina was four and a half, with her shining red hair, and big green eyes. She squealed with laughter when Nicholas tickled her, and he put Marina to bed himself, and then returned to the living room to tell Zoya his plans.

"Well, Mama . . ." He hesitated, smiling at her, and she sensed that something important was happening.

"Yes, Nicholas? Am I supposed to wear a serious face, or are you just trying to

frighten me?" She had been expecting it
for a while. He had been seeing a charming southern girl. He had met her when
he was in South Carolina, checking on the
mills. She was very beautiful, and a little
spoiled. But Zoya never commented on
that. He was a grown man, and free to
make his own choices with his life. As she
said to Paul, she respected his judgment.
He was a sensible young man, with a kind
heart, and a mind that had been honed by
running Simon's businesses.

"Will you be very surprised if I tell you
I'm going to get married in the fall?" His
eyes played with hers and she laughed.

"Should I be surprised, my love?"

"Elizabeth and I are getting married,"
he proudly announced.

"I'm happy for you, darling," she looked
at him and smiled. He was a good man,
and both his fathers would have been
proud of him. "I hope she makes you
happy, my love."

"She already does." Zoya couldn't have
asked for more, and she offered to help
her find a wedding dress the next time
they spoke, remembering to herself Sofia's
inquisition before she and Simon had gotten married years before. Simon's parents
were long since gone, and his uncles after

that. She had never been close to them, but she had seen to it that Matthew visited them often before they died, and they were grateful.

She reminded herself not to be difficult, when Elizabeth swept into the store and was rude to everyone. The wedding dress was the least of it. She also seemed to expect Zoya to supply her entire trousseau, and buy them an apartment. Zoya felt a tiny chill run up her spine, as she stood at the wedding after that, watching Matthew carefully balance the ring on the cushion he held, and Marina swing a tiny basket of rose petals, as she waved at her grandmother in the front row, and Zoya smiled proudly at them.

But Nicholas carried on valiantly, supplying her every need, meeting her every demand, catering to her every whim, until he could stand it no more. Almost four years to the day that Zoya had watched Marina tossing rose petals at them, Nicholas sent Elizabeth home to her parents. Marina was nine by then and Zoya was taking her to ballet class every day. It had been her only passion in life since she was five. And this time, Zoya was determined to do everything she could for the child, still feeling that she had somehow failed

Sasha. She left the store at three o'clock every day, picked Marina up at Miss Nightingale's, and took her to the ballet classes where she did the same tours jetés, the same pliés, the same exercises that Zoya herself had done a lifetime ago in St. Petersburg with Madame Nastova.

It was odd how things repeated themselves again. She told her about the Maryinsky School, its wonders and joys, and how demanding Madame Nastova had been. And when she and Nicholas went to her recital, she sat quietly and cried. Nicholas looked over and touched her hand, as Zoya smiled through her tears, watching Marina.

"She's so sweet and innocent." Life was just beginning for her. And she worked so hard at everything she did, she was such a good and earnest child. Matthew was like a brother to her, although they were seven years apart, not unlike Nicolai when she was growing up herself. It was odd how it all happened again and again, generation after generation, her own passion for the ballet reborn in Marina.

Paul gave the budding ballerina a tiny bouquet that night, and after Marina went to bed, chattering excitedly about how the recital had gone, he asked her the question Zoya had dreaded hearing from him for years. His wife had finally died of cirrhosis several months before, and he looked at Zoya quietly in the silence of the library after Nicholas was gone, back to his own apartment.

"Zoya . . . after twelve years, I can ask you now. Will you marry me?" He reached for her hand, and she looked into his eyes with the smile born of a love long shared, but never fully brought to fruition. They had been together for twelve years and she loved him deeply and valued his friendship, but that time was past for her. She had never wanted to marry again after Simon. She was happy watching Matthew grow up, and Marina dance. She still bustled around the store with almost the same energy she'd had before. At fifty-six, she was barely slowing down. But marriage wasn't what she wanted now, and she gently touched his fingers with her lips and shook her head.

"Paul, my darling, I can't."

He looked wounded as he listened to her, and she tried to find the words to explain it.

"I'm past that now. I'm too old to marry anyone."

"Don't say that, Zoya, look at you! You

haven't changed since the first time I saw you." She was still so very lovely.

"Yes, I have," she smiled pleasantly, "inside. I want to grow old quietly, to see Matthew on his way, and Marina become exactly what she wants to be. I want her to have the luxury of doing exactly what she wants to do, to be who she has to be . . . and that's what I want too."

He had feared that, even before he asked her. He had wanted to marry her for years, but he couldn't. And now that he was free, the moment had passed for her. He wondered if things would have been different if Allison had died sooner. His weekends with Zoya were less frequent now, but they still went to his house in Connecticut from time to time, but in recent years the weekends were less important to her. It was their friendship she loved, and she would have wanted more than that of marriage. She would have wanted passion. The children were her only passion now. The children, and still, the store. Always that, in memory of Simon.

"I can't be anyone's wife again. I know that now. I gave everything I had to give to Clayton and then Simon, a long time ago. Now there's me. The children, my

work, and you, when we both have time
for it. But I couldn't give you enough of
myself to justify marrying you. It wouldn't
be fair to you. I want some time for myself
now, Paul, as awful as that must sound.
But perhaps now it's my turn to be selfish.
I want to travel when the children are
old enough, to be free again. Maybe to go
back to Russia again one day . . . to visit
St. Petersburg again . . . or
Livadia . . ." She knew it would be painful for her, but it was a dream she'd had in
recent years, and each year it was more
possible. All she needed was the time, and
the courage to go back. But she knew she
couldn't do all of that with him, he had his
life, his house, his work, his gardening, his
friends. His life had slowed down considerably in recent years. "I think I have just
grown up, finally." At sixty-six, he suddenly seemed much older, but Zoya didn't
say that. "I was so busy surviving for so
many years. I finally discovered that there
is a great deal more than that. Perhaps if
I'd known that earlier . . . perhaps
things might have been different for
Sasha." She still blamed herself for her
daughter's death, and it was difficult to
look back and see what she could have
done differently, and it didn't really mat-

ter anymore. For Sasha, it was much too late, but not for Matthew, or Marina, or even herself. She still had some living to do, and she had chosen to do it on her own, no matter how much she loved Paul Kelly.

"Does this mean it's over for us?" He looked at her with sad, wintry eyes, as she gently leaned over and kissed him on the lips, and he felt the same fire he had always felt for her since the first day they'd met.

"Not unless you want it to be. If you can accept me like this, I'll be here to love you for a long, long time." Just as she had been there for him during the years when he was married.

He laughed quietly, "Just my luck, the world has finally come of age, people are doing things that would have shocked the world twenty years ago, sleeping with each other openly, living in sin, and what happens? I offer you respectability a dozen years too late." They both laughed as they sat comfortably in her library. "Zoya, you're too young for me."

"Thank you, Paul." They kissed again, and a short while later, he went home. She had promised to spend the weekend in Connecticut with him, and he was somewhat mollified when he left. Zoya tiptoed to Marina's room then, to watch her as she slept, and she smiled again. The world would be hers one day. Tears filled Zoya's eyes, as she gently bent to kiss her cheek, and dreaming peacefully, Marina stirred beneath her grandmother's loving hand.

"Dance on, little one . . . little ballerina . . . dance on . . ."

Chapter 50

The Kennedy years were exciting ones for
Zoya at the store. The young senator's
wife set exciting trends that everyone followed. And Zoya admired her greatly. She
was even invited to dine at the White
House, much to her older son's delight.
Zoya was still as beautiful, as elegant, as
she had been when he was a child. At
sixty-one, Zoya was recognized by everyone, as she strode proudly into her store,
straightening a hat, frowning at something she didn't like, changing the flowers
with a practiced hand. Axelle was gone by
then, and her shop only a memory, but
Zoya had learned her lessons well from
her.

Marina was at Juilliard by then, dancing
professionally occasionally, and whenever
Zoya saw her dance, she could almost feel
her own heart leap again, as she danced
for Diaghilev more than forty years be-

fore. Matthew graduated from Harvard in June of 1961, as Zoya sat in the front row with Nicholas and applauded for him. He was a fine young man, and she was proud of him. He was going on to business school, and then to work in the store with her. Nicholas wanted him to work with him, but Matthew was more interested in retailing, he confessed. Zoya had promised to keep the store open until he was ready, and both boys laughed.

"You wouldn't close your doors if the place burned to the ground," Matthew teased, and she laughed. She knew her boys well and loved them deeply. She was chatting distractedly with Nicholas on a flight back to New York. And finally she turned to him. It was easy to see he had something on his mind, and she decided to ask him.

"All right, what is it, Nicholas? I can't stand the suspense anymore." Her eyes danced as he laughed nervously.

"You know me too well." He straightened his tie and cleared his throat.

"I should after all these years." He was thirty-nine years old. "What are you hiding from me?" and suddenly she remembered her brother taking her for a ride a thousand years before, and teasing him about his dancer. She knew without his telling her, that the source of her son's embarrassment was a woman.

"I'm getting married again."

"Should I applaud or cry?" She laughed, "Will I like this one better than the last one?"

He looked at her quietly, a handsome man with her own piercing eyes. "She's an attorney. In fact, she's going to work for Paul Kelly. She lives in Washington, she's been working for the Kennedy administration. She's funny and bright, and a terrible cook," he laughed, "and I'm crazy about her. In fact," he looked uncomfortable again, "I was hoping you'd come to dinner with us tonight, if you're not too tired." For more than a year they'd been commuting back and forth between New York and Washington, D.C.

Zoya looked at him with serious eyes, hoping he had made a wiser choice this time. "I was going to work late at the store, but . . . I could be convinced otherwise." They both laughed as he dropped her off at her apartment on the way to his own. Julie was already waiting there for him, and he told her he'd invited his mother to have dinner with them as she stared at him with terror in her eyes.

"Oh, no! What if she hates me? Look at this dress! I didn't bring anything decent with me from Washington."

"You look wonderful. She won't give a damn about that."

"The hell she won't!" Julie had seen photographs of her, and she always looked impeccable and was dressed in the best of the latest fashion.

Zoya looked her over carefully that night, when they went to dinner at La Côte Basque. It was near the store, and it was her favorite restaurant. And she was everything Nicholas had said she was, amusing, bright, excited about life, intent about her work, but not to the exclusion of all else. She was ten years younger than Nicholas, and Zoya was certain she would make him a good wife. So much so that she made an important decision that night when she left them. She was going to give them the imperial egg as a wedding gift. It was time to pass it on to her children.

She walked quietly back to the store by herself after that dinner, and let herself into the silent halls with her key. The night watchman wasn't surprised when he saw the light under her office door. She came by often late at night, just to check on things, to take some work home with her. And as she went home again, she thought to herself how nice it would be to have Matthew working with her one day. He had remained the light of her life, the child she had thought she was too old to bear. Simon had been right. He had kept her young, even now, as she walked home, spry at sixty-two, to Marina, anxiously waiting up for her beloved Grandma.

It was midnight when she got home, and heard her granddaughter call out to her from her bedroom.

"Grandma, is that you?"

"I certainly hope so." She walked into her room, took off the hat she'd worn to dinner with Nicholas and Julie, and smiled at the child who looked so much like her. Her red hair was as long as Zoya's still was, though hers was now white, and Marina's was cascading over her nightgown. "Guess what! I've been asked to dance at Lincoln Center!"

"Now there's a coup! Tell me what happened." She sat down on the edge of her bed, listening to her chatter happily. She lived only to dance, but there was no denying it now, it wasn't just grandmotherly pride, the child had enormous talent. "All right, now tell me when." She had reeled off the names of the entire cast, the choreographer, the director, their life histories, the music, to her the when wasn't as important.

"In six weeks! Can you believe it! I'll never be ready."

"Yes, you will." Her studies had suffered a little bit in recent years, but to Marina that didn't matter either, and Zoya found herself wondering frequently if this time, the muses would sing, if Marina would one day be a great dancer. She had long since told her about dancing for the Ballet Russe in Paris in her youth, and once with Nijinsky, and then long after, she had told her about Fitzhugh's Dance Hall. Marina loved to tell the tale, it made her respectable grandmother seem far more exotic.

And six weeks later, the performance went beautifully. She was reviewed for the first time. At fifteen, she was on her way. Marina was a real ballerina.

Chapter 51

Nicholas's first child, a daughter, was born in 1963, the same year that John Kennedy was shot, and that Matthew came to work at Countess Zoya. And Zoya was deeply flattered when Nicholas and Julie named their baby girl Zoe, it was an Americanization of her own name, and in truth, she liked it much better.

Marina was dancing full-time by then, at seventeen. She had taken Zoya's Russian name and was known as Marina Ossupov. She was working hard and traveling all over the country. Nicholas thought she should be forced to go on to college once she finished school, but Zoya didn't agree with him.

"Not everyone is made for that, Nicholas. She already has a life. Now that you're a father, don't be so stuffy." Zoya was ever open to new ideas, always excited about life, never boring. And Paul was still deeply in love with her. He had retired several years before and was living in Connecticut full-time. She drove out to see him whenever she could, and he always complained that she was much too busy. The store seemed to be enjoying a whole new life. She had brought in Cardin, Saint Laurent, Courrèges, and now Matthew went with her when she went to Paris. He chased every model he could, and enjoyed staying at the Ritz. At twenty-four, he was full of excitement and mischief, not unlike his mother. And instead of slowing down, as she had promised to do, once he came on the scene, she only seemed to work harder.

"Your mother is amazing," Julie told Nicholas, and unlike most daughters-in-law, she really meant it. The two women had lunch together from time to time, and by the time little Zoe was five, Zoya had bought her her first tutu and ballet shoes. Marina was twenty-two by then, and a star of major proportions. She had danced all over the world, to rave reviews. She was the darling of ballet devotees everywhere, and the previous year she had even danced in Russia. She had told Zoya excitedly about her visit to Leningrad, which had been St. Petersburg, she had seen the

Winter Palace, and even visited the Mary-insky. It brought tears to Zoya's eyes as she listened to her. It was like a dream come true . . . all those places she had left more than fifty years before, with a piece of her still there, and now Marina had been there. She still talked about going to Russia herself, but claimed that she was saving it for her old age.

"And when will that be, Mom?" Nicholas teased on her seventieth birthday. "I'm getting old faster than you are. I'm almost fifty. The trouble is you don't look it, and I do."

"Don't be silly, Nicholas, I look absolutely ancient!" But the amazing thing was that she didn't. She was still beautiful, the red hair now white, but always exquisitely groomed, and the neat suits and slim dresses she wore showed her still lovely figure. She was an object of envy to all, and a source of inspiration to all those who knew her. People still came to the store and begged to see The Countess. Matthew was always telling funny stories of people who absolutely insisted they *had* to see her.

"Rather like the Louvre," Zoya said dryly, "only somewhat smaller."

"Now, Mother, don't be modest. Without you, the store would be nothing."

But it wasn't true anymore. Matthew had applied the merchandising techniques he had learned at business school, and in his first five years, had doubled their sales. He added a new perfume called, of course, "Countess Zoya" the year after that and in the first five years, the sales once again doubled. By 1974, Countess Zoya, the woman and the store, was a legend.

But with the legend came inquiries that interested Matthew, but terrified his mother. Federated wanted to buy the store, as did several other chains, a liquor company, and a company that sold canned foods, but wanted to diversify their investments. Matthew went to Nicholas's office to discuss it all with him, and the two brothers conferred for days. Nicholas was only surprised that the offers hadn't come sooner.

"It's a tribute to you," Nicholas said quietly, looking fondly at his younger brother. But Matthew only shook his head, and moved swiftly around the room. He was a man who was always in motion. He picked up books, glanced at things in his brother's bookcase, and then turned to face him again as he shook his head.

"No, it's not, Nick. It's a tribute to her. All I did was the perfume."

"That's not entirely true, Matthew. I've seen the figures."

"It's not important. But what are we going to say to Mama? I know what she's going to think. I'm thirty-five years old, I can find another job. Mama is seventy-five. For her, it'll be all over."

"I'm not so sure of that," Nicholas pondered it. From a business standpoint the offers were too good to refuse, one in particular, which they both liked. It kept Matthew on for five years, as chairman and consultant, and gave them all an incredible sum of money, including Zoya. But they both knew that it wasn't the money that interested their mother. It was the store and the people and the excitement.

"I think she'll see the value of this." Nicholas was hoping she would as Matthew laughed and collapsed momentarily in a leather chair.

"Then you don't know our mother. She's going to have a fit. It's what she does after that that we have to think of. I don't want her to get depressed over this. At her age, it could kill her."

"That's something to think about too," Nicholas added wisely, "at seventy-five, we can't expect her to be there forever. And it's bound to change once she's gone, even with you there. She adds something to the store. You can feel it come alive when she walks in." She still went to work every day, although now she left promptly at five and was driven home by a chauffeur. Nicholas had insisted on that several years before, and she gave in gracefully. But she was there every morning at nine o'clock, come hell or high water.

"We're just going to have to talk to her," Matthew finally decided. But when they did, she had the fit he had so wisely predicted. "Mom, please," he begged, "look at what they're offering us." She turned to him with icy eyes that would have been worthy of her mother.

"Is there something I don't know? Are we suddenly destitute, or are we only greedy?" She looked pointedly at her son, and Matthew laughed. She was impossible, but he loved her dearly. He had been living with the same woman for the last five years, and he was convinced that the only reason that he loved her was because she was of Russian origin, had red hair, and looked vaguely like Zoya. I know, it's very Freudian, he had admitted more than once. But she was also gorgeous and smart and very sexy. Also not unlike his mother.

"Will you at least give it some thought?" Nicholas asked.

"Yes. But don't expect me to accept it. I will not sell the store to a dog food manufacturer just because you two are bored," she turned to her youngest son, "why don't you invent a new perfume?"

"Mom, we're never going to get another offer like these."

"But do we want one?" And then, as she looked at them, she understood, and there was no denying that it hurt her. "You think I'm too old, don't you?" She looked from Nicholas to Matthew, and she was touched by the respect and love she could see there. "I am. There's no denying that. But I'm in good health. In my own mind," she squinted her eyes, thinking, "I was thinking of retiring at eighty." And then all three of them laughed and she stood up and promised to think it over.

For the next four months, the battle raged as new offers came in, even better than the last ones. But the real issue was not how much, but if they were going to sell at all. And by the spring of 1975, when

Paul died quietly in his sleep at eighty-six, Zoya began to understand that she would not live forever. It was unfair for her to keep a grip on her sons, and refuse them the right to do what they wanted. She had had her life, and her fun, and she had no right to alter the course of theirs. As hard as she had fought them before, she capitulated gracefully late one afternoon, at the end of a board meeting, stunning everyone into silence.

"Do you mean that?" Nicholas stared at her in amazement. He had all but given up by then, and had resigned himself to keeping the store, if only for his mother.

"Yes, Nicky, I do mean it." She said it quietly, she hadn't called him that in years. "I think it's time."

"Are you sure?" It suddenly made him nervous that she was willing to give up so meekly. Maybe she wasn't feeling well, or she was depressed. But as he faced the piercing green eyes, she didn't look it.

"I'm sure, if it's what you both want. I'll find something else to do. I want to travel a little bit." She had promised Zoe only a few weeks before that she would take her to Paris in the summer.

She stood up slowly then, and looked around at the entire board. "Thank you, gentlemen. For your wisdom and your patience, and the joy you have given me." She had started the store almost forty years before, before some of them were even born, and she went around the table and shook everybody's hand, and then she left, and Matthew wiped his eyes. It had been an extraordinary moment.

"I guess that's it," Nicholas looked at him sadly for a moment when they were alone again. "How long do you think it'll take for the deal to go through?" They had already agreed on which one they wanted.

"A few months. We should be settled by the summer." Matthew looked moved and excited.

Nicholas nodded, looking somber. "She wants to take Zoe to Europe. I was going to discourage it, but I don't think I will now."

"Don't. It'll do them both good."

Nicholas nodded and went back to his office.

Chapter 52

The day dawned bright and sunny as Zoya sat at her desk for the last time. She had packed her things the day before, and Matthew had given her an incredible party. The store had been filled with every name anyone had ever heard, the luminaries of society, and two visiting royals. They had all kissed her and hugged her, and remembered. And now she sat and remembered them, thirty-eight years of them, as she prepared to leave her office. The driver was probably waiting for her outside, but she was in no hurry to go, as she stood at the window and looked out over Fifth Avenue, looking down at the traffic. So much had changed in forty years, so many dreams fulfilled and others broken. She remembered how Simon had helped her start the store, how excited he had been, how happy they were when they went to Europe together on their first buying trip. It seemed like a whole lifetime, now gone in only a moment.

"Countess? . . ." A gentle voice spoke from the door and she turned to see her latest assistant, a girl who was younger than her oldest grandchild.

"Yes?"

"The car is waiting downstairs. The driver wanted you to know, in case you were waiting."

"Thank you," she smiled graciously, her back straight, her eyes proud, "please tell him I'll be down in a moment." Her words and her manner still bespoke nobility, more than her title. No one who had ever worked for her would ever forget her.

The door closed silently, as she looked around the room for a last time. She knew she would be back again, to visit Matthew, but it would never be quite the same. It was theirs now. She had given it to them, and they had chosen to sell it. But she suspected that Simon wouldn't have disagreed with them. He was a shrewd businessman, and so was Matthew.

She cast a last look over her shoulder, and closed the door, her back straight in a new navy blue Chanel suit, her hair swept up and carefully knotted. And as she left her office, she almost collided with Zoe.

"Grandma! I was afraid you'd left. Look! Look what I have!" Nicholas had agreed to the trip to Paris long since, and they were leaving in two weeks, but not by ship this time. They were flying. There were no ships left that she wanted to take, and Zoe didn't mind. She was jumping up and down, full of twelve-year-old exuberance, her hands full of brochures as Zoya laughed.

"What have you got?"

She glanced over her shoulder as though she'd been followed and whispered conspiratorially, "Just don't tell Daddy. Once we get there, he'll never know the difference." The brochures she held out to her grandmother were not of Paris, but of Russia. The spires of the Winter Palace looked at her boldly from the pictures. The Catherine Palace . . . the Alexander . . . the Antichkov . . . as Zoya's eyes met hers in silent wonder. "Grandma, let's go to Russia!" She had been promising it to herself for years, and maybe now, with little Zoe, she was ready.

"I don't know. Your father might not want you to . . ." And then, as she thought of it, she smiled. She had left with her grandmother more than half a century before, and now she could go back with her own grandchild. "You know," she beamed, as she slipped an arm around the child's shoulders. "I quite like it." She stepped onto the escalator with her, glancing at the brochures, thinking of their plans, her mind racing.

They reached the main floor, and she looked up, startled to see hordes of her employees, standing there, many of them crying openly. She shook their hands, smiled, kissed one or two, and then suddenly, it was over, she and the child were on Fifth Avenue, as she waved the driver away. She didn't want to drive anywhere. They were going for a long walk, as Zoe rattled on excitedly about the trip.

"And then . . . we could go to Moscow! . . ." Her eyes danced, just as Zoya's did as she listened.

"No. Moscow was always very boring. St. Petersburg . . . and perhaps . . . you know . . . when I was a child, in the summers we went to the palace in Livadia . . . in the Crimea. . . ." They walked down the street hand in hand, as Nicholas's limousine drew up slowly. He couldn't bear the thought of her leaving the store alone, and he had come to take her home, and then suddenly he saw them . . . the straight back in the Chanel suit, and his own daughter, her dark hair flying as she talked animatedly about something. The old and the new. The past and the future, going home hand in hand. He decided to leave them alone, as he walked slowly into the store to see Matthew.

"Do you suppose we could get there, Grandma? . . . to Livadia, I mean . . ." Her eyes were filled with love as she looked up at her, and Zoya smiled.

"We'll certainly try, darling, won't we?"

MER